1

GORAN VOJNOVIĆ

THE FIG TREE

Translated from the Slovene by Olivia Hellewell

istrosbooks

First published in 2019 by **Istros Books**
(in collaboration with Beletrina Academic Press)
London, United Kingdom
www.istrosbooks.com

Originally published in Slovene as *Figa* by Beletrina Academic Press, 2016

© Goran Vojnović, 2020
The right of Goran Vojnović to be identified as the author of this work has been
asserted in accordance with the Copyright, Designs and Patents Act, 1988.

Translation © Olivia Hellewell, 2020

Cover design and typesetting: Davor Pukljak | www.frontispis.hr

ISBN: 978-1912545247

This Book is part of the EU co-funded project *"Reading the Heart of Europe"*
in partnership with Beletrina Academic Press | www.beletrina.si

Co-funded by the
Creative Europe Programme
of the European Union

The European Commission support for the production of this publication does not constitute an endorsement
of the contents which reflects the views only of the authors, and the Commission cannot be held responsible
for any use which may be made of the information contained therein.

FREEDOM
TO **WRITE**
FREEDOM
TO **READ**

Supported using public funding by
**ARTS COUNCIL
ENGLAND**

This book has been selected to receive financial assistance from English PEN's "PEN Translates" programme,
supported by Arts Council England. English PEN exists to promote literature and our understanding of it, to
uphold writers' freedoms around the world, to campaign against the persecution and imprisonment of writers
for stating their views, and to promote the friendly co-operation of writers and the free exchange of ideas.
www.englishpen.org

TRANSLATOR'S NOTE

There comes a time when the stage of your life appears to be set: you know the characters, the plot is seemingly sketched out ahead of you, and you've been cast in your role. But what if we had made other choices? Who would we have been, and where would the plot have taken us? Who, or what, might we be, if we could break free from the scenes that we have found ourselves in?

Sitting in a sun-lit classroom at the British Centre for Literary Translation in July 2019, this is how author Goran Vojnović began to explain the starting point for his third novel, *The Fig Tree*. I was there with Goran to lead a week-long translation workshop at the BCLT's Summer School, where along with seven wonderful participants, we would begin to unravel the many threads of this multigenerational family saga. The workshop was funded by the AHRC and formed part of Dr Cecilia Rossi's Open World Research Initiative project, 'Literary Translation Workshops: Bridging Communities Affected by Past Conflict'. The workshop was also kindly supported by the Slovenian Book Agency. During that week, the group translated two short sections of the novel, both of which remain unaltered in this published version*.

The opening scenes of *The Fig Tree* unfold in 1950s Istria, in the relatively early days of Tito's Yugoslavia. Through narrator Jadran's eyes, we see the six central characters navigate their changing existential landscapes. These landscapes will undoubtedly introduce new contexts and references to a reader in English, but even as borders are drawn through homes and lives, the novel remains quietly focused on the cracks that can appear between us as people, and the feelings borne of these fates. One episode which might be helpful to contextualise, however, is one that Vojnović depicts through the character of Safet, Jadran's Bosnian father. In February 1992, not long after Slovenia had declared independence from Yugoslavia, around 25,000 formerly Yugoslav citizens were erased from the register of permanent residents. Those who did not, or were unable to, apply for citizenship in the newly independent state of Slovenia were stripped of all their legal, economic and social rights that had previously been accessible to them as Yugoslav citizens. Overnight, these 25,000 people became 'illegal aliens' in their own homes, and would later come to be known as *Izbrisani* ('The Erased').

Another unmistakable feature of *The Fig Tree* is the use of languages from across the former Yugoslavia. The characters speak Slovene and they speak *naški* (nashki; 'our language', which for these characters would today be known as BCS, or Bosnian-Croatian-Serbian). Safet speaks *naški* and Vesna speaks Slovene, and many of the characters, like Vojnović himself, experience the world in more than one language. In my translation I considered marking the language shifts in a visual way, such as using italics to denote the *naški*, but italics already have a very significant function in the novel, as they distinguish between layers of narrative voice (active dialogue in the present, and dialogue as recalled through memory, or perhaps, imagination). I never really considered leaving the *naški* and providing footnotes, either. I first read *The Fig Tree* as a reader, without the knowledge that I'd one day be translating it (although the streams of pencil scribble in the margins attest to a hope that I might), and so my approach was always guided by the conviction that *The Fig Tree* is an immersive, meditative reading experience. So, occasionally, I leave some *naški* in the text – a song lyric, or a simple hello or goodbye – as a reminder of the novel's rich linguistic fabric. Where the text dictates that the language being spoken is named, I describe Safet as speaking Bosnian, because we know he is from Bosnia, and likewise with grandfather Aleksandar, I refer to his occasional phrases in *naški* as Serbo-Croatian, as we know he is Serbian by birth, but living (for the most part) in Croatian Istria. And elsewhere, I ask readers to go with it: even though *The Fig Tree* is unmistakeably rooted in Vojnović's world, it is, after all, a book about stories. It's a book about the stories we tell ourselves in order to make sense of the world around us, even when there is seemingly little sense to be found.

To Katja Cvahte, Florencia Ferre, Melita Koletnik, Ana Krkovič, Mojca Petaros, Paul Townend and Miha Žličar: the ideas and insight that you all brought to the text undoubtedly made this translation better, and what's more, made me a better translator. The first paragraph of Chapter IV, part 4, and the first 50 lines of Chapter XVI, is your work.

To the two of them

A BRIEF NOTE ON PRONUNCIATION

C, c	tz (as in *pizza*)	Dolanc (Dolantz)
Č, č & Ć, ć	ch (as in *church*)	Vojnović (Voynovich); Černjak (Chernyak)
Đ, đ	dj (like the j in *judge*)	Đorđević (Georgevich)
J, j	y (as in *yellow* or *boy*)	Jadran (Yadran); Jana (Yana)
Š, š	sh (as in *dish*)	Saško (Sashko)
Ž, ž	zh (as in *pleasure*)	Pražakova Street (Prazhakova)

I

The year was 1955, and in the town of Buje, Croatia, Commissioner Risto Marjanović was awaiting the arrival of incoming forest warden, Aleksandar Đorđević, in the manner as was customary for his region. He had laid the table in his office with all the delicacies that his wife Jovana had brought with her from Serbia. The famous cheese curds, pork scratchings, sausage, lardo, apricot brandy – all this awaited Aleksandar, making his way from the neighbouring republic of Slovenia, but who was, by the sound of his name, a fellow Serb; a man with whom Risto could exchange a few words in his mother tongue. Risto had only just taken up the post as Commissioner in northern Istria, but already he longed for home, already he felt conscious that his dear Yugoslavia was home to foreign folk, folk who did, it was true, speak an almost intelligible language, but who nevertheless remained unintelligible to him. They were strange, these people here in Buje. Risto preferred to avoid them, and instead of breathing down their necks, recruiting suitable candidates to the Party, and removing the unsuitable ones from society, he preferred to leave them well alone, to forge their own paths, and above all make sure that they had as little to do with him as possible, and he with them. When he was informed that a young man by the name of Aleksandar Đorđević was coming from Ljubljana, he was cheered by the news, as if they'd announced the arrival of Josip Broz - Tito himself. Something told him that Aleksandar would immediately understand what was wrong with the people of Buje, and that Risto would be able to say things that would not otherwise be permitted within the bounds of brotherhood and unity; that just like him, Aleksandar would notice that it was not possible to speak, nor drink, nor fight with these people in a brotherly way; that he too would see for himself how these people could not be saved by socialism, would understand how it was better to leave them in peace, and not expel the image of God from their strange heads. Risto hoped that he would not have to pretend to Aleksandar that he spent day and night fighting for the advancement of his homeland, and that instead, he'd be able to admit that he preferred to stay in his office, out of sight, with locked doors, pretending not to be there when they knocked; he hoped he'd be able to admit that he preferred to drink his brandy and think about his native lands and about how, if only he could, he'd immediately retreat back to the forest, among the partisans, had his wartime courage not deserted him and had he not become cowardly now there was peace; he hoped he could admit that he waited until dusk every day before creeping around town, the town he crept around like a wartime fugitive, in spite of it being under his command; but he was more scared of these people, these Istrians, than he had ever been scared of the Germans. Risto wanted to tell Aleksandar all of this, though he knew that as soon as they sat opposite one another it would be hard to find the right words, and that he didn't know this Aleksander at all, who was actually younger than him – for all he knew, this man from Ljubljana was just as strange as the strange people of Buje. Risto even wondered, after a few too many drinks, whether there were any normal people like him left anymore; that perhaps even the people of his hometown, Užice, were different now, that they would also let you speak, uninterrupted, just like they did here, and not only that, but with staring eyes wide open, so that there was no way of telling what they were really thinking. Maybe there's no longer anyone, anywhere, Risto thought, to whom he could confess his fear of staring eyes like these, that swallowed him like quicksand; no one, to whom he, a political commissar, member of the communist party, could confess that he was afraid of the people who did nothing but stand before him and listen. Aleksandar Đorđević was, for this reason, his final hope; he had to understand it all, he had to know what Risto was talking about, because he was one of his kind and they had to think the same and see things in the same way.

But as he impatiently awaited Aleksandar's arrival, nibbling at the cold meats and draining his bottle of brandy, Risto could not have known, of course, what kind of person was hiding behind that Serbian-sounding name. He could not have known that Aleksandar Đorđević was not, in any sense, a typical representative of his nationality, for the nationality to which his surname alluded was not something that he could claim at all. Born in Novi Sad in 1925, Aleksandar initially bore the surname of his mother, the nurse and bookseller Ester Aljehin, and his first name, so his mother said, was his father's. But other than the fact he was born in Ukraine, was supposedly called Aleksandar, and supposedly had the same strong, bushy eyebrows – something which my grandfather always doubted until the day he died – he never learned a thing about his father. For Ester, who inherited a small bookshop in Novi Sad from her father Moš, the war had begun long before the first Nazis marched through Novi Sad; and she began fighting her own battle for freedom long before those who will be remembered by history as freedom fighters. The morose, wet spring of 1937 was cause enough for her to seduce the dentist Milorad Đorđević, convince him to marry her, and then, as Mrs Đorđević, leave her new husband and home-town for Belgrade without the slightest explanation. She arrived in Belgrade as Branislava, finding work as a nurse, which is what she had trained to do, and introducing herself to everyone as Milorad's widow. She even went to church and lit candles for him; little Aleksandar, meanwhile, had to learn to pray for the soul of a man that was neither really his father, nor really departed, and learnt to attract the pitiful gazes of the women of Belgrade, all so that the image of Mrs Đorđević and her son kneeling before the altar would be engrained as deeply as possible in their minds. Everything in the life of Ester Aljehin, or Branislava Đorđević, was premeditated and predis-posed to her one simple aim: survival without humiliation or oppression. Not once did my great grandmother ever feel obliged to introduce herself by her real name, never did she feel the need to be sincere with anyone, and never did a single person earn the right to know the woman behind the mask. She held this world – a world which so flagrantly displayed its vulgar hatred of all that challenged convention – in contempt, and she took particular pleasure in brazenly deceiving it, pretending to be exactly the type of person that this wretched world wanted her to be. She performed her role as one of them with dedication, internalising their ignorance and primitive natures, their fears and prejudices. Like a chameleon she adapted to the surroundings she despised; she would smile politely, curtsey, and perfect her deception with each passing day, until she became lost within it. And all the while, the cunning, calculating, pious Ester Aljehin, who would quietly read Joseph Roth at home to the young Aleksandar in German, gradually vanished behind the fictitious façade of the feeble Branislava Đorđević, who would explain to male admirers in horror that once a married woman, always a married woman, and that they ought to be ashamed of their sinful thoughts. And yet, as she caught sight of the first Nazi uniforms in the city, and when she heard of the mysterious disappearance of Dr. Štiglic, and when she heard whispers of nocturnal goings-on at the old Belgrade marketplace, this Branislava Đorđević was unable to suppress Ester Aljehin's fear. Fear was what drove Branislava Đorđević from Belgrade, a place where nobody had endangered or threatened her, where no one knew her secrets; yet Ester Aljehin harboured great fear, and an even greater will to survive, and so in the February of 1942, Branislava and Aleksandar Đorđević arrived in Ljubljana, in the hands of the Italians at the time, of whom Ester was for some reason less afraid than the Germans. Besides, the Slovenes seemed less intimidating than the Serbs, mostly because Ljubljana was even further removed from Novi Sad, and there were certainly fewer people among the Slovenes who could know her secret. But her fear did not subside upon arrival in Ljubljana; it only increased, for the Slovenes would stare at her suspiciously, in a manner similar to how the locals of Buje were to stare at Risto Marjanović thirteen years later. It was a suspicion of outsiders, but Branislava couldn't work out why exactly she was so intriguing to the people of Ljubljana, nor what their stares were accusing her of. And so in Ljubljana, Ester Aljehin withdrew even more. She quietly carried out her duties at the hospital, and after work she would shut herself away in her modest home. She didn't go for walks around the town, she didn't go to church, she didn't go to the square; she certainly didn't walk amongst others, she made no effort to assume new roles, she had no wish to be part of the crowd, because this crowd was so very foreign to her that it superseded her acting capabilities. And so, in the evenings, Aleksandar would teach his mum Slovene – the language he would speak with school friends, but which she never spoke with anyone. He also taught her Italian, which they spoke at school, and she taught him German, as she had learned from her father. It was the language of the enemy, but it was also the language of Joseph Roth, she explained. Nothing in this world was black and white, the woman who looked askance upon this maddened world would say to him. In her eyes, the world's conflict was not divided into good and evil, or ours and theirs; the war had ultimately divided the world into Ester and Aleksandar on one side, and everyone else on the other. And from one day to the next she would fight her own war, always on the lookout, Ester Aljehin, eternal prisoner of a fear that first stirred inside her in Novi Sad, 1936, when a man entered her bookshop and said the days of books for some, and pitchforks for others, would soon be over; and that a new order was coming soon. These fears grew within Ester Aljehin, to the extent that in Ljubljana she wouldn't even let Aleksandar turn on the light anymore; and then she started whispering to herself, and walking home from the hospital at increasing speed, always looking over her shoulder. In late 1944, when Ljubljana was still under the Germans, Aleksandar came home from school one day to find Ester on the floor by the front door. Her heart had succumbed to the fear and she had collapsed in a city that had paid her no attention, that hadn't known her secret; that hadn't, and never could have, understood what she, Branislava Đorđević, a former bookseller, widow of Milorad Đorđević, a nurse who performed an exemplary role at Ljubljana hospital, had been so afraid of. But unexplained deaths were not uncommon during those times and no one was alarmed, no one was surprised by the young woman's heart attack, no one thought it out of the ordinary in these extraordinary times. They came, expressed their sympathies to Aleksandar, and carried on as before, leaving him alone in the flat, where he didn't dare turn on the light nor raise his voice above a whisper, so as not to startle his late mother.

In lonely Commissioner Risto Marjanović, who in 1955 was waiting in Buje with what remained of the food he had laid out and an almost-empty bottle of rakia, Aleksandar Đorđević recognised the remains of a world that had frightened Ester Aljehin; a world which ought to have been his, but which was anything but; a world which he hated and feared in equal measure. He, Aleksandar Đorđević, an outsider with a local-sounding name, who Risto Marjanović pictured as a future friend – a desperately needed kindred spirit – could not have been a more unsuitable companion for this unhappy man. And Risto likely sensed this the moment Aleksandar stepped into his office. There was something in Aleksandar's posture, in his serious, silent manner, in how he waited patiently for Risto to start speaking, in his deferential form of address, in everything. Another one of these foreign, incomprehensible people, someone else to hide from and avoid, thought Risto, disappointed; as he examined Aleksandar standing at the door awaiting instruction.

Let's go. The sooner we find you somewhere to stay, the better.

Risto led Aleksandar across the road to a house that stood at the far end of the main square. Risto opened the door and walked in.

I don't have the keys, but you won't need them here. No one will bother you. They're more likely to run away from you.

He showed him the kitchen, bathroom and bedroom. He opened a wardrobe that was full of clothes.

If you need space, you can move these or throw them away.

Risto took a few dresses down from the rail and dropped them at the bottom of the wardrobe.

Whose are they? asked Aleksandar.
These? I don't know. Some Italian's.
But where are they?
Who? The Italians?
Yes.
How would I know? Gone somewhere.
Without their things?

Risto had already run out of patience with Aleksandar and his questions.

Look, tomorrow morning I can send someone to clear out the wardrobe if you want.

I can't live in this house.

Why?

People clearly live here.

What would you have me do? Build you a hotel? All the houses are like this. They left, we arrived. That's life.

And what if they come back?

Make them a coffee and offer them something to eat.

When Risto had left, Aleksandar went back into the bedroom and picked up the clothes that Risto had flung on the floor. He hung them back on the rail, closed the wardrobe door and went down to the kitchen. He walked carefully around the table, not wanting to touch anything. In a cup on the draining board he could see, beneath a thin layer of dust, the solidified remains of coffee; on the cooker, the bottom of a pot that was encrusted with burnt bits of food; and in the stove, charred wood lay nestled among small bits of newspaper with sooty edges. His eyes met a light rectangular patch on the wall, the trace of a picture or photograph that used to hang there. Aleksandar imagined it might have been pocketed by someone, perhaps Risto, or someone else who had taken the liberty of entering the abandoned house. He was already tired and went back into the bedroom, but stopped in front of the bed, realizing that he couldn't allow himself to lie on someone else's bed sheets. So he lay down on the floor between the bed and the wardrobe, placed his jacket beneath his head, and soon fell asleep. Fortunately, his young body had not yet become accustomed to the comfort previously offered by his soft Ljubljana lodgings.

The next morning, Aleksandar told Risto once more that he could not stay in the house. The Commissioner was, owing to an unbearable headache, sat in the dark behind closed shutters, and with eyes closed explained to Aleksandar that all houses in the town were like that, and that if he would like a new build, he would have to build it himself. Of course, Risto and his pounding head had not been serious, and had merely wanted to get rid of the irksome forest warden as quickly as possible. However, unfortunately for him, the curious young man thought it easier to build a home of his own than move into the home of a stranger.

When Risto realised that Aleksandar had not understood, he opened his eyes and adjusted his tone.

Listen, Đorđević, if we can all move into these houses, then so can you. Understand? Don't play the saint in front of me. Stop pissing about and get back to your house.

It's not my house, comrade Marjanović.

Not yours?

No, it's not.

Everything belongs to all of us now, does it not?

Yes.

So if I say that house is yours, it's yours.

'Ours' is not the same as 'mine'.

Are you taking the piss, Đorđević?

No.

Come with me.

Risto led Aleksandar out into the street and pointed north.

See that hill over there? That's the extent of my command. Up to the border. And that's where you can build your house. So you can see Slovenia from your window.

And thus the pounding head of Risto Marjanović laid the foundations of Aleksandar's house in the village of Momjan, right on the Slovene border, three miles out of town, thinking that this was the best way to punish the young forest warden for his impertinence.

Precisely one week later, Aleksandar and his pregnant wife Jana were making the three-mile trek from Buje to Momjan. Every few metres or so, Aleksandar would look expectantly in the direction of his wife, expecting a look of disapproval; expecting the tired Jana to stop and ask if her pregnancy had perhaps escaped his memory, and whether they were far from their plot. But on strode Jana behind him, in silence.

Aleksandar knew to be wary of a woman's silence, and knew that he would not be met with smiles upon arrival at their destination, but he had no choice other than to continue, not wanting to worsen the situation with a careless word. Never, neither before nor after, would the journey from Buje to Momjan seem longer than it did that morning, never were so many steps taken, never would there be so many steps still to take; never had the path ascended so steeply, never had it wound so tightly around the Istrian hills.

In spite of her visible bump, Jana did not tire. However briskly he marched, she would march too, and Aleksandar knew that this could not be good, and he hoped Jana would stop before they got to Momjan, and that before they arrived she'd unleash the words stewing inside her. But Jana was silent, even when Aleksandar stopped and opened his arms.

Here we are.

He pointed to the bay, basking in the sun at the foot of the hill, and with his finger traced the coastline all the way down to Umag, lost in the springtime haze; and he pointed out Buje, which from afar looked to be a tiny, tightly-packed village not much bigger than Momjan; and the Republic of Slovenia, which extended from the foot of their hill.

Like nature kissing my eyes, is how Aleksandar described the view to Risto, wishing to let him know that his punishment had in fact been a blessing. Blessing was the name that Aleksandar, a committed atheist, had given to his plot with the intention of provoking another atheist, more committed than he; not realising that the depressive, desperate Commissioner would not be the first person he would provoke.

Blessing.

Jana never shouted, ever. When she was angry, she would slowly utter single, choice words, one after the other, with long pauses, barely audibly and with a coldness that would send a shiver down all spines in her vicinity. She would stare vacantly ahead, as if the blood had halted in her veins, which roused fear first in Aleksandar, but later in her children, and eventually even her grandchildren. Yet Aleksandar always said that her stare had never been as chilling as it was that morning in Momjan.

Blessing, Jana said, and not a single word more until they got back to Buje; back to the house on the edge of the square, where they would make their bed in the evenings with a mattress on the kitchen floor; where they would take their things out of a box and put them back again; where they would eat and drink out of pans they'd brought with them from Ljubljana, and where they had made their own temporary shelter inside a large, foreign home.

Jana's single word told Aleksandar everything: it was the story of a pregnant woman's journey from Buje to Momjan, an ode to the house at the end of the world, and a lamentation for their home in Ljubljana. That word was a rebellion against everything, but in his youthful enthusiasm Aleksandar still believed that he could get Jana onside in this story, and he began to build the house in Momjan, believing that once it was built, she too would find her home there.

Who could say whether what drove him was a desire to stand, for the first time in his life, on his own plot; to finally be able to take refuge in a place of his own and subdue Ester Aljehin's fear, or whether it was his sheer self-righteousness that motivated Aleksandar Đorđević to trudge the six miles from Momjan to Buje and back, rather than lie in someone else's bed. That, along with his belief that just because others were doing something, it didn't make it right, nor acceptable. Whatever the reason, one thing was clear. Day by day, with each foundation stone laid, Aleksandar was beginning to enact the words of his mother; the woman who taught him that it was normal for everyone to lose their minds from time to time, and that submitting to the will of the crowd was not always enough to survive.

Jana did not accompany him to Momjan and instead stayed in Buje. With tiny, barely perceptible steps, she made the foreign house they were forced to inhabit her own. The previous owners' belongings were moved far from Aleksandar's sight. She removed the pots from the kitchen, the clothes from the wardrobes, the sheets from the bed, even the curtains and curtain rails were taken down and stored away in the cellar. She stripped the house and exiled its soul, doing everything so that Aleksandar would be able to move into it; while he, meanwhile, carried on putting down roots up there, at the end of a long, winding road to nowhere.

Every stone he laid brought him closer to that small, gifted piece of land, and took him further away from her. With every drop of sweat that dripped from his brow and soaked into the red earth, the more he became absorbed into that world. He could now say that a tiny piece of the world was his: not shared, but his, and his alone. He noted the distinction, and he wasn't ashamed; indeed, ownership gave him a feeling of justice, repayment for the years of homelessness. He would spend many an evening sat outside, alone, on his piece of land, and he would look out towards the sea, and wonder whether this was the happiness of which people spoke; if this was that contented feeling of simply being; not wishing to be anywhere else, feeling as if you could remain, in complete stillness, without ever having to move again.

Aleksandar and Jana each built a home of their own, and each spent their days enticing one another over. It was a childish game of two premature adults; two immature lovers enacting alternative performances of adult life. His excuse was a childhood spent with Ester Aljehin's fear, hers was not yet being twenty years old, and their joint excuse was love: a magnetic force that could not be disentangled, and which simultaneously attracted and repelled them, and would keep attracting and repelling them for the rest of their lives.

One morning, Aleksandar decided to take a slight detour from his usual route through the town and stop off at the house, to see Jana. During the day he was usually busy with work, the majority of which he'd find for himself, and so he would often simply be wandering aimlessly around the forests and marking out trees to be cleared, and he'd then spend the afternoon in Momjan, where the house was beginning to take shape. But he felt like disrupting that inevitable pattern, and wanted to surprise his wife with an unannounced visit. For the first time in a long while he stepped into the house, glowing from the midday sun, and could instantly see what Jana had done. There, right before him, was everything that his weary, evening eyes had failed to notice. All those alien objects had vanished, and that strangers' house was now brimming with the two of them. Their leftovers; their dirty washing; their pots; theirnewspapers.

He went up to the bedroom and saw that the bed was made with fresh sheets of their own, and the wardrobe was home to his shirts and her blouses. The clothes that Risto had discarded on the floor had gone. All traces of the people who used to eat and sleep here were gone too. Finally they were alone in the house, finally there was no one lingering around, no one who would silently creep up the creaking stairs, who would slip between rooms in a blink of an eye.

Now the only thing he saw in the house was Jana, downstairs in the kitchen preparing dinner, hanging washing on the line fixed across the street, between the houses; he saw her leaning against the window and waiting for him to return from Momjan, tired; he saw her getting into her nightdress in the bathroom and standing at the door, whilst he pushed the table to one side and set up the mattress on the kitchen floor – she, waiting for the bed to be ready so they could both lie down. And he knew that the reason he saw her was because his memories had filled every corner of that house and had ousted those other, alien ones. The house had succumbed to them, and he was overwhelmed by a desire to lock himself inside and make love to her, to forget the boundaries of day and night.

Only then did he realise that Jana wasn't even in the house, and he flew out of the door and ran through the town, panic-stricken, trying to find his pregnant wife.

Jana, meanwhile, was weaving around the walls of Aleksandar's unfinished house in Momjan, caressing the stones with her fingertips, as if wanting to strip them of his attachment to this place at the ends of the earth; as if she wanted to touch it, feel it, absorb it.

She walked between the walls and imagined him there in the afternoons, competing against the dying light, trying to do as much as he could whilst he could still see; before the dusk fell upon him and his house, and forced him back to the town, back to her. She pictured her husband standing before the bare walls, like a painter before a canvas, trying to paint his own home. Something warm, crackling, with the aroma of simmering stew; with walls as smooth as bare skin. She saw him, enveloped by these walls, with her and their child, hidden away from everyone, and everything, that existed outside of their trio. She'd never asked him how he pictured their home, but now she saw clearly how Aleksandar was shaping their warm sanctuary with his own hands.

And then it started. She clutched her tummy and knew instantly that she would not make it back to Buje, that she would give birth in this very place, in Momjan, by the skeleton of Aleksandar's unfinished home. She stepped onto the road and glanced around, searching for someone, anyone. But just as when Aleksandar had first brought her here, there was not a living soul to be found. The houses on the street appeared empty, but empty is how the houses in Buje always appeared, even though there were still people living inside. Phantoms that she caught a glimpse of, peeking through the window, or crossing the courtyard in the distance. Sometimes, from across the square, she'd hear indiscernible voices which seemed to be coming from those who had lived in her house, chasing her, the intruder, out; and she'd close the window in fright, and hide in the kitchen amongst a clattering of pans.

But now phantoms were what Jana wanted to see. She wanted to hear their voices, the sound of footsteps on the floor, the scrape of a knife peeling potatoes, the wipe of a cloth along the draining board; anything to betray their presence behind closed shutters. She did not want to believe the eerie silence, nor did the imminent child, and she leapt at the nearest door and started to hammer on it. Her fists pounded against the solid wood as hard as they could, and she thought she might have heard voices, just like the frightening, indiscernible voices in Buje, but carried on knocking, because the imminent child did not know fear, and nor was it afraid of phantoms, and the doors had to open; they had to open for the baby that wanted to come in to the house.

This baby was no intruder; it did not wish to hide itself away – it wanted to be amongst the phantoms and the humans, who it saw as all the same, all discernible; and so it kept on knocking, until finally its calls were answered. Then the tiny eyes of an old lady looked upon the baby and said something indiscernible, but now even Jana was able to discern every word.

Coming up the hill and staggering from exhaustion, Aleksandar caught sight of the old woman standing in the middle of the road. She looked as if she were waiting for him, and he thought he was hallucinating. But he had seen her, and she continued to pace outside her house, silently moving back and forth ahead of him. She disappeared behind the corner, and then she looked straight at him, and beckoned him over. Even hallucinations are better than despair, thought Aleksandar, and he followed the old woman inside, and followed then the sound of a baby's cry, growing closer as if spellbound, until he was stood next to a stranger holding his daughter in her lap.

A blessing, he said, when the stranger placed the tiny baby into his enormous hands. *Blessing*, Jana's exhausted voice could be heard behind him, and only then did Aleksandar catch sight of his wife on the sofa in the corner. He sat next to her and tried to kiss her, but she pulled away.

Promise me, she said, and stopped short. Her body was still quivering from the exertion she had endured.

Promise me that you'll never let them move us… all three of us… around the world ever again.

I promise, he said, and kissed her sweaty brow.

Indiscernible voices resounded around the room; voices that cared for them, embraced them, and sang to them. Aleksandar's eyes sought those of the old lady.

Grazie, donna sante.

For the first time since the war, he spoke in Italian. He broke his own spellbound state and could suddenly understand the voices of the house. Strangers whispered about how beautiful his little girl was, about her mother's eyes and her father's lips.

Over the years, this blessing would come to be described by Aleksandar as an omen that determined which of the two houses would become their home. He took it as an omen that their firstborn daughter did not arrive in Buje, but in Momjan – which actually remained her official place of birth. And so the Đorđević-Benedejčič family stayed in Momjan, and left the house in Buje to new intruders.

Jana, on the other hand, preferred to talk of punishments rather than omens; Aleksandar missing the birth of his daughter was punishment from God, punishment for his stubbornness and for forcing his wife to trudge from Buje to Momjan. To which he would respond, every time: *If that's the case, then God's a bloody fool.*

II

1.

I took a book from the footstool, the one my grandad used as a bedside table, and opened it at the page marked by a shred of newspaper. He had never been one for leather, cotton or paper bookmarks, and so rather than between pages they rotted away in untidy drawers and other ransacked corners of his house, while other flat or pointed objects at hand – pencils, toothpicks, coins – would perform the task instead. His later life amounted to the sum of insignificant details: stains encrusted on shirts, clumps of food on plates, different coloured shoelaces, burnt-out lightbulbs, chipped glasses, old biros, out-of-date I.D cards, faded horoscopes, keys without keyrings and keyrings without keys. All of these were tiny trivialities of no consequence – things he was not inclined to waste his limited time on.

Because time was always against him, Grandad never searched the house for things that were designed with a specific purpose in mind, like keeping a page in a book, because he, consistently stubborn, considered there to be plenty of other objects that could do the job – or any other job – just as well. Coffee was stored in a mayonnaise jar, tipped into the coffee pot, stirred with a gas lighter and poured into a yoghurt pot, while Grandma's beautiful ceramic sugar, salt and coffee jars, gilded coffee spoons and porcelain cups sat gathering dust in the cabinet.

Mum flew into a rage when once he used her driving licence as a book-mark, which along with the book was then returned to the library, only to reappear when the book was taken out again. It was at this point that she furiously went on a hunt for bookmarks – raiding drawers, moving armchairs, wardrobes, and even the fridge; she got under tables and beds, and eventually placed seven bookmarks on Grandad's footstool with a loud huff, and insisted that he use them. Against all her expectations, he promised that he would.

But Grandad would only read within reach of the footstool in the evening before he went to sleep, and it housed very few of the books he actually read, so it was not long before random things reappeared between the pages, from electrician's business cards to Jehovah's Witness leaflets. Usually he would just tear off a piece of newspaper, and once, when he was reading some particularly heavy tome, an obituary and photograph of Julia Morosin could be seen protruding from it for several months.

From the table in the living room, from the arm of Grandad's chair, from the oven, from the dresser in the hallway, even from the bathroom floor, my eyes were met with Julia's look of resignation. Many a time I pored over her eighty-seven years, her three daughters and their families, and the days leading up to her funeral, before I'd have to avert my gaze just to be on the safe side, before I rescued poor Julia from her posthumous duties and replaced her – Grandad style – with an article about a regatta.

Yet in spite of the boundless freedom granted to objects in his house, where beach towels would bask on the bedroom floor and dictionaries would relax on the toilet cistern, my scatterbrained Grandad was an incredibly disciplined reader. Never would he stop reading in the middle of a page, least of all mid-sentence. Neither the doorbell nor a stew boiling over on the stove would interrupt his reading. He always read a chapter from start to finish, but if the chapters were too long, he would stop reading at the end of the first sentence on the left-hand side. It was therefore easy to establish which had been the last sentence he ever read in his life.

I opened the book that I'd found on the footstool at the place marked by a piece of newspaper. At the top of the left-hand page was only the last part of the sentence, so I turned back and read the paragraph from beginning to end:

An eventful century or so ago, my paternal ancestors left behind what was then Galicia, the easternmost province of the Austro-Hungarian Empire (now Western Ukraine), and resettled in Bosnia, which had recently been annexed to the Hapsburg domain. My peasant forebears brought with them a few beehives, an iron plough, many songs about leaving home, and a recipe for perfect borscht, a dish previously unknown in that part of the world.

As I read, I became aware of the coroner standing behind me, waiting for me to move out of his way so that he could examine the hypostasis on Grandad's neck, check the dilation of his pupils and the transparency of his corneas, and establish the time of death; but just like my grandad, I couldn't stop reading until I'd reached the end of the sentence. It was my obligation: an overdue apology for all the cancelled visits. I knew the apology would not reach its intended recipient, but nevertheless I carried on reading until I reached the final word, and stopped exactly where he had stopped the previous night.

'It's rare to see people with a book on their lap. Some women perhaps, but men hardly ever. They like to have magazines and newspapers in their hands, or more likely, a remote control. These are the times we live in. People don't realise that with the help of books, they create the images of their dreams themselves; that reading develops and tends to their imagination, whereas television thrusts these images upon them. When we read, the images we create are our own, but on TV we're watching foreign ones. Television programmes violate our dream world. All the pictures that we watch enter into our subconscious, which is why we're increasingly distracted and restless. The scenes of our subconscious are scenes of horror.'

I turned around to look at the young man from Piran, who had found work on the Croatian side of the border and who stood, most likely as he was trained to do, at a respectful distance from the grieving party and looked at me, tentatively, with sadness. Deaths were his trade and he was relaxed as he spoke, but with a sincerity in his voice that sought to create the impression that for him, every corpse he came to examine was a new story, and that he was yet to succumb to the apathy that comes with routine. It seemed to me, though, that as some post-mortem handbook had taught him, he was deliberately filling the silence which prior to his arrival had flourished around the corpse, and that his clichéd remarks were just one of his professional duties.

I was tempted to break the pattern, to stop politely nodding, and ask him in all seriousness how then, in his opinion, did all those unrealistic, obscure images as described by medieval dreamers enter into peoples' subconscious in the Middle Ages; what, in his opinion, were nightmares made of, before the existence of film and television; where did our ancient ancestors get all those three-headed dragons and one-eyed cannibals from, if not from the night-time programming on commercial television.

Instead I kept quiet and let him move past me to get to the bed, where Grandad's body was lying.

Grandad's death was my first. I turned away from the body lying on the bed and felt terrified. My eyes went flying around the space, searching for a nook where they could rest, but everything around me stared back. Grandad's glasses for watching television were on the dining table, carelessly discarded on the dirty tablecloth. Beneath the table were several large breadcrumbs, having escaped his palm cupped at the edge. There was a pile of old newspapers in the corner with a basket buried deep inside, having been filled long ago. A single sock hung from the edge of the bed, which he had most likely taken off in his sleep a night or two before. It crossed my mind that his smell was still likely to be inside it, his odour, and a hole or two as well, made by his hastily cut toenails. On the floor beneath the window lay two books, splayed open, having fallen off who-knew-when. On the other side of the room by the television there was an empty glass, probably stuck to the dusty cabinet. The rug was turned up at the corners and I pictured Grandad tripping over it. Two out of four drawers in the chest were slightly ajar, both entrapping some item of clothing. From underneath the sofa I could make out the shadowy outline of a spoon, which he had probably knocked from the table a few days ago without realizing. Or, most likely, he didn't fancy bending down and simply left it lying there.

Grandad was everywhere, only there, on the bed, was he absent. He wasn't there behind his speckled grey-green eyes, nor behind his flyaway white eyebrows and beard, which for the first time obediently lay flush against his face. I was sitting right beside his motionless body, almost touching him with my hand, but I had yet to comprehend his death. Everything in the house was as it always had been, so normal. A dense smoky smell was still filling the room, noises in the street drifted by the old windows and particles of dust danced in sheaves of light. At first glance, nothing had changed since my last visit. Except Grandad had died.

I repeated those words to myself, and the coroner confirmed it. Mum nodded.

When Grandma died, everything was different. Only after the funeral did I go back to the house, after Mum had sorted through Grandma's things and had given the place such a rigorous clean that a photograph above her bed, in which she didn't even resemble herself, was the only trace of Grandma that was left. That, along with her toothbrush.

Mum believed that death should be no obstruction to life, and that traces of the deceased were to be tidied away as quickly as possible; scrubbed, cleaned and washed, carried out of the house, piece by piece, just as the corpse was carried out before them. Thus, only a day after Grandma died, her clothes were packed into old leather suitcases which atop of wardrobes had been waiting patiently for their final journey; Mum took them to Caritas, put Grandma's jewellery into a plastic ice cream tub, and gifted it to the neighbours' granddaughter, and threw the make-up in the bin.

All Grandad could do, meanwhile, was watch in silence; but when Mum brought him two toothbrushes from the bathroom, and asked which was his and which was Grandma's, he said *I don't know*. Thinking that he hadn't understood, Mum explained that she'd like to throw Grandma's away, so asked if he could please tell her which was the one he used to clean his teeth. But Grandad persisted with his *I don't know*. Mum took no notice of this lie, and repeated her question just as stubbornly, and so Grandad changed his response.

They're both mine. Put them back in the bathroom.

Then could you tell me which one you like the best? she asked him.

Why?

It doesn't make sense to have two toothbrushes.

I can have as many toothbrushes as I like.

Would you like me to leave Mum's toothbrush as a memento?

If I'd have wanted to keep something as a memento, I'd have kept hold of one of her dresses. Or a necklace.

Did I ask you if you minded me getting rid of them?

Yes.

And what did you say? That I should go ahead as I saw fit, no?

Yes.

And now you're telling me that you'd like to hang on to a necklace or a dress.

I didn't say that, Vesna.

What did you say then?

If I wanted to keep something as a memento, I said. If.

If that's not an accusation, what is?

It's not an accusation.

What is it then?

It's not an accusation.

Whenever Mum had a guilty conscience, she would bite. She held the toothbrush in front of Grandad's face.

You've got three seconds to decide which is yours, because after that one of these is going straight in the bin.

I like both of them.

Three, two, one…

Mum let one of the brushes fall from her hand and into the rubbish bag in which she was collecting items to be taken away.

Grandad said nothing, and Mum thought this was the end of the toothbrush saga, but when she returned the next day, standing in a cup in the bathroom was a new toothbrush, one that Grandad had bought that morning. He used it to clean his teeth until the day he died. The old one, either Grandma's or Grandad's, the one which didn't end up in Mum's rubbish bag, remained beside the photograph, never to be used again. Since then, on the edge of the washbasin, two toothbrushes have stood in the red plastic cup, covered in limescale and other grime. And there they still stand.

'One could not wish for a better way to go. To die in one's sleep means to die without pain. It's what we call a royal death.'

So said the coroner, putting his shoes on in the hall. He was one of those persons who removed their shoes even when the hosts insisted that it wasn't necessary. Mum nodded, I closed the door behind him, and then we went back to Grandad. I was still holding the book in my hand.

'Every morning he read to her, over coffee. One chapter each morning. Like reading to a child.'

'Well, she was a child,' said Mum.

She was. A child with wrinkled hands which gently took hold of you and delicately drew you in close. A child that looked at you with eyes seeking safety, eyes with a childlike curiosity, which were heavily draped in sagging, mottled skin, completely covered in moles.

I remember that child from Aunt Maya's story, the child that turned to her daughter, who had driven over one afternoon for a brief visit, and accosted her in a quiet, timid, childlike voice.

Excuse me lady, do you know my mother?

Yes, answered my aunt, who had never known her grandmother Maria; a seamstress, who died young from tuberculosis.

Could you call her and ask her to come and collect me? said Grandma. *I'd like to go home.*

An alarmed Aunt Maya began to call for help; she called out to her father, who she supposed would know how to answer such a question; who she supposed would know what to say to the frail child sitting beside her.

An alarmed Grandad came flying out of the kitchen, but when Maya explained that Grandma would like to see her mother, he turned calmly to his wife.

We've called her already, she'll be here soon.

Maya could not fathom how he had told this lie with such tremendous ease. To her, what Grandad had said was unacceptably deceitful; it was a discourtesy that Grandma had done nothing to deserve. Her father seemed insensitive, and she was shocked to see him so casually invoke his mother-in-law back from the dead.

Whilst she's on her way, why don't you play a game with this lady, Grandad suggested, going back into the kitchen.

Maya wanted to call out after him, but Grandma got there first.

Do you know how to play hangman?

He read to her every morning. Grandma would sit on the edge of the sofa, leaning forwards over the table, towards the coffee and biscuits, while Grandad sat in the armchair beneath the window. He always held the book in his left hand, while with his right, he would raise his glasses so that he could look beneath them over to her, as if mindful that she might escape whilst he was reading. Then he let go, so that the nose pads were back resting on the tip of his nose, and the letters came back into focus, and he read on. Always slowly, one word after the other, sentence after sentence. When he read, time would lazily disperse around the room, like thick honey rolling over the rims of jars. Heroes fell in love, went their separate ways, were born and died; yet his rasping voice would proceed, undisturbed, never entirely adapted to the tale he was telling. His attention was always on her, poised for any indiscernible movements, waiting for something within her to stir. Yet she would continue to sit motionless, only journeying with her fingertips among the coffee cups, taking a sugar cube or teaspoon, and then replacing them on her lap. This was their ritual; cut off from the rest of the world.

When she listened to his metronomic voice, her inaudible drifts of thought would become tangled in impossible knots, and in pursuit of them she was led to a place where words no longer had meaning, and where thoughts were nothing but obscure images. Her eyes became vacant, her breathing shallow, her hands settled; until eventually she sat suspended in a daze. My grandfather's breaks were the quietest times of the day. And when he finished, he put the book and his glasses down on the table, and carried the coffee tray back into the kitchen. The only thing he left on the table was her coffee cup. That cup would stay there, in front of her, right until the evening, as a reminder that they'd had their coffee that day, that yet another one of their finite mornings had been spent.

When Grandad returned from the kitchen, he would bring her back round. Sometimes she responded, suggesting that he ought to take the dirty coffee cup away; sometimes she would merely stare back at him searchingly; and sometimes he didn't wait for a response. The day forged ahead, and it was time for other duties, for other rituals.

You don't have to be alone to be lonely, he once said to me, though I never understood that sentence back then. Or rather, I didn't try to understand it. I didn't take it in; I thought he was talking about himself, that he was talking about Grandma's drawn-out departure, about the passing of memories, about his despair. Back then, I didn't think about how much of his consciousness was lost along with hers; I didn't consider how, without her, there was no more them; that she was the only other one who preserved their story, and that for all those years he had to watch it all vanish before his eyes; that he had to watch himself slowly die away in her.

I never thought about how agonising that moment must be, when you realise that the person sleeping under the same duvet no longer recognises you; when the eyes which once reflected you, in all of your nakedness and goose-pimpled flesh, now see you as a stranger. How you are left, at that moment, so very alone. And so very lonely. Interminably lonely.

I thought, extremely naively, as is always the case when our own selves and our own personal grief are not immediately concerned, that the hardest thing for Grandad was to watch my deteriorating grandma suffer; to be faced with her forgetting on a daily basis, to come up with ways to help her remember to take the green tablets before lunch, and the yellow pills before the black and red ones; to repeat ad infinitum that it was only midday and that yes, if she went to bed now she wouldn't be able to sleep at night; to introduce her to her own daughter, to convince her that he wasn't lying and that they really were at home, and the house really was theirs. I thought the hardest thing would be to live in eternal fear, to be scared that whilst you were out queuing for bread or paying the electricity, she would wander out of the back door, which you'd possibly forgotten to lock – because you're not young yourself, and you also forget things – and that she'd step out, onto the road, alone, and that nobody would see her, because older people are never really seen.

It never occurred to me that the care and compassion were the only things that actually helped Grandad survive; they were the only things keeping his head above the surface of solitude, preventing him from being embedded in a vast world of bitterness. It must have been so tempting to feel cheated; it would have been so easy to give in, but Grandad never did. He never stopped caring, he never lacked compassion.

Mum sat across from me at the table and she seemed unusually calm and considerate. Her only movement was to draw her right hand to her face at irregular intervals, before moving it away again. Her middle and index finger were slumped against slightly parted lips, like the days when they used to hold cigarettes. But every time Mum became aware of the imaginary smoking, her hand would suddenly flop back down onto the table.

'We should tidy up a bit. People are going to start arriving soon.'

She didn't wait for my response, and instead she got up, went into the kitchen and started washing the dishes that had piled up in the sink. Just as when Grandma had died, she was wiping away traces of the dead. Steam was rising from the sink, and she watched the crumbs of Grandad's last supper disappear down the drain. But, as if something had made her change her mind, she put the unwashed coffee pot back on the side and, using the tea towel to wipe her hands, came back into the room.

'Do you know what just came into my head? I'm not sure if this is the time… but seeing as it's just the two of us… When I was younger, when I still lived at home – I must have been, I don't know, fifteen, the time when I used to really read a lot – he had this awful habit, where if he saw you reading, for example – if he came home from work and I was reading in my room, he'd come up to me and start explaining something. Nothing important – just stupid stuff. And he'd never ask if he was bothering me… he never used to read back then. He didn't have time for books. And those of us who read seemed to rather get on his nerves. Because he wanted to chat. He loved to chat with us. And now look… all these books. He died with a book in his hand… But I honestly don't remember the last time we had a conversation, you know, a proper conversation…. Everything really did change at that time. That Egypt of his changed him. Him and her. All of us. As if the whole of Cairo had wedged itself between him and the rest of the world, keeping him away from us. He used to belong to us so completely, to us alone. Full of some special warmth that made you want to be near him. I know this sounds strange, but there was something feminine about him… Something so soft, gentle… But then…'

Even though I knew Mum would not let herself cry, I stepped forward and gave her a hug. She wasn't the cuddling sort, but she leaned on me and put her arms around my shoulders. For a moment we stood there, in the midst of time and space, and she let the tea towel slip from her hands onto the floor.

The ring of the doorbell late at night took me by surprise, and I sat there, sure that it would be some wandering soul or other, who would soon realise their mistake and be on their way. But then it rang again, and when Mum got up and reluctantly headed towards the door, it dawned on me who was standing behind it.

The door opened and a long silence ensued. I was not best placed to see, and could only keep an eye on Mum standing at the door from a distance, but I could picture the similarly motionless figures on the other side. For a moment I was afraid that Mum was going to leave them outside, something that was certainly possible, in spite of the dead body that was lying to the side of me, but she did eventually take a step back.

She remained standing in the middle of the tiny porch, where it was hard for people to squeeze past; or rather, was impossible if one of those people happened to be Aunt Maya. This meant that the visitors were yet to step inside the house. Stepping inside would have meant bumping into Mum, or barging past her at least, which would have been the first contact between the two sisters for more than seven years.

As Mum moved aside, Maya stepped through the door and into my line of sight, and stood there awkwardly, not knowing whether to go inside, or whether to wait for Mum to make more room. Maybe she was waiting for my assistance, but I wasn't interested in playing their games, and I avoided making eye contact.

As if she'd had enough of the embarrassment, Maya strode into the house, threw her arms around Mum and clutched her tightly to her chest. Both of them were in view now, and Dane too, who had fought his way through to the foreground.

A bewildered Mum was patting Maya's ample back as she sobbed, and I was amused to see Dane try, unsuccessfully, to close the door behind him whilst remaining inside, without touching the two sisters – something that was impossible due to the basic laws of physics.

Eventually he decided to take his shoes off, but quickly gathered that they'd have nowhere to go. So he held onto them, did a full turn, but the shoe rack was right behind Mum, exactly where Dane was unable to reach.

At that moment, Maya came towards me, wiping her nose on her baggy cardigan sleeve. She and Dane had always been an unlikely couple; he was ironed to professional perfection, but she was untidy, even in her evening wear with a freshly coiffed hairdo. It wasn't just her size; there was something unkempt about her, as if supporting her husband, Secretary of State at the Ministry of the Interior, had taken its toll on the lady from Human Resources at the Faculty of Education.

'Why haven't you covered him up?'

Maya turned to look at me, but the covering of the departed was not something I knew anything about, and I even mumbled something about it being a custom subconsciously lifted from American films.

'We wanted to wait until you'd arrived,' said Mum, who had sensed that Maya's question was aimed at her. Mum always impressed me with how she knew how to play people so easily. She could sense what people wanted to hear, and whenever she was in the mood, would pander to them with incredible spontaneity.

'Thank you.'

Moved by the fabricated gesture, Maya began to weep as she drew the sheet over Grandad's body. Mum went to help her, but Maya signalled that this was something she would like to do herself.

The sheet was trapped underneath the weighty corpse, and Maya, clearly not wishing to disturb it, coaxed it out from underneath his thigh an inch at a time, then a little from under the shoulders, and then a bit more from his behind, where the sheet offered the most stubborn resistance. Maya persevered, as Mum and I, and Dane, who meanwhile had managed to put his shoes down and come inside, could do nothing but watch in silence. It was like a funeral ritual in advance of the funeral; she moved around the body so slowly, as if conducting the last rites, and her clumsiness and short arms, too short to reach where was needed, were the only things to shatter this illusion.

But when Maya eventually managed to free the sheet and began to cover Grandad, I turned away. I wasn't ready to see the covering of his face. The symbolism of the scene was too much. As comical as it was, and as awkward as my aunt was, this was an act of farewell in which I did not want to participate. I went into the kitchen and got myself a glass of water. I wasn't thirsty, but I didn't want Mum to know that I'd intentionally removed myself.

'Dane, before we leave, would you be able to go with Jadran to get that table from the garage that we were talking about?'

Maya liked to decide what needed to be done, and how, when and by whom. Dane did not protest, at least not in front of me, as if he dutifully accepted his subservient role. In actual fact, it was impossible to understand what bound this couple together. It couldn't be the children, as Miha and Špela had long since broken free from their parents. Miha was forging a brave new world with the million other technological geniuses in Silicon Valley, while Špela had moved out to the small town of Postojna after numerous arguments with Maya, and only came back to Ljubljana on occasion. Dane and Maya lived together in a residential neighbourhood close to the centre, in a flat which was too big for them, and their cohabitation remained a mystery to me.

'We ought to be going soon.'

'Well then go and see to it straight away.'

Dane relented on behalf of the both of us, and signalled for me to follow him with a twitch of the head. Mum turned away, not wishing to get involved, and so I was left with no choice other than to go with him.

We stepped out of the house into thick darkness, but the well-trodden path that led through the garden was familiar to both of us, and we walked, one behind the other, towards the garage without waiting for our eyes to adjust, or for the outlines of the house and trees to reveal themselves. Dane was in a hurry, and wanted to complete the task at hand as quickly as possible, and get back to Ljubljana.

The light above the garage was obscured by the singed bodies of curious moths, and offered only a feeble glow. Dane paused beneath it, and held up Grandad's ample bunch of keys, the majority of which served locks that had long since been changed, and cars that had served their time. His hands were shaking. As he stepped closer to the lock and tried one key after the other, his face caught the light and his forehead gleamed from the gathering beads of sweat.

'For fuck's sake!'

Dane picked the keys up off the floor and started again. He gathered himself this time, separated the keys that he'd already tried from those he hadn't, and soon found the one that unlocked the garage door.

The open garage revealed stacks of obsolete items, the kind of items that fill every store room, shed and garage the world over. Grandad's garage was just one of many halfway houses en route to the dustbin. Somewhere amongst all the rotting and rusty junk was the table that Maya had sent us for, though it wasn't easy to make out in the dark.

Dane took his phone out of his pocket, illuminated the makings of a pathway and stepped forward, but after two steps was forced to stop.

Frantically he shone his light onto plastic canisters, a pram, two wooden deckchairs, a TV antenna, three car tyres, a pile of yellowing comics, a chest freezer, a can of antifreeze, an umbrella, a spade, and several other items indistinguishable in partial darkness. He was constantly getting caught in things as he did so, as if he were tangled in a spider's web and everything in the garage was clinging onto him.

'Ff...'

A clatter rang out, and with it, the light from Dane's phone bolted across the garage ceiling, past me and back onto the floor; its shadow bounced backward and collided with something glass on the wall. As the overturned items rolled along the floor, and the clattering and banging subsided, I could hear Dane's deep, laboured breathing. He hurried out in a panic, and angrily slammed the garage door.

'For fuck's sake! Who sends someone into a garage for a table in the dark! It makes no sense. Half the garage needs emptying before you could get to it. Some idea that is, Jesus!'

Dane walked away back towards the house without waiting for any response from me. I don't ever remember seeing him so on edge, and I wondered if the unease that he'd long felt around me had eventually turned into fear.

It was possible he was afraid of what I knew about him, about him and my father Safet, about Dane's role in his departure. I doubt he knew what Mum had told me about events prior to Safet's disappearance, but he probably had a feeling that I'd found out nearly everything there was to know.

Dane had, as a matter of fact, been avoiding me for a long time, and it had been years since we had been in such close proximity, let alone just the two of us, face to face.

When Dane disappeared back into the house, I was left alone in the dark of the garden. I didn't hurry after him; by then my eyes had grown accustomed to the darkness, and I could easily make out the contours of Grandad's small garden. I walked over to the fig tree, under which Grandad had installed a wooden bench, so that he could, in his words, observe the fruits of his labour. My arm reached out to touch one of the branches. I couldn't make out its colour in the dark, but from its plumpness and softness I could tell that it was fig season; the season of Grandad's fig jam.

But before my mind could be flooded with sweet memories of harvesting figs, I saw Grandad scaling the thick, strong branches of the fig tree, as if seeing a tomorrow that would never come; I saw his dry, slender hands picking the ripe fruit hidden behind large, leathery leaves. I saw him pick up the phone and let Mum know that the figs were ripe, and that she ought to come and get some. He knew that she wouldn't, but he also knew how much she loved figs, and it was one of those rare phone calls that brought him joy. But her answer was always the same. He could pack the figs on to a bus, or wait for me to visit.

I saw Grandad carefully placing the figs into Vesna's tub, which is the name he gave to his largest plastic container; I saw him making fig jam for me, for pancakes; and I saw him taking his fig ice cream out of the freezer, which was never offered to anyone, as it didn't bear the slightest resemblance to ice cream.

I saw him. He was stood right next to me, leaning on the trunk, and it occurred to me that even though Grandad wouldn't be harvesting his figs this year, the tree would keep on growing regardless, and that it would go on to bear its sweet fruit, even if he were no longer around to climb its branches like a kid.

It wasn't memories of him that got me in the end. His death didn't change those. What got me were the images of a final few days which had been taken away from us. And I was overcome by the sad image of the tree, which stood, lonely, in front of Grandad's empty house, looking at its closed doors.

I started to feel suffocated. On the ground in front of me I could see a plump, ripe fig, torn by the weight of its juice from the branch. I looked at it, decomposing sadly on the ground, and my eyes clouded over. I slumped down onto the ground, keeping my back against the tree, and let my head sink down towards my lap. It finally hit me that Grandad was gone.

2.

When I went back into the house, Maya and Dane were already leaving. All apologies about their leaving so soon had been made, and Mum had already accepted them on our behalf. All that remained was the exchange of forlorn expressions. No one felt the need to say anything else as they said goodbye. I felt Maya's silent sobbing as she hugged me. Dane offered me his hand and a sympathetic expression.

'Look after your mum,' he said.

Maya gave one last glance towards Grandad, covered by a sheet. Dane, meanwhile, opened the door and let her out of the house, while I stood as if I'd wanted to say something else, but had changed my mind. I waited until the porch light had aided them to their car before closing the door and returning to Mum.

I found her sitting at the table, which was covered in old photographs. She had tipped them out in front of her and was rifling through them, holding them up and gazing at them. She was completely engrossed in the pictures, and when she spoke, she didn't raise her eyes to check whether I was listening.

'Do you know, there are no photos from their wedding? Not a single photo of them when they were young. No photos of Maya and me when we were little, from holidays or birthday parties. Nothing. They have passport photos. The first photos of the two of them together were from my wedding. Before that – nothing. Nothing to immortalize their story. We only know their story as they told it. Like in books. The only way their story can be told is the way they wanted to tell it. Isn't that beautiful? Like a fairy tale. The only pictures we're left with are the ones our minds created, as we listened to their storytelling.

I crouched down under Grandad's bed and picked up a small, empty, brown bottle from the floor. It was familiar. There used to be blue and white capsules inside. Grandma's blood pressure tablets. The bottle had been lying there ever since her death, I thought; like so many other small objects, it had rolled around in corners of Grandad's house, and gathered dust out of sight. But it wasn't dusty; which meant it had been down there for a day or two at the most.

'Look, there just aren't any photos of the two of them together. Here's Grandad at some conference. Here he is with his colleagues. Here's Grandma with her sister. They were so good-looking, weren't they? This is Grandad on a union excursion to the Plitvice lakes. I remember him talking about how they found the director floating in the lake one morning, naked and semi-conscious. Here are their school photos. Look at those haircuts. Nowadays, when everything is photographed, filmed, recorded, anyone will be able to tell our stories; everyone will think that they can tell them, until eventually, our own stories – the ones we tell about ourselves – will be just one of many, buried amongst all the others. Stories will no longer be written from memory; no more romantic stories, tailored to fit our own wants and needs.'

Maybe Grandad had used Grandma's pill bottle to store things of his own; rubber bands, buttons, screws. I wouldn't be surprised if he'd even kept salt, nuts or bay leaves in there. Maybe the bottle seemed like the perfect size for any of those things. I could just picture him, empty-ing Grandma's medicine drawer and opening the little bottle, shaking its contents into the toilet bowl, giving it a quick rinse, and then funnelling sugar, pepper or seasoning into it. And I see how easily the little bottle slips out of his hand, and rolls under the bed unnoticed.

'How much do you know about their wedding? Anything? They arranged to meet after work, outside the town hall – did you know that? Grandad was late because he forgot to buy flowers and only remembered when he was halfway there; Grandma was waiting for him at the Robba fountain, and was so tired that she sat down on the fountain and dirtied her wedding dress – it wasn't really a wedding dress, but a normal one that she'd go to work in – but it didn't matter, because it was more or less over as soon as it began: they read their vows and exchanged rings, and then they all went to Café Evropa for cake, the two of them with Daria and Milenko. Someone was playing beautifully at the piano, and Grandma and Grandad shared a dance. What photos do you need? Photos would ruin the story, don't you think? The story would long be forgotten if they'd have had photos, but I still remember it; and even now I can see them dancing, every time I pass Evropa I see them, dancing, accompanied by the piano. And I see them holding each other tight on the bus, and how Grandma's flowers get squashed, so that all she comes home with are bare stalks, and says *it's a good job we're not superstitious*, and puts the bare stalks in a vase; and then the next morning, a fresh flower bud appears and Grandad says *it's a shame we're not superstitious, that'd be a good sign*. Even if it had been captured, a photo could never have done that flower justice. Photos would have also shown the stain on Grandma's dress. And you'd see Grandad's funny moustache. And their small, run-down flat that they rented – that disgusting stove in the corner, and the black sooty marks that spread halfway across the room. This way you see them in each others' arms, in love, happy. Exactly how they wanted to see themselves, when they looked back.'

It could even be that Grandad had a similar health condition to Grandma, and that whenever he was running low on medication, because he never liked going to the chemist, he used her old supply. He never believed in expiry dates on food, let alone on medicines.

'Their story was theirs alone. Even if it was fiction, it was more truthful than all of ours; all our documented stories. What an ugly expression. "To document". We document our entire lives these days; our weddings, births, leaving school, graduation, travels – we document it all, whereas they remembered these things; talked about them, gathered their memories in boxes and turned them into stories. They stuck them together however they wanted, because making a beautiful story, and appearing beautiful in it, was all that mattered. Why would you want to tell horrible stories, just because they were true? Why would you remember those things? Life really was, for them, what they chose to remember; whereas we're forced to remember everything, our own life, shaped by the wants of others, is forced upon us. We're not free anymore. Because freedom is in the alteration; in the deception, in the invention, in the act of misleading. Misleading oneself, and others. That's what freedom is. Seeing yourself as you want to be seen, not how others see you. We're not free because we accept our image in the mirror. . . Oh, he finally shaved off that awful moustache here. This ought to be the photo on his headstone, what do you reckon? He looks the most like himself in this one. And he's around the same age as Grandma was in the photo we chose for her... Isn't he? I'm not sure, I'll have to ask Maya what she thinks.'

If a film scene depicted a small, empty bottle on the floor beneath the bed of a deceased man, viewers would immediately suspect a suspicious death. But we don't do that in real life, because we don't believe that suspicious deaths, such as the suicide of an 87-year-old, could ever actually happen. At least not here, and not to us. It might be that something similar happened in 1963, in the Philippines, or in Wales, but we read about it in the *Believe it or Not* column. And we didn't believe it.

'Look, here they are at our wedding. Look at us. You see, our story is fixed already. All those drunken faces, funny outfits and slack ties, sweat patches on checked shirts, white tablecloths over red ones and artificial flowers in plastic vases. You almost forget about us when you look at these photos. We're just not there. You see Metod in the chair, Darinka and Peter with their arms around each other, singing, Irfan asleep at the table, Roman, Blanka and all that lipstick and rouge that was fashionable at the time; you see everything, yet we're nowhere to be seen – just two faces in the photographs. If you look at these, they tell a different story to the one I'd tell you. The story you know is one from the photographs. The drunken version of our wedding. And you know the story about how, the next morning, we carried the tables outside and ordered breakfast on the restaurant lawn. Even the waiters ate with us. There on the lawn, at ten in the morning, your Dad and I sang *Bila je tako lijepa*. That story's still beautiful, because everyone had stopped taking photos. The photographer was still in bed and the two of us sang, and not for the camera. And then everyone else joined in. That really was a beautiful morning.'

And now I don't believe it. I play about with plot lines in my mind, with policemen who question us about Grandad's past, gather fingerprints around the house and ask us not to leave the country. None of it was actually possible. And so I imagine Grandad approaching the medicine drawer and pulling it out clumsily; more forcefully on the right hand side, because that's his strongest hand. The drawer comes out at an angle and gets stuck, but Grandad stubbornly persists. Only when he's out of breath does he stop, push the draw back in, then tease it out again, slowly this time, so he's adjusting as he goes. It's not premeditated, and yet it is; he knows and yet doesn't know what he's looking for in the drawer. He doesn't know which medicine he'll find in there, but he senses it, senses the fatal potential of such treasure. He has already made his mind up: he'll die in his own bed, just as she did – he doesn't wish to collapse on the floor, unsupervised, in the middle of the house, in the kitchen or the doorway; which is why his pyjamas are already on, he's going to get into bed, take the tablets and go to sleep. That's the only way to do it, so that no one will suspect that he's killed himself. His death is his business, and that's how it must stay; nobody needs to know that he invited it. And so he takes the small brown bottle of blood pressure tablets out of the drawer. A full glass of water, which will wash the tablets down, is already waiting on the bedside table, and Grandad lies down, and turns out the light. Soon afterwards his snoring can be heard in the darkness. And then silence.

'Look at Safet in this picture. He's already drunk before the wedding's even started. Can you imagine – he turned up drunk to his own wedding! Out on the lawn the next morning was the most sober he'd been. He looked at me and gave me that smile of his, and told me that in Bosnia they had a saying: *a wedding night in the tavern makes a marriage full of song. And wine.* And he laughed. I can still hear that laugh of his. He made that up there and then, I knew it, but that was just how he was, and I liked that about him. Ever the improviser.'

I looked over at Grandad's bedside table, and suddenly I could no longer play about with the image of the suicidal old man as casually as I had done before. There really was a glass of water there, next to a book.

There was still a sip or two of liquid left in it. Fortunately, Mum was still sifting through photos and didn't notice me turning white.

'Do you know which other story isn't documented? The story of when Safet met Aleksandar. There we've got two stories, their stories, which don't entirely match up. I was there when they met officially, when I introduced Safet to Aleksandar. Straightaway, they seemed weirdly polite, especially Safet; Grandad knew how to behave himself, but Safet didn't have his usual front, he didn't try to impress with his jokes and didn't start telling him stories. And Aleksandar didn't perform any of his tricks either. That's what usually happened when I introduced a boyfriend or friend to him – he'd ask them if they knew who Bata Živojinović played in the film The Battle of Sutjeska. That's the kind of question he'd ask. What did Nikola Tesla do when his light bulb burnt out? That was another of his. He once admitted that he'd never been worried about any of my boyfriends, because he knew that none of them would last. Maybe that was true, but to this day I don't know what he saw in Safet. Because I wasn't there the first time they met.'

She carried on talking, while I stared at Grandad's dead body. It's probably no easier to understand the suicide of a seventeen-year-old than it is the suicide of an 87-year-old. It's probably pushing the same limit. There is nothing more extreme that a person can do than take their own life. There is nothing harder to fathom. And at the same time, there's nothing more human. To resign from life is to reach out beyond our animalism, beyond the innate will to survive. All the atrocities that people commit against others are more understandable.

'The only part of their stories that matched up is the part where Aleksandar was head of sales at the Lesnina furniture store, and Safet worked there for a month. Student temp job. Safet always related that story as a joke; as his, Irfan and Roman's big swindle. In their one month of working there, they used the Lesnina warehouse to renovate all the beds in the student dorm. Who wouldn't want a bed that didn't creak? Who wouldn't want a sturdy wooden bed for their small student room, a spare bed for a friend? They supplied them for next to nothing, plank by plank; Irfan and Safet would even build one for a few extra dinars, it was good business, but they were soon caught out. *You can't hide a bed in a drawer*, Safet would always say, but in actual fact, that's just the start of the story. Instead of causing uproar and marching them to the police, Aleksandar placed an advert in the paper, with the manager's approval, saying that Lesnina had decided to give away thirty-two beds to the student halls in Ljubljana, and gave Safet's contact details for further information. He knew that taking the beds back from the students could end badly, it might cause another revolt of some sort, but gifts always went down well. The Party were also very pleased to see Lesnina supporting the youth in such a way. And then Safet was called in for a chat. Aleksandar always said that it was instantly clear that he was dealing with a certain breed of Bosnian, and if he could have patented and exported one like him, Yugoslavia would have been a world superpower. And Safet said Aleksandar was a typical bigwig, so typical that he could've been lifted straight out of the Party handbook, and he laughed, at himself – well, you remember that laugh of his. No one will ever know what they spoke about exactly, during that meeting, or how they came to an agreement that got them both out of that mess, saving Safet from the wrath of swindled students, and Aleksandar from questions from high up about giving gifts to students at a time when they weren't exactly the regime's closest allies. Both of them, outcasts as they were, wisely kept quiet about it, and even when I introduced Safet to Aleksandar, both of them were as polite and friendly as could be, like thoroughbred Slovenes, and it would have been easy to think that something was afoot. But I was in love…'

'How long had he been sleeping in this bed?'

'What?'

Mum looked up from the photos, but it wasn't clear whether I'd managed to call her back from the era she'd been lost in.

'Didn't he sleep in the living room? On that sofa bed?'

'Who? I don't know… why?'

'When was the last time you saw him?'

'Who? Grandad, you mean? I don't know…'

This wasn't something I was able to verbalise, but Grandad did not die in his own bed. Grandad didn't die in the bed he'd slept in for the past five, maybe ten, years; but in the bed that he'd shared with Grandma. He died in the same bed as her.

'What do you mean, you don't know?'

Mum was too honest a person to hide what she felt. Or what she knew.

'So you don't even know which bed he slept in?'

Maybe he simply sensed that he was about to die. They do say that the dying can sense an impending end. Maybe he lay down in her bed because he sensed that night would be his last.

'I saw him last week... but only briefly...'

She withdrew back to the photographs. She hadn't been going to Momjan regularly. She would only give her dad a very occasional phone call. But then she went to visit him, without telling me. Only a few days before his death.

'Look, here's one of us all together in front of the house. It used to be such a happy place here, didn't it? And we always had to take photos. Because we were all here together, and we never knew when the next occasion might be. It all seemed so daft at the time, but then, all of a sudden, we were never here together again. This is the only photo of us all together. It was just after Aleksandar returned from Egypt. And can you see Grandma in this photo? Can you see... this is why I don't like photos... my memory of it is... nicer... it's nicer... and now I see how she was, and then... if it weren't for this, all I'd remember was that we were happy to be together. Now I see this, and...'

Her voice cracked. She cracked. For a moment she was frozen, but continued to stare at the photo in her trembling hands. I sensed that she had to finish her story. To overcome herself and see the story through to the end.

'That's why I'd like to tidy everything away after him. That is why I tidied everything away after her. I don't want... I... don't want anything to alter my memories, to remind me of the things I've forgotten. If I've forgotten something, then it's right that I have. And I don't want... I don't want anything… none of this… no photos. Look at her here… I'm going to tidy everything away and get rid of it. Everything. Every last bit.'

She quickly got to her feet, took Grandma's grey Italian shoebox and put the photos back inside. They were protruding haphazardly above the rim and it was clear the shoebox wasn't going to close, but Mum balanced the lid on top and carried it, unclosed, back to the wardrobe. The gap between the shelves was too narrow, so she put the box on the floor, and then pushed both hands down on the lid, as if wanting to squash the photos with her bodyweight.

Then she stopped, sat on the floor, removed the lid and took the photos out of the box. Now she carefully ordered them by size, neatly arranging each pile, distractedly wiping away the dust and using her nails to scratch off the specks of dirt that had gathered around the edges. Her hands appeared to be in charge of themselves.

'You don't have to sit here because of me you know. I'm not going to do anything stupid.'

That was a request for no further questions. I bent down towards her, and just as I always do when saying goodbye, I touched her right cheek. And she, just like always, places her hand on mine and leaves her fingers to slowly drag as I walk away.

III

I don't remember the last time I was at home on my own in the middle of the night, without Anya and Marko. It must have been before Marko was born. I made myself a cup of tea and let my tired limbs sink into the sofa. I'd long forgotten the sound of a night free of Anya's gentle breathing and Marko wriggling in his cot. I'd forgotten the sound of silence. I didn't want to dwell on Grandad's death, on the small, brown bottle, or the glass by the side of his bed. Or on Anya and her departure. Not yet. My time was without limitations and that was of comfort. No journey to nursery or work was waiting for me on the other side, and I was free to draw out the night until morning.

Every part of my life was neatly compartmentalised. Half an hour for coffee before work, twenty minutes of sitting around after lunch, an hour for beer after basketball, half an hour of watching TV before bed. Everything had a pre-determined time frame. Because there had always been something waiting for me. But now I found myself outside of schedules. I wasn't expected to be anywhere. Grandad's death had gifted me that small luxury, and I revelled in it shamelessly.

But thoughts were already moving in on me. Thoughts permeated with her.

I tried to relive that Tuesday, the day before Anya's departure; tried to search for signs of what was about to happen, but it was a day like any other, in every way possible, and as I replayed it, I caught myself layering scenes and conversations from other days. I was no longer sure whether Anya was still asleep, or already in the bathroom, on that Tuesday morning, as I gazed at a sleeping Marko and touched his head, as I do for luck – my only superstition. The image of Anya curled tightly into a ball on the right-hand side of the bed was being distorted by the sound of running water. My only clear memory is of Anya calling me before midday, saying that one of the nursery teachers had informed her that the previous day, Marko had pushed Teya, knocking her to the floor. I asked if she had been hurt, but all Anya said was *she could have been*. For some reason which now escapes me, I didn't want to continue the conversation, and I said that we'd see each other at lunchtime, and Anya said *yeah*, wearily – maybe curtly, even – and hung up.

When I got home, Anya and Marko had already eaten. Anya apologised, saying that they were too hungry to wait. I used to hate eating alone, but with Marko it had become routine. Sometimes I even relished the chance to eat without having to answer Anya's questions when I was tired.

The afternoon of her departure had almost been erased from memory, except for me avoiding a conversation about Teya. We left Marko to play in his room; Anya may have asked me to go and get him, I may have told her to call him, but we weren't listening to one another, and Marko stayed where he was, playing undisturbed. I forget what the two of us were doing. The TV was on, our laptops were on, the newspaper was spread out on the dining table, and we must have been talking at one another, but words plummeted down into the empty space between us.

Could you take us to Mum and Dad's when you go to basketball training? she asked that evening, and I drove them to Stanka and Miro's without asking why. All I asked was how they'd get back, and Anya said they'd sort something out, and that I was not to worry. Then she asked when I'd be home, even though I always got home from basketball between ten and ten-thirty.

She gave me a kiss before she got out of the car, which wasn't something she normally did, but I let the kiss remain a kiss, and silently watched her cross the courtyard with Marko. Marko turned around at the door and waved to me; Anya didn't look back.

The flat was dark when I got home from basketball. I crept into the bedroom to give Anya a kiss goodnight, as I always did when she fell asleep before I got home, but our bed was empty. I guessed she must've fallen asleep with Marko when she put him to bed, and I carefully peeked my head round his bedroom door, only to be met with Marko's wide-open eyes.

Where's Mummy? I asked, though I ought to have pretended to know the answer to that question in front of him.

His big eyes widened even further. I had thrust an unanswerable question upon him and it was too late to take it back. Marko's face was already crumpling and letting out a quiet whimper, which would become a loud howl at any moment.

I picked him up and held him against my chest.

It's alright, it's alright. Shhh, shhh, Mummy's sleeping.

We rocked back and forth and he calmed down, and his eyes started to close. But I knew that if I were to lay him back down, he'd wake up. I carried him into the bedroom and lay down with him on my chest. Marko happily settled on my left shoulder, while I searched for an answer to the question that had frightened both of us.

I don't know how many times I had thought of abandoning my phone on the kitchen side and walking out, just as Anya had done. To a place where I'd get my time back. To somewhere I could be alone again, and could sit and listen to the endless night. Thoughts of running away had hounded me too, and I had also toyed with images of another life; one where evenings were not entirely predictable before even stepping out of bed. I imagined a place where I'd introduce myself to strangers, name and surname, before charming them with story after story; a place where I was no longer myself, but where I could be rewritten for anyone, and where I could access a thousand different selves. I imagined a place free from traces of a previous life where I, a stranger, could have secrets again. There, I could play again, and when the game was up I could return to the boundless night and listen, like now, to the hum of stillness. The hum of freedom.

Exhaustion got the better of me, carried me into the antechamber of dreams where scenes from my past happily mingled with each other. Strangers shook each others' hands, hugged one another and chatted away like old friends. Wednesday morning was interlaced with Friday evening and all of Thursday night; everything morphed into an indistinguishable mass, and even though I briefly managed to extract a couple of Anya's words – to catch her eye or glimpse how she rinsed her hands in the kitchen sink – uninvited voices were already intruding; anonymous faces that I'd met over the past few days, and Anya was once again lost in a whirlpool of images, blurring into one.

Weary from dozing, I stepped out onto the balcony to clear my head in the fresh midnight air. I stared into the dark of the courtyard, at the vague outlines of trees and bodywork, listened to my shallow breathing and fought back the images appearing before me. But images of Sunday lunch at Pleteršnikova soon began to force their way into my fragile midnight meditation, dragging me back there against my will, sitting me down at the enormous dining table, carved from a single piece of dark oak, from where I looked out onto the garden, where Anya and Neja were running around after the boisterous little ones. Marko tripped over, driving his knees into the damp lawn, greenish-brown stains on his new trousers, not knowing whether to cry, or get up and chase after Tilen, as if nothing had happened; he waits for Anya, who has turned towards the window, towards me, the only one who persists at the dining table after lunch, drinking coffee; there's nothing particular about the way she looks at me, but I know she's not happy about me sitting there; she recognises my small act of protest, and maybe I am deliberately distancing myself from Matjaž and Miro, who light their cigarettes in the garden after lunch; maybe I don't want to listen to the rest of Matjaž's story about the bankruptcy of some company that manufactures car seat covers, and of bank loans that ended up in untraceable offshore accounts; maybe I am avoiding Miro's kindness, maybe I don't want to hear, yet again, how I don't need to worry because all that stuff with Anya's work will soon sort itself out; maybe I would like to be untraceable, hidden behind the window; maybe

I don't want to pretend to everyone that I'm not bothered by how Anya announced, over lunch, that she'd been fired, and that her Dad got a more detailed explanation than I did: about how her boss Saško couldn't tell her to her face, and instead waited until she'd got home and then told her over the phone; maybe I don't want to hide the fact that I would have preferred Anya to have kept this from her family, especially Miro; maybe I don't want to pretend that I'm not offended by this, because Anya and I had agreed that we wouldn't mention it, and she had agreed that we'd work it out ourselves; but then she was explaining how Saško apologised for calling outside of working hours and started reeling off about how they didn't get the not-for-profit housing development project they'd bid for – it was probably already a done deal with the mayor – and there was nothing he could do about it; Anya also explained how Saško was throwing figures at her, about the drop in earnings last year, rising costs, projections for the coming quarter, and how he apologised for not being able to promise her anything but an incredibly small, symbolic redundancy package, as he's got no idea at the moment whether or not the company would survive the present market conditions; she spoke and nobody, including me, interrupted her; not once did she look at me, she only looked at him, at the nodding Miro, straight into his sympathetic and understanding eyes, eyes which held the answer to all our problems; with every word she moved further away from me and closer to him, her Daddy, who was always so very happy to help his youngest daughter wherever he could, whenever he could take care of her, and she knew it, and this was why she confided in him; it was so obvious that he'd be able to help her again, and that it would make him happy again; she gave away yet another of our secrets, and yet again our problems weren't private to us, our lives weren't private to us; yet again we didn't keep the two of us between us; instead Anya declared us, and the two of us became all of us – her redundancy was no longer our problem, but everyone's problem, apart from one detail, which is that Saško concluded by saying that these things happen these days, in a tone that left her no choice but to understand, which made Anya so angry that she hung up the phone.

That terminated call was now the only part of the story that remained ours; everything else had been given away, and our problems were now Miro's problems, and yet again we were merely his incapable children who needn't worry about anything, because he would sort everything out. But I didn't want to be free of worries, and I felt defeated; through the window I watched Miro extinguish his cigarette and put the ashtray on the windowsill, where Stanka would later collect it, as he headed over to Anya; I watched him striding across the garden with calm, confident steps; he has a white beard that fills people with trust, and tiny, reassuring eyes; Miro is a man who could never say the wrong thing and never shows the wrong emotions; he is devoted to Anya and devoted to us, everything's alright in his book – whatever we say, whatever we do – and that's why he'll now draw Anya close, Daddy's here, Anya; he'll hold his little girl close and let her know that it's not her fault, he's good at that, he'll look after her, he'll click his fingers and her problems will disappear, magical Dad will once again magically save her world; whilst meanwhile I'll be a mere bystander behind the window, alone with my rejected requests that she no longer lean on him when the car needs a service, when she'd like to go to a sold-out theatre performance, or skip the dentist's waiting list. Once again Anya had ignored me, once again she'd let her fear of Miro being offended about being kept separate from our life get the better of her; she was scared that it was the only way he could show his love, and that he'd think he'd offended her, that he wouldn't understand her cutting loose. That's how she explained it, but I sensed that Anya was still afraid of a life without his help, of a life with only me and my limited resources, because I didn't have a miracle phone line that could solve all of her problems; I didn't know how to comfort her, she didn't believe me when I said that everything would be OK, because I couldn't click my fingers like Miro did; all I wanted was to be alone with her and Marko, but I couldn't replace Miro; all I wanted was to drive him out, which is why, as Anya leant against him, resting her unemployed head on his broad shoulders, I could do nothing but watch… I saw how it calmed her, how she was back to being a little girl in the arms of her wonderful father, with

Miro's weighty, soft hands stroking her upper arms; everything was fine, life was beautiful and the two of them happy, Anya and Miro, as if Saško had never even called. While I stood there, by Miro and Stanka's display of holiday souvenirs from the Dominican Republic and Bali, in Australia and Tunisia – all those pseudo-exotic destinations befitting a company director and his wife – I stood there before those gaudy, carved trinkets that didn't appeal to any visitor besides Marko, who would eagerly reach for them every Sunday, and I had to hold myself back from smashing them against the wall, or dropping them, walking over them and crushing them into tiny pieces with my bodyweight.

Watch out! Jesus, Jadran! Anya shouted, when I failed to spot the pedestrian on the crossing. *Could you please watch the road?* she said, while I, without saying a word, let some distance grow between us and the yellow Twingo that I'd become much too close to. *Would you like me to drive?* she asked, when I narrowly missed colliding with a car when it stopped suddenly at an amber light at the crossroads, thrusting her forwards, forcing her to grab the seat in front with both hands.

I'd been waiting for her outburst the whole way home – maybe even trying to provoke her – and when I stopped at the traffic lights, Anya opened the door.

You know what, we'll walk: you can drive yourself around town like that, she said, grabbing Marko out of his car seat, and headed towards our apartment block, while I drove alongside her, waiting for her to tire and get back in the car.

In the garden of his old family home by Lake Cerknica, sitting under the old apple tree, Miro had told me at length about how, in most cases, it was almost always better to pay an honest price for things in life, rather than beg for them, as things that appeared free were rarely so, but that unfortunately, such was the state of organised chaos that we lived in, we were lured into a vicious cycle of exchanging favours, which made our lives more and more complicated and costly, even though to me and many others, particularly young people, it might seem otherwise. He spoke with disappointment about this world of his and ours, as if he'd become caught up in it accidentally, as if he'd been forced to live a life in which he had it all. He sounded like a man without choices, his voice full of regret; to me, Company Director Černjak didn't ought to sound like that; he ought to sound ruthless and satisfied. It seemed to me that people like him shouldn't be allowed to be like me; they should leave the disappointment to those of us who had good reason for it.

As I drove alongside Anya walking with Marko in her arms, I felt as if I were caught amongst the powerful roots of Miro's old apple tree, as if its branches had sprawled over me, encircling and crushing me. And as if wanting to tear myself free, I opened the window, leaned out towards Anya and yelled: 'Oi, Sanela, sweetheart! Sanelaaaaa, jump in – we're gonna get the lad circumcised aren't we, did you hear me sweetheart? We're gonna get him circumcised!'

I knew that Anya would hate the glances of passers-by, and that's why I shouted. I knew that Anya would hate being seen by strangers as Sanela, particularly Sanela with such a primitive husband, yelling out of his car window in a thick Bosnian accent, because she was the daughter of Miro Černjak, Mr Company Director Černjak.

For that brief moment, in front of three, maybe four strangers, I enjoyed ripping her away from her father's world, that impossibly idyllic world filled with devotion; I enjoyed the illusion of drawing her closer to me, while knowing at that moment, as she got back in the car and let me drive her and Marko home, that we had never been further apart.

Every morning, Ljubljana awoke from hibernation. In spite of its early bedtime, the city rose with eyes clamped shut and took so long to get on its feet that nobody knew if the new day had really begun. When the last city buses had quietened down and windows were no longer rattled by their engines, disturbing those sleeping behind them, it seemed as if the night went on and on, even when the sky was beginning to brighten and the delivery lorries had started to reverse outside the Mercator supermarkets.

I stood on the balcony and waited for the end of one such endless night, even though voices on the street below had already started speaking at full volume, calling out children's names and leaving their dogs to bark. I went to bed only as I heard the sound of the postman's voice. When I woke up, it was half-past five in the afternoon. I had a missed call from my mum, and a message from Stanka to say that Marko was with her, and that I should ring her as soon I could. Last night's feeling of freedom had vanished. Boundaries were firmly drawn once again.

When I arrived at Miro and Stanka's house, Marko was sat on the floor in front of the television watching a cartoon. He must have heard my voice as I spoke to Stanka at the door, and he's been able to recognise my footsteps for some time, but he didn't flinch as I approached him, not even for a second. Stanka, standing behind me, gave me a consolatory pat on the back.

'He doesn't see or hear anything when he's engrossed in those cartoons of his. Would you like anything to eat?'

There were some people whose voices lent themselves to sadness, whose eyes could show you death before you'd even been able to picture it yourself. These people expressed their condolences so as to make others feel their loss even more acutely than the time they'd huddled around their loved one's grave. Stanka was one of these people, one of the finest, and when she let me in, she hugged me as if I'd been missing for years, and whispered my name as if to bid me farewell.

I sat down on the sofa next to Marko, who was still not going to be distracted. Stanka left us and we sat watching the cartoon in silence. Heroes were constantly dying in cartoons, but this was of little help when death had to be explained in a non-cartoon world. Life was not a cartoon, even though I often wished I could conjure up anything Marko wanted.

I wanted us to be at home, away from Stanka's curious ears; to be able to tell Marko a story about how his great-grandad had gone home. At home, I could tell him about how all of us – he, Mummy and me, Grandad Miro and Grandmas Stanka and Vesna – are actually from a place called

Lullaby Land, where we had a house made of Wotsits, where our baths are brown because there's chocolate milk instead of water, and where it's always daytime and every day is Sunday, and where we draw rainbows and play football with snowmen, and that we're here, on Earth, on holiday – that we're sent here to grow and learn and work, and then when we've learnt enough and done our bit, we can go back, to our actual home which can be reached by toboggan, a huge toboggan that Great-Grandad Aleksandar is riding now, and at the end of the track, Great-Grandma Jana is waiting for him with ninety-five turquoise puppies – animals on Lullaby Land can talk, I'd explain – there's no difference between people and plants and animals, there we're all the same, and we play together in one big sandpit, as big as the sea. I'd tell him that when he's as old as Great-Grandad Aleksandar, he'll go to Lullaby Land on the toboggan too, and Mummy and I will be waiting for him at the end of the track, and so will Boots, his teddy, and he'll be a real bear, because objects in Lullaby Land can talk and eat and dance too, and that we can write to Great-Grandad in Lullaby Land, we can send him kisses and tell him to say hello to Great-Grandma.

I couldn't tell him any of this in front of Stanka. When it came to matters of life and death, heaven and hell were the only fairy tales she recognised, and in her eyes, all other fairy tales merely made a mockery of hers. Stanka was convinced that people mustn't invent imaginary worlds, even for the purpose of explaining to a child that his great-grandfather had died, because that child will then think that what is written in the Holy Bible was invented to comfort people, and that the story of Jesus is just one of many imaginary tales. For Stanka, life after death was certainly not child's play.

Which is why, when the cartoon finished, I told Marko to gather his things because we had to get home straight away, but he settled himself down next to me and put his head on my lap. He knew already, at three years of age, that adults could be manipulated, and if it had been any other day he probably could have persuaded me to stay a bit longer and watch one more cartoon at Grandma and Grandad's.

'Grandma's made dinner,' he said.

'Yes, if you're hungry Jadran, there's plenty, really,' Stanka's voice came from the kitchen.

'Thanks, but we have to go. Come on, Marko, we're going.'

At that moment, a key turned in the door. Miro would have seen my car parked outside, and his consoling eyes were searching for me the moment he stepped through the door.

'Jadran.'

He took my hand, and with his other hand patted my shoulder, and then also stroked my face.

'How's your mum?'

'Coping.'

'Really? Stanka sent a telegram.'

Miro and Stanka always did what was expected of them. They always stuck religiously to unwritten rules; rules that I was not familiar with. Which is why, despite being rooted in good intentions, their actions, and words too, always upset me slightly. And on this occasion, their considerate behaviour had led them to send a telegram, rather than picking up the phone and calling my Mum to offer their condolences in person.

I walked around the flat behind Marko, and waited for him to ask where his mummy was, but rather than a question I was met with his big, small eyes, as he waited for me to come up with something to comfort him. I watched his short steps hurry towards his room, and thought that perhaps I, of all people, know what it's like to be abandoned; that the only thing keeping me here with him and Anya is the painful experience of betrayal, and that's why I don't succumb to temptation and leave, just as Anya had left.

My temptation had gone by the name of Tadea. She was an old friend, an old school crush, almost a girlfriend back then, now a graphic designer who had stepped back into my life to renovate the website that I wrote basketball predictions for; or tips for those with sports betting dependencies, as we called them.

Tadea was the one who asked me, as we sat having coffee after a meeting, filling in the gaps of our life stories that had taken divergent paths since leaving school, whether I felt guilty for doing what I was doing.

She was being provocative, but I didn't back away. I said that I'd learnt to live with a guilty conscience, and turned the question on her. Did she, a university-educated artist (placing special emphasis on the "artist"), feel guilty for designing websites for companies like ours. Now I was the one being provocative, and was enjoying it; I submitted to a game where I didn't know the rules.

Tadea began to tell me about her childhood dreams, about painting and the moment that she realised she would never be an artist. A part of her had died inside, she told me, when she came to terms with that. She was open, just like she always had been, and I wanted to be open too, and I told her something that I'd never told anyone, not even Anya. I told her that I consoled myself with the fact that I do all of this for Marko, but I don't believe myself, because it isn't true. The only reason I do this, I admitted, is because it's all so easy; because there are no disappointments. I've always been afraid of disappointment, and I'd rather back away before I dare admit that I'm not a gifted journalist or writer. I'd rather be a conformist in the eyes of others, rather than a bad writer in my own.

I'm afraid of disappointment, I repeated once again. *In everything, but especially in love.*

Tadea became increasingly attentive as she listened.

That's why I never asked you to be my girlfriend at school.

I tried to say it as a bit of a joke, but it didn't sound like one. She knew that I meant it, and I knew that she knew.

It didn't just happen. I allowed Tadea and I to become close. I didn't have to tell her what I told her; I didn't have to confide in her, but I did. Never have I come so close to succumbing to desire, to no longer fighting myself, as I did with Tadea. I came so close to it that the thought of her still frightened me. I knew that Anya was the person I should be closest to now. Now, when she was left without a job, and when she needed my understanding and companionship more than ever, I had allowed myself to drift away. I had allowed Anya's quiet sadness to creep in between us.

I closed my fist around Marko's tiny fingers. How close to separation I'd let us come, I thought to myself; again I was taken aback and I hugged him but he, oblivious, wriggled free from my arms and tottered into his room. I heard his footsteps and pictured him standing there, in the middle of his room exploring it anew, as if his room were the big wide world.

'Marko! Are we going to brush those teeth please? And put those pyjamas on?'

'Now?'

'Sooner than now.'

Water was running in the bathroom, and I closed my eyes and saw how he stood on his tip-toes, reaching for his toothbrush. And how the first thing he does is reach out his hands under the water, then shuffles forward a bit, opens his mouth and sticks his tongue out until it touches the water, and how he lets the water fall over his tongue so that it splashes up all over his face.

'Marko! Without soaking ourselves please! Come on, brush your teeth. And put your pyjamas on.'

'Where are they?'

'Under the covers.'

'Under which covers?'

'Next door.'

The rustling of covers and clothes could be heard, and then the patter of Marko's bare feet, which ran towards me, growing closer and closer, until he jumped on me.

'What are you doing here? Get to bed.'

'I'm sleeping here.'

'Where? On me?'

'On you. Full stop.'

'There'll be no full stop.'

'Full stop.'

That phrase – "full stop". Anya would say it to him when she ran out of patience, and now he was saying it to me. He placed his head on my chest, and we lay there on the sofa.

When I opened my eyes it was already one-thirty. Marko and I had been asleep on the sofa for nearly three hours. Careful so as not to wake him, I carried him into his room and into bed. I gently placed my lips upon his hair, which by now nearly covered his whole forehead, and then went back into the living room.

Somewhere en route from Marko's room, I wandered off into another night. I had just got back from the smoky basement bar on Trubarjeva, head full of Tadea, vibrations, and ringing in my ears. I could feel the avid thirst for alcohol; warm, flat beer swilled around in my mouth and I felt the imprint, like a permanent mark, of her soft cheek lent against mine. Her smile was everywhere, like glaring light; her smile which drew closer through the haze, which draws closer and closer, I see it patently, like a slow-motion replay, even though I know that it all happened so quickly, and then it vanishes into obscurity, and I see her hands touching me, her head fits my shoulder like adjoining jigsaw pieces, the nape of my neck, my face; I feel her soft, warm cheek against mine, we're pressed tightly against one another and I can feel my body flooding with desire, I feel it expanding, rising from somewhere, wanting to flow outward; everything is in slow motion again, every second punctuated again, and we still have our arms around one another; I can't make out the music, voices are drowned out, smoke hangs in the air, everything stands still, our cheeks brush against one another, it was nothing – a hug, that's all – yet there's so much more stored inside me, safely hidden away; we're not guilty yet, we're only hugging, but then, as if something brewing inside spills over the edge, my head starts to turn towards hers, my lips travel towards her face, they want to kiss her, they want to lean against her warm cheek, leave their trace; I'd like to turn my head back, but I can't, because it's just a memory and I'm powerless, memory is where past desires reign supreme, and they're leading the game again and again they're leading my lips, suspended, opening, drawing closer to her face, but it's just a face, a face is not a forbidden zone, a kiss on the cheek says nothing and no one will hear my thoughts, my desires will remain my own, some drinks were had that evening, too many, I tell myself now, but memory doesn't lie, memory knows, it recalls the touch of my lips, of her cheeks, it recalls meeting the corner of her smile, this moment is long, infinite; all of a sudden I'm drawn towards her smiling dimples, I'm swaying, as if I'm tipping towards her, drowning in bliss, it's not right, I tell myself, I shouldn't stay here, against her cheeks, I should be quick, my lips should pull back immediately, but it's just a memory, and memory doesn't lie; now it's coming to a standstill and I see myself kissing her and something rising from me, spilling over and then flowing, flowing outwards unrelentingly, but still no one sees, only I can see; me, watching my own memory, unable to turn away, everything playing out before me and inside me and I feel myself boiling over again, as if her cheeks were kissing my lips, and I know what comes next, I'd like to look away, I'd like to switch off this mind game, to end what has already ended, erase the images, discolour, fade, soften, disperse them, yet the opposite happens, everything comes into focus, because memory doesn't lie, memory is playing with me as I hide behind closed eyes like a child hiding behind their hands, I see everything, everything put before me; I see her head turn, her smile coming closer, my lips no longer resting at the threshold of her smile but almost touching her lips, her breath now gliding over mine and my lips flee from hers, or maybe they're pursuing them; now I'm pretending not to know whether her lips are moving towards mine, or whether they are moving towards my cheek, we're too close, I know that now, way too close, but memory measures proximity differently, desire presides over memory and memory therefore knows that I wanted to move closer that evening, and it knows she didn't draw away either; it knows the proximity was no coincidence, our lips brushed against each other, maybe it wasn't even a real kiss, but they made contact, they passed over one another, and it was more powerful than a kiss, it was unfulfilled, and now the desire lives on in memory, which is toying with me, taking me back, and her lips are moving over mine again, and it isn't only a moment of awkwardness, drunkenness; memory knows it and I know it, I gave in, I know it wasn't just coincidence, it was more than an accidental touch; I'm pretending that it was nothing, that nothing happened, but it did, something big, enormous, there was a thirst for the kiss, from both sides, maybe from a distance it even looked like a kiss, through the haze; her eyes came too close, I shouldn't be returning that look, her eyes should not be watching me from this close-up, I know that now, but memory doesn't know, her eyes reflect my desire and hers is mirrored in mine, uncovered, unadulterated; we were laid bare, now everything stands still in memory and now all is on view, that moment of being laid bare, our mutual desire exposed, now I'm afraid again, again I don't know how to back away from her, I feared this desire, I was scared it would never subside, that's what I was scared of, I was sobbing and shaking that night when I returned home; it was such an ordinary night, the only unusual thing being me and my desire, an unwelcome desire, a desire which took hold of me; yet again my memory had awoken my fears and a cold sweat crawled over my body, the kiss, which wasn't, or which was, I don't know, her gaze piercing through me, desire in her eyes, responding to mine, she consented to it, it was not a rejection, she detected my desire because it was real, my desire left my body, met with hers, then I clasped her against me, so my memory says, so as to disguise our desire in a hug and the night ran away, on it continued, smoke began to swirl around the close basement atmosphere, people started to move, the proximity between our bodies was no more, but the other thing was still there, more dangerous, the desire for her, that night, when I arrived home; I opened the bedroom door and looked at Anya, sleeping on her side of our bed, and I could still see Tadea's smile, a double exposure, everything mixed together; I was looking at Anya and wanted to feel desire for her, drive away that other, forbidden desire, I undressed my Anya, I wanted to take hold of her naked skin, press my hand between her legs, I wanted to be fuelled by the thought of a naked Anya, a tarnished thought; I turned her over onto her stomach and looked at her from behind, lustfully, crudely, but still the image would not focus, memory remained most vivid, the desire for Tadea resisted and punched through my lust, I lay down next to Anya and felt her breathing, gently placing my arm over her sleeping body, conjuring up memories of the two of us, of our innocent debauchery, my thoughts travelled down between her legs, drawing them apart and guiding my tongue over her sex and I saw her head between my legs, her lustful smile, everything, so as to just drive away the memory, drive away the desire that I had no desire for, for it to be superseded by Anya, by desire for Anya, for the mother of my child, by a just desire; how unfree, acutely unfree I felt, like never before; how trapped, how powerless, how weak, pathetic, helpless, as I let my hand fall away from her sleeping body and down between my legs, all of this is for us, it's all done with good intentions, there's nothing wrong, it's all so I can drive away Tadea's smile and the touch of our lips and her eyes, the way they read my desire; I didn't fall in love with her, I don't want to be in love with her, I forbid myself from falling in love with her, I want to drive her out of me, but memory doesn't lie, memory is present and it knows, which is why we're back on the train, at night, we're alone in the carriage, which is why you're unbuttoning my fly again, which is why I'm trembling with arousal again, which is why you're taking me in your hands again and letting your head drop down and you're taking me in your warm, soft lips again; which is why we're back there, so that those images smother me entirely, so they cover all the other images, which is why, why we're back in your car again, in your red Peugeot, and I'm sitting in the back seat and you're sitting on top of me, rocking back, and forth, back, and forth, I see it all so clearly and it's getting clearer, back, and forth, back, and forth, there's no one else's smile, no one else's gaze, it's only me and you in your red Peugeot, in our secret place, still young, still insatiable, still in love, back, and forth, I feel that desire for your body again, desire impatiently tugging at your black underwear, desire which pushes, gasping, into you, not sparing a thought for your goose-pimpled body, back, and forth, I am released, I release myself next to you, sleeping, I release over memories of us, I won, I won for us, we were stronger, we released ourselves over memory, which doesn't lie, over memory, which knows, we covered it over with images of our own, with our memories, which don't lie either, and now I'm crying, Anya, next to you, sleeping, because I'm powerless, I feel so unfree that it paralyses me, I'm clenching my fist and pulling the covers over me, quietly crying, silently sobbing, because I don't want to wake you, because you get up early; Marko is still young, he's still a baby, he starts crying early, not like the person who's crying next to you now, who you don't hear, who's crying because I'm scared, because I don't know if my forbidden desire can be suppressed, if I can rid myself of it forever, or whether at some point it will overcome me, prise me apart from you, which I don't want, I don't want to be apart from you and I don't want to be apart from Marko, I know what it's like to be abandoned, but desire is strong, stronger than I am perhaps, our lips made contact, I kissed the corner of her smile, her eyes read my desire and it made her happy, I don't know if I'm going to be able to suppress that desire, if I'm going to be strong enough, which is why I'm crying, because I'm scared, scared to death, I've never been so scared in all my life and at the same time I've never felt so un-free, so trapped, I could scream, I could run away, smash things, I could do all of those things, but you're sleeping and Marko's sleeping and I mustn't wake you, neither of you can see me like this, you mustn't see my fear, because you'll want to ask about it, I'll have to beat this, I have to, have to, have to, I have to, for you, Anya, and for Marko, because I love you both, I love you both, I adore you and I adore him, you're my world, so I have to beat this, I can't be beaten by her and her alluring smile, which draws closer, in slow motion, I have to beat this memory, crush it until it dies, until there are no memories left to force me back there, so I don't have to live through it again, I need time, I just need time, Anya, I mustn't see her again, I mustn't make new memories, everything will be OK; I promise you and I promise Marko that I'll never allow her that proximity again, I'll never allow her breath to brush the surface of my lips, everything will be OK, everything will be OK, Anya, just sleep, sleep peacefully, I'll cry this out and I'll go to sleep and everything will be easier in the morning, in the morning I'm going to squeeze you tight and I'm going to squeeze Marko too, I just have to make it to the other side of this night, it's nearly morning already, soon sleep will get the better of me, I know it will, sleep will overcome me and memory will overcome me too, memory which doesn't lie, everything will go to sleep and she will go to sleep within me and will never awaken again, I promise, to Marko, to you and to myself I promise, because we have to stay together, because we're us, because I know what it's like to be abandoned, and I still know that now, as I merely remember the memory which doesn't lie, as I merely remember that night and know that two years have gone by since then and the desire has been defeated, it's no longer inside me, and that the memory which doesn't lie is no longer alive, that all that remains are dead images, just as I wanted, but tonight you're not lying beside me, Anya, on your side of the bed; tonight you're somewhere else, and I'm being hounded by desires again, forbidden desires to run away, for freedom, for no limitations, I need you again to help me beat them, so I can quash this thing inside me, threatening us, so I can hush my fears, but you're not here and I'm scared because I don't know what has driven you away, I don't what it is inside you that's threatening us, I'm afraid of you, because I don't know you like I know myself, I don't know those memories of yours that don't lie, I don't know your forbidden desires, I don't know what you're quashing inside you at this moment, or what, at this moment, is quashing you; I'm scared, because I know how hard it is to suppress forbidden desire, it's hard to crush it, and I'm wondering whether you've maybe succumbed to it already, or whether you're still fighting, for us, for Marko, for all of us, or whether, somewhere, you're still fighting, alone. Anya, I love you, and I'm scared.

IV

1.

The year was 1975. Although the words DON'T KNOCK were emblazoned on the door, he knocked, entered, and said that his uncle had arranged for him to see comrade Mahnič immediately. *And your uncle is?* she asked, to which he looked her up and down in mild astonishment, wishing to inform her that this was something she ought to have known, working here, as she did, for comrade Mahnič. *Stane Dolanc,* he then proffered, only as clarification, but all this did was provoke a loud, involuntary guffaw, despite the fact that even smiling upon mention of that name was inadvisable. *I expect you're a trainee here,* he added, and she nodded, still laughing. *You find it funny, do you, that Stane is my uncle?* he asked, by now imitating the authoritative air of the Party Presidency's Secretary of the Executive Bureau. *You are funny,* she retorted, *if you think you can jump the queue with that sort of Bosnian wind-up.* He put on his very best horrified expression. *Bosnian wind-up – please, comrade! What is your name?* The nephew of the Secretary of the Party Presidency's Executive Bureau was becoming more authoritative than his uncle. *I'm Vesna,* she said. *Vesna Benedejčič.* Despite all the gravitas with which he'd delivered his words, it was clear he was not getting through to her, and so he marched forward to her desk and picked up the telephone. Now things were serious. *So then, Vesna. I can also give my uncle a call, and then he'll ring comrade Mahnič and you, comrade Benedejčič, will be able to have a chat with them about Bosnian wind-ups.* He took a dramatic pause, like he'd seen actors do in films. *Or you can immediately let me through and we can forget all about it.* He was sure that he had now managed to convince her of the gravity of the current situation. But she, in the calmest of voices, replied: *My mother is the second cousin of comrade Dolanc, and I know full well that he does not have any nephews, particularly none of the sort that speak with a Bosnian accent, comrade.* Now she took a cinematic pause. *What did you say your name was again?* They stared, studying one another: Stane Dolanc's nephew and the daughter of his second cousin. It would be difficult to say who was enjoying this game the most. *My name is Safet, comrade Vesna, and I'm incredibly happy to have such a beautiful relation,* he said, offering his hand, which she refused, and instead shook her head disapprovingly. This, too, was reminiscent of film stars of the time. At which point, comrade Mahnič stepped into the office, glanced at Safet, and asked Vesna if this comrade was next in line. Yet before Safet could respond, Vesna began to explain that the comrade was here by mistake; he hadn't known that they didn't employ persons with vital organ defects. At the mention of vital organs, comrade Mahnič stopped and carefully eyed up Safet. He didn't quite understand what it was all about, but it sounded like he ought not to enquire any further, and so he nodded, and then instructed his young secretary to send the next candidate through. Vesna sent in a frightened fair-haired boy who wiped his sweaty palms on his trousers before entering comrade Mahnič's office. When the doors had closed behind him, Safet said: *Pretending to be the daughter of comrade Dolanc's second cousin is a serious offence, comrade Vesna,* to which she replied: *In a world where you are his nephew, I will easily be forgiven.* Safet slowly came to realise that even if he'd been Stane Dolanc himself, he was not going to get past her and into comrade Mahnič's office that day, and that the battle was lost; but now she, comrade Vesna Benedejčič, daughter of the second cousin of the Communist Party's second in command, was of more interest to him than the job of night porter at a construction site. Now, as he took his time and a closer look at her, she seemed at least twice as valuable as the month of reliable employment that he'd come for. *So if you're the daughter of the second cousin of my uncle, we're not that closely related, are we? I don't think it would be too incestuous of me to ask you out to dinner?* He had placed his cards on the table, expecting to be disappointed, but Vesna, who had had an answer ready since the very beginning, replied: *This dinner will have to be approved by your uncle, comrade Safet.* There was not a more unambiguous way of telling somebody to clear off in those days, but Safet would not have been Safet if he hadn't taken her reply as an invitation. To him life was, in one way or another, just one large, impossible knot to be disentangled. All the more so in matters of love.

If comrade Dolanc confirms that his nephew can take the daughter of his second cousin out to dinner, will you come, in that case? he asked.

If comrade Dolanc approves that, then you can take me to Dubrovnik as well.

The year was 1984. Safet had somehow managed to drag himself from Bar Katrca into a taxi, but tiredness and inebriation overcame him to such an extent that he barely succeeded in making eye contact with the driver before his head fell backwards and he was out, dead to the world, in the passenger seat. Zdenko, who was a small, round man from Zagorje, listened to Safet's snoring for a few minutes, and, trusting that he knew where he wanted to go, patiently waited for him to wake up before mustering the courage to give his shoulders a tentative shake. Yet so deep was Safet's slumber that you could have whizzed him round in a blender and he would not have stirred. Zdenko, who was not a man in possession of a firm hand, was left with no option other than to carefully reach into Safet's inside jacket pocket, remove his wallet and look for his home address on his identity card.

Zdenko gave Safet one more nudge, and checked one last time to see if he was still sound asleep, and then took out a few dinars, too, enough to cover the journey.

Zdenko Bajuk was an honest man, who turned off the radio and drove a sleeping Safet home in silence, and wondered what he ought to do in the event that he did not wake up by the time they reached his home. When Safet opened his eyes, just before the railway crossing, Zdenko was momentarily relieved.

Almost there, he said to him, reassured.

But Safet began to glance around anxiously, and when he recognised the market in front of him, and Eli's flower kiosk on the right hand side of the street, he let out such a long and loud 'Woooahhhhh', that Zdenko slammed his foot on the brake in panic, halting his Renault 18 in the middle of the road.

What an idiot! I can't go home empty-handed! Today's my fifth wedding anniversary! a distressed Safet cried. *I need flowers. A bunch of flowers.*

It was three thirty in the morning. The only places open in Ljubljana were the police station, the emergency department and the train station bar.

I could take you to the cemetery. It'll be the only place with flowers… at this hour.

One mustn't steal from savings books, my friend, let alone gravestones! But – we need tulips, you and I! White ones! Those are her favourites.

Not only did Zdenko have no clue where to find tulips in Ljubljana at three-thirty in the morning, nor had he ever seen a tulip in his life, but Safet already had an elaborate plan.

Listen up. Let's take this one step at a time. First we go to Popit, then to Ribičič, then to Dolanc.

Zdenko was not even close to following what Safet was talking about. The only thing that was clear to him, upon hearing those familiar surnames, was that he had not taken nearly enough money from Safet's wallet to cover the journey ahead.

You be the lookout, while I get the flowers. OK?

Zdenko did not dare question the drunken romantic, who was a whole head taller than him, and so Safet and Zdenko were soon driving across Ljubljana in search of white tulips, which Safet was convinced grew in the well-tended gardens of old townhouse villas belonging to the communist aristocracy.

When Zdenko, further diminished in stature by the fear, finally dropped Safet off outside his block of flats, the day was already dawning. Safet stepped out of the Renault 18 with a fistful of beautiful white tulips.

I risked exclusion from the party for you, said a proud Safet to his wife Vesna, handing over the flowers.

You're not in the party, you idiot, she replied.

Fine – maybe not exclusion, but death by hanging for sure!

Vesna took the flowers from Safet and tossed them on the floor.

For a start, our anniversary isn't for another three weeks, and second, we need to be in Jožica Jamnik's office in two hours.

She waited a moment for her words to safely reach Safet's drunken brain.

Sober!

Vesna marched straight over the tulips and into the bedroom. It slowly began to dawn on Safet that the big event which Eli's flower kiosk had prompted him to remember was not their fifth wedding anniversary, but was, instead, a meeting with Jožica Jamnik. She was the reason he had the day's date, the seventh of April, etched in big letters somewhere in his brain.

The meeting with Jožica Jamnik was in fact a more significant event than their wedding anniversary, as it would determine whether or not the Dizdar family would be allocated one of the flats in the up-and-coming socialist development of Fužine, which were being handed out to employees of construction giant SCT, Vesna's employer.

Yet the odds of this were minuscule. Partly because they gave priority to families with two or more children; but partly, as well, because the waiting list was shaped by the unwritten regulations of Yugoslav bureaucracy: anyone could jump the queue, if only they knew the right person.

Which is why Vesna had arranged the meeting with Jožica Jamnik, housing queries clerk, way ahead of time, so that she and Safet could win her over, and, with her help, be rescued from a precarious life of subletting.

Vesna's hopes and fears were now coming back to Safet's drunken brain. In the hall of their creaky, claustrophobic flat, he held the most beautiful bunch of white tulips, as they once were, and quietly cursed his absent-mindedness. It wasn't the first time he'd screwed up, but now he was no longer only screwing himself over, but his wife and five-year-old son, too.

He headed into the largest of the two rooms, shoes on, and sat himself down on the floor by my bed. He was shielding his face behind the tulips, but I immediately sensed his agitation as he whispered *it'll all be OK, it'll all be OK my little one*, stroking my head, with hands quivering as much as his voice. He stroked my cheek until he had calmed down and his breathing was no longer as shallow. It wasn't long before his head succumbed to the edge of the bed in exhaustion, and the tulips scattered across his lap.

I was woken again by a clattering in the bathroom, the kind I would normally hear when Mum was late for work, and couldn't find her hair clip or mascara. Things were falling on the floor and bouncing along the tiles. Then I heard Mum's footsteps and the opening of the door.

If it's aspirin you're looking for, we're all out.

I'm not looking for anything.

Wrapped in his towel, Safet went into the kitchen and started opening cupboard doors.

There's no Cedevita either!

Mum's voice was snappy, just like when she'd hurry me into bed.

Cedevita's no good anyway, replied Safet, returning to the bathroom. Shortly afterwards, a strong jet of water could be heard.

Mum stopped at the bathroom door, left slightly ajar.

If you so much as mention that you have a headache, I'll make sure it's aching alright!

Safet's singing in the shower could be heard by way of reply.

Lijepe žene prolaze kroz graaad, ja na uglu stojim sasvim saam…

As I got dressed, Mum checked to see that the collar of my jumper was straight and that my trouser legs weren't tucked into my socks, and then opened the front door and ushered me out so she could put her shoes on in peace. Safet eventually emerged from the bathroom, looked at Mum and gave her a wink.

One wink at Jožica, and she'll be giving us three apartments!

You just be careful you're not sick all over her office, said Mum, heading for the door.

Wait! Safet shouted.

His voice echoed down the staircase, through the open door, which Mum then instinctively closed, leaving me alone outside.

What is that?

These are twins!

What twins?

It was clear, even to the five-year old listening from behind the front door, that Mum was losing patience. Then everything went quiet, and I got scared. I didn't understand what sort of twins they were talking about, but I was old enough to recognise the silence that set in; the silence that arrives once the words have stopped. I was worried that they were never going to open the door again, but I was also scared to knock, to interrupt that soundless strain. I was worried that so much as a touch of the door would be enough to start me shaking.

Mum came out holding my pillow and hurried down the stairs. *We're late!* she said, and then she was gone. Meanwhile, Safet was closing the door with one hand and putting his shoes on with the other. He was in a hurry now too.

An hour or so later, the young, happy Dizdar family were stepping inside the office of Jožica Jamnik. Safet held the door for me and Mum, and then pulled out a chair so that she could sit down. She dragged her feet across the floor, and let out a rasping groan as she carefully lowered herself into her seat. When she was finally in place, she let out a sigh of relief. Then, she placed her hands on her stomach and looked at Jožica.

Eight months.

I was sat beside Mum, resting my head on her tummy and waiting for Jožica Jamnik to look at me.

They're kicking, I said to her.

They? she repeated, surprised.

Safet nodded his head, proudly.

They're kicking, both of them. One shot, two rabbits. Boy and girl.

I also felt pride. I had successfully carried out my mission.

How lovely, said an empathetic Jožica, beginning to sift through papers on her untidy desk. She quickly gave up.

Well, it's obvious that there will soon be five of you, isn't it?

We nodded.

I'll just need to see the doctor's note.

What doctor's note? queried Safet.

The note that confirms your wife is pregnant, so I can approve your apartment before the birth.

That's all?

That's all.

Mum turned to Safet. But Safet was Safet.

No problem. I'll bring it to you first thing tomorrow. One for each baby, if that's necessary. Do you need a photo as well?

Jožica did not follow.

These days they have some new equipment, ultrasound or something – they take photos of the babies inside the tummy.

Jožica was yet to hear of ultrasound and couldn't imagine how it was possible to photograph a baby inside its mother's tummy.

Oh, no, a doctor's note will do, she muttered, rescuing us all from our torment.

Safet took her hand, whilst I helped my pregnant mum to her feet.

Say goodbye to the lady, Jadran, she said to me.

Goodbye, I said, and Jožica gave me a friendly smile.

We walked slowly down the long corridor towards the exit. Mum was still performing a pregnant walk and supported her bump with her hand. Only when we reached the car park did she take it away.

Do you need a photo as well?! Have you lost your mind? Ultrasound? What ultrasound would that be, you thick idiot?!

Mum pulled the pillow from beneath her blouse and angrily threw it on the floor.

Where would you get an ultrasound scan? Of twins? Where? Where would you get that, you idiot?

She grew increasingly red in the face, while Safet remained calm, as if he were starring in an alternate movie.

The cigarette kiosk, maybe.

Jean-Paul Belmondo. Mum always said that Safet looked like Jean-Paul Belmondo. Never had he looked more like him than he did as he uttered those words.

The year was 1990. The two-and-a-half bedroom apartment on Marinkov Square was overflowing with leather holdalls and nylon beach bags, and was waiting for Safet, who had gone over to Dane's to borrow his Golf. Our Renault 4 was too unreliable for the journey to Lošinj and I felt sorry for it and I didn't think it was fair that we were going to the seaside without it, but Safet didn't think overheating en route was fair either. Mum explained to me that Safet had the travel jitters, which meant getting scared before travelling, and that was why he was complicating things, because he'd never driven such a long distance before.

It was the first time we'd gone to the seaside on our own. The three of us. We were used to spending summers in Momjan, from where Grandad would drive us to the beach in his Škoda, but in the spring of that year, Safet's firm had bought a holiday home on the island of Lošinj that it let out to employees as a symbolic gesture. After months of hints whispered in the bedroom, Mum succeeded in persuading Safet to put in an application and get permission for a week's holiday. Just for us.

It had been agreed that we'd get on the road early, but midday came and we were still at home. Safet wasn't back yet, and Mum was pacing around the flat, worried that he and Dane were raising a toast to the vehicle swap, which could easily set back our departure until the next day. She had the jitters too, it seemed; it was also the first time she'd packed for an extended trip to an unknown region, and she stood in the hall and for a third time read out her list.

Three pairs of pyjamas? Check. Two large towels? Check. Badminton rackets? Check.

I sat down at my computer and smashed the Salzburg racetrack record in a 600 cc motorbike, when I heard her footsteps quickly approaching.

Jadran, come and look at this for me. We'll get all this in the Golf, won't we?

I pressed pause and followed her into the hall, took a quick glance at the pile, nodded, and then went back into my room, even though I could already see Safet stepping through the door and saying *Just as well you didn't pack the kitchen sink!*

But the only thing Safet said, when he did come home shortly afterwards, was *Fuck this country!*

Mum and I froze and waited, each of us at our own end of the apartment, to see whether Safet was going to elaborate, but all he did was step over the holdalls, sit down on the sofa and repeat himself, this time even louder and with added emphasis.

Fuck this fucking country!

Silence reigned over the apartment, the sort which signifies something terrifying is about to take place in films, and I turned the computer off just in case, and carefully listened for what was going to happen next.

What's wrong? I heard Mum's quiet, frightened voice. Safet let out a heavy sigh.

I went into the living room, and when Safet saw me he told me to sit down. I was scared that something bad had happened, like that time in Chernobyl, but Safet explained that he'd gone to work that morning to get the keys to the holiday home, but Miftar the porter said that the director had come to take the keys last night, and had set off to Lošinj already, for a fortnight with his family.

You are kidding me!

Now she, too, sat down beside him and put her arm around him, and it was just like the time when Safet's Aunt Fadila died.

Well, we shall go to Momjan, Mum said.

Only then did it dawn on me that we weren't going to Lošinj, and I could have almost cried, but Safet jumped to his feet, opened the drawer beneath the television and took out a blue envelope in which he kept some German marks, sent to him by his sister Anila.

What are you doing? Mum asked.

Safet transferred the money to his wallet, then went into the hall and picked up the heaviest holdall.

The director's family is no better than mine. If he's taking his to Lošinj, then I'm taking mine to Italy! Let's see about that!

I turned to Mum, hoping that her face would reveal that this was all a wind-up, just another of their games. I wanted to go to Lošinj; Italy sounded so improbable, as if Safet had just announced that he were planning on flying to the moon, a holdall in each hand.

Come on, get your passports. I'm taking you to see the leaning tower of Pisa!

A fine display of Bosnian defiance, is what Grandad said, laughing, when we told him about it later; Mum said it was like he'd been hypnotised; but whatever it was, Safet was deadly serious. He had all of our savings in his shirt pocket. All of the currency that they'd been saving in the drawer all year, three-quarters of the caravan that Mum had been dreaming about; the new Yugo that he wanted for himself, and at least three BMX bikes of mine. Safet was prepared to blow it all on a trip to Pisa. All that remained of our future, in his eyes, was just a single leaning tower.

Mum probably sensed that at that moment there was no use in trying to explain to him that you can't just go to Italy without preparation, that you can't set off on such a long journey at two in the afternoon, especially when you have no idea how long it takes to get to Pisa, nor any idea of how to get there. She didn't even attempt to change his mind, or make him see that a smarter idea would be to set off the next morning, having borrowed a decent roadmap of Italy and some sort of guidebook, and having chatted with someone who was more accustomed to long journeys.

Instead, all she did was take out our passports, which lived in the same drawer as the Deutschmarks. Perhaps she sensed that this was a once-in-a-lifetime opportunity for a holiday to that mystical, unreachable foreign land, long-promised by Safet; or perhaps it sparked a mischievous sense of rebellion in her, and so to take revenge against the country where the company director can take away the keys to your holiday, she consented to a trip to capitalist Italy.

Whatever the reason, it was madness, because prior to that point neither Mum nor Safet had been further than Ponte Rosso, and neither of them had so much as dreamed of how many worlds there were between Trieste and Pisa.

Yet the madness that got us behind the wheel in Ljubljana could only get us so far. Beyond the border we were met with roads not yet fit for cars, and signposts bearing the names of unknown places. All around us thundered the horns of Italian drivers, warnings were yelled in a language unintelligible to me and Safet, and which Mum did not wish to translate, and everything was telling us to turn around and go back to where the roads were quiet, and where signs were intelligible.

We were still closer to home than we were to Pisa and its leaning tower, and I, rapidly losing courage, started to think that we'd be better off accepting that it was just too foreign for us here. From the back seat I observed Safet, neck protruding, head almost touching the windscreen, and both hands gripping the wheel as if he were afraid it might slip from his hands.

The further we drove, the more I wanted us to pull over and go for a walk through one of the meadows we passed by. We'd be on our own there, with nobody hurtling towards us, nobody overtaking. The meadows were free of crossroads, and the need to stop and guess whether we ought to go left or right.

But when Safet did eventually pull over, all I wanted was for him to drive on as soon as possible, because the sight of him was scaring me. He was gripping the wheel more tightly than ever and staring ahead, motionless, at the narrow road that led through an avenue of trees. Mum said that we could ask someone for directions, but all Safet said was *I'm thinking*.

Mum looked out of the window in desperation towards a field, on the edge of which stood a large sand-coloured house. Its shutters were closed, there were no cars parked outside, and it looked to be abandoned. My eyes searched for sheep or goats in the pasture, but it seemed that the animals had abandoned the place too. There were no birds in the sky, which was covered by a large grey cloud, and I sensed that we'd reached the end of the road.

This is our first big adventure, Safet had said, whilst still on our side of the border and before he'd been subdued by frightening forking routes leading to every corner of the Italian wilderness. Not long after we crossed the border, he turned off the radio so that he could focus on the road, and in silence we drove, as if the road had seized us and was driving us, powerless, into the unknown.

Safet started the engine.

We'll park up by the road somewhere and sleep in the car. Everything will be easier in the morning.

There wasn't a word from Mum, who carried on staring out of the window, whilst I was happy that we were on the move again and that Safet was no longer deep in thought. It looked as if he might even be whistling to himself. After a while, Mum turned to face me.

It'll be your first night in a car tonight. You'll be able to see what it's like, and then she gently caressed Safet's neck with her hand.

We parked up in a small lay-by. On a few metres of strewn sand. Safet stepped out of the car and took in his surroundings, which were sinking into darkness. Mum followed him and I heard her ask: *Where do you think we are?*

Through the window I could see Safet, really not looking himself, shaking his head, and Mum moving in closer, giving him a hug. They stood there for a long time in each others' arms, in front of the car, in silence, in the middle of the unknown, holding one another up. Through the window it was difficult to work out who was comforting who.

Mum then got back in the car, and from the cool bag took a sandwich wrapped in tin foil and handed it to me.

Dinner, she said.

She opened the window and called out to Safet, who was by now obscured by the dark shade of the trees.

Would you like a sandwich too?

From the dark Safet shouted back:

Turn the lights off so you don't run the battery down.

Mum turned off the light above the rear view mirror. I ate my processed ham and mayonnaise sandwich, anticipating the bite of gherkin when I reached the middle. The outline of Mum's head was resting on the headrest in front of me.

Jadran! Come here, Jadran! Safet's voiced sounded out.

Your Dad's calling you, said Mum, taking what was left of my sandwich so that I could open the car door.

She didn't ask me where I wiped my hands. It wasn't important at that point.

Jadran, come and look at this.

I followed Safet's voice. He was crouched down by a bush, looking at the ground and signalling for me to come closer.

Look at him.

He reached out towards me, searching for me in the darkness and pulled me towards him, whilst pointing to something black on the ground with his other hand.

Puž. Slug, he whispered.

He touched the slug, and then he picked it up, placed it on his palm and lifted it up to me. I turned away.

Don't be frightened. It's not poisonous. We used to look for these as kids and put them down people's backs.

As I watched the slug on his palm, Safet's free hand tickled my neck, but I already knew that trick of his and I wasn't scared.

He put the slug back on the ground. He didn't appear to be anxious anymore.

Puž.

Then he stood up and put his arms around my shoulders.

Tomorrow you'll see the leaning tower of Pisa. It'll be like nothing you've ever seen.

2.

The first day after my father's disappearance, the fifth of March 1992, Mum existed solely on the telephone, while I was listening to Guns n' Roses in my room, briefly overhearing snippets of her conversation in the gaps between songs, and gauging the tone of her voice. I didn't believe that anything had happened to my Dad; I was convinced that he'd just gone out somewhere and got off his head. Down there in Bosnia the war had started, and the piss-ups had gained new impetus up here in Slovenia. Dad's friends were drowning their fears; fears for the lives of their parents, brothers, sisters, and it was no longer so easy to remain standing, as they did, until the final round. That's why it seemed like Mum was overreacting, and if she was so worried, instead of calling Aunt Maya and Uncle Dane, Irfan's wife Rufija, the police, Dane and Maya again, the emergency department, and then Danilo, Roman, and I don't know who else, she should instead head out to Emona and to Borsalino, the cafes and bars that usually swallowed my Dad's time between leaving work and arriving home.

That evening, I sprung into action. Partly to calm Mum down, partly so that I didn't have to hear her repeat, for the three-hundred-and-sixtieth time, that Safet had not been home since yesterday morning. It was my first ever tour of the local bars, and I roamed from one to the next, every bar in the area; those that Dad frequented often, and also those that he'd never set foot in, not even if you carried him in blind drunk. I came across a few of his friends, including Irfan, but no one had seen nor heard from him.

Tell your mam not to worry herself. He'll be back, as soon as he's drunk his fill, was Irfan's advice.

Mum was on the phone when I got back, but she was no longer explaining anything. All she was doing was listening and absently nodding, and when she saw me she said that she had to go and put the phone down before the voice on the other end could protest.

Come on, we're going to the police.

At the police station we were told not to worry, that Dad would probably come back of his own accord, that we did the right thing in reporting his disappearance, but given that no incidents had been reported in recent days with victims matching Safet Dizdar's description, there was no reason to suspect that anything had happened to him.

More than likely he's got waylaid somewhere, madam, said the eldest policeman, who did not appear overly concerned by Mum's story. Mum had to repeat for a third time that Dad didn't come home from work yesterday and hadn't been seen since, before the policeman noted it down.

They like getting waylaid, these people, he said. I was too young at that point to understand what he meant, but Mum knew all too well. She picked up a stapler from the desk and hurled it at him with all her might.

You bent bastards! she yelled. Bastards! *You like getting waylaid somewhere! The lot of you head out and get waylaid!*

Two policeman grabbed hold of her and dragged her towards the exit, while a third came up to me, firmly took hold of my hand and held me back until Mum was outside.

I suggest that you calm yourself down right now and go straight home, one of the policemen said to Mum, when we were all stood outside. The other two stood beside him, one hand on their belts, the other holding their hats.

When I woke up, the second day after my father's disappearance, Mum gave me the fright of my life. I was on my way to the toilet, certain that Mum was at work and that I was alone in the deathly silent flat, when I saw her motionless body, standing in the middle of the living room. I was so frightened that my feet leapt clean off the ground. There was no reaction from Mum, as if she hadn't even seen me.

What are you doing?

Nothing. Waiting for Dane to call me. He promised he'd ring around and let me know if he found anything out.

Why aren't you at work?

I became acutely aware of the expression on her face. I'd said the wrong thing.

Is this all a fucking joke to you? Do you also think that THOSE people like to go off and get waylaid? That it's normal that he hasn't been home for three days? That I'm crazy for not sleeping all night?

Did you not sleep at all?

Oh what the…

Mum's voice cracked. She cracked. She was sobbing and shaking. She pushed me away, went into the bathroom and locked the door behind her. The sound of sobbing was soon drowned out by running water. When she came out of the bathroom, she looked straight through me again.

Shouldn't you be at school?

Half-day today.

She nodded. I sat down next to her on the sofa and there we sat, motionless, waiting for Dane's call.

Later that morning, the phone rang numerous times. Dane let us know that he didn't know anything; Maya called to comfort Mum and tell her not to worry, that everything would be OK; then Dane called back and said that he'd checked with an acquaintance who worked at the prison at Povšetova, and Safet definitely wasn't there. Then they called from the health clinic and a friendly woman told Mum that they hadn't treated anyone that matched her husband's description in the past twenty-four hours.

When I got back from school, Mum was no longer at home and the telephone had stopped ringing. Dusk was setting in, but from the balcony I looked down at the square in front of our block, waiting for Mum and Dad to appear. That was the first time it occurred to me that Dad might never come back. I gripped the balcony railings as hard as I could and clenched the muscles in my face. I was trying to tense my body so that the fear wouldn't escape. Then I dropped to the floor and did twenty press-ups. Then twenty more. And twenty more. Then an extra thirteen. I didn't cry, and that seemed like a good thing to me.

The third day after my father's disappearance, Mum and I went back to the police station. This time Dane was there, and a plain-clothes policeman who listened to us very attentively. He asked Mum things that the others had not.

In the time prior to his disappearance, did you notice any changes in his behaviour? Had he been to see a doctor at all? Had he fallen out with anyone? At work? Or with a neighbour? Have you contacted all of his relatives? Forgive me, I know this will be a difficult question for you, but have you considered that he might have gone to fight in Bosnia? Quite a few have gone over from Slovenia, to the war. Something flips inside them and they just leave. In circumstances like this too, overnight. They normally say goodbye, granted, but there are different stories. Does he have anyone down there?

Mum shook her head.

Everyone loves him, she said. *He's always laughing. Constantly laughing. People recognise him by his laugh. Everyone knows his laugh.*

Dane explained to the policeman that Safet only had distant relatives in Bosnia, that his parents and brother had died, and that his sister lived in Australia, so he hadn't been to Bosnia for years. Mum tugged at his sleeve, dragging him towards the exit. Dane then took the two of us for coffee. Maya came too.

If he's not blind drunk, then he's popped off to shoot someone. Tomorrow they'll be saying he's out kerb-crawling. Do you know how demeaning that is? No? They're just doing their job, are they? A job they're paid to do.

Mum became louder and louder and people on neighbouring tables were turning round to look at us. Maya drew her finger up to her lips, and as a reflex Mum's left hand swatted in her direction. Maya gasped at the pain, and Mum stood up and walked away from the table. Her chair tipped over onto the floor, knocking over some glasses, but she wasn't taking any notice of anyone anymore. I wanted to run after her, but Dane held me back.

Leave her. Let her get some air.

Dane returned to work, and Maya took me for pizza. She said I had to eat something. During the good hour that we spent together, my aunt uttered only a few sentences, which were not dissimilar to the questions posed to Mum by the plain-clothes policeman. Then we took ourselves to the shop, where Maya bought two bags full of food, pressed them into my hands and sent me home.

Pop those things in the fridge, were the only words Mum said that evening.

The fourth day after my father's disappearance, Mum turned into a detective and we went to visit Kolinska, Dad's place of work. She hurtled past the security guard and I was almost running behind her along the lengths of corridor to his office. People turned around, wanting to say something to her, but she was too fast and all they could do was stand and watch.

At Dad's desk was a thickset woman who, as Mum entered the office, immediately stood up and removed her thick-rimmed glasses. Everyone in the office fell silent; the phone was ringing but no one picked it up. I think it must have been ringing the whole time we were there.

Mum was rifling through things on Dad's desk; opening and closing drawers, spending a long while sifting through papers that she found in a cupboard, and then she listened to Dad's colleagues, who willingly came up to her, offered coffee, called colleagues from other offices, and some lady in a greenish two-piece said that they'd all thought Dad was quieter than usual on the last day they saw him, but it was that sort of day, she quickly added. The only man in a suit and who was therefore probably Dad's boss, said that the police had phoned and that he'd spoken to everyone, but that nobody knew anything, that they'd already gone through his desk, but they hadn't found anything out of the ordinary. Mum was nodding and shaking things out of the drawer onto the desk, carefully checking every bit of paper; two ladies helped her to empty the cupboard, and then all of them, some five or six people, inspected all the stationery, even opening boxes of staples, blank envelopes and fax paper.

More than twenty people had steadily accumulated in that small office, each of them wanting to be useful, everyone wanting to help. One lady, Zdenka, who had worked with Dad the longest and who I knew the best, squeezed me so tightly that I thought she was never going to let me go.

Then the crowd that had gathered around Dad's desk started to disperse, and I saw Mum fighting her way through.

Let's go, she said.

As I glanced back down the corridor in the direction of Dad's office, I saw a procession walking behind us, as if at a funeral. I got the feeling that these people knew something, but didn't want to tell us. They moved along the corridor at a snail's pace, as if all linked together, all with the same lengthened postures, the same conciliatory looks on their faces, all dragging their feet along the floor in the same way, all remaining silent.

After that, we went to the Emergency Department and Mum showed Dad's photo to paramedics, until a bald-headed doctor asked us to leave before he called the police.

The fifth day after my father's disappearance, Mum finally fell asleep before sunrise. I brought a chair out into the hall, closed the living room door, and sat down next to the phone so I could pick it up as soon as it started to ring. People were now calling to ask how we were, or if we needed anything. Calls from Mum's colleagues, wanting to find out if it was true that they still hadn't found my father, saying how awful it was, leaving their best wishes; calls from the mums of my school friends; calls from people I didn't know, saying they were friends of Mum and Dad. Our neighbour Minka came round to ask how Mum was, and placed a whole pie in my hands.

Why didn't you wake me? Are you mad? Have you any idea what time it is? said Mum, as she walked past me on her way to the bathroom.

How could you let me sleep in? Christ's sake, Jadran. You're not a kid anymore, she said, coming out of the bathroom.

What's that? she asked, as she caught sight of the pie on the floor by my feet.

Minka brought it.

What? Here? She called round and brought pie? People have gone mad. Are you just going to leave it there on the floor? I nearly trod on it!

Jožica and Dunja rang. They send their best wishes…

What do I care. What good are best wishes? Christ, everyone wants to know how I am. How am I supposed to be? Nobody knows anything. Not a single person has seen him. No one! He's vanished and nobody has seen him. Fucking useless bastards. Dane always knows everything, he's mates with everyone, and now all of a sudden no one can help. Fuck them all. Tear me off a piece of that pie, please. Thanks. Why aren't you at school? Oh, half-days this week, that's right. When are you going in?

At twelve.

At twelve.

Borut said not to worry about going in to work, that you can stay at home if you like, and that Neža has sorted out sick leave for you.

They're all acting like he's already dead. Those smug fuckers. No one is out looking for him. No one is looking for him. No one. No one is looking for him.

I never made it to school that day. I turned right out of our block, and went to his favourite bars, and then to all bars in the area. I stepped inside the stale rooms and searched corners thick with smoke, and barmen asked me who I was looking for, but I didn't respond; all I did was turn around and head out, on to the next smoky establishment, until there were none left. I peered through shop windows as I walked by, on the off chance I might see Dad's face, and I inspected passers-by on the street; I inspected all of them, and from a distance, a few men looked like they might be him, and I waited until they came closer, or, if they were walking in front of me, I'd follow them, until I was close enough to see that they in fact had grey hair or a beard. Then, in the distance, I caught sight of somebody who walked just like my father did. He was far away and walking towards a car; I was worried that he was going to get in and drive away before I could get a look at him, and I ran towards him, I ran about 100 metres, and when I reached him he was still standing by the car and was taking something out of the boot. He looked nothing like Safet Dizdar; he was older and had a round face, whereas Safet Dizdar had an elongated face, which is why I continued running and ran for some time without taking anything in around me. Then I walked along the river and looked from one side of the riverbank to the other, I was looking for a body washed up on the riverbank, and just like in films, I could see my father falling from the bridge, the river taking him away; I walked faster and faster so I could check every inch of riverbank as quickly as possible, and soon I was running again and I thought I really saw a body, but it was just a black plastic bin bag and on I ran, all the way to the castle, and I ran under the bridge and on ahead towards home, and then I came to a stop and watched how the water carried my father's body towards Zalog and beyond, I couldn't run any further, the path had come to an end, and it was also getting dark.

The sixth day after my father's disappearance, we got a phone call from Irfan. Without saying hello, he told me to put Mum on the phone, and she took the receiver from my hand, raised it to her ear, listened, and then she handed it back to me, for me to put it back down, and then she said *Safet is in Bosnia*, exhaling deeply and closing her eyes, and then she draped herself onto me and there we stood, in the middle of the hall; I didn't dare move, and I looked out of the window that had blown open – it was unusually warm outside and the air was still; there was no wind in Ljubljana, there was never any wind, just like in our flat, which never caught the slightest breeze, despite us facing East.

He's in Bosnia, that's all I know, said Mum as she opened her eyes. She picked up the phone and placed the receiver to her ear. Then she started to dial the numbers.

I have to call Maya, the police, work.

She put the receiver down and placed the phone back on the shelf. She leaned on me again.

Only once had we all been together in Bosnia, I thought to myself – in Bihać. I couldn't remember why we'd been there. I was only young, but I knew that we'd sat on the grass behind the house, by the water. I was the only child, so I was bored; it was just older people sitting around, drinking coffee at the table. I wanted to kick a ball about, but they didn't let me because the ground was uneven and the ball would have rolled into the river. That's what they told me, when I told them that I'd be careful – but nobody had the patience for me, and they took the ball away and told me I ought to sit down. Then I sat with them at the table and didn't want to eat or drink, not that anybody took any notice of me. Strangers came and went; Dad, meanwhile, greeted them sincerely, more sincerely than usual. Maybe someone had died, but I couldn't remember who.

That, to me, was Bosnia; and when Mum said that Safet was in Bosnia, he was there again, at the table on the sloping lawn, behaving again as if I weren't there beside him; once again he was some other, serious person, and I was tugging at his sleeve and telling him that I wanted us to go home. I didn't like him like that, I didn't like that Dad in Bosnia, Dad who talks differently, sits differently, drinks coffee which he never drinks at home. My Dad was the only Bosnian who didn't drink coffee, but he drank it in Bosnia; there they put it in front of him and he drank up, and didn't say a word, only slurped loudly from the small cups that were lost amongst his large fingers.

Ring Maya and tell her that Safet is alive and well, that everything's fine, he's in Bosnia… No, wait, I'll do it a bit later… Or maybe you do it… No, it's OK, just bring me a glass of water, I'll ring her… I'll do it now.

3.

It was seven years since Safet had been to Bosanska Otoka, the birthplace of his father, the town in which he should have been born and where he should have lived, had his father, chemical engineer Fuad Dizdar, not taken a job six months before the birth of his son at the military hospital in Banja Luka, from where he was then soon sent over to the military hospital in Kragujevac, in Serbia. Kragujevac, instead of Bosanska Otoka, was to become Safet's hometown, the first of many foreign cities that he would call home. Even as a child Safet seldom went to Bosanska Otoka, as vague family and friendly ties were steadily loosened by time, but he would go there maybe once or twice a year, to weddings and funerals. Until there was a lack of people to visit in Bosanska Otoka.

The last time Safet had been here was 1985, at the funeral of his youngest brother Vahid, the only one of Fuad's three children to have returned to their would-be hometown. After the funeral, Vahid's widow Tijana sold their house by the bridge and moved to Sweden. Safet had asked her what would become of the old house, Nana's house, as they called it. It was no concern of hers, he was told. They were in touch only once after that. She'd let him know that she was going to remarry in Sweden. He didn't have anything against it. She thanked him, and that was the last time he heard from her. Tijana most likely never went back to Otoka. And neither did Safet.

Every year, for Eid, my Dad's sister, Aunt Fadila would call from Bosanska Otoka, or he would call her. Her son Dado would occasionally get in touch, when he took a van across to Germany and would stop over in Ljubljana. They'd meet up in front of some warehouse or other, and quickly swap news. Then one day, Dado came to visit us at home and told Safet that Aunt Fadila had died whilst he had been on his way to Bucharest.

That's life, my cousin. My mother's Janazah couldn't wait.

Dado's brother Nihad had wanted to call Safet to notify him of Fadila's death, so that he could go to the funeral, but he couldn't find his Ljubljana phone number. Fadila had never written it down anywhere, Dado said. She had all the numbers in her head. He could have asked Ismar, Safet said, and Dado went quiet. It eventually transpired that Ismar and Nihad weren't speaking to one another.

Not long afterwards, Dado moved to Germany. It was as if he had been waiting for Fadila to die. He and Nihad sold her house, and off he went. The last time they met before his departure, he'd said to Safet that he couldn't bear to watch the situation down there anymore. Safet couldn't understand what he was talking about. From Ljubljana it looked like everything down there was fine.

Nihad died on the first anniversary of Aunt Fadila's death. Safet couldn't remember who told him, but again the news took a while to reach him. Ismar was the only one left.

Ismar Bašić was the only person in all of Bosanska Otoka with a good understanding of who Safet Dizdar was. And he was therefore the only person on that day, the sixth of March 1992, who Safet did not wish to bump into when he returned to Bosanska Otoka after seven years. All he wanted was to go back to *Nana's house* without being recognised. He hoped to avoid a single greeting. To be left alone, to arrive at the house unnoticed, without a sound. After that – and Safet knew this – there'd be people in town who knew him, but none of them would call in on him. Some would wait for him to call in on them. Some of them wouldn't even do that. Except Ismar.

If I could just make it to Nana's house, was his only thought, as he stepped out of the car onto the bridge. He didn't even want the taxi driver to know where he was going. Which is why he asked him to drop him off, even though his destination was still a good twenty minutes' walk away. Safet waited for the taxi to pull out before getting on his way. The house stood in solitude, outside of town, and there he would be left undisturbed for as long as he might need. Nobody would take such a detour and climb the slope just to greet a stranger. Wives might encourage their husbands to invite him round for coffee. *That's just how we do things*, they'll say. Because of his father, because of Fuad the engineer. And the husbands would say that he ought to be the one to come and say hello. *That's just how we do things*, they'll say. If he's any son of Fuad the engineer. The only exception was Ismar. He wasn't interested in how things were done. Ismar's curiosity was the only thing that worried Safet. He sensed it as he walked through the town, how it stayed with him, how it drew closer. Ismar was Vahid's godfather. A bus driver.

Nana's house had been empty since Nana's death. Nana, as everyone called Safet's mother Enisa, died on the eighth of February 1984, on the day of the Olympic opening ceremony in Sarajevo. Sometimes, when Safet's sister Anila used to visit from Australia with her children, the house was so full that children and grown-ups had to take it in turns to use the dining table, but after Enisa and Vahid had died, there were no visits from Safet in Ljubljana, nor from Anila in Melbourne.

Poor Nana had left her house and her land to all three of her children. Nothing was divided up. In her mind, Vahid, Anila and Safet would continue to gather there, celebrating Labour Day and Eid. The grandchildren – Safet's Jadran, and Anila's Elvis, Mensur and Adisa, would spend summers there together. The attic was their dedicated space. Nana made up a room for each of her grandchildren. But none of that made sense after Vahid died.

One evening, Ismar had been behind the wheel. On his way to Bihać, drunk, he veered off the road as he turned a corner which he'd driven around four times a day for the past twenty years on his local bus service. Vahid died at the scene, while Ismar only suffered concussion and a few broken ribs.

After the funeral, Tijana banished him from the house. She saw him drinking and she lost it. That night, she told Vesna that she was going to leave Bosanska Otoka. She asked Vesna to tell Safet, and to ask him not to try and convince her otherwise. She knew that if she were to see Ismar drunk at Lela's one more time she would kill him, and so it was better if she went away. She also said that every time she drove to Bihać she was gripped by the thought of veering off the road on that corner herself. And that she knew that at some point she really would. Being pregnant wouldn't stand in her way.

Safet respected her wishes and didn't try to convince her to stay. He said nothing. God was his witness. He, the atheist. Even though he sensed that he'd never see Vahid's child that she was carrying inside her.

None of his people were left in Bosanska Otoka, none of the Dizdars. Just Nana's empty house. And the graves of Fuad, Nana and Vahid. More than likely that was why Safet returned after seven years. Because there was nobody there to ask any questions. Nobody that required any explanations. Nobody that he had to apologise to. He could be on his own here; and that, on the sixth of March 1992, was all that Safet wanted.

He felt relieved as he arrived at the house, as if he'd just escaped a starving pack of wolves. He didn't come across a single soul during the long walk, apart from some children playing at the roadside who took no notice of him. He had been careful to keep his head down as he walked through the town. He didn't want to be intercepted by anyone and be forced to say hello. He didn't want anyone to greet him. The very thought of somebody watching him was unbearable. Let alone the realisation that someone might ask who he was. That they might guess what he was doing there.

That day he wanted to avoid all that. That day, at the very least, he wanted to hide from everyone. Shut himself up in Nana's house as quickly as possible. Because in truth he wasn't really there, in Bosanska Otoka. That day, he was still in Ljubljana with his wife and son, whom he had left behind.

Safet knew that not many people walked this way, and that each passer-by would rouse curiosity. Which is why he was almost running despite being tired and barely able to lift his legs. He hurried and hoped that no one was leaning out of the window, that they would be busy with other things.

Standing before the two houses, but with the cover of the forest, Safet felt like he'd made it. Even if anyone were to see him now, he wouldn't know. Just a few more steps and he'd be there. At Nana's house.

For eight years the house had stood empty. No one had stepped over its threshold, not even uninvited. Everyone knew that it was Nana's house. They were different times, times when that still meant something to people, and no one went anywhere near it. The front door was still locked after all this time and Safet had to climb in through the bathroom window. Just like he did as a small child. Nana used to get so cross at him for that. Someone might see him and climb into her house themselves, she'd say. Yet no one but he came in through that window. Children find ways and means where thieves do not. But now was a time when people would find a way, even when there were none.

Safet didn't wish to loiter in Nana's room on the ground floor. He, whose life had just been transformed into a scattered heap of memories, didn't want to remember. From the bathroom he went straight up to the attic. To Jadran's room, as it was known to everyone, even though Jadran had never actually been there. He opened the window to let in some air. The window looked out onto the Una, and all it would take was for someone to sail by, right by the river bank, to see that it was open. He laid down on the dusty bed, fully clothed. The only thing he removed were his shoes, because he could hear Nana's voice saying that if you lay down in your shoes, the night could send you on your way.

Despite not having eaten a single thing all day, he didn't feel hunger. Nor tiredness. He felt nothing. He'd reached the end of the line. No one would look for him here. No one could call him here. He had fled from everyone and left his life far behind him. He lay there and stared at the ceiling. He sensed he could spend days lying there, on that bed. Weeks. Months. He knew he could. There was nothing to get up for. He lay there all afternoon and evening and for a large part of the night. He fell asleep towards morning. It was only a full bladder that woke him. He relented, and went to the bathroom. He tried to pull the chain, but all that could be heard was a dull rumbling sound. The house had no water. Nor electricity.

This fact momentarily returned him to reality. His stomach rumbled. He had a dry mouth. I can bathe in the river, he thought. But he would need drinking water. Food. Probably electricity too. The nights could get a lot colder than the previous one. His only thought until now had been of lying down on the bed at Nana's house. But now, having confined himself, he didn't know what came next. His wish for solitude was no less than the day before. The hunger and thirst weren't unbearable yet. So back he went to the attic and laid down on the bed. He was calm again. He felt a strange sort of contentment, one that he'd never felt before. He could hold on for a while longer without water, he thought, looking out of the window and observing a new day pass by. It was like a drug. Lying there. On Jadran's bed. Body and soul were soothed. Both wanted to be nowhere else but there. Safet didn't try to understand any of that. He lay there until late afternoon, until a horrible thirst forced him to get up.

People in that part of the world are wary of strangers. If they don't know you, they'll pretend that they're not interested and will turn the other way, before then secretly observing you once you've gone past. And in Bosanska Otoka, not even those who feasibly could know him, knew who Safet was. He had been away for too long. And besides, time passed more quickly there.

That afternoon, when he arrived in town and took at seat at Lela's to have something to eat and drink, it was a long time before anyone approached him. Then Lela hoisted her ample and by now rather tired body up from the neighbouring table to ask him what he would like. He ordered, and she brought what he'd asked for. He drank, ate, paid and left. Without saying another word. As he returned to his new home, he sensed that not a single passer-by had so much as glanced at him. He felt invisible, and he liked it.

He hoped that the next day would be the same. But because he came back, he caught people's attention. Now they knew where he lived. Maybe they even knew who he was. He was greeted by Lela this time. Three men, sitting with her at the next table, nodded to him. But not because they were being friendly. Because they were curious. Because they wanted to know what he was doing there. Safet did not reciprocate. He ordered, ate and left, just like the previous day. He was still not fond of superfluous words, and didn't want to listen to their questions.

On the way back to Nana's house he passed a small cluster of children playing, and they watched him, and then started to follow him. He heard a woman's voice calling them back. He also heard a man's voice, calling Denis. Denis had clearly not listened to the woman's voice, he thought to himself.

No one greeted him at Lela's the next day. Not even Lela. It still seemed, though, as if they were waiting for him to say something. By now they were visibly staring and waiting. But they were waiting in vain. He hoped, as if he didn't know the locals, that they'd slowly get used to him and come to accept his secretive ways, and that he'd be able to roam like a ghost once again, without any one of them staring at him. He hoped he'd be able to come and go undisturbed again, but the looks on their faces told a different story. Their unease was palpable, and he himself became uneasy in their presence.

When he'd finished and paid his bill, he said goodbye. But now it was their turn to say nothing. On the way home, he lifted his head and took his first look around the town. He got the feeling that people were trying to hide from him, not the other way round. There were no children playing in front of the neighbouring house this time. A man stood in the garden, leaning on a spade. He was staring straight at him. Neither said a word. The man seemed to be afraid, so he looked away and carried on home. He heard the man's voice shortly afterwards. He couldn't quite hear, and he was soon gone, vanished behind the front door.

The next morning, they were knocking on his door. Three armed officers in uniform. The door remained locked, and Safet was without a key. He was worried they might break it down, and so he opened the window and asked if he could help them. They asked him who he was. A refugee, he replied. From where, the eldest officer enquired. He had unusually small eyes, these two black dots centred on an oval face. From Slovenia, he told him. They wanted to know what he was doing there, in that house. The house was his, he said. They asked for his name. He gave it. They asked what he'd fled from. From the madness, said Safet.

One of the younger guys laughed out loud. He had a protruding jaw which, as he laughed, moved independently of the rest of his face. The old guy said that he must be mad to have left the madness for the madhouse. He wasn't smiling. Safet replied, saying that he may well be right. Then the old guy put his gun down, leaning it against the door. He was clearly unsure of what to do. The two younger officers were waiting for him to come up with something. He then asked who had previously lived at this address. Safet told them it was Nana. *My mother, Enisa*, he quickly added. *Aha*, the old guy said, though he didn't appear to know who Nana Enisa was. He's clearly not local, thought Safet. The old guy then asked him what he'd been doing in Slovenia. And in which city he'd been living. Safet feared the interrogation would continue until he gave a wrong answer. But all of a sudden, the old guy turned and started to walk back towards the town without saying a word. The young guys followed him, one of them stopping shortly afterwards to stare back at Safet, who was still leaning out of the window. He picked up a stone and launched it in the direction of the house. It thumped against the door, a metre or so away from Safet. His mate laughed and picked up a stone for himself. But his fell a few metres short of the house. The older officer, meanwhile, was already well ahead, and was not concerned with what was happening behind him.

Three days later, when Safet was sitting at Lela's one afternoon, he was approached by a man with a long scar across his bald head. He asked if he could sit down. He did not wait for an answer.

What's going on in Slovenia? he asked, taking a seat.

I don't know.

Are you really Vahid's brother?

Safet nodded.

Good, said the man, waving towards the middle of the bar. Lela brought them both a rakia and placed it down in front of them without saying anything.

I'm Ismar's brother, said the man with a scar. *Ismar died last year. He killed himself.*

Again Safet nodded. The man with a scar raised his glass.

To souls at peace, he said, a few drops of rakia spilling onto the floor beneath the table.

Our mother was a Serb from Valjevo, he whispered and let out a loud burst of laughter. It seemed as if he were trying to make his laughter travel around the room.

If you need anything, just say.

I need water and power.

The man with the scar laughed loudly again.

Everyone needs something. These are the times we're living in.

Once again Safet nodded. The man with the scar stood up, turned to Lela, pointed at the two empty glasses on the table and then at himself, and then turned to look at Safet.

Don't do anything stupid.

I won't.

On his way home, Safet stopped in front of the post office. He looked at the long queue, winding its way out of the building along the street, all the way back to the bakery. People were waiting to use the phones. Safet joined the back of the queue, without knowing who he wanted to call. Ismar's brother had thrown him. At first he tried not to listen to other people's chatter in the line, but it proved impossible. A woman in front of him was loudly recalling to a friend about how she'd been at her sister's in Banja Luka, and how her neighbour Dragana hadn't come out for coffee all week.

I saw her at the window, and she saw me, but she didn't come out.

Another one was saying that she wasn't happy about her husband walking into Bihać and she'd asked him to stop.

Here everyone sees everything and knows everything, she kept saying.

As Safet drew closer to the phone box, he could hear a female voice, sobbing.

Don't be silly, don't be silly. They're lying, sweetie, they're lying. Don't be silly.

A woman stepped out of the phone box and ran towards the exit. All of a sudden Safet found himself standing in the phone booth, receiver in hand. A long line of impatient people stood behind him. He dialled Irfan's number. He told him where he was, and asked him to tell Vesna.

He found it hard to say her name and he hung up before Irfan could ask any questions.

By the time he got to the house it was already dark, and from a distance he noticed that a light was on in one of the ground floor rooms. He ran towards the front door, convinced that the officers had broken into the house. But the door was locked. Safet rushed to the window, through which he clambered into the house. He had to get to the illuminated room as quickly as possible. It was Nana's bedroom. As he approached it, the only sound was that of his own footsteps and he felt like a small, frightened child. Warily, he opened the door and looked over to Nana's bed. The room was empty. All he could think at that point was that they'd turned the power back on. He switched on the light in the hall. Then in the kitchen and the living room, too. He went into the bathroom and ran water into the sink. A thick, brown liquid spurted out of the tap. He let it run, and watched as it turned clear.

He had a wash, and then took a walk around the house. Everything was just as it was when Nana was still living there. Untouched. There were even a few food packets in the kitchen cupboards. A mild stench was emanating from them, which he'd smelt as he walked into the bathroom. He took them and carried them out, and shook out the contents, along with all the pests that had been residing in there, onto the floor out the back. From there he went into the shed. Only now, with light, could he see everything that had accumulated in there. It was full of Vahid's things, and even some of his father's. He was forced to retreat by a suffocating stench of damp, a sea of cobwebs and the sound of scurrying creatures. But then in the background, behind a stack of garden chairs, he caught sight of a spare tractor wheel. He immediately recalled how, as little kids, he and Vahid used to float along the Una, sitting in those tyres while flicking through comics. He fought his way to the back and dragged the tyre out. He pulled out the inner tube and took it back with him into the house. Then he turned out the light and went up to the attic.

The next morning, he was awoken by shouting. He went over to the window and looked out towards the neighbouring house. There was a car parked outside, and the man with a spade was standing beside it. A woman, presumably his wife, was standing at the fence, while he was shouting at her and hurrying her back inside. She was saying something as well, though Safet couldn't work out what. The man's piercing voice was the only thing that cut through the morning air. Next, a man in uniform stepped out of the car and placed himself between them. Safet couldn't hear what he was saying to them; the woman turned in anger to go back inside, while the man with the spade got into the car. Only now when the voices had quietened down could dogs be heard barking in the background. The dogs were calling to one another, and soon the entire street was barking.

He had to get away from there, to leave everything to calm down a bit. And so he picked up the inner tube and went to the shed. He'd rooted out Vahid's bicycle pump, and began to fill the inner tube with air. It took time, but time he had. Besides, he enjoyed physical work. He liked feeling his body sweat, becoming increasingly out of breath. With each drop of sweat, each gasp of air, something was driven out of him. Something heavy. He tossed the pump aside and started to blow up the tube with his own breath. He puffed into the tube with all his might, counted the breaths in and out, and felt encouraged. Only ten more, only five more. And another ten. And another five. He was dizzy, but he didn't want to stop until the tube was inflated and he was lying, exhausted, in front of the shed.

At that moment, a woman's voice could be heard coming from the neighbouring house, shouting to her children and shooing them back inside. He got up and headed to the river.

He walked upstream along the river for almost two hours. It was still just as beautiful as it had been when he was a child, when he came here with his parents to visit Aunt Fadila. Green. Luminous. There were no Una fisherman anymore, though. He didn't meet a single one along the way. Nor were there any of those first, early summer bathers. There were no longer any young guys in the ice-cold river, trying to prove that they were real men. Just him with his tractor tyre on his shoulder. And the birds. They were the only ones taking any interest in the upcoming spring, he thought.

As he caught sight of a bend up ahead, the one where Vahid and Ismar veered off the road, something stopped him. He didn't want to get any closer. I must be at least three miles out of town, he thought. It was far enough. He fought his way through the tall growth between the trees and found a way to the water. He placed the tyre on the water's surface. He had to keep a firm grip, or the current would have pulled it away. It was all much easier when he was a child. *Kids don't know the meaning of impossible*, he heard his father's voice say. Small children's bodies could climb everywhere. But now he was afraid of being too heavy, and of capsizing or going down with the tyre. Into the cold, March waters of the Una. Or of getting swept straight into a rocky bank. He could hold on to the tyre no longer and had to make a decision. As he didn't have the strength to pull it back towards him, should he jump, or let it go? He jumped. The tyre beneath him rocked vigorously, his arms and legs flailed in the air, but he stayed in. He was floating.

The current wasn't too strong in that section of river and he could control his course. That child with a comic in his hands was awoken, and all at once everything was so familiar, so at-home. The Una was his river. He soon surrendered himself to it entirely, letting it take him wherever the current chose. He drifted beneath the shade of the riverine trees bathed in warm, March sunshine. He ran his fingertips through the water and surrendered to the moment. The freshness of the water and the gentle midday heat washed over his body.

And just then, the sound of shots fired out. Judging by their volume, they couldn't have been too far away. It has begun, he thought. Finally. The Una was carrying him slowly towards Bosanska Otoka. There was still a good hour of drifting ahead of him. Shots fired out again. Even louder this time, even closer. Hard as it was to understand, it seemed as if the shots were what truly calmed him down. Only then did his voyage become complete. Everything is just as it should be, he thought. Him, in the middle of the Una, encircled in Vahid's tractor tyre, the warm midday sun, and war. A war that he deserved. A war that they all deserved.

When I reach the town, he told himself, I'm not going to stop. I'll let myself drift through, all the way up to Aunt Fadila's house and beyond.

Stone after stone, house after house would disperse all around him. The town would slowly fade away, until there was nothing along the banks of the Una. No pain, no sin, no debt, no remorse. No more former lives and former loves. There'll be nothing; nothing worthy of celebration, nothing worthy of commiseration. Everything would be blank and he would be blank. At last, he'd no longer feel a thing.

He closed his eyes, tipped back his head and allowed the water to carry him away.

4.

The first ruined house never leaves your mind, the first burnt out village you pass through is etched into your memory and all the ruins you see afterwards fade away over time; you know they used to be there, you know you saw them, but they cannot be recalled. After a while you don't even see the ruined houses, it's as if they were untouched, or were never there at all, but the first house and the first village remain, and so I keep returning to that window on the bus to Bihać, unable to look away from the charred gaping window frames and the bare blackened walls, from the invisible faces moving through violently ripped-open rooms, where stoves were once inevitably full of leftovers stuck to the bottom of trays, and where sideboards displayed delicate china coffee cups, patiently waiting, year after year, never used because war, as it always does, arrived ahead of their special occasion.

I'm sixteen years old. Old enough to board a bus and get myself to Bihać to visit my father; too young to understand what's pulling me there, or why I'm looking out, across from a sleeping, unshaven man, at ruined houses by the road, instead of being at home, sixty miles north, retaking the history exam that we have on Monday. When she reads my letter, Mum will know that I'm lying, that I'm not camping with Jerec and Igor; perhaps it will occur to her that I'm here, but she'll immediately drive that thought away – too frightening, too open-ended – and she'll find some other, alternative, explanation.

I asked you where you were you going, not who you were visiting, the border guard said, smiling, as if he'd told a joke, but I felt we were standing too close to burnt-out houses for me to laugh at him, and so I glared, solemnly, at the guard who shook his head in disdain. I, the dimwit, didn't get it; the dimwit who wasn't from round here, which is why he gave up, stopped talking, and handed me back my passport as I told him I was going to Bosanska Otoka. But he had lost interest, having established that I didn't speak his witty language, and went up to the next, unshaven, person in line.

And how are things in Sweden? he asked, when he looked up from inspecting the passport.

Cold, answered the unshaven man.

Cold, the border guard repeated, as if not knowing what to do with that word.

Neither one of them smiled, nothing was funny anymore and all travellers, serious as can be, waited for the conversation to continue, a conversation which was already over, not that we knew it. The border guard turned back towards his colleague standing a few metres behind him.

The things a man learns at this border, he said, and the other man nodded, the one with a moustache standing in front of me, and whispered *motherfucker* under his breath, though no one except me, who turned around to look at him, heard.

Is your old man from Bosanska Otoka? he asked, and I nodded, even though I felt I ought to shake my head, because my old man had never been from Bosanska Otoka; his father was, but not him. He was born in Kragujevac and grew up in Split, and whenever he was asked where he was from, he'd always say *from round 'ere*, except when he was drunk, and then he'd say *my mother, where d'you think, and not out of her arse*.

But, yes, now he was from Bosanska Otoka, that's what he'd decided, or so I believed; he went there of his own accord, he made the choice to be from there. From Bosanska Otoka. I turned back to look at the border guard, now at the tail end of our line, recognising the same smirk on his face that had been directed at me, but the man standing before him did not see the funny side. The guard was sifting through the few pieces of paper that constituted his documents

Get your things, he said, and the man went over to the bus and took a green sports bag out of the luggage compartment, then walked with the border guard towards the container.

The doors closed behind them. As they signalled for us to get back on the bus, an order we obeyed, I was the only one to look back at the closed doors that were concealing our fellow passenger; nobody wondered whether it could have been any one of us, they acted as if he was chosen at random because he was last in line, or because he had a slightly offset jaw, or because his trousers were too short. All the passengers seemed vulnerable to me; any of them could have had forged papers, nobody seemed entirely confident that they'd make it across the border, because nobody believed that there was an actual, clear set of rules that get you across to the other side. We all knew that we had found ourselves in a changeable world, especially now, of all times; which is why we all breathed a sigh of relief that we weren't the ones who had ended up in a container, and that we'd been allowed to get back on the bus.

As I climb back onto the bus, the images disappear. My first few miles of post-war Bosnia consist only of smells; they are just the odour of tired and anxious passengers wafting out from their unwashed armpits, their neglected oral cavities, their heads of greasy hair laced with cigarette smoke, from skin that is clammy with moisture, from the discomfort of sleeping in cramped communal spaces, from lungs breathing out the air of factory canteens and station diners, from worn out shoes that have wandered through refugee camps, the department for foreign citizens, humanitarian aid distribution centres… I feel sick; I don't want to touch anything on this bus any longer, I'm scared of these foul-smelling people, I'd like to get off the bus and go home, I'd like freshly laundered sheets and clean bathroom floors, I'd like air freshener in the toilet; I don't dare look anyone on this bus in the eye anymore, their eyes are black holes, their nails are claws, and my stomach can't handle unpasteurised milk and I get skin allergies. I'm not from Bosanska Otoka, I don't belong on this bus, on these seats that let out clouds of dust particles when beaten; I'm from somewhere else and I'd like to go back there, because here the stench of people is suffocating me, the stench of burning and gunpowder and blood, but I smell of *Malizia* aftershave, even though my body doesn't yet secrete unpleasant odours as I'm only sixteen, and have only got the odd hair sprouting here and there; I don't have bad breath, because my toothpaste prevents tooth decay, I can't see anything out of the window, my fellow passengers' putrefying bodies are obscuring my view, I don't know what Bosnia's like, I don't even want to know, I want to go back, back home; why wasn't it me that got led into the container? That would have saved me from having to disembark there, where the roads have no pavements; from having to disembark at Bihać bus station, where he promised he'd be waiting for me.

First he promised he was going to come to my leavers' ball, not that I actually wanted him to come. It was already stressful enough without him: sixteen-year-olds dressed up like clowns, with ties and bow ties, feeling stupid in our big brothers' shirts and fathers' suits. There was no room there for Safet, I was already nervous enough without him, I already felt sick enough as it was, without him, and I threw up all the red wine and cola fifteen minutes after drinking it, and I was more sober than I'd ever been, and I didn't even dare go up to Mirela, let alone try to kiss her; all I wanted, even without him, was for the leavers' ball to be over as soon as possible. My Dad's unfulfilled promise was actually the only thing that cheered me up that day; the only thing that offered me at least a small amount of relief, and one less thing to worry about. But in truth, I never really believed that he would make it, because Mum had told me that he couldn't be relied on, Mum was angry at him for saying he was coming, *he could have at least kept quiet about it*, she kept saying; because she knew he wouldn't come, and she prepared me for it, she helped me keep my mind on Mirela and what I was going to say before I kissed her, if anything at all, or if I'd be drunk enough to not chicken out at the last minute, and over-think whether or not she'd kiss me back or if she'd slap me; there were so many other thoughts, that the one of Safet and the announcement of his arrival was driven away.

But it was only driven away until the day after the leavers' ball, when I woke up feeling disappointed and angry at myself, that I had been the one to run away from Mirela, away from temptation. Instead, we sat in

Cubana drinking brandy and coke, managing three rounds before we ran out of money, and so we sat behind our tower block until three a.m.

Fuck Mirela, I said, though either no one was listening to me, or they thought I was drunk.

Fuck my dad, I said, but they just burst out laughing at me, because I was gone after three drinks, and they said that I was the biggest backwater goofball in the history of Fužine.

The only reason I started thinking about my Dad the next morning was because I didn't want to think about Mirela. I started thinking about why he didn't come when he'd promised, and it hurt, it seemed deceitful, and it made me cry; it was only afterwards that I realised just how much I'd wanted him to come, to see him. I thought about him there, looking at me in that clownish suit and saying *pretty as a picture* and me adding *yeah, a picture of shit*, and him slapping me on the back while giving me a wink. That's how I imagined him, because that's how I imagined a Bosnian father might talk with his almost-grown-up son; I didn't know that Safet wasn't that type at all, that he'd never say anything of the sort. I even thought I'd be able to tell him about Mirela, that we'd be able to have a chat about her attributes.

The second time he promised to be there was when I invited him to watch me play in Novo Mesto, at the Cadets Championship Final Four. He wouldn't be able to miss it, I was sure; he'd want to be one of the proud fathers in the stands, he'd want to tell the referee to get fucked three times over, just as I imagined all Bosnian fathers did, he'd want to give me a few tips after the match, he'd mention legendary basketball stars Mirza Delibašić and Ivo Daneu, he'd go over the action in the black and white footage from the world championship in Ljubljana, which he was at, he'd congratulate me after the match and say that I was going to be even better than Dražen Petrović. I didn't know him, and in my head, Safet was just like all other Bosnian fathers; he was built from my Bosnian friends' anecdotes about their own dads, he was a mosaic of stereotypes and teenage exaggerations. Maybe it was for the best that he didn't make it that time, because he wouldn't have met my expectations; he wouldn't have played the role that I'd assigned to him, he probably would have hidden away quietly in a corner of the arena, different, just as he was that time when he left five years ago, because he was probably just like the person who was waiting for me at the bus station in Bihać: scrawny and greying, oddly dressed, the sort of person who offered his hand and asked how my journey was, and whether I was hungry; the sort who, after I replied that I was, glanced around confusedly, not knowing where to take me to get something to eat; unprepared, lost.

He's as much of an outsider as I am, I thought to myself that time, as I walked around Bihać behind him, and he looked around in confusion, searching for somewhere to get čevapi or burek or anything – anywhere – where I could get something to eat.

Let's go here, he eventually said, heading towards a dilapidated kiosk and sitting down at a dirty plastic table outside.

You alright here? he asked.

I looked around, trying to spot another restaurant. But there didn't seem to be anywhere else.

I'll find out what they've got.

Safet stood up and walked towards the door. He spoke quietly and I couldn't hear the conversation between him and the woman in the kiosk.

They've got cheese pasties, he said when he came back. *Will that do you?*
I nodded.

We could go somewhere else!

I shook my head.

Something to stop you dying of hunger.

I nodded.

But we can leave if you'd prefer.

I shook my head.

There's definitely somewhere to get čevapi somewhere round here.

I shook my head.

If you want čevapi, that is.

I shook my head.

You only have to say.

I pictured him at the final against Krka, with the other dads in the arena, standing with all of them who already knew one another, who knew the names of my teammates and the Krka players, the referees, the coaches, the people in the crowd, and I saw those familiar faces turning to look at him, asking who he was and where he'd appeared from, dressed like that, looking so lost, *who invited the tramp*, I heard the mob whisper; they were sniggering behind his back, at his shoes, at his white socks, at him.

My first thought, when I caught sight of him at the bus station in Bihać, was that it was a good job he didn't come to the match. I was ashamed to think like that, I was ashamed to feel ashamed of him, but the way he looked would have made people in Ljubljana think he was homeless, or at least an alcoholic; but more than anything, Safet looked like the people on the bus from Ljubljana to Bihać, similarly unkempt, smelly-looking, broken, spent, done-in. But I didn't know that then, when I was surveying the Novo Mesto arena, ignoring the logic which dictated that Safet would not just turn up in the stands. I waited for him to call, I waited for him to come, I waited, and when Mum said that he probably wouldn't come, for the first time in my life I shouted at her, I told her where to go, for the first time my word was final, for the first time she just stood there in silence; she was powerless, caught between what I wanted and Safet's inability to make it happen, and she herself could hardly wait for the weekend, for us to play in the semi-finals against Maribor, and then the final against Krka, too; she was rooting for us to win, but not so much for the victory, but because she hoped that my happiness would outweigh Safet's broken promise, she hoped it would drown out the disappointment. But it had the opposite effect, and the disappointment drowned out the happiness; I was still looking around after the match, into the crowd full of parents, brothers, sisters, friends, who for me were bigger competition than the guys on the court; I wanted to beat them, I wanted to prove something to them, to all of those dads cheering for their sons, I wanted to show that I was better, that I was faster, stronger. I played my two best games out of spite, but they didn't count, because Safet didn't see them.

Whilst the others were showering, and chants of *we are the champions* sounded out from under the showers, I sat in the changing room and decided that I was going to go to Bosanska Otoka, go up to Safet and say *go fuck your Bosnian self, you're a dickhead, that's what you are, I don't want to hear from you again, don't call, don't write – screw you*. And then I stripped off and went for a shower, with the other team mates, Jure and Kapo put their arms round me, one on each side, and I jumped and shouted *we are the champions* with them, shouting for all of us, except Safet, who was certainly no champion of mine.

I didn't tell him to go fuck his Bosnian self. I didn't say anything at all. I ate my lukewarm cheese pasty and kept a discreet eye on Safet, uncomfortably installed on the seat beside me, turning away so I could eat without the feeling of being rushed. A glass of water was all he ordered for himself. He requested it politely, addressing the waitress formally despite her not being much older than me. He didn't know her by name, as I imagined he might have done. I actually thought all Bosnians knew all waitresses by name, and they theirs. I thought that people on the streets of Bihać would greet Safet, saying *O, Safete, đe si, šta ima, kako je*, and that he'd take me to his local where the bartenders would hold out their hands and say *Is this your son, Safet? He's just like you! A dead spit! Maa sha'Allah, Safet, Maa sha'Allah!*. I had imagined Safet making my arrival cause for local celebration, but now here he was, drinking tap water, and patiently waiting for me to report back on the cheese pasty that he'd ordered for me.

Will that be enough for you?

I nodded, while Safet got up to get a napkin from the next table, so that I could wipe my mouth. Then he went up to the counter and paid, politely smiled and said *Doviđenja*.

The waitress mumbled her farewell. She seemed to be wondering where on earth we'd emerged from, but maybe that was just me wondering the same about Safet.

He wasn't a Bosnian, at least, not the sort that I'd had in mind; the sort that I thought he ought to have been. He was too quiet, withdrawn and shy, and certainly too polite. I wasn't prepared for this sort of Safet, and I wanted to get up and run back to the bus station and take the first bus out of there as quickly as I could.

Safet put his hand on my shoulder, and gestured that I should follow him over the bridge. He walked a metre or two ahead, hands in pockets, engrossed in his entangled trails of thought. At the bridge's midpoint, he turned around and offered to carry my bag, as if he'd suddenly remembered that I was there, but I said I was fine and on we walked. Just before we reached the end of the bridge, Safet stopped once more. He pointed to the river.

That's the Una.

I wasn't interested in the Una. It was just a river like all others, but I did stop and look into it, out of consideration for my guide, who seemed to think that of all the things he could have told me, the name of the river we were walking across was the most important. It was his river, which would later enter into many of his stories.

He stood next to me and left me to observe it in peace, even though I was only pretending to look. We then carried on downhill along the riverbank, until we stopped outside the entrance to a barber shop. Safet cautiously peeked inside.

Dobar dan.

A man in a white smock was sweeping the floor and did not immediately turn around. Only when he'd put the broom back in the corner did he turn enquiringly towards the front door.

Is Meho here? Safet asked him.

The barber shook his head, as if he didn't know who Meho was, but he was softened by the look of disappointment on Safet's face.

Any minute now. He should be here by now.

Safet and I remained outside the barber shop. He didn't seem to think it necessary to explain why we were waiting for Meho, and I didn't think it polite to ask too many questions.

Pop your bag on the floor, he said to me, after we'd been standing there for over five minutes.

Now we were both gazing into the Una. It was summer, and the surface of the water was so low that the river appeared to be crawling along the riverbed, weary, as if the difficult years of war had tested and drained the life from the Una, just as it had been drained from the surrounding streets. There was no one to be seen for miles around, folk had fled from the scorching midday heat, and it felt as if Safet and I were the only two people in town.

You can sit inside and wait for him, the barber's voice said after a while.

No, we're fine, thanks, Safet called back from outside, and we continued to wait, still in silence, still motionless, in spite of our bodies being baked in the Bihać heat.

Then Safet shifted about, and moved close enough for me to catch a whiff of his sweat-soaked body. It was an unpleasant odour that put further distance between me and this reserved individual. The thought of having to live with him – use his bathroom and eat from his plates – was turning my stomach. Everything about him repelled me. Stained plastic sandals, dirty feet and yellowing toenails; stains on his trousers, faded marks on his shirt; a dull, unshaven face; thinning, unkempt hair; sunken, colourless, lifeless eyes; chapped skin on his hands; everything.

I had the feeling that my body was rejecting him, that it didn't want to accept that the person standing next to me, waiting for someone called Meho, was my father.

Meho, it turned out, was an ageing gentleman with an enormous belly and short legs, whose weight transferred from one side to the other as he moved towards us at a snail's pace.

Here you are, he greeted us, then panted his way past us into the barber shop.

He looked funny, as he sat on a stool that was too tall and too narrow for him, and then tried in vain, being wedged on it, to sit more comfortably, until he gave up and remained in what was a visibly uncomfortable position.

I'm just having my hair cut then we'll go, it won't take Fudo long, Meho said, while Fudo stood, waiting behind his ample back, with a comb and scissors.

You take your time, Meho, said Safet, *we're not in a hurry.*

I now understood that Meho was our lift to Bosanska Otoka; Safet probably didn't have a car and was dependent on people going into Bihać to run errands, kind enough to take him along with them. It occurred to me that Safet might have come into Bihać at the crack of dawn, just so that he could be waiting for me at the bus station at eleven thirty, and that he might have been sitting in the bus station all that time.

A quiet, unobtrusive creature, hidden away in a deserted corner of the bus station, tensed-up as if cold, with scrawny legs crossed in a ladylike fashion, with head hung low and right foot gently swinging, which was the only thing about him to show any sign of life. This is what Safet was for me now. That was my Dad. My Bosnian Dad.

Fudo really was skilled with the scissors and comb, and Meho's large, round head was soon freshly coiffed. Now it looked even bigger and even rounder.

Salam alaykum, said Meho, as he somehow managed to clamber down from the barber's stool.

Alaykum salam, Fudo replied, already sweeping the floor.

Safet said *Doviđenja* and Fudo nodded, and then the two of us followed Meho, who was waddling over to his Passat.

It's not locked, Meho said to me.

I opened a rear door and sat inside. Safet got in the front. It was hot and suffocating, and the Passat smelt like two sweaty men of two contrasting body types. Meho started the ignition three times, before he eventually managed to set off and I was rescued by a gust of fresh air coming in through the window.

She's not sounding so good, he said.

Let's hope she hangs on in there, Safet said and then they both sat in silence, so that Meho could concentrate on the road.

We were driving from Bihać towards Bosanska Krupa. On the way, Meho told Safet about how his phone had been disconnected; about Nedim, who ought to have sorted it out ages ago, but who was now talking nonsense and sending him to Aida, who had already phoned around the whole of Bihać seven times, to no avail. Meho was talking, Safet followed his narrative with the occasional sigh and interjection, while I soon lost track of who had phoned who, who was whose brother and who ought to be doing what but hadn't, and I stared vacantly at the Una as we followed its course.

I allowed the images outside to be blurred by the speed of Meho's driving, and tried to empty my head. I wished the journey would go on and on, so that we'd never arrive at Bosanska Otoka, so that Safet and I would never be alone together again, and I wouldn't have to talk to him. I became increasingly averse to the inevitable disembarkation from Meho's Passat, and increasingly I wanted to be somewhere else, anywhere else, so long as it got me far away from here. I wanted to be at home, with Mum, in my own bed, on my own. I never wanted the stocky man behind the wheel to leave Safet and I; I never wanted his confusing story about his disconnected and reconnected telephone line to stop filling the space between me and my Dad; the Dad I did not recognise.

By the time we sat down in front of Nana's house, looking out at the river, it was getting dark. Safet opened a beer, poured a small amount into a glass and offered it to me, without asking if I had yet started drinking. And as we watched a fisherman pack up and go home on the opposite bank, he was the one who spoke. He was talking about something of no interest to me, and which was impossible to follow. I can't remember a single word of what he said. Safet was talking past me, but on he went, constantly, as if he were afraid to stop. In the meantime the temperature had dropped, and his face had become shrouded by dusk; but apart from the sound of a fresh can being opened in the darkness, and a momentary interruption to his story from the spurting beer foam which Safet had to contain with a quick slurp, his speech maintained the same steady rhythm, irrespective of me and whether or not I was paying any attention. And when he'd finished, he stood up, stretched, took the not-quite-empty glass from my hands, and took it back into the house. I thought he was going to come back and continue his story, but instead, I heard the flow of water in the bathroom sink. Safet had a wash before bed, and then he paused briefly at the front door, said *Laku noć* and left me in the dark in front of the house.

He left me with her; with the person I'd come without, and after whom he had not asked; with the person who had not been mentioned all evening. She sat right beside me, looking at him, and then she got up too, said *Lahko noč* and followed him into the house. I heard her opening Safet's bedroom door so clearly, and saw her disappearing behind it. She, unmentioned, who remained at home, but who was with us the whole time. Even in Bihać, she was with me as I got off the bus, and not for a moment had she left Safet and I alone.

In the morning we ate our breakfast in silence, or rather, I did, while Safet sat down with me. He'd bought me a loaf of bread, three meat spreads and a bottle of milk. Ever since I was a child I had been so crazy for the Argeta chicken paste, that I'd even eat it on its own, without the bread. I wondered whether Safet had remembered that, or if there was just nothing else at the shop.

Are you not eating? I asked him.

I'm not keen on eating in the morning, he said and went into the kitchen.

I saw, even though he had his back to me, how he poured himself a tot of rakia and downed it in one, before quickly tidying the bottle and the glass back in the cupboard. He didn't drink a lot whilst I was staying with him. Nothing at all during the day. He would have a beer or two during the evening and one rakia in the morning. But while the evening beer was shared freely with me, he'd drink the morning rakia in secret, as if it were a sin.

He turned and asked if I'd finished, swept the crumbs onto the floor with his hand, and carried the remains of breakfast back into the kitchen.

Jadran, do you fancy going for a swim?

To the swimming pool? I asked.

What pool, you twit. There's no swimming pool round here. A swim in the river.

I forced a smile, even though I didn't like the fact he'd called me a twit, and swimming in the cold river did not appeal; but by now I didn't care about how we passed the time before my departure that evening. As long as I made it to my seat on the bus, as soon as possible. Besides, the thought of a walk was preferable to the idea of more sitting around with Safet.

Come on, let's go, he said, walking towards the water.

I followed him along the narrow path, and we gradually left the town behind, its voices fading out completely after a while, and it was then that Safet veered from the path towards the river. Between two trees there was a narrow strip of growth, about a metre wide, that he was able to make his way through to reach the water. I assumed this was to be our swimming pool, as he crouched down, but he got back up and offered out his cupped hands.

Look how clean the water is. You could drink it, he said, sniffing it, before moving his hands apart to let the water pour down onto the grass.

That's the war, that is. The factories stopped, time stopped, everything stopped. Only the Una kept moving. Now it's clean again, like never before. Like when we were kids. There's no river in the world more beautiful than this.

He walked past me, heading back to the path, before turning again and looking out towards the opposite riverbank.

You see that island? That there, that's an island. On the river. See it?

I nodded, even though from where we were standing it was difficult to make out where the land, the land that Safet was calling the island, separated from the riverbank on the opposite side.

That island was ours, once upon a time.

He hurriedly recounted the story of his great-grandfather, my great-great-grandfather Džemaludin Komić, who in his day was a wealthy tradesman that owned a large portion of Bosanska Otoka, including the island in front of us. But just as Nana chose not to divide her home between her three children, so Effendi Džemo chose not to divide his fields and forests between his daughters, my great-grandmother Fahira and her sister Hajra. After Džemo's death, the distribution was left to his sons-in-law, my great-grandfather Yusuf, and Hajra's husband Rusmir.

The division of land was something that Yusuf procrastinated over for months, as Rusmir had a reputation for being a formidable fraudster, not a penny nor pair of shoes to his name, who had succeeded in convincing the wealthy tradesman to consent to him marrying his youngest daughter. In contrast was his great-grandfather Yusuf, known to be a reckless and extravagant man who much preferred to spend his money rather than earn it, who took on Džemaludin's market hall and large family home, in which he and Fahira lived with her long-dying father. He was known not so much for his skills as a tradesman, but more for his habit of closing the market in the middle of the day, at its busiest hour, to go riding on his white horse. Out to Krupa, to Bihać, sometimes to Banja Luka and apparently even further, to Vienna, so it was said, though there was no actual evidence of that journey. It was only Fahira's persistent pressure that eventually persuaded Yusuf to divide the land with Rusmir, so that they'd be able to sell a small portion of it and repay one of their many debts. And so that time Yusuf really did mount his horse and ride to the other side of town, to Rusmir. Only the next morning did he return home, if being carried back by your horse, blind drunk, can be considered a conscious return. Fahira, whose eyes had not closed all night, in anticipation of his arrival, did not let him fall asleep; she poured a bucket of cold water over him, so that he could tell her about the arrangement he'd come to with Rusmir. The river Una, said Yusuf, now demarcates what is mine and his. All of Džemaludin's land on our side of the river is now mine, and the land on Rusmir's side belongs to Rusmir. Fahira's heart stopped dead. All that's on our side of the river is our house and that worthless piece of land behind the neighbour's house, with the hill covered in overgrown forest, and nothing else, that's all, black-hearted Yusuf, that's all, sobbed Fahira, while he asked is that not enough for you, Fahira? Are you lacking something? Is the house and land and forest not enough for you, for one lifetime? What about the island, which is on neither our side nor his, asked the despairing Fahira. Rusmir thinks that it's his, Yusuf replied, but the island belongs to the river; it always has, and always will, belong to the Una.

We're Yusuf's blood, you and me, no changing that, Safet concluded the story, and trod carefully towards the water in his sandals while I continued to stare ahead at the island, which might now be Safet's, and could one day be mine. It was an island, a real island in the middle of the Una, embraced by the river on all sides, as if the island belonged to no one but the Una , and I pictured myself on it, waiting for my Ljubljana friends to come so I could proudly show off my tiny piece of land, my own little island kingdom.

Safet's swimming pool was a good ten meters' worth of riverside clearing, and a metre, maybe two, of shallows where you could easily paddle through the water. This was not a deep section of the Una; it meandered calmly and maybe at first glance it could actually look like a lake. But to call it a swimming pool would be an exaggeration; a bathing pool would be more appropriate. Safet took off his sandals and waded in up to his knees, then turned to face me.

Come, bathe.

I'd never bathed in a river before and wasn't moved to take a dip in the shallows now either, but I was waiting for Safet to think better of it, for him to leave me out of his ideas.

He had understood my hesitation.

What good are swimming trunks here? he said, looking all around him.

There was nobody but the two of us for miles around. I quickly got undressed and quicker still, launched myself into the water. It was seriously cold and my body felt as if it were screaming. The worst thing was that the clear water did nothing to hide my nakedness from Safet, who was standing only a few metres away. If only he'd at least turn the other way, I thought to myself. I stripped off in front of my teammates every day after training, got under the showers with them, but now, in front of Safet, in front of my father, I was embarrassed.

I swam away from the riverbank, even though I was cold, hoping that Safet would move to one side, so that I'd be able to get out of the water without having to go past him. But he just sat there, on the riverbed, soaking his legs in the water and bathing his face in the scorching sun.

He was my Dad, and yet he wasn't. I didn't want him to be my Dad; at least, I didn't want this stranger who caused me to freeze up in his company. I wanted him to disappear, or for me to disappear myself. Maybe, in that moment, I would even have said that I hated him.

I started to swim towards the bank, jumped out, and put my clothes back on as quickly as I could. I was standing with my back to him, now dressed, but I still felt exposed and tried to avoid his gaze which I could feel on my back. I wanted to cover myself with my hands, to crouch down, curl up, hide, but all I did was stand there and keep my eyes fixed ahead, at the impenetrable riverside thicket.

Then I heard his footsteps. Safet was heading back to the house and I waited long enough for him to disappear from sight. There was no stopping my impending departure, I reassured myself. Only a few more hours, and I'll be waving goodbye to Safet. And that goodbye will be final. Never again will I return here, never will I see him ever again.

When I got to Nana's house, Safet was waiting for me with the glass that he'd shielded from view that morning.

Drink up, he said, pressing it into my hand. *It'll warm you up a bit.*

My throat tingled, and the burning heat quickly spread across my body. It was a pleasant sensation, but I didn't want to let on. I handed back the glass.

Thank you so much for coming, he said.

He was saying goodbye, and I had failed to carry out what I came to do. I hadn't asked what I had wanted to ask; I hadn't said what I had wanted to say.

But I no longer had any desire to do either of those things. It was too late. Nor did I want to mention her.

Thank you, I said, and I went into the house to pack my things.

V

Domen's message came as a reminder that time beyond my own front door was coursing onward, unhindered, and that nothing had come to a standstill because of Grandad's death. Time is not mindful of our deaths, natural or unnatural; it doesn't stop to wait for those of us who have stopped.

Nothing had happened on the outside. Grandad hadn't died, and Anya hadn't disappeared. On the outside, Nuša, Luka, Jera and Domen would be sitting outside our usual bar on the embankment at eight o'clock this evening, having however many beers – they'll sit at a table and someone will ask where we've got to, and Domen will say that we've flaked, and after the third round Luka will say that he's got theatre rehearsals tomorrow, and Jera will say that Domen's mum is pestering them to go and pick up both their little ones, Domen will say that there's no need to take her seriously, but he'll stand up anyway, and Nuša will ask what's going on with Jadran and Anya, and they'll all look at each other, wondering what might be going on; they're just snowed under, they couldn't make it today, but we should make sure we get together soon – and then they'll go their separate ways, and time, none the wiser, will keep on moving forwards.

I was sitting in bed, looking at Domen's message, and I could see the evening and my friends sitting at a table by the river. But they were in some sort of parallel universe, and I was no more able to join them than I was able to join characters on a cinema screen. I couldn't even send a message out there. I couldn't imagine us together; me and them, us, who together had morphed from children into what we were now.

From here, where I was now, all I could see were kids in ripped jeans and stretched woollen jumpers, impersonators of the god Kurt, sons and daughters of melancholy, full of bitterness because the world was turning in the wrong direction; sad because the revolution turned out to be just the kind of whore that Primož Habič sang about; angry, because anger was still sexy in those days. I watch and I see us, not yet jaded. I know those kids and I know that we were anything but jaded.

From here I saw Anya, changing the music at three-thirty in the morning and forcing the last remaining revellers to listen to the troubled voice that sings *Sometimes I feel like I don't have a partner*.

Back then we enjoyed feeling alone, like outcasts; it was us against the fakers and in that contest we were the favourites, though Anya would say she was going to study medicine and work for Médecins Sans Frontières. But she didn't believe herself, even back then; she already knew that she was one of them, that she was a faker.

But I didn't know. I really did care about stuff. Now I see myself, too, wanting a name for myself so that I could write a book, I see myself celebrating because I've been accepted onto the journalism course, it's the Bubbles Party at El Dorado and I'm falling on the floor, drunk, and I get lost amongst the white foam, with my head between strangers' feet, but I know that tomorrow will be different – I believe that – because tomorrow I won't be just anyone, because tomorrow I'll have made a name for myself.

Maybe we're just older. Maybe we just googled our names and realised that no one was watching or listening; we grew tired of the shouting, which did not bring peace and prosperity to the people of Sudan. Maybe our idealism was rejected along with those olive-green jackets with little German flags on the sleeves.

Maybe we were fakers all along, but with the cynical smiles of powerless, yet dignified, underdogs. Instead of talking about the plight of refugees, now we talked about the weather in clear conscience, weather which really ought to be letting us sit out by the river by now, instead of keeping us inside, stuck at the table between the smoking booth and the toilets in Daktari. Maybe we're just older.

Three months ago was the last time we all sat together, Domen, Jera, Luka, Nuša, Anya and I; we're seemingly still the same old school friends, yet we're so different. I watched us then, and was struck by the feeling that all of us, each in our own way, sold out on our secondary school selves, that we all succumbed to the fates inadvertently ascribed to us.

Maybe it was that feeling of treachery that prompted me to start talking about an email from a colleague, with a photo gallery of favelas; about photos of Indian, Brazilian, Mexican and Nigerian shanty towns, about scenes of poverty which, in spite of all the photographs, remained beyond our comprehension, beyond our life experience, because we really can't imagine that level of nothing, because that level of nothing is still a long way off the level of nothing known to us, and which isn't really nothing at all.

They all knew the sort of photos, circulated as some sort of attempt at saving the world, but because the conversation looked like it might be turning to chain e-mails with old jokes that we got from our parents, I quickly added that I'd urged my colleague to please not send me such things in future, as it would help neither me nor him to aid the less fortunate.

Maybe because we were two rounds in and we'd become slightly unreasonable, or maybe because he was just after a reaction which we would sometimes use to rouse and spice up our evenings out together, Domen asked me why I was so cynical, and I responded, in complete earnest, that what was cynical was the sending of those newsletters. Something about the tone of his question stung, and so I said that what seemed cynical to me was the pitying and easing of consciences by raising awareness about problems in the third world, and that those who truly pitied those people, and who have genuine ambitions to save the world, would be better off handing in their resignation and never again agreeing to being paid a thousand euros for work that would earn someone in Vietnam thirty dollars.

I didn't know where my anger was coming from. Luka stood up, said that I was a fine example of the damage that chain e-mails could do to people's well-being, and went to the smoking booth. Nuša followed him. The debate was concluded as far as they were concerned, and I felt that I'd said my piece too. But Domen chose to carry on, saying that there was no greater cynicism than the belief that there's no point in doing anything and therefore no point in even trying; but for me, it seemed worse to consider yourself a humanitarian and feel good about yourself, even though we all know that nobody can have any sort of tangible impact with that sort of humanitarian initiative.

I felt the roll of Jera's eyes. I tried to catch Anya's eye, wanting her support in this nonsense, but she was facing the other way, as if our conversation were of no interest to her. And then Domen said that it was the easiest thing to sit in a bar with a four-euro beer in hand, spouting the Žižek brand of cynicism, and added that some people still gave a toss.

I was on my own and I should have walked away, but I couldn't. Domen really pissed me off, with his fair-weather moral compass, clearly deciding to find favour with his socially-conscious girlfriend, and all of them pissed me off, all opting out in front of me, once again being scared of a sharp disagreement. I finished my beer, and said that poor people in favelas gained precisely nothing from him or Jera or any one of us giving a toss, and that they don't make the slightest distinction between us; that we're all arseholes to them, we're all rich, we don't show any solidarity; in their eyes we are all that one percent that they slave away for. I also added that he shouldn't be under the impression that he was any better than market gamblers, politicians or American foreign agents in the eyes of those who have nothing, just because he cares and feels sorry for them, and because he protests outside parliament and the stock exchange.

Everything went quiet after I'd said my piece, they were all waiting for it to quickly blow over. I looked around for the bar tender, Domen went to the toilet, Anya said something to Jera, trying to change the subject, Luka and Nuša came back and Nuša said that she'd seen me through the smoking booth window and I looked just like that time when we all argued about whether Eurovision should be abolished; Anya and Luka burst out laughing, Luka said we ought to watch Eurovision together again this year, it could have been the end of it all, but I didn't want it to end there, and I said that it just wasn't true that I didn't give a toss. Domen looked away, I had no idea if anyone was actually listening to me, but on I went, saying that it wasn't about whether or not someone gives a toss, because there wasn't a single person who would look at those photos and feel cold – we'd all wish a better life for the less fortunate, but that it's gross for someone to appropriate all concern for those people.

Domen was now making a point of ignoring me, he'd had enough too, but I turned to Jera and Anya, and said that I was pissed off at people seeing me as heartless, as someone who didn't care about the world just because I didn't see the point in those philanthropic schemes; that I was pissed off by all those career activists looking at me like I was the head of a bank or owner of a factory full of slaves, and those people are just like me, actually, no better than me; it's not the poor accusing me, I said, but the same conformists, just like me, who live in the same apartments and drive the same cars and have the same rich fathers-in-law.

Do you get what's bothering me? I asked them.

Jera was quiet, she couldn't be bothered, she sensed that Domen had gone too far with me, but she didn't know what nerve he'd hit. All she knew was that there was no sense in drilling down into my pain. Anya, however, shook her head.

I don't get it.

What don't you get?

Anya didn't want to understand me. She refused to show any under-standing, she refused my request for it.

What don't you get?! People play at revolution, attack the stock market and whine some dumb slogans into a megaphone and think it makes them better than the rest of us, who apparently don't give two shits about all the people going hungry in Africa, or getting killed in Syria or all the refugees from Libya. To them we're propping up the system! Criminals, for fuck's sake!

Her head was tilted back between her shoulder blades, rigid. She answered quietly; lifelessly, even.

The only thing I get is that earning your living from gambling, and enjoying it, eats away at you. You feel dirty – you, the one who's always been so pure, and it hurts if others see your job in you, if they associate it with you, if they overlook everything else about you, or what you think is about you, rather. You'd like them to see past your job, straight into your unspoilt soul; you'd like them to look past the fact that all day long you watch millions of basketball matches and advise addicts where to put their money; you'd like them to see that that's not really who you are. And it hurts you because they don't see that. That's what I get. But why should you be seen how you'd like to be seen, rather than how you appear to them? Why should they overlook what you do every day, the clothes that you wear, the car that you drive, the beer that you drink? Why should they see past all that? Why should you be seen as a sensitive and righteous person, who stands with the oppressed and the vulnerable, if that's not what you seem like to them? Do they have to anticipate what you're like beneath the surface? To guess? People have every right to see you as an apathetic conformist who's paid to watch basketball and who doesn't give a monkey's about anything else. And the fact that they see you that way is not their problem, but yours alone.

Hearing those words didn't surprise me, I'd heard them before; but what did surprise me was hearing them in front of our friends. Until now, her frankness towards, and intolerance of, my weaknesses and self-delusions had remained between us, but now it was reverberating around Bar Daktari, and I sensed that Domen, Jera, Nuša and Luka wanted to back away from us, but they didn't have anywhere to go; I sensed their embarrassment, caught with us here, between the toilets and the smoking booth, between our accusatory stares. All they could do was wait for the conversation to end and be forgotten.

Perhaps I could have said *Yes, OK Anya, I admit, I'm in the wrong;* perhaps I should have taken back what I said in front of everyone, because for three years I have been spending my days watching recordings and highlights of evening and late night basketball games, because for three years I've been earning a solid wage writing substantiated predictions with statistical and technical analyses for upcoming games and using those to help people who can't decide whether to put their money on the Atlanta Hawks or the Memphis Grizzlies, or on Real Madrid or Fenerbahçe. Perhaps I could have apologised for helping people waste their money, for no longer being pure. Yet I was incapable of that admission.

So does working for a betting company mean I don't have a right to say what's bothering me?

She didn't answer. Anya sensed that we had gone too far. Yet I was pushing for us to go further. On a subconscious level it was probably getting to me that I had inadvertently switched sides in this conversation I was having with myself, and that I was now defending that which I had not long since judged; that I was putting a question to her that I'd already answered myself.

Suddenly there was no longer anyone else around us, the tables behind Anya had emptied out, the place had gone quiet. The two of us were left there alone.

Should I hand in my notice just so I can say when something pisses me off?
Yeah.

Cool, why don't I hand in my notice and then we can both be out of a job.

Eyes and ears were swarming around us again, all of them watching and listening to us. Nobody knew about Anya losing her job. Before heading out that evening, Anya had asked me not to say anything yet, and I promised her that I wouldn't. I broke the promise, betrayed her, just as she betrayed me when she spoke of my impure soul in front of the others. It was our first betrayal. As I stood up to go to the toilet, I felt my muscles ache. I was exhausted. My body was collapsing under the weight of the accrued impurity.

I replied to Domen, saying that we didn't have time this evening and that they should have a round for us. I didn't care what they might make of our absence. I even felt relief at not having to be in their company that evening. "OK" was Domen's reply. Perhaps my reply had pleased him, too, I thought. Then I got out of bed. I remembered that Marko was still at home, and breakfast at nursery was probably over already.

For as long as she remained out of a job, it was Anya who took Marko to nursery. I would leave for work whilst they were still asleep. Each of them would stir as I kissed them goodbye, and sometimes they'd look at me with sleepy eyes, but the jangling of my keys, the turning of the lock, and the fading sound of my footsteps heading down the stairs would soothe them back to sleep. For as long as she remained out of a job, Anya was without routine. Her inactivity dictated a new set of rules, and made her indifferent as to whether Marko had breakfast at nursery, or whether they stopped at the German bakery on the way there for a chocolate croissant.

Anya was afraid of the recurring day-to-day that came with unemployment, and she would purposefully break the patterns established by me going to work, and her staying at home. Disorder was her emergency exit from the abundance of time at her disposal, and it was impossible to predict her days in advance. It was brazen, almost, how she abandoned herself to chance, and gave in to the slightest whims, starting with an extra hour of dozing in the morning.

In the evenings, which herded us back from our different worlds, back around the same table, she would frequently choose to ignore my question, always the same, about what she'd done that day. She'd say *Nothing special* or *Everything under the sun*, and the conversation would trail off. It was rare for her to describe her day in any detail. On those occasions, it seemed that she'd made a conscious decision to commit that chosen day to her memory, as well as mine. Some days were recounted in such detail that it was as if we'd spent them together.

But all of Anya's days would begin in the same place, right here, where I'm standing now, in the playground at Marko's nursery, where children's voices were drowned out by the rumble of a city emerging, full of drivers, the overturning of dustbins and the peep-peep-peep of reversing delivery lorries approaching shop entrances. Here, in the morning hustle and bustle, even the children wanted to leave their parents and run as quickly as possible to the peace and quiet of the cloakroom, but Marko just stood there and gazed at me, as if he were waiting for me to start disappearing into the distance, while promising that we'd see each other again soon.

Anya spoiled him. She started taking him in later and later, and coming to collect him increasingly earlier, sometimes even before the nursery teachers had put him down for a nap. The solitude was becoming too heavy to bear, and she needed Marko; his voice, the sound of his footsteps. Perhaps that was why Marko waited for me to promise that I was also going to come and collect him straight after lunch.

When I told Borut about my grandfather's death, he said that I was entitled to a day's leave after the death of a close relative, to which I could add two days of unused leave from last year. I reminded him that they expired in June, but he said he wasn't interested and that he'd see me on Monday. And so there I was, with time that I had no idea how to fill. The nature of time quickly changes. Up until last night it had calmed me, but today it filled me with fear.

I didn't know how Anya experienced her abundance of time. I didn't know if the time frightened her, or if it made her tense. I never asked her how all those empty hours felt. I didn't attempt to imagine myself in her situation; a self that doesn't go to the office, that doesn't predict the evening's basketball scores, but who stands in front of Marko's nursery, motionless. I didn't know how an unemployed person moved; I didn't know if they walked fast, or made stops along the way and whether they looked around, or whether they knew where they were heading, or if they even wanted to be heading anywhere at all.

I walked towards the centre of town and wondered whether I had accidentally woken up in one of Anya's days, in one of the one hundred and thirty-seven days that had passed since Saško's phone call; days which we hadn't counted, but of which we both knew the total at any given moment. I remember one of them she told me about. A Tuesday or Wednesday. A good three weeks ago. And I saw her in front of me, and I recognised her gait from a distance, even though now it was slower, hesitant, as if her feet weren't walking the streets of her hometown.

On Tuesday or Wednesday, Anya went straight from nursery to the Tea House for breakfast. She turned off Trubarjeva down one of the narrow streets that lead down to Petkovšek Embankment, and then walked along the river to the main square and onwards, across the Triple Bridge, past the Robba Fountain towards old Ljubljana. She walked the way she'd walked countless times before, but on that Tuesday or Wednesday she imagined that she was in town for the very first time. She was a literary historian from Belgium, roaming in search of Central Europe's lost soul; an attendee at a seminar on Japanese mythology; or maybe she was a French archaeology student from Dijon, interested in the latest excavations from the Emona period.

Whoever she was, that Tuesday or Wednesday, Anya looked upon Ljubljana as if seeing it for the first time, and could not understand the scribbles on noticeboards or the words spoken in bars as she passed by. At the Butchers' Bridge she fought through the tables, down to the riverside where she took a few photos with her phone. Ljubljana castle above the Kresija building. The Butchers' Bridge with Plečnik's arcades. She then stared into the green water beneath her, just like people in other cities stare into the Seine or the Danube.

Perhaps, behind her back, she felt people's glances and unspoken musings about the reasons for her being there, but she didn't turn around. There, in a foreign city, she didn't know a soul and her eyes looked beyond people's faces, travelling upwards to the upper floors of Ljubljana's houses. Perhaps she hoped to catch a glimpse of faded memories, long gone but close to her heart, but Ljubljana was not a city that had survived its own history. Its inhabitants liked to forget, and the city was forced to evolve time and again, to become unrecognisable and draped in the present, down to the very last brick.

Disappointed, she looked away from the gleaming, renovated facades and gazed at passers-by on the main square. As they looked back at her, she wondered what an absence of smiles might say about a city and its people. Maybe smiles don't come cheap in Ljubljana, she thought, and wondered about their price. If she'd have spoken their language that Tuesday or Wednesday, she would have certainly stopped the stern older lady with her shopping trolley to ask her the price of a smile.

Maybe it was just a desire for unpredictability that was hiding behind Anya's game; a need to escape from the day-to-day. Maybe she only wanted to walk around the city without stumbling over traces of herself.

But she impulsively went to the Tea House, where the staff knew her by name and served her without having to ask what she'd like. Maybe she wanted them to bring her back, to click their fingers and call her back round; maybe she'd grown tired of being an outsider.

'You on your own?' Aleš asked me, surprised, as I took a seat at one of the tables outside.

'Yeah, I'm enjoying,' I replied, and thought how, on that Tuesday or Wednesday, he would have also thought it unusual to see Anya, and that she, too, probably pretended that it was a completely ordinary day.

'Mudan, special green, and a flatbread, no ham?'

I nodded, and Aleš nodded back. Two pretty tourists were waiting for him at the neighbouring table.

One summer they had a garden in the interior courtyard, completely surrounded by tall, chipped and cracked facades. Anya and I fell in love in that rustic space, which had something of the Middle East about it, at least that's how it seemed to us, and we'd go there almost every evening, drink tea by candlelight and soak up the surroundings of old, yellowing photos.

In that courtyard, which was in swing for that one single summer, we – and I know this now – were retreating from the city. It gave us a sense of how it would feel to be somewhere far away, somewhere where the winds ruthlessly revealed the colours of the houses and laid their ages bare, somewhere, where all we had was each other.

At home you're never alone, yet the two of us so loved to be on our own, distanced from her story and from mine, from the clutches of Miro and Safet. Away from home, our thoughts and dreams were aligned; with distance from home, the gulf between us diminished to the point that it vanished completely and we became one.

But at home, she went back to being Anya Černjak and I was Jadran Dizdar. And increasingly so, the two of us would sit, just like now, at the same table, each in our own present moment.

Anya and I stopped getting to know one another, I thought. I never knew the Anya who went alone, on a Tuesday or Wednesday, to the Tea House. I wouldn't be able to guess what she ordered that day. I didn't know the unemployed Anya, and she didn't know the Jadran who had traced her day, as if under a spell.

These days it seems that time changes us faster than we're able to learn about one another. The slightest lapse of attention, a momentary absence, and before you know it you find yourself next to a stranger; their words become unintelligible, their thoughts inaudible, their views unrecognisable. And you can neither grant their wishes nor fulfil their needs. And they withdraw, upset, while you have no idea how to bring them back.

On that Tuesday or Wednesday, Anya went from the Tea House to the Museum of Modern Art at Metelkova. There, she spent a long time standing in front of a television screen showing an hour-long recording of a street, shot through the window of a moving vehicle. A straight road through American prairie, an hour of constant filming, an hour of uninterrupted driving. She watched the video and wished she understood it; she wanted to be one of those people who understood, and she drew nearer to the screen so she could take a closer look. In the unwavering image she searched for a clue which might uncover its meaning, and became angry when she found nothing to explain the sense behind a one-hour recording of a car driving down a straight road, and she was about to ask someone, maybe even one of the custodians, sat bored in the corner of the gallery, in the hope that they might give her a clue as to what it was all about; she needed to understand and she approached the screen a little closer, hoping for a written explanation that she hadn't wanted to read at first, believing that art ought to speak for itself and that it was all a scam if you needed the help of an explanatory note to unravel it. Yet all there was beneath the screen was a list of fifty pieces of music, a list of songs by Michael Jackson, Madonna, Depeche Mode, unknown singers with Jewish and Arabic names. Her eyes went back and forth between the list and the video and she still didn't understand, but now she really needed to – her curiosity was too intense, and so she read the description of the Israeli artist, Palestinian perhaps, who asked fifty of his friends and relatives which song they would listen to if they could drive for an hour without being stopped by police patrols. Then he went to Texas, hired a car, drove it for an hour and listened to their musical wish list. That was the recording, only Anya hadn't noticed the headphones until now, hanging there above the screen, and she hadn't listened to the music that accompanied the image of the landscape through the car window, a landscape without confinement, without police. For the first time in her life modern art had made an impression on her; for the first time in her life she had understood.

Things that might seem self-evident to us are unimaginable and unattainable to others, she said to me that evening, on that Tuesday or Wednesday.

Something so simple, like driving for an hour without interruption, is an unfulfilled dream for the people of Palestine.

She was enthused, and she didn't know whether it was thanks to the art itself, or because she'd been capable of understanding it, but she didn't care; the most important thing for her was that day, that Tuesday or Wednesday, had not been without purpose.

Anya liked to wander around museums, she would wander from one installation to the next, from sculpture to sculpture, but only so that she might come up with meanings and messages in the art work, that she might scoff at them, that she might have fun imagining what those scribbled blotches or sculptures of unrecognisable forms were supposed to represent. She gave herself permission to be silly and shameless, and enjoyed standing in front of an exhibit by a renowned Lebanese visual artist and whispered to me that the piece attests to the postmodern hesitancy towards classic geometric forms, and that in positioning the introverted nature of the artistic object at the centre of the viewer's interest, we see the possibility of alternative ways and forms, which signifies a continuation of his obsession with premonitions, something which his previous works have alluded to; and then she took a small step back and said, rather loudly, that she didn't get it at all, that it looked like the shape of a woman's toe mid-menstrual cramp; she moved again and said that she could make out the two dimensional image of the digestive tract of a bark beetle.

Then we would snigger and the people around us would turn their heads, and more often than not we'd have to leave the museum to avoid being thrown out due to Anya's sniggering becoming out of control. She liked to wander around modern art museums in every city we found ourselves in; we sought them out, in Vienna, Bilbao, Lodz, Zagreb or Singapore, together we uncovered mysteries all over, it was a small vice of ours, but we stuck at it, even when it became unacceptably childish, even by our standards, because the vice was so very much our own, because we thought we were that very couple, the giggling couple, the shameless Eastern European tourists, uncultured and uncouth; that that was exactly who we were and if we were to get serious and look seriously at the exhibitions in silence just like everybody else, then we would lose ourselves. That's what we thought and we carried on sniggering, even when it wasn't funny anymore.

I wandered around the Museum of Modern Art and looked for the video with the hour-long car journey along the straight road, but it was no longer there. Just as Anya was no longer there. Her sniggering was nowhere to be heard. I walked behind her, but no matter how hard I tried, I couldn't catch up with her; soon I would have to go and collect Marko from nursery, tomorrow morning I have to go to Zagreb, to the crematorium, and she would still not be here. I watched the tall, thin, bald-headed man who was sitting on a chair in the corner, and I thought about asking him whether he remembered seeing a cute brunette staring at the Israeli installation, and whether he could help me figure out who she was.

But the tall, thin, bald-headed man was looking the other way, absorbed in his own thoughts; perhaps he was composing a lecture in his head, for his child who had to take a re-sit, or maybe he was writing a song. When I got a better look at him, he no longer had the appearance of someone who might remember visitors, even if they were as attractive as Anya. I left him there and headed for the exit and to Marko's nursery. I wanted to pick him up before they put him down for a nap.

On that Tuesday or Wednesday, Anya also went to pick him up before his nap, and then she took him to the train station to watch the trains and eat ice cream.

VI

1.

'He really was something, your Grandad!'

Mum's voice greeted me as I picked up the phone. She didn't wait for my response.

'You'll never guess what he's written. Listen to this: I would like my obituary – it says in brackets that there's money enclosed for one to be published in *Voice of Istria* and another in *Delo* – to announce to all friends and relatives that there is no need to attend my funeral, particularly not in the case of inclement weather. The funeral should be, for those who are going to come anyway, as short as possible, without any sort of ceremony. Please note, flowers count as ceremony. I'd much prefer people to save their money for something useful, rather than spending it on wreaths. He writes, in brackets, that money for the funeral is enclosed. He's crossed out "I'd like to be", and then writes "I insist on being", cremated, and in brackets again, writes that money for the cremation is enclosed. But that's nothing – listen to this – I expect Maya and Jadran to persuade Vesna that my wishes be respected. And all of this had been scribbled down in such a hurry that I could hardly work it out. Didn't he used to say that he couldn't care less about what happened after he died?'

'Yeah, but he didn't want to be a burden, even when dead.'

'Do you think we ought to respect it?'

'Does it not say that I need to convince you of that?'

'But are you going to?'

'I suppose I should really.'

'Do you reckon?'

'Yeah.'

'OK, bye for now.'

I've always believed that funerals play an important role in the grieving process. Their organisation demands a moment of composure from the grieving parties, who, adrift in a parallel time and space, are caught and called back to the here and now. Funerals aren't designed for those who have died, but for those who continue to live; though people seldom know how to surrender to their sorrow, to let it cover them, just as the earth covers the coffin at the bottom of the grave. They seldom know that, when the time comes, we have to let ourselves feel sadness. And it will leave, all of a sudden, just as abruptly as it arrived.

But Grandad looked upon these things differently. He was a radically practical man, and in his eyes, funerals were a waste of time for the young, who surely had much more important things to be doing than crying over deceased elders who would be just as dead with or without their tears. You can't hear kind words from your box, he would say. Nor can you smell the roses through thick wood – the thickness of which is usually proportionate to the stupidity of the grieving party. You're paying for a banquet for the worms. When I die, go for a walk on the beach instead. Or for an ice cream. That's what Aleksandar Đorđević used to say.

About a year ago, he mentioned to Mum on the phone, in passing, that instructions for his funeral were in a blue folder in the drawer under the television, along with the money to cover it.

I've done the sums and it ought to be enough, he said.

He left a little bit extra, just in case things were more expensive by the time he passed away. Mum had pretended not to hear him, as she didn't want to talk with him about death. It didn't seem right to bury someone before they'd died, but Grandad could not ignore that practical whisper in his ear which told him that such conversations might be difficult when dead, and that these things must be decided whilst a person was still alive.

Maybe we'll never really understand our grandparents. Maybe it's impossible to bridge the years of distance between us, and those sharp edges hidden behind the softness of their exterior will always remain out of reach. Maybe, long before we were even born, they hid themselves away from us, from those of us too young to understand. Maybe we cannot comprehend the time that inhabits their bodies, because we don't know that frost of days gone by, the humidity and hazes of old. Maybe they simply choose to ignore the fact that meanwhile, we also grow, and they forget to introduce themselves by their proper names.

Maybe. Mum would always say that Grandad changed over time, that she remembered him differently too. She did perhaps know who he was, but that was something I couldn't know; I merely heard stories and made assumptions. I had merely imagined a young Aleksandar and Jana arguing and laughing; I could only guess what they had laughed about, and how they used to laugh, all that time ago. People laugh differently when they're young, so they say. Time stifles laughter, silences it, so they say.

I'd like to feel their unease. We're all uneasy about something, and unease is our biggest giveaway. Unease says something about us, which is why I'd like to feel it, but I can't. Before I'd learned to decipher traces of unease behind Grandma and Grandad's eyes, they'd already learned to disguise it, and had removed it from their soft, wrinkled faces. All I was left with were stories of their fears and superstitions, yet even if I were to hear everything, from the first to the very last word, I could never know who Jana was, in the Istrian town of Buje, surrounded by the shadows of others, turning a strange house into a home of her own; nor could I know Aleksandar, who built walls at the ends of the earth so as to shut himself away. To me their story is only words; words which don't amount to the two people I loved so very much.

Sometimes I think that words aren't fit to describe a single one of us, because our internal vocabulary is comprised of inhales and exhales, and I can't say how Grandad was breathing when he told Grandma that he'd broken the promise he made in the house of *Donna Sante*, when he agreed to be seconded to Egypt for a year. I don't know how she was breathing when she heard that. All I can do is imagine their faces, just as readers imagine the faces of their literary heroes; I can imagine scenes, I can even imagine their thoughts, I can imagine their lives from birth until death, I can imagine every day they spent together, but I cannot imagine the two of them as they truly were.

Yet in spite of knowing that the image of Grandma and Grandad that I have in my mind may not resemble Jana Benedejčič and Aleksandar Đorđević in the slightest, I am nevertheless compelled to imagine them. I have to listen to every word uttered one more time, I must return to the memories, mine and Mum's, I have to seek them there because I need to find that person capable of surrendering to death. I'd like to get to know that person, because Grandad, at least as I knew him, had no reason to wish for death. My Grandad didn't want to run away from life. Yet Aleksandar Đorđević killed himself; or maybe he killed himself, I don't know. If he did, then a trace of the man who committed suicide must somewhere lie amongst the memories, a trace of a man in his seventies, who opens a brown bottle of blood pressure tablets.

I have to reach that man and stare into his darkness. I imagine it as a giant, ingurgitating, hole. That darkness is full of her, Jana; I can feel it, that darkness is full of Mum and Maya and maybe me as well, we're all in it, Safet and Dane too. Maybe the darkness is the only thing that binds us together. That darkness is now my Grandad, that darkness is me, which is why I must stare into it, my eyes must adjust so I can make out the outlines of what lies within. I have to feel Aleksandar's unease.

I know that is impossible, but I'm left with no choice. I have to know why he chose death, if he did choose it. I have to edge towards the darkness, to plunge down inside, even if I can no longer stay afloat, because I know, I can feel it, that we are all hidden inside and through it leads the path to everything, through it leads the path to me. Perhaps within it lies my home. In the darkness.

The phone, which I was still holding in my hand, began to ring again.

'He'll be cremated at ten o'clock, the day after tomorrow, in Zagreb,' Mum said, and then she hung up.

2.

'God's a bloody fool. If he said that once, he said it a million times.'

It must have been gone midnight by this point. Early the next morning we had the journey to Zagreb ahead of us, but Mum was in no mood for sleep. I hadn't been especially keen on spending the night at Grandad's house either, but Mum insisted that we drive together from Momjan to Zagreb, and then go back there after the cremation. I was prepared for another sleepless night.

'The war in Vietnam, Chernobyl, Yugoslavia being knocked out of the World Cup in Spain. He didn't believe in God at all, but he was always going on about him. I mean, he lived by his rules. Both of them lived by his rules. But nobody confesses piety to atheists. They pretend not to be god-fearing people, but if Aleksandar and Jana weren't god-fearing people then I don't know who was. If anyone were ever to accuse them of it though, they'd probably get a clip round the ear. Rubbish! Those two – not a chance! They were partisans, as you know. And God is a bloody fool. But that didn't stop them forever squabbling about blessings, signs and punishments. It was their own little game that they'd been playing for decades. And I remember when he told her that time, that her giving birth in Gini's house was a sign from God, that it was God's way of saying that he'd been right. The way she looked at him – you could see that she had no idea what he was talking about, and that it was something else she'd forgotten, but he didn't want to admit that, and so he continued the conversation without her, saying that it wasn't God's punishment and nothing would convince him otherwise; I was scared that he'd lost his mind, because it was as if he were talking to himself – sign, punishment, sign, punishment – while she just stared at him, probably wondering what this madman was doing, talking to himself, there, in her house. Do you remember that?'

'Yeah.'

'Do you know, he never told me why they moved to Buje? I mean, he said that he got a job there, but back then they didn't just send you a hundred miles away for work – there was plenty of work around for everyone. That's what it was like with him. He'd tell one story a hundred times, but some he'd never mention once. Not all stories were for sharing, in his view. He once joked that as a young man he'd thought Momjan was an improvement on the prison on Goli Otok. But if he was anything like his mother, and I'd say he was a lot like her, then it's very possible he went there to get away.'

'Get away from who?'

'From the communists.'

'But he was a communist … ?'

'He was about as communist as he was Serbian. He was as communist as he needed to be in order to get a bit of peace from the communists. He couldn't "be" anything. He wouldn't have been capable of believing in God, nor the Party, nor the state, even if he'd wanted to. His life's motto was *"you keep your distance, and I'll keep mine"*. He was incapable of making connections with anyone or anything. Being part of something simply wasn't in his DNA. He loathed cooperation. He didn't get it. He was never "we". He was always just himself. On his own. Aleksandar Đorđević. He couldn't even belong to his own name. Because it wasn't his. And now, just imagine Yugoslavia in the early fifties, the anti-Soviet paranoia, those dogged, vindictive communists. And him. If you don't see yourself as "one of us", then you can't see others as "one of them". And for those people that was an even bigger problem. He was probably actually very lucky to not get sent to Goli Otok.'

'But he was in the Party, though. Wasn't he?'

'He was. And more than that. They expelled him and then reaccepted him. But he wasn't overly principled in that regard. Or rather, that version of principle didn't particularly appeal to him. He was way too practical to be a dissident. He had his own core values – don't kill, don't lie, don't steal, that sort of thing. *Don't be a Party member* wasn't one of his commandments. He liked to say that he'd already fought one occupation, and it was now someone else's turn. He wasn't short of things to say, basically, considering the times he lived in, and he said many a thing which others wouldn't have dared, but thankfully they never took him seriously. And then one day, they sent him to Buje. He just didn't believe that he could change anything. He knew it was a losing battle, and he didn't like losing. And that's why he became so self-interested, I reckon. Just the like the majority of people under communism. True communists, who believed in communism, were few and far between; there were a few more of the self-serving nutcases who liked to make life difficult for others; a handful who resisted, making life difficult for themselves and their loved ones, and then the rest, who more or less hustled their way through life. And if Aleksandar was good at anything, it was hustling. His whole life, from birth onwards, was just one big hustle. For him it was about making sure that in one way or another, he and his family lived without interference; about keeping the promise he made to Grandma when I was born, to leave politics at the door and that family life would go on without any communist meddling. And he almost succeeded. I had such a wonderful childhood. Life was so much more idyllic for us then than it is for anyone these days. But in the end, he got caught up in it. That project in Cairo came up and he left.'

'Do you really think he had no other choice? Did he have to go to Egypt?'

Mum went quiet. She took a deep breath. I waited.

'I don't know. He agreed to go. That's all that matters. Maybe he really was needed over there, for his knowledge, experience… I don't know. Maybe he really did have to go.'

'But do you reckon he ever came to terms with it, or was it something that bothered him right 'til the end?'

As I uttered *the end*, it gave me a shiver, and I sensed Mum shivered too. Nobody really believes in an end; nobody really dares believe in something so unfathomable. Of all the things people believe in, to me, an end seems like the least likely thing of all.

Mum, I sensed, was letting *the end* ring out.

'I think it did, but I'm not sure… probably…'

'Did you ever talk to him about it?'

'Oh, Jadran…'

'Did you?'

'Back then I was angry at him for leaving, and I told him as much, too. Back then. At the airport. Before he left. Though I'm no longer sure if it was the right thing to do. I told him that he didn't have to go. That he shouldn't go.'

'And what did he say?'

'Nothing. He gave me a kiss and said that he'd let me know when he got there.'

3.

He could feel it as soon as they touched down. It suffocated him, exerted a downward pressure so that he could barely move. Here the heat was as thick as Ljubljana fog, rising from the blazing asphalt beneath his feet. This was a dry heat, they told him, it was more bearable than those in Asia, but it was summer and he was dripping, even when he had lain down on the bed in his apartment. Even the air was struggling to move in this heat, he thought, looking through the open window out at the town which extended beyond the hazy horizon. On certain days you could see the pyramids from there, so his guide, interpreter and assistant, Ahmad, told him – he was the first Egyptian Aleksandar had ever met, and he didn't meet many after that. The majority of his colleagues were Lebanese, his neighbours Palestinian, and the taxi driver he managed to hold a brief exchange with was Iranian.

What he wouldn't give to feel a bit of a draught – usually the mortal enemy. He was too old to adjust to new climes, he was too old to get used to drinking hot tea in the height of summer, he was too old to start understanding everything that he'd spent his entire life judging and criticising; he did keep quiet, though, when Ahmad explained the Arabic custom of saying things they didn't mean, and making arrangements which they might keep, but also may not. That's just how it is in Egypt, Ahmad told him, it's all part of the culture here, it's our way of life; but he was too old to start a new way of life, Aleksandar thought to himself. He could have already done without the one he reluctantly grew accustomed to in Ljubljana – the Yugoslav way of life was already unstable and unpredictable enough as far as he was concerned; he'd already heard enough empty words from Yugoslavs to last him three lifetimes, and he really didn't need to listen to people blathering on in Arabic as well.

He was too old to be working from dawn until dusk, in smoky corners of restaurants; too old to sit on the floor as the Turks did, smoking shisha. If he could at least have a drink, it might at least help to pass the time, he thought, though Ahmad reassured him that he was doing well, brilliantly even, that he'd soon be an Egyptian; his European soul just needed a little more time to settle, and then everything would get easier.

Polako, said Ahmad, slowly, *Mr Aleksandar, polako.*

He explained that the difference between them and us was that Europeans looked out at the street and thought that the Cairo traffic stood still because nobody was moving; yet Egyptians knew that no matter where they were at sunrise, by sunset they'd always be elsewhere.

Aleksandar wanted to clarify that he wasn't European, he was Balkan, which was something entirely different, but Ahmad shook his head. *I studied in Belgrade*, he told him, *I travelled across your Balkan lands, and all I'll say is that Westerners always find the East in places where it's yet to even begin*, so Ahmad told him, laughing loudly, so that Aleksandar felt a little offended by his honesty. But why? Because Ahmad had failed to acknowledge his non-European identity; his own Eastern roots? Had he really meant to chide him by saying that, or was he, in his own Egyptian way, paying him a compliment? In Slovenia he would sometimes get called a 'southerner', and he'd been called a 'Byzantine' on countless occasions. Why should it offend him, if Ahmad saw him as a European?

Aleksandar often felt completely lost in the middle of Cairo, as if it were the first time he'd ever come down from those northern European hills; he was aloof with people, closed off and unfriendly, and above all unaccustomed to the unbearable southern heat, which dried up all the snot in his nostrils, which made his inner thighs moist, which made his shorts and trousers chafe and caused tingling rashes, and fevers that led his shoes to steep in his sweat, where the stench would then waft out from the hall and around the entire flat. What sort of southerner was he, Aleksandar Đorđević, here in the middle of this baking city, with enormous sweat patches under his armpits, shirt stuck to his back, and big beads of sweat running down his forehead which signalled to each passer-by that he was an outsider from a cold, distant north. Whenever children on some narrow street stared at him, and whenever stall holders at the bazaar asked him where he was from, he felt he was too old to be introducing himself anew, too old for new coordinate systems, for new placements. He concluded these endless internal monologues by saying that he was too old, full stop, and telling himself that he ought to be sitting at home, with the grandchildren, with her.

It was hard for him to believe that he missed her. He'd long been convincing himself that it wasn't what he thought it was; just a need to have someone by his side in this enormous city; someone with whom he wouldn't be obliged to explain what he was trying to say. He just needed time, he convinced himself; he'd get used to it eventually, he was no longer the same adaptable young man he once was, the young man who could effortlessly adjust. Now he was that old dog who couldn't be taught new tricks, which is why everything was taking longer. But then he started to meet up with other Yugoslavs, people from his part of the world; he'd go to receptions at the embassy and mingle, yet a feeling of perpetual emptiness stayed with him. Something stayed with him; something which kept calling her name.

Maybe I'm just homesick, he thought; an alien thought from the man who believed that mankind only forges connections with people, not places. Man is born without roots and dies without roots; everything else is an illusion, he always said, but now he didn't want to admit that the pull he felt was her, and he convinced himself that it was his homeland that he was pining for.

The person he met with the most was Ljubomir, a Montenegrin from the Yugoslav embassy, who by Montenegrin standards was surprisingly small in stature, something which he attributed to life on the breadline and a small bed which stopped him from stretching out his legs as a child. They would meet at a restaurant in Zamalek and joke about their encounters with the locals, or the Pharaohs, as Ljubomir would say. They'd get drunk on wine and toast their inability to adjust to the never-silent city. Ljubomir told him about how he'd dreamt of having a volume control in his room which he could use to turn down the noise outside his window, and a button that could instantly hush the sounds of Cairo's screeches and horns. Aleksandar laughed; he felt at ease in his company, because Ljubomir spoke Arabic and was known to people; they smiled at him and offered their hands, and also to him, the stranger sat next to Ljubomir. And when the wine had instilled sufficient courage in him, he too would tap the waiter on the shoulder, just as his Montenegrin friend did, and it was then that he felt entirely at home, even thinking that perhaps the Egyptians weren't so different after all.

He observed how people were fond of giving their children kisses, and lovingly drawing them close, just as Balkan folk did; he saw them sitting and smiling in restaurants, and drowning each other out with their never-ending stories all evening, and how quickly they'd get worked up and start shouting and waving their hands in the air; he saw them, and Ljubomir agreed with him, too. *They're not so different*, he said, *they're maybe more similar to us than the Swedes or the Danes; if it weren't for their religion they'd be the dead spit of Serbs*, a drunken Ljubomir joked. Aleksandar laughed and they pointed out guests around the room, guessing at which famous Yugoslavs they resembled, and sure enough, Ljubomir would always find someone on the next table who looked just like the actor Bora Todorović. And as Aleksandar drove home, he would say to himself: you see, all of this is just homesickness, just a little taste of home out here in Zamalek, and now everything's alright.

But by the following morning, usually a Saturday when Aleksandar was without obligations and free to stay in bed feeling worse for wear, that sense of satisfaction would vanish. Beneath him was a soaking sheet, crawling with a layer of stale, drunken sweat, the Cairo dust visibly stuck to him, not that it made him feel dirty. The only thing he felt was a longing for her, for the one who could be sitting at the other, as yet unused chair at the table, listening to his disjointed sentences about Cairo, Ljubomir and Ahmad.

He wanted to tell her about Ahmad most of all; about the dark-skinned, giant, friendly bear of a man, who wasn't one of us, but who spoke like us; about that strange sensation of not speaking a common language with someone, though both are using the same language to speak; about how misunderstanding can take countless forms, the majority of which have nothing to do with the language we use; about how Ahmad invited him into his home and how uneasy he felt, sitting there with him and his wife and four children. He wished she could help him uncover the source of that discomfort which he couldn't get his head around; that she could help him understand why his conversations with Ljubomir were so different to those he had with Ahmad, of whom he was equally fond.

He also wanted to tell her about the Lebanese bunch – about Said, Karim and Fadi – about how they make no secret of their hatred for the Israelis, the reason for their fleeing to Cairo, and how it's something they share freely with him on a daily basis, not knowing that he was of Jewish descent himself. He wanted to tell her how it felt to hear them so openly voice their hatred, how weird it seemed to him, to a person who came from a country where hatred was palpable and in plain sight, but where it was never called it by its real name, as if everyone were scared to admit their hatred. And even yesterday, he would have sworn that he'd never hated anyone, but at times it now seemed as though their hatred towards Jews was contaminating him. He'd like to talk about that with her, about the fear he'd been contaminated with a resistance to a part of himself; he thought, even, that perhaps he'd always hated his Jewish history within, and had merely been waiting for the opportunity to base that hatred on something.

He knows, recognises, that it's all odd, that his thoughts are scattered, but he was increasingly starting to believe – and this is what he wanted to talk to her about – about how subjugated identities are never really subjugated; that they function on subjugation, constantly, and when they come to the fore they can be the most harmful of all, because everything that's despised and discarded has some sort of special power that can take hold of us in an instant, take hold of everything that we think we are.

He never spoke of these things, nor did he think of them often, but now he was alone with a lot of time on his hands, and more importantly he got the feeling that in Cairo he was getting to know himself rather than Egypt and the Egyptians. Perhaps that's why he felt the need to speak, to her, only to her, to tell her all these things, to tell her about himself, about everything which, even if he had wanted to, he had nobody to tell it to in Cairo. Because it wasn't possible to talk about himself with Ljubomir, nor with Ahmad, nor with the Lebanese bunch. Nobody would understand him, nobody knew him; he was equally unknown to all of them. Nobody on this earth except her would understand what he was talking about, nobody except her knew who he, Aleksandar Đorđević, was.

And all of a sudden he could no longer excuse the fact that he had stopped confiding in her, that he had not spoken to her about Mihelčič and the others who had pressured him; but he had been persuading himself, and was in the end convinced, that he could stop her from getting hurt. He could no longer excuse the fact that he had withheld what Mihelčič had told him about her father during the war, and his post-war attempts at escaping; nor that he had decided to take all this on alone, without her. Perhaps, back then, he really was afraid that she might confirm everything, perhaps he was scared of discovering that Mihelčič was telling the truth, but now he felt ashamed of his fears, and could no longer find justification for them.

He knew, he had to know, he told himself, that Franc Benedejčič did not rent out his places to the Nazis in exchange for money and services, but that they were confiscated against his will; he knew him, his father-in-law, and he knew there's no way that he'd have gone there, he wouldn't have gone to collect rents and he wouldn't have gone to their recitals, because Franc Benedejčič was a man who never asked anyone for anything, least of all the Germans. In any case, this was all so long ago. But who knows, Ahmad would say, if the sun was first seen in the Nile, or if the Nile was seen sparkling in the sun; and the doubts resurfaced, and the remorse resurfaced, and with it resurfaced his longing for her, for an honest conversation with her.

All this became mixed up in the muggy heat of a summer's night in Cairo, during which Aleksandar could no longer tell if he were awake or asleep. So rarely did these nights grant him a deep, restful sleep that it wasn't long before he began to avoid his bedroom. When dusk fell, he moved out onto the small balcony, stepping out from the kitchen, as if there, in the ever-present pale glare of the big city lights, he were hiding from a restless darkness, and he would sit and wait for tiredness to take him down, for it to start closing his eyes and dragging him away towards his spacious bed. It was easier to keep his thoughts in check this way, he liked to believe; to prevent them from running riot in the antechamber of sleep, from taking over and leading him to places he did not wish to go. That's how our biggest fears emerge, Aleksandar believed. Which is why he preferred to spend his nights sitting on the balcony, and day was often already breaking by the time he headed to bed, half asleep, and instead of lullabies he would listen to the hum of the city, the azan from a nearby minaret, the opening of shops on the street below, the voices of street traders, car horns, children on their way to school.

But the longer he observed the synchronous shut-down and start-up of Cairo life, and the more he stared hypnotically into the distance, as if waiting for his eyes to eventually get used to the dark, until they could even see the obscured pyramids there on the tip of the horizon, as Ahmad had promised him, the more his thoughts turned to Ljubljana. And to comrade Vekoslav Mihelčič.

He had been tempted, he really had been tempted, when they happened to bump into one another that time, when Mihelčič suggested a coffee in the Slon Hotel, as colleagues, as he put it; he had been tempted then to tell him the whole truth about why Jana Benedejčič hadn't taken his name after they got married, why she didn't become Jana Đorđević. He was tempted to tell him – a person who purported to know everything – something that he couldn't have known, he was tempted to see him visibly shaken by the tale of Ester Aljehin, her fear, and the Đorđević surname. He knew that he could, at least for a second, close the mouth of that Mihelčič, that architect of coincidence, at least for that one rainy afternoon, but he thought better of it, and simply reminded himself that it was their own private matter.

What did Mihelčič care about his reasons for not wanting his wife to take his surname, about why he didn't want his daughter to take it? What did Mihelčič care about his reasons for keeping his surname as his cross alone to bear! Nobody would care about that, least of all him. Let the curiosity kill him, Aleksandar thought at the time, let that be another truth for him to concoct. He didn't tell anyone, and nor would he tell him, the man who already knew so much more than he ought to.

On his Cairo balcony he even felt a trace of satisfaction about it, for having kept a small, incredibly insignificant, piece of knowledge from him. But he was aware that the war with comrade Vekoslav was lost, that he'd surrendered without a fight, and that admission was still a source of pain.

There will come a time when what has been forgotten will be forgotten no more, Mihelčič said to him in the Slon that time, and those words were what had scared him most of all. He couldn't escape those words, nor what was hidden within them, and Aleksandar knew this all too well. The persecution was all too familiar to Aleksandar for him not to be afraid of it. If the architects of coincidence were on the prowl for past sinners, hunting for forgotten sins to resurrect, then he'd need to go further than Egypt and Cairo, he thought.

As he stepped on to the street, the midday call to prayer had already resounded. Aleksandar sauntered through the hustle and bustle of Cairo, thinking it might dispel those troublesome thoughts; that it might drown out the longing for her, which had been with him since the moment he woke. He walked along the wide French boulevards and tried to surrender himself to them, looking around in curiosity. His eyes followed the women in niqabs, as they walked behind their bearded husbands in crowds. He paused to examine the ornate decoration on the minarets. He noticed the Cairo traders, standing in front of their wares on display, greeting familiar passers-by, their polished routine of seduction and charm, a routine of unspoken invitations. He studied their choreography, the practised movements of their hands, facial muscles and eyes, all directed at potential customers. The bazaar, including this one, conceived of by former European rulers on wide boulevard pavements, and intended for

Cairo's wealthiest citizens, had its own musical notation, to which everyone played along. The town and its dwellers were at the mercy of its habits and customs, its way of life, of everything that Aleksandar missed about his own blustery city, a city at the intersection of countless winds which had transformed Ljubljana into a dazzling exhibition of diverse customs, so diverse that people no longer knew how they ought to greet one another in the street.

As he walked past the windows of Cairo's finest shops, his eyes looked beyond the vendors and set upon some colourful displays. When he stopped in front of one, he discovered that the cost of clothing was much lower than in Ljubljana, and he recalled what Ljubomir had said, about it being possible to live like a sheik in Cairo, and that he knew European women, Eastern European too, who had so many dresses that they'd pass them on to their cooks and housekeepers after only one or two wears. He'd thought that Ljubomir was exaggerating, but now he felt these beautiful dresses made of the softest cotton, and he thought he could easily indulge. He started lifting them off the rails and looking at them, gliding his fingertips over the fabric to feel their silky softness.

He'd never bought her a dress, he thought to himself. Aleksandar did not like walking around the shops and he was even proud of that old-fashioned attitude of his, which deemed it unbefitting for a real man to be overly concerned about his appearance. But now he was picturing her in the dress he held in his hands, and wanted to watch the moment she'd take it in hers; he longed to feel her gratitude. He wished he could buy her all of the dresses hanging before him, the man who decided long ago that gifts were childish, and who said time and again, every birthday and anniversary, that they were too old to play lovebirds and give each other earrings and ties, things that nobody really needed, except for those who sold earrings and ties.

But now he felt like he wanted to buy her something, anything, or everything, rather. He stood before the shopkeeper, who was showing him that the dresses he'd picked were three different sizes – for three different women. No, replied Aleksandar, what did he mean, three women?

There's only one woman in my life, well, my two daughters as well, but this is for my wife, my only wife. Then he fell silent. He didn't know his wife's dress size, and he was embarrassed in front of the friendly, smiling shopkeeper; he was embarrassed by his childishness and sudden desire to buy her a gift. After all, he was no longer a besotted teenager, he chided himself, and placed the gold, blue and dark grey dress back on the clothes rail and walked out, back on to the street. He lowered his head and quickened his pace, to get as far away from the dress shop as quickly as he could.

I'm homesick, he said to himself, as he hurried home; I'm not used to being away, that's all, it's got nothing to do with her, it'll get better soon, it'll soon pass. He then hailed a taxi and asked to be taken to Zamalek. It was the first time in Cairo that he hadn't heeded Ahmad's advice and agreed on a price beforehand. That day, he didn't care.

4.

Even though Aleksandar was being despatched to Cairo for several months, it seemed to Jana, after Safet's car had disappeared around the corner with Aleksandar and his four suitcases inside, that he'd left without really saying goodbye. They hadn't really spoken of his departure and she'd never really consented to it. He said he was leaving, and with that he was gone. All those months preparing for his departure were reduced to one nebulous moment, one single image of an open wardrobe, suitcases splayed out on the floor, which she'd had to fight her way past to get into bed every night for the last few weeks. And then, the wardrobe was closed, and Safet was carrying the suitcases to the car, and her bedroom was emptier than it had ever been before. There was now a gaping space between the wardrobe and the edge of the bed, which without Aleksandar's suitcases resembled an infinite wilderness in which she could become lost.

It was a few days after he'd gone before she could set foot in the bedroom. She was afraid of its empty space, and chose to sleep in Vesna's room, full of Vesna's things, carelessly discarded and now of comfort to her. Stepping over boxes of books, and moving piles of beach towels from the bed to a chair, so she could lie down every night didn't bother her. None of it was too much. As long as she didn't have to lie down there, in that big, empty room, suddenly freed of all his shirts and all his jackets and all his tie pins that she'd given him as New Year's gifts. When she finally set foot in there, the fourth day after his departure, and sat on their bed, she knew that she could no longer stay in that house. He was all she saw; the one who was no longer at home. His absence was holding her captive.

The next morning, she was already sat on a train, heading for Ljubljana. She told herself it was only temporary, as she waited at Divača for the

Trieste train, that packed red train on which she'd never find an empty seat. *It's only temporary*, she told Vesna, who was waiting for her, and who accompanied her to the Ljubljana apartment on Bratovševa Square. There were just a few things she had to sort out, then she'd be straight back to Momjan, she explained over the phone to Maya, when she invited her over for lunch. I'll spend a week or two here, she thought to herself, as she sat out on the balcony, and looked into the multitude of windows and other balconies; at the women hanging out their washing, and the men in their vests, keeping an eye on the children playing on the square below.

Jana had never really made herself at home on the fifth floor on Bratovševa Square. She never came to terms with the fact that she had moved into that flat, which Aleksandar had acquired from his company when he became head of sales, as Mrs Đorđević, and from day one the neighbours saw her as just another thing that belonged to their new neighbour, comrade Đorđević. This was comrade Đorđević's flat, on the square below stood comrade Đorđević's car, and she was comrade Đorđević's wife. That's what they said and that's what they thought; her place on Bratovševa Square was clearly defined, and it was never home to Jana Benedejčič.

If she didn't hang the washing out in the communal space on the staircase, it was because the other wives didn't do so. If she was overly polite with neighbours her junior, she did that for him, for comrade Đorđević. Nothing said or done in that block, in that community, was motivated or justified by her alone, by Jana.

But now, it was Jana Benedejčič sat on the balcony. Vesna had gone, and she was left alone in the apartment. There was no comrade Đorđević, and nor was there a Mrs Đorđević, either. All that stood behind her was just a flat, just a kitchen, a living room and a bedroom, just a wardrobe, tables and armchairs, just walls with a few pictures, an out-of-date calendar and a decorative plate with an image of Dubrovnik. The flat was hers alone at long last, and inside it she was her own person.

She knew that people would soon forget comrade Đorđević, because those who aren't around tend to be forgotten, and then perhaps they'd also notice that on the door, next to Đorđević, the name Benedejčič was written too. Perhaps they would start to greet her as Mrs Benedejčič, maybe even Mrs Jana, Aunt Jana to the children, maybe even just Jana by the end. She heard their voices saying *Hello, Jana! How are you, Jana? Jana!*, she sensed that the world around her was changing and she was glad. She took pleasure in the thought of being Mrs Benedejčič again, of not being asked about her husband again, of being invited to meetings of the tenants' council, and being sent invitations to New Year's Eve celebrations and Victory Day rallies. Not that she would respond to them; but the thought that someone would be expecting her and her alone was a source of great joy.

Night fell, balconies packed with washing disappeared into darkness, men in vests called their children inside, while she sat and pictured her new life and self, someone who went to the theatre. Alone. She pictured the clerk at Drama's ticket office looking up to check whether the lady was perhaps mistaken, or whether she really would like just one ticket.

Yes, one ticket, please, Jana Benedejčič says to her, on the balcony of her flat on Bratovševa Square.

'Oh, her stoicism got right on my nerves. I couldn't stand it. I was convinced it was an act, that my mother was hiding her feelings from me, that she was bottling everything up and not admitting that she was hurting. I would meet up with her, just the two of us, on purpose, so that it'd be easier for her to open up, to talk – but nothing. She would sit opposite me, eat her scoop of ice cream, compliment the whipped cream, while I sat there, patiently waiting for her to stop blathering on about the history of Ljubljana's ice cream, and about the weather and the films she'd been to see; I'd steer the conversation towards him and to Egypt, but nothing. I could have throttled her, but I was considerate – yes, I was considerate – I believed it was all a front, that under all the chatter about Woody Allen, there lay a very real pain that I had to respect, that I had to be patient about; many a time I had to bite my tongue and smile at her meticulous re-enactment of scenes – and he said this, and she replied like this, and then he … Christ, I hated Woody Allen because of her, I could have snapped, but I was a good daughter and kept quiet, I didn't pressurise her into telling me, just once, that she was sad, that she was disappointed, that she missed him; that it was normal, that it's the only normal thing because you can't, for the love of God, be completely unaffected by your husband packing off to Egypt one day. I didn't know, back then, that I was projecting my own feelings, my own anger, onto her; that I was waiting for someone to validate my own hurt, to confirm that it was natural for me to resent my father, to bitterly resent him for disappearing to fucking Egypt. And when I failed to uncover those feelings in her, I was disappointed; I started to think that it had messed her up, that Dad had let her down so badly that she'd lost her mind; that she'd turned into some cold, heartless lover from a romantic comedy. The only explanation I could come up with was that it was all such an enormous shock to her, and that I ought to leave her be, to calm down and let her settle into things; but instead of settling, Mum just got weirder and weirder. She started ringing me to tell me how much she was enjoying life in Ljubljana, can you imagine – it was the eighties, no one was enjoying life in Ljubljana – no one except her, obviously, she was enjoying it. But what was she enjoying, I ask you? Because she wasn't a kid, who could enjoy a microwaved pizza slice and some French skipping in the square. Did she enjoy the rusting candelabras, the queues at the counter, the empty streets, the gravel, the fog, chips wrapped in newspaper, plum brandy and raspberry soda? What was it? She would tell me about how she went to the library, or the theatre, or to Maximarket for a slice of cake, and to the cinema, of course; she'd go to the cinema and then back to the library, she'd chat with the librarians; she was beavering around non-stop, but I began to avoid her; I couldn't stand to see her in a good mood, I felt the urge to scream at her cheerful face to stop the madness immediately, to stop making a fool of us all, embarrassing us with her enthusiasm, because there really wasn't a single thing in that city to be enthusiastic about. But all I did was smile; we'd meet up on my way home from work and I'd hear about some new Italian film, and about some new show at the theatre: we would be standing in the middle of the street, I'd keep repeating that I really had to get home, I couldn't take any more, but she was like, just one more thing, just one more thing, and she wouldn't stop, and we stood there in the middle of Trubarjeva, as if I were chained to her; I was on the verge of screaming *Egypt! Egypt! Egypt!*, I couldn't play that game of hers any longer, I wanted to run away, while she was giving some rambling explanation about some young actor about that Boris Ostan being a phenomenal Hamlet, you lose track of who's who when Hamlet's speaking with the ghost she said, you have to see him, I was incredibly lucky to be able to witness that, she said, and it was then that I couldn't take any more and I told her: no chance, I've got plenty of acts and actors in my life already, without witnessing them on stage as well. She didn't get what I meant by that, she really didn't, she hadn't a clue what I was talking about, and I felt quite bad because her confusion seemed genuine; it was hard to believe that she'd become so lost in her role as a happy woman that it had ceased to become an act, and she could no longer distinguish between her act and reality; I was worried about her, I really was worried about her. How naïve and ignorant I was. I know, now I know, but back then I really was worried about her, I even spoke to Safet about maybe taking her to see someone, a psychologist, but there weren't as many around in those days, because for me the normal thing for her to do would have been to sit in a corner and weep, or at least spend all day cursing that goddamn Egypt and the idiot who'd gone there. I don't know, I had it all wrong back then; I pictured what it would be like if Safet had packed up and left me for Egypt, I just didn't know any better, and I expected her to feel what I would be feeling in her situation, I thought that I could put myself in her shoes, but I couldn't. Which is why I decided to put an end to all of those secrets, to start talking openly with her, asking her what was on her mind. It sounds silly now, but we never spoke about things like that; to me, it would have been the equivalent of asking how her sex life was going – it was such a big thing for me to ask her why she seemed so pleased about Dad being in Egypt; I set my mind to it, I prepared myself, but she beat me to it, she called me and said she had something to tell me, I never dreamed anything of the sort. And how could I have done? It was a total shock.'

She taught herself to stop thinking about him. At first she thought it would be easier that way, and she consciously banished every thought of him; then she grew used to it, and any mention of his name would simply wash over her. It was better that way, she felt; and maybe she was right about that too. He was there and she was here and his thoughts were there and hers were here. It made sense. In response to the question whether she missed him, she would nod, though she wasn't exactly sure what they were asking her. Missing someone was not something she understood. She lived in Ljubljana, alone in the flat on Bratovševa Square, and her life was different from the one she had before, when they lived together. There was nothing missing in that new life of hers. She never admitted that, but that's how it was. Maybe she really didn't miss him, she thought to herself. But that was never something that could be uttered out loud, because people would misunderstand. Which is why she avoided conversations about him and about Egypt. She purposefully steered conversations with her two daughters in other directions, far away from him. She knew that neither Vesna nor Maya would understand.

How could they understand that there was no longer space for their father in their mother's life? How could they understand the sort of space she was talking about? Love was different to those two; they had a more naïve understanding of it. For them, love was a space to be filled by one person alone, a single, designated person, irreplaceable. An absence of that person must therefore bring a sense of emptiness, of wanting. But Jana didn't want for anything. Her space was full. She'd filled it with freedom. It was simple, yet impossible to explain.

She sometimes wakes and asks herself where she'd like to go that evening, but then doesn't go anywhere at all. In summer, when Ljubljana evenings are warm, she reads a book on the balcony. The balcony light doesn't work. She's changed the bulb, but that didn't help. She ought to call the electrician, but she got used to reading by candlelight. She thinks it's romantic. Nobody else has a candle on their balcony and nobody else reads books in the evening. It's another reason why Jana feels lucky to be able to spend entire evenings sitting on the balcony with a book in her hands.

If she were to tell Vesna and Maya this, they'd think there was something wrong with her. They might even force her to go to the doctor. Nobody can be alone and happy at the same time.

We live under communism and happiness is something we only experience as a collective, Jana says to herself. She's pleased with that idea. *Women can't possibly be happy without their husbands,* she says. *It's probably forbidden. If I wanted to talk about my happiness in public, I'd have to invent a secret imaginary lover. Or rather, they'd have to invent him for me.*

But Jana wasn't good at playing the pathetic woman. It really didn't agree with her. She couldn't play the suffering, abandoned woman, wearing stiff dresses in drab colours, walking around absent-mindedly with tired, heavy steps. She didn't know how to pretend, and so she was forced over and over again to face the surprised, dubious, and even outright suspicious looks of those who didn't agree with her cheerful disposition, and who didn't approve of the smile on her face whenever they met out on walks in Tivoli Park.

Or at Lake Bled. She would never forget the expression on the face of Vera, a former colleague, who spotted her on the terrace at the Lakeside Hotel.

What are you doing here, Jana? she asked, as if she'd bumped into her in her own bedroom.

The word 'alone' wasn't used, but Jana heard it loud and clear.

I'm eating a cream cake, she replied.

Most stubborn of all was Vesna, her expression the most piercing, her eyes were permanently looking daggers and boring holes into Jana. It's why she found things with Vesna hardest of all. She felt they were too different to see eye to eye on emotional and personal matters, too different to use the same words to describe those things. Vesna would put it differently; she'd use her own terms for Jana's feelings, and suddenly Jana would be someone else and her life entirely different to the one that she was actually living.

But Jana had exactly the sort of life she wanted. When Aleksandar left, a year had seemed like an eternity, but then that eternity grew shorter, and when almost six months had passed since his departure, the eternity didn't seem long enough. She began to think about how she could extend it, how she could turn it back into a perfect, endless eternity, the kind she had once been so very afraid of.

'She told me she wanted a divorce. I thought she was winding me up, that she'd just called round because she was bored, that she fancied amusing herself by seeing the look of surprise on my face. I felt like telling her that I had a young child at home, and a husband that couldn't even make himself a coffee, that I didn't have time for her pranks, but then I realised she was being serious. She wasn't the sort of person to go behind people's backs, she said; she liked to lay her cards on the table, she didn't want anything untoward to happen. I stared at her, as if she were telling me she were from Mars, it felt like I was dreaming – Mum, I mean, my Mum – I couldn't believe what she was saying to me; I asked her if she were having an affair, I felt so awkward, it's not something I ever thought I'd hear myself saying, especially not to my Mum; affairs were for women in films or romance novels, not for women of her age, in Ljubljana. She said that she wasn't, and so I asked, in that case, why she wanted a divorce, and said that being married didn't stop her from going to the theatre or the library. She asked me what I had against her library. I've no idea why she asked me that, I expect I sounded like I was taking issue with the library, who knows; I said the library wasn't up for discussion, I couldn't care less about the library, I'd rather hear her reasons for wanting a divorce. She said she didn't know, she just wanted one, she was scared of what might happen. With you or Dad, I asked; I asked if she were scared he'd met someone in Egypt; oh come off it, she said, it's your father we're talking about. I was hurt, I don't know why, I felt she ought to have more respect for him, for her husband, and it's not as though I thought your grandfather was capable of an affair at his age either, but there was an air of contempt in her voice, an air of derision, and I took issue with that, I told her that the same "oh come off it" could be said about her, which she didn't really like, but admitted I was probably right, even though she certainly didn't agree. I then said to her that she couldn't get divorced if Dad was in Egypt, and that she ought to speak with him about it, not me, and that she was – if she were asking my opinion – just lonely, and missing him, and that was what was driving this nonsense. She told me that I didn't understand, and I told her that I had no wish to understand her, and I got up and walked out. The divorce was never mentioned to me ever again, we never spoke of it, nor of anything of the sort, after that I gave up and started to play along with her, and talk about the library and films and Woody Allen, because I was scared, scared to death, that the divorce might come up again. In her company I acted as if I were closing my eyes and hoping to wake from this dream, and for everything to be how it used to be. I was waiting for Aleksandar to come home, I was counting down the days and cursing him, while trying to stay out of her way, as if that might somehow help.'

Mum stopped. Just as it had done many times before, her story stopped here. Never was the story told beyond this point, as if she were still waiting for Grandad to return from Egypt.

I wanted to ask her whether Grandad had ever found out that Grandma wanted a divorce, and if he did find out, when and from whom; I was curious to know whether he'd been upset by it, I believed he would have been, but I wanted confirmation and I don't know what was holding me back.

Was it a sense that Mum wouldn't like the question? Was I being considerate? Did I already know the answers, and was afraid to hear them out loud? Or was I afraid that her answers might contradict my assumptions and destroy the logic of my story? That I'd be left without a story?

VII

1.

I was in love with her; with her loud, wanton fits of laughter, with the way she twirled her hair as she listened to you, with her big eyes that opened wide when something took her by surprise, which shut tight and pretended not to be there; with the way she tutted right before she said *Oh, come onnnn!* Nobody else could say it so sweetly, so innocently. I was in love with her voice, especially with those whispers as she turned around in the middle of class; with her quiet, suppressed fits of giggles.

I was in love with her, but she was in love with Željko, a student at the Economics Faculty two years her senior, who played handball and went to the Balkan nights at Club El Dorado and hung out at the bar with his teammates until he'd drank enough to go and hover at the edge of the dance floor, obligatory whiskey and coke in his right hand, nodding his head and feebly wafting his left hand in the air. But he was also tanned, with dark features, darker than mine, thick hair and even thicker eyebrows, and dark eyes, which hid beneath his forehead. I don't know where Anya met him, he was probably a good friend of a friend and they'd gone out together a few times, but there was probably nothing going on between them, because he had a girlfriend.

There was, however, enough between them for Anya to follow him and his handball mates to El Dorado every Wednesday – a place which I, a skater, and she, a stoner, hated. But the hatred was not strong enough to keep her away from Željko, nor was it strong enough to keep me away from her.

Anya knew that I was in love with her but she never said a word. And I was also waiting for something to happen that might make her say or do something, despite her having announced, via Eva, that I didn't have a chance. *I'd go out with Edo before him* she said. Edo was the school caretaker. He had a moustache. And only a couple of teeth.

Eva was also the one who encouraged me to follow Anya to El Dorado. *You know what girls are like when they've had a few drinks,* she said to me.

Eva thought all this was hilarious. When she fancied someone, she went up to the guy and told him. And then they were going out. Which is why she could not understand why I found it so hard to admit I had a crush on Anya. She didn't understand why I didn't dare tell Anya that I liked her, why I didn't ask her out for a drink or to the pictures, or, more straightforwardly, why I didn't go up to her at the school dance and make out with her. She suspected that all I wanted was to get Anya into bed, and that I was only pretending to be in love with her. And the fact that I wanted to – in her eyes – use romance as a guise to trick her friend was not reason enough for her to take issue with me. The rules were different at secondary school; or rather, there were no rules, and Eva was happy to help me get Anya into bed, probably thinking that it'd be easier than getting us to go out together. She believed that I'd fare better at taking advantage of a drunken Anya, rather than seducing a sober one.

It seemed to me as if Eva didn't actually know Anya at all. In actual fact, no one at secondary school knew Anya very well, because secondary school Anya was a confused and complicated creature, and lovesick on top of that. And this confused, complicated and lovesick creature would follow the object of her affections to El Dorado every Wednesday, and secretly pine for him whilst he nodded his head and waved his arms in the air.

And one Wednesday, the confused, complicated and lovesick creature necked four vodka and orange juices and made a courageous beeline for the dance floor, wrapped her arms around Željko's neck, and took them both down onto the floor. Željko got up immediately, and tried to help Anya to her feet too, but she sat there, buried her head between her knees and curled her body up into a ball. Only after a while, when almost everyone had forgotten about her, and dancers started accidentally treading on her, did she get up and run to the toilets.

More than two hours later, some other confused, complicated and lovesick creature was standing at the bar and keeping an eye on the door to the ladies, waiting for Anya to emerge. For over two hours I watched the long line of girls wait for the one remaining toilet; I watched Anya's concerned friends as they went in and out, and who eventually gave up and went to sit at a table in a corner of the club, which, in the meantime, had emptied out. Željko had been sat for a while with his mates, keen to get an update from the ladies, even going up there once himself, standing on his tiptoes and peering over the heads in the queue, trying to see what was happening inside, but eventually he collected his jacket from the cloakroom and left. With a friend, who no doubt persuaded him that Anya would be fine. They thanked the bouncer at the door, both of them in good spirits, satisfied with their night out, thoughts already on getting a burger in Tivoli Park.

Once they'd gone, the coast was clear and Anya came back out. As soon as she spotted me, she realised that her embarrassing incident had not only been seen, but that it had also been noted. I, the person she'd turned her nose up at just a few hours earlier, letting me know how pathetic I was for following her out to clubs, had been witness to her humiliation.

She strode up to me furiously. She was still drunk.

What is it? By y'self? No friends is it? Shouldn't you be off 'ome? You got 'owt to say? Huh? What d'you want?

I didn't respond. I turned and walked past her to the cloakroom, got my jacket, and headed for the exit, but Anya followed me.

Don't you have a jacket in there? I asked her, when we got outside.

What's it to you, she hissed.

I was walking towards Bavarski Dvor. Anya was following a few metres behind.

Shame you're such a loser, 'cos you're kinda cute, she said and grinned, while I felt my cheeks burning up.

D'you not think it's a bit sad that you go to El Dorado on your own? Like, couldn't you find a mate to go with? So you didn't look like such a loser? Cos standing at a bar like a loner isn't a good look. Didn't you see everyone lookin' at you?

She finally stopped talking, as we walked past a couple of starving souls jostling, waiting for their takeaway outside Petica, and we carried on ahead in silence. The distance between us grew shorter, and it wasn't long before we were walking side by side, so that she was back in view. She'd lowered her head and wasn't looking around anymore. Her arms were stuck down by her sides and she was shivering.

Want my jacket? I asked, but she shook her head.

It was five past three when we arrived at the bus stop. There were no buses.

OK, well, see you at school tomorrow, I said, and headed over the road to where the number eleven stopped.

Yeah.

Anya stood there at the crossing, looking at me running across a red light.

Jadraaaaan!

She beckoned me back across the road. I ran through a red light again. I didn't look left and right that time, and the taxi driver who had to swerve to avoid me made his feelings known. But I didn't care.

Have you got any change for the bus I can borrow? Anya asked me.

Where's your pass?

In my jacket.

She pointed in the direction of El Dorado.

I'll get it tomorrow.

I reached into my pocket for mine, which had got my last few tolars stuffed in with it. It wasn't enough.

I've got seventeen. If you roll 'em up like this…

Our heads collided; her lips touched mine. Her tongue was in my mouth. She was kissing me. She was properly kissing me, but I'd frozen, and it took a few seconds for my tongue to start moving in rhythm with hers, which was eagerly circling inside my mouth. At that point her hands clasped my head, while mine continued to hang by my side as if they'd malfunctioned. I decided to lift them and place my hands on her back, but by then Anya was already pulling away.

Thanks.

Okay.

It was like neither of us knew what had just happened. We stood staring at each other searchingly, as if to ask what the kiss meant and how we ought to act now it was over. Luckily, at that moment the first buses started to appear, and our heads were turned by the deep hum of approaching engines.

It's the number six, Anya said.

Yeah.

She headed for the stop, whilst I, for the third time, ran across a red light to my side of the road, even though the eleven wasn't there yet. Anya's number six pulled into the bus stop, and she'd already vanished behind it by the time I looked around. I soon caught sight of her again, getting on and choosing the seat right behind the driver. I kept my eyes fixed on her until the number six pulled out, though she didn't once look in my direction. She must have known, though, that I was still standing there, looking at her.

Anya and I didn't become a couple after that night in El Dorado, we didn't start going out, we didn't hold hands and kiss in the corridors, but we did start doing things that we hadn't done together before. We spent break times together, or went for a coffee after school, sometimes on our own, sometimes with someone else; sometimes I'd walk into town with her after lessons, when she went to buy new Converse, or an Adidas tracksuit top from the second hand shop. Sometimes I'd call her in the afternoon for no reason at all. Sometimes she called me.

Anya said she liked that I wasn't pushy and knew how to listen, that there was some stuff she found way easier to talk to me about than with her best mates, and that she found my shyness sexy. I was just happy to be with her, just the two of us, to have her attention and for her to want mine.

These days, we'd probably describe what went on between us as *it's complicated*, but back then we didn't have a phrase for it, and so officially there was nothing going on between us, except that everyone knew there was something. Eva said that we were seeing each other, and looking back, that seems like the best way to describe it.

And then one night, Anya asked me if I had time to go to Pražakova with her after school. I didn't know where that was, but I said yes. I'd have said yes to anything.

When we arrived, Anya stopped outside the entrance to one of the buildings. She pulled a bunch of keys out of her bag, and jangled them with a look of mischief in her eyes. I was confused; but she unlocked the outer door. Then she looked around, as if she'd just broken in, and when she found the key she unlocked the main door and stealthily gestured for me to follow her. I followed her up the stairs to the second level. There was no doormat in front of the flat we were outside, nor was there a name or number above the peephole. Anya turned to look at me again with another of her mischievous expressions. This time the door opened with the first key she picked, and we stepped into a large, spacious flat with far-reaching rooms, high ceilings and windows with the original wooden frames. We went into the largest room, which resembled a small gymnasium. Especially after Anya ran into the middle of the room, did a cartwheel and ended up on the opposite side. She wiped the hair away from her eyes, and turned to face me.

What d'you reckon?
What is this place?
A flat.
Whose?
Mine.
Yours?
I mean, my Dad's.
Really?
Yeah. He got it.

Got it?

I mean, they gave it back.

Gave it back?

De-nationalisation. It used to be his grandma's, until the communists took it. Now he's gonna do it up and sell it. But not straight away, he's doing his sister's place first. So it's empty. I got spare keys done. I do work here sometimes. Listen to music. Cool, right? We could have a party here sometime. Something chill. Right?

It's cool, girl. Real cool.

You're the first person I've said anything to. Don't tell anyone. Not even Eva. OK? 'Cos my Dad doesn't know. It can be our secret now. It's cool that we've got a secret, innit?

It's cool.

Anya had been getting closer to me as she spoke. Now she was standing right in front of me. She put her hands on my chest, before leaning against me and pushing me against the wall.

Swear you won't say anything?

I swear.

Honest?

Honest.

She kissed me. It was our first kiss after that one at the bus stop; it was the kiss I've always wished was our first, even though I knew that we wouldn't have had this one – completely different, so much softer – without that drunken one which left us both feeling confused. Our tongues caressed one other, rather than clashing like swords; it was a kiss that wove us together as one.

Her hands were still resting on my chest, while I wrapped my arms around her and drew her close. My fingertips felt her bra through her shirt, and when her hands slid down from my chest, she pressed hers against mine. The feeling of her small breasts pressed up against me, even through a bra and two shirts, was enough to overwhelm me with an unbearable desire.

The sound of a nearby building site, the voices of Bosnian workmen, the clanking of hammers, whirring of machines, the thundering boom of iron pipes all infiltrated the flat; you could hear the manoeuvring of a crane and the echo of boots on scaffolding. These sounds took on a whole new meaning for me that afternoon, and from that point onwards, whenever I walked past a building site I'd be transported back to our kiss; to the invisible impression of Anya's chest upon mine, to the traces of her fingertips along my back, to my clammy palms sweeping over the contour of her bra, to the unintentional discovery of bare skin at the base of her spine, to her hair falling over my face and sticking to my lips, to her hands touching my face as she moved her hair out of the way, to the tickling sensation of her soft, warm skin, to attempts at taking a breath without severing the kiss, to the feeling that along with oxygen we breathed in one another, to our bodies pulsating in unison, impossible to distinguish from the beating of our hearts, to the straining of my trouser fabric, that I surreptitiously attempted to graze against her, to wishing that the kiss would never end, that we would never end, to a gratitude for something extremely indefinable and indescribable; for Anya and me, for us.

The sounds of the building site became our soundtrack to afternoons at Pražakova. We'd later laugh about drowning out an entire construction company with our teenage desire, and I, for some time afterwards, would find myself feeling aroused by the wooden and iron, blunt, sharp and hollow sounds of a building site.

That spring saw everything in my life explode, whirl, merge, and flow. We'd head out to the flat on Pražakova every day after school. As time went on, my hand grew braver and found its way beneath her shirt to her naked back; with time it unfastened her bra and nervously approached her breasts, being careful to avoid the nipples; with time the other hand slid down her back to rest on her behind; with time the kisses went lower, to the neck and below, seeking naked flesh while hands forged a pathway; with time the kisses became licks, and hands slid up and down her back and thighs; with time my fingers unfastened her belt and traced the edges of her underwear; with time my head lowered to her breasts and my tongue met her nipples; with time my eyes delighted in the curves I'd exposed; with time my fingers felt the softness between her legs; with time her head tilted backwards and her breathing became heavier and faster and louder; with time fingers started to tease, learning to provoke gasps; with time the gasps became moans, quiet at first, but then increasingly louder; with time Anya gave herself over to me; with time I learned how to give her pleasure.

You're not like everyone else, she said, looking at me, as if expecting an explanation.

Why?

I don't know, you're different. You're a good guy. It feels like you'd never do anything I didn't want you to. You actually care about me. You care about people. Know what I mean?

It sounded good, so I nodded.

The words of Bosnian workers echoed around the room, water and sand ground together into mortar, welders came and went and the house across the road grew taller. The building site got bigger and closer, drills drilled and hammers hammered, while the two of us were fixed in an embrace, listening to the clanging over the road.

We need a mattress, she said.

We can't just be on the floor, she said.

I got goose bumps, because I knew what she was talking about, and I couldn't believe that I was so close, that I was almost there, that a mattress was the only thing standing in my way. A mattress that I would need to buy, because I couldn't lie Anya down on a mattress out of a skip. I'd have to bring it there myself, because I couldn't ask anyone to help me carry it to Pražakova, revealing our secret location. I had neither a car nor a driving license, only a bus pass in my pocket, and I was unlikely to be let on carrying a mattress. My Mum's old bike would buckle under its weight.

I was so close, yet so far. I didn't even know where they sold mattresses. I was seized by the thought of Anya and I walking through town carrying a mattress, and had visions of us walking down the school steps with it, everyone knowing where we were headed and giving us knowing smiles. And so I suggested to Anya that maybe a blanket would do, a few of them maybe, so it'd be easier to get them to the flat, and we could pile them up so they'd be almost like a mattress. But Anya didn't agree, because it wouldn't be as comfortable for us.

I started to think that she regretted that sentence. *We can't just be on the floor*, she had said, but I was no longer sure that she meant what I wanted her to mean. Maybe it was just me, and she'd meant it innocently. She didn't want to discuss the mattress, it had irritated her, and our touches were hurried, our pleasure was hurried, and we rushed off out of the flat.

I was scared she was avoiding me, that she'd changed her mind, that she wouldn't want to anymore, even if I brought a mattress.

My life was saved by Top Shop and the miracle that is Turbo Maximus. Turbo Maximus was a blue, inflatable mattress, designed for camping, or as a guest bed in homes where space was tight. Or, alternatively, for unfurnished love nests. I called up at the first opportunity, and they also threw in an electric pump, and a sense of my own genius. Yet when the woman at the other end asked for my address, I was quickly deflated back down to the level of imbecile, with a head spinning at the thought of a delivery man placing the Turbo Maximus into my mum's hands and explaining that the Turbo Maximus could also withstand up to two hundred kilos, no problem.

The charade continued after a brief pause, thanks to one performer suffering a temporary lack of blood flow to the brain, and I asked the woman's voice whether this miraculous mattress, which didn't take up entire spare rooms or cellars, and which I could easily transport to Anya's flat without the whole town knowing what I was hoping to do there, could be collected from one of their stores or warehouses. The momentary silence before her reply was the longest of my life. The Turbo Maximus, the woman's voice eventually said, was available for me to purchase at all of their retail outlets, which open at nine o'clock every morning.

The next morning I skipped maths and history, and at ten to nine I was standing outside the shop doors. By ten past nine I was holding the Turbo Maximus in my hands. I emptied my school bag onto the sales counter and crammed the small white box inside. The sales assistant was watching me with great interest. I felt as if I were in a sex shop, buying an enormous pink vibrator, a leather whip and handcuffs, as mortified as in those dreams where I found myself standing naked at the front of the class. In the middle of the store, with a box-shaped rucksack and a handful of exercise books under my arm, I wondered how on earth I was going to turn up at school like this. The assistant informed me that the Turbo would easily fit inside a two-person tent, and that the electric pump had an adapter which could be attached to the car engine. I looked at him as if he were speaking to me in Chinese, convinced that he was using some Top Shop code to take the piss out of me, but he, probably out of pity, pulled a plastic bag out from under the counter. I put my school things inside and got out of there.

On the street, at the bus stop, on the bus, everywhere, I felt as if people were turning around, as if someone might stop me and ask what I'd got in my rucksack, and demand that I open it. *We can't just be on the floor*, I repeated to myself, looking out of the bus window and daydreaming about the two of us on the Turbo Maximus.

I, the atheist, prayed that Anya wouldn't yell *Sicko!* at me, that she wouldn't run crying into the toilets with her friends, that I wouldn't be subjected to everyone's jokes and stares at school tomorrow, that they wouldn't chant *Turbo! Turbo! Turbo!* behind me, that the girls at school wouldn't form a ring around me, the pervert, that the social worker wouldn't call Mum into school, that they wouldn't ask her if I was abused as a child.

Even as I caught sight of school in the distance, I faltered. I couldn't go any further with my school things in a carrier bag and a Turbo Maximus in my rucksack. I didn't know how I was going to let Anya know that I'd meet her at Pražakova after school. I decided to get away from school, away from the danger of prying school friends, and sit in some bar to think it through one more time.

The world was instantly clearer the moment the waitress placed a small beer down in front of me. Suddenly everything was simple. I'd leave my rucksack and the bag here, at the bar, and walk to school, find Anya and explain everything, then come back for my things. It was so simple that

I ordered a second small beer to celebrate before I'd finished the first, and it wasn't long before I headed back to school, emboldened, and arrived just as lunch break had started.

Anya was standing in front of the school in a small crowd of girls. Eva and Tina were smoking, the others were tolerating the first few drops of rain in solidarity. I waved to Anya from afar, and as she came over, I changed my original plan of meeting after school. I asked her to come with me somewhere, because I had a surprise for her.

Anya could smell beer, but luckily she was sufficiently curious.

What's that? she asked, as I opened my rucksack in the bar.

You said we couldn't be on the floor. This is a mattress. You blow it up, and then it's a mattress.

You blow it up?

Yeah. You get an electric pump, too.

And what are you gonna do with it?

What do you mean what am I going to do with it? We're gonna blow it up in the flat.

Are you joking?

No. Like you said, we can't just be on the bare floor. We need a mattress. This is a mattress. See, look at the picture.

It looks like a beach towel.

But it's not. It's a mattress.

It's plastic.

So what!

You think that's going to hold two of us?

Of course it will. It can hold up to 200 kg.

I'm not sure.

Shall we go?

What, now?

Yeah. Why not?

We've got a maths exam fifth period.

Yeah and I didn't revise.

Me neither.

Shall we go?

My bag's at school.

We can go back for it. We'll go back for final period. I'll say that my grandma's in hospital and we went to visit her.

The flat was quieter than usual. The workers across the road were on their break, or were doing something without machinery. We moved around the room cautiously, as if we'd broken in and as if every square inch hadn't already been completely saturated with our kisses.

Where shall we put it? I asked.

Anya shrugged her shoulders.

I'm gonna put it here, so it's close to the socket, I said, carefully putting my rucksack down. I opened the box, pulled out the blue plastic canvas and unfurled it on the floor. Then I got the electric pump and plugged it in. I pressed the power button, but nothing. I checked whether the plug was in the socket properly.

The electric's probably not turned on, Anya said.

Her voice faltered.

What are we gonna do now?

I'm gonna blow it up, I replied.

I took hold of the Turbo and started to puff. My arms were shaking. I started to burn up immediately, thanks to the beers and the increasing nervousness before the big event. I felt the sweat seeping out of my pores and soaking every part of my body. I puffed with all my might, but the Turbo Maximus did nothing. My head was spinning, and the blue canvas remained flat.

Meanwhile, Anya anxiously paced up and down the flat, looking out of the window. I recalled the Anya who had once, in that same space, done a cartwheel and smiled at me mischievously from behind a curtain of hair. There was some other girl here now, quiet and shy. Perhaps I should have stopped and waited for my Anya to come back, I thought; the lively, naughty Anya.

At which point someone turned the key in the front door. Anya and I looked at one another. She went white. We distinctly heard two male voices, and in walked a grey-haired man in a black suit and a younger guy with ripped jeans and a baggy checked shirt. Both were more surprised than we were. The grey-haired man's eyes wandered from me, to the Turbo Maximus and back again, before quickly turning to Anya, and then to his younger friend, and back to me and my inflatable mattress. He was holding the keys to the flat in his hands. It was obvious who he was. My heart stopped dead.

The grey-haired man was also far from comfortable. He turned to the man in ripped jeans and pointed at the pair of us. As he spoke, his index finger, which was aimed at me, trembled slightly in mid-air.

Yes, so this is my daughter Anya and her friend, they're here, I think, I think they're here to assist you, to assist you with the measurements or whatever else you might need, I asked them to come over today and I forgot to mention that they'd be here with you, as I've got to get back to work, I'm running late already actually, but you take your time and have a look around, if you need anything at all, just let these two know, Anya has everything covered, so you can ask her anything you might want to know, and we'll be in touch regarding your decision.

Anya's father then extended his hand to the man in the ripped jeans, and left without saying another word. The man stared at the door for a few moments, stunned, but then he pulled a tape measure out of his pocket and passed it from one hand to the other, no doubt not knowing whether to start with the measurements or to make a run for it himself.

I mean, everything's basically the same as in the plans, isn't it?

Anya nodded.

The man in the ripped jeans craned his neck to take a look at the other part of the flat, as if he were rooted to the spot he'd been standing on since he arrived.

Yeah, so I see, it's all good. Great. Thanks, both. That's fine for now, he said, and then he was gone.

It must have been several more minutes before Anya eventually moved and locked the door behind him.

Anya and I never went back to the flat on Pražakova. Around a month later, we did the deed at a summer camp in Croatia. Doing the deed was just what it was; it was over far too soon, she found it painful, and both of us were happy to have finally got it out of the way, to no longer be virgins and to be able to start enjoying ourselves. It wasn't memorable, that night in the tent in Poreč. I've no recollection of the noises outside, and I doubt Anya does either; only of the rustling of my sleeping bag beneath our bodies, of Anya asking, *Do you think anyone can hear that?* and my response of *There's a storm, everything's rustling* – the impatient reply of an impatient boy, who didn't have a clue whether the light sea breeze could actually be classified as a storm, but whose only concern was whether or not Anya might change her mind again.

That night didn't come close to being as special as our afternoons on Pražakova, the ones where kissing was as far as things went. And for a long time, I actually convinced myself that losing my virginity in that borrowed tent, on a roll mat covering the prickly forest floor, was the right thing; it was right that it didn't happen in that luxury bourgeois apartment that was returned to the Černjak family thanks to denationalisation. The fact that it had been our escape for more than two weeks, and was home to our very first mutual orgasms, was already a complete contradiction of my youthful, punk principles and ideals. The ones which only applied when my jeans were zipped up.

2.

Back when I was still admiring her secretly in the breaks between lessons, and imagining us sat on the bench outside school, kissing, I thought that the hardest thing would be to tell her that I loved her; that it would be impossible to utter those words. After that night in El Dorado, I thought that we'd never be anything more than awkward potential loves. When, at Pražakova, we shared our first real kisses, I thought I'd never be able to live up to her expectations. I didn't know what those expectations were, and all I could do was hope that everything would be easier once we'd succeeded in having sex for the first time.

But then Anya suggested that I go over to her house to meet her parents, and led my anxieties in an unexpected direction. Until that point, I'd only thought of parents as phantom-like apparitions who went to parents' evenings and then complained about unauthorised absences and detentions; just these people who made you come home before midnight. All the mothers and fathers in our stories were the same mum and the same dad; they all spoke the same way and they all did the same things. If they didn't conform to this predetermined ideal, you adapted them. Or you just made them up.

As such, in Anya's back garden, with her mum Stanka and her dad Miro, the grey-haired man who I'd met on Pražakova, I found myself completely unprepared. I knew that I couldn't roll my eyes and say 'fuuuck', or 'maaaaate'... only 'please' and 'thank you'. We spoke about our exams, and how both Anya and I had chosen history and geography, and that neither of us were very good at German, and how that one same teacher got on our nerves. About everything, therefore, that teenagers talk to adults about when they're pretending to take an interest in everything to do with school and pedagogical achievements.

We were sitting, chatting and drinking apple juice, and Stanka even offered me a coffee. At some point, Miro decided to join the conversation, and latched on to our remarks about German. For his generation, he said, German was forgotten, not studied.

We were under communism back then, you see, he said, going on to say that forgetting was something he did very well, and that by the time he'd finished school he'd managed to forget all but four German words.

Ein, klein, bier, bitte, listed Miro, counting with the fingers on his left hand. Try as he might, he could just never forget those four words, he said, and it was clear that this was one of those stories that Anya and Stanka had heard countless times before, but they were polite enough to laugh as if hearing it for the first time.

He seemed like a talker. I wasn't to know that Miro only told his old stories when he didn't know what to say. I didn't know that he felt uncomfortable around me, that he didn't know how to play the role of girlfriend's father, that he was only sat there for Stanka's sake, and that he himself had never wanted to meet his daughters' boyfriends.

I can meet them at the wedding, he said, antagonizing his wife.

If I hadn't have ignored you dimwits, I would have throttled you with my bare hands, he later confessed to me. I was old enough by then to understand what he was saying.

But that afternoon, he sat in the garden at Stanka's behest, being all smiles with me, the horny eighteen-year-old, who was pretending that his desire was noble, that it was almost love, even. He couldn't think of anything to ask me without giving himself away. And Stanka probably didn't want Miro to say what he was really thinking either.

Anya tells me that your mum works for SCT, she said.

Mum works there, yeah, I confirmed. *No idea what my dad does though. Don't know anything about him.*

I don't know why I lied. I looked away, thinking that they could all tell I was lying and that they were about to come down on me and ask me to leave. Yet all Miro and Stanka did was nod, and the conversation resumed after a short pause. Stanka deftly led the conversation far from my absentee father, but I remained stuck in that moment where I had, without knowing why, renounced Safet and our thirteen years of family life.

I don't remember Miro and Stanka saying or doing anything that afternoon, or Anya ever saying anything, that would make me want to keep Safet's name, and the fact he lived in Bosnia, a secret from her parents.

I rarely spoke about Safet because people rarely asked about him, but I had never disowned him like that before. In the garden of Anya's middle-class home, with an ornate, white garden table beneath a large beige parasol, was the first time I'd felt afraid to utter Safet's non-Slovene name. It was the first time I felt his name might ruin everything; that I'd become an intruder in Anya's nice orderly home, in a world of carefully tended lawns, spacious porches, and people carriers under factory guarantee.

I returned to that afternoon countless times, and during the visits that followed I studied Stanka's garden almost obsessively, trying to understand what exactly had happened there. I grew to know Miro and Stanka and I waited for their words to uncover the heart of my fear, the fear that was asking me, *Who are you, Jadran Dizdar?*

That question was ringing inside me that afternoon, as if Anya, Miro and Stanka were screaming it in my face. *Who do you belong to, Jadran Dizdar? Where do you come from, Jadran Dizdar?*

Yet as I recall, all Stanka and Miro did was laugh politely; as I recall, nobody said a word about Bosnia and Bosnians, about the outskirts of Ljubljana and its tower blocks, and its melting pot of ethnic groups.

We spoke about exams and about our school friends, and then we ate Stanka's apple strudel and I said that it was just like my mum, Vesna, made it. Something made me feel the need to mention Mum's Slovene name. I had a china saucer in my hands, and a teaspoon with a gilded handle, and her name seemed to befit the occasion more than mine. Vesna could belong in a world where water was infused with slices of lemon.

I don't know how that feeling of displacement managed to creep right into the most everyday of realms, into a day-to-day where mums serve apple strudel to daughters' boyfriends, and they make conversation about rehearsals for the final dance, and the dads politely smirk at remarks about teachers who favour the boys over girls, and where the girls say *Dad, stop it, you're so embarrassing*, when they tell them that they really ought to do a day's work one of these holidays, so they can see what it's like and earn some money for trips to the coast. And yet, the feeling of displacement that reared up inside me that afternoon remained.

I never did tell the Černjaks about Safet. I only told Anya, bit by bit, and not the whole story even then. I asked if it could be our secret, without knowing why I wanted that. Nor do I know why, after all these years of knowing them, I still wish to keep a part of me hidden from the Černjaks; why I still don't want Miro and Stanka to find out who I, Jadran Dizdar, really am.

As if I were cultivating a gulf between us on purpose; as if I were afraid to become part of their world. I sometimes think that for some reason, that afternoon, something sparked a resistance to that world inside me, and it prevented me from truly stepping into the garden at Pleteršnikova, to Anya.

3.

In truth, it wasn't at school that I fell in love with Anya. Nor was it that night when she kissed me at the bus stop. Nor did I fall in love with her at the flat on Pražakova, nor in the tent in which we went all the way for the very first time. I just thought I was in love. We told each other that we loved one another and believed it. We longed for touch, felt butterflies, and pushed the boundaries of pleasure, convinced that that was love.

I told her that I could see love in her eyes, and that she was gazing at me like they do in the movies, and she replied by telling me to be quiet, because she knew full well that my legs went to jelly when I looked at her. We made fun of each other, unaware of the love that was yet to come.

At the end of the summer we were heading to lake Bohinj for the weekend, to a house owned by Anya's grandparents. Stanka was trying to persuade us that the weather was always bad at Bohinj, and there was no point in going with such a dismal forecast, but Miro answered for us, saying that we wouldn't see the rain from the window, and he was right. We didn't care about the lake, or the waterfalls, or the Alpine scenery. All we saw in Bohinj was an empty house, and we couldn't wait to spend two days closed up inside.

Come with me, I've got something to show you, said Anya, stepping out onto the terrace and disappearing around the corner.

I was standing in the middle of the kitchen with a bag full of food that needed to go in the fridge, and I heard Anya's footsteps crunching on the gravel at the front of the house. And so our romantic weekend begins, I thought to myself, putting the bag down and rushing out after her.

When I caught sight of her again, she was standing next to a rocky outcrop which separated the neighbours' house and ours. It towered as high as the roof, while the branches of the trees that extended from it wound even higher, and cast shadows over both houses together. When she was sure that I was following her, she started to climb and soon disappeared through a narrow crevice between the rock and the side of the house. From where I was standing, it looked as if the house was leaning against the stony mount. Anya peeped back round.

You coming?

I followed her, carefully treading along the damp, mossy trail. The crevice was perhaps about as wide as she was, and I could barely get through its widest point. There wasn't enough space for the two of us on the other side, which offered a nice view of our courtyard, and so I stood on one leg, balancing between the rock and the side of the house supported by both hands. Anya, meanwhile, was having a great time. She grabbed hold of the thick branch above her head and hauled herself up with little steps up to the peak of the rock. I stepped into the space she left behind, and took hold of the branch myself. But I was going to need more room, mainly because the footholds were tiny, barely visible nuggets of rock which my large feet found it difficult to feel supported on. Between the house and the rock behind me there was a narrow drop of a few metres, and the branch from which I was hanging no longer seemed so strong.

Anya was standing above me and grinning gleefully. I was too immature back then to be able to admit my fears. My left foot found the lowest foothold, and I pulled myself up with all my might. As my right foot was searching for the second foothold, I tried to grab the rock with my free hand, but I couldn't find a firm hold anywhere. I lost my balance, and Anya burst out laughing.

The peak of the rock was visible behind her. A few metres of sloping, grassy surface, from which the outline of the lake could be seen through the trees. I approached the edge and stared down. In truth I was retreating from Anya, embarrassed by my awkwardness and cowardice.

This is my hill, she said. *It's where I always played when I was a kid.*

I turned around and saw a little girl before me, scaling her very own mountain; a skinny little girl in sports clothes, who wasn't interested in Barbie houses, and who didn't care if the Converse on her feet were imitation or real. I saw a shy girl, ashamed to admit that she had her own hill she loved to climb, and so she told her friends that she was bored at Bohinj, because she didn't like playing monopoly and walking with her parents and sister around the lake.

So you were a bit of a tomboy when you were younger? I ask her, already picturing the girl with short hair, a flat-chest, in wide-legged trousers and baggy t-shirts; a fresh-faced girl who loved to exercise, who loved to hang out with her cousins, play football with them, and whittle wooden darts to launch at pigeons.

And so what if I was, says Anya.

Now she's the one who's embarrassed, and even though she's at least five metres away, she's closer to me than ever before. I love her, I think to myself, this girl, who's standing here, right now, blushing.

When we get back into the house, we don't have sex; we make love. We caress one other and lie in each other's arms, and for the first time we are more than the lust we feel. I clutch her to my chest, my arms squeezing tighter and tighter, as if I wished our bodies could mould into one, like two pieces of plasticine. Nothing can sate my need for closeness, and even when I release inside her, I don't want to pull away from her; instead I stay, protecting the tight embrace. I feel the beads of sweat gathering between our bodies and I know that the slightest of movements will shatter everything.

VIII

1.

Mum believed that death was the end of it all. She didn't believe in another side, a side from which her deceased father would be watching over her, checking to see that his final wishes were being fulfilled. Grandad didn't believe in God. *Just to spite him*, he liked to clarify. It seemed as if Grandma, though, never stopped believing, despite giving the outward impression of being a model atheist, who never once mentioned God, crossed herself or prayed. But both of them, Grandma and Grandad, were raised by religious people, whereas Mum and Maya had been raised in the spirit of God-adverse times. That's how Mum turned out to be a non-believer that rejected every kind of spirituality.

Nor had Mum ever been superstitious. *I don't need black cats to bring me bad luck – it seems happy enough to turn up on its own*, she used to say. But her childhood world had been infected with superstition, which she, as a young girl, had absorbed, and so she would touch a button when she saw a chimney sweep, and would avoid clipping her nails in the evening. But by the time she'd reached her teens, she was rebelling against Grandma's superstitions to the extent that she'd open every umbrella in the house, right in the middle of the sitting room, positioning herself in front of all five, and would spend her day preventing her parents from closing them. It wasn't long before Grandma and Grandad weren't even allowed to touch wood in her presence.

What Mum hated, in actual fact, was only doing things because they were expected of her. She scoffed at the conformists who lit candles for relatives or acquaintances they never liked anyway. Maya was one such conformist, whose ritual of taking flowers to the graves of Dane's parents on the first of November was something Mum took offence to. She was certain that her sister had every right to hate her departed mother-in-law freely, out in the open.

Nevertheless, something would not allow Mum to ignore Grandad's dying wish. It probably wasn't something she understood either, but she felt a duty to obey him one last time. She wouldn't have rung me otherwise; she would have simply forgotten about Grandad's envelope. The upset wasn't because of what he'd written, either; because she could have guessed the contents of the letter, word for word, without even opening it. No; Mum had been angry because she was incapable of putting the old man's funny note out of her mind. Something inside her was at odds with everything she held dear, and could not be reconciled with what was, in her mind, an indisputable fact: dying wishes were an oxymoron, and fulfilling the wishes of dead people was the epitome of human stupidity. She was being betrayed by something inside, and it was contradicting her deepest convictions.

We exchanged no more than a few words on the journey from Momjan to Zagreb, but it felt as if I spent the whole journey listening to the thoughts going round in her head. She was opposed to the very idea of cremation, and I sensed that she was constantly trying to find sense in complying with Grandad's final wishes, but could find none. Yet compliantly she sat in the passenger seat, and only passed intermittent comments on the morning fog above Gorski Kotar, or on how it was the first time that she'd travelled along the new road between Rijeka and Zagreb.

Any potential evidence of Grandad's suicide was going to be cremated along with his body, and I'm never going to find out how he died, I thought to myself, as we came off the motorway and headed towards the city. I was going to be left with the unresolved hypothesis about Grandad's final hours. But it was too late to start that conversation with Mum now.

'How many times have I said that next time I'm in Zagreb I'm going to go to Mirogoj cemetery and visit Dražen Petrović's grave?'

'Why don't you go today?'

'Today's really not the day.'

'Well, why not? We'll be finished up at the crematorium quite quickly. It's like a production line in there.'

'I'm not sure I'll be in the right frame of mind.'

'Up to you.'

'Are you going to direct me or shall I stick the sat nav on?'

She sat up straight in her seat and stared out of the window.

'A few years ago, maybe more – no, it's got to have been about a year ago, or maybe more – one of my uni friends, Anita, was cremated in Mirogoj, after she died from cancer. It sounds absurd, to hear that out loud. Anita did have cancer, but if she died of anything, it was of Zoran, her ex-husband, or the Weasel, as we girls affectionately called him in later years; turn left at the lights. Zoran really was a weasel of the highest order; he used to be a super guy: smart, easy on the eye, too; he studied journalism in Zagreb and was the first of his generation to get a job at *Vjesnik* newspaper before graduation, which really was incredible in those days, now go straight on, I'll tell you when; I think he even won a young journalist award, I don't know more than that, but anyway – he always seemed very pleasant to me, a well brought-up boy, polite chap, as Grandma would say, but then there was some disagreement at *Vjesnik;* it was the late eighties then, he was always too clever for that lot, and he handed his notice in and sold his parents' house on the coast: he told Anita that it was pointless going to the same place every year, the weasel, and that from then on they were going to holiday all over the world, somewhere different every year, a bit further, there, up to that red house; and he had the idea of starting up his own newspaper, independent, an alternative, like *Mladina*, he said; he was smart, but, as Dinka used to say, he was more ambition than intellect, so, basically, go right here, then up the hill, that *Mladina* of his folded spectacularly, he couldn't get over it – male ego, that incurable disease – the thing would still be up and running if he'd caught on that it wasn't happening straight away, but the weasel didn't want to admit defeat, the Croats were getting more and more fascist by the day, he meanwhile was working for this mildly anti-fascist weekly paper, bad timing; Anita pleaded with him desperately, now just continue along here, but not a chance, so yeah, bad timing, he thought he was a genius and that was that, there was no way he could fail, he was the reason that the whole of Croatia bought *Vjesnik*, straight on, and then, typical hard done by bloke, he started drinking, instead of giving himself a kick up the arse and getting back out there with the journalists, writing tabloid crime pieces, anything; he'd begun to dream about starting a business, the debts stacked up and he was left without a choice, I mean, he had choices of course, he had every choice, but he was just the sort of person they looked for: intelligent, a good writer, on a downward spiral and in debt, disillusioned, and so they bought him, here, look, you'll see the car park on the left; President Tuđman and his henchmen bribed him to write articles, some in his own name, even more under various pseudonyms; it's sad, because he was schooling the young talent in how to write propaganda, I don't know the half of it anymore, but he was a different person by then, look, there it is – park here, the crematorium's just over there – we all met up once, in Zagreb, and I could see that he wasn't the same; not just in appearance, but in how he spoke, the sort of things he was saying, everything; Anita told me that his family didn't talk to him, that he'd fallen out with all of them, there's a space here, he was a different person, you wouldn't believe; then about a year later he and Anita got divorced, though only on paper – she didn't have the heart to kick him out, she thought it was an illness that he was going to recover from, and she took him back, let him talk her round and they made up, I couldn't bear to listen to all this – oh, did you lock the car? – good, the entrance's over there; all I know is that it was all bullshit, he gathered and coordinated a mob who wrote this stuff on forums, I mean, can you imagine? All those nationalist fallacies of theirs, all that barbaric shit, he wrote it, under the guises of semi-literate people; one day he was Jozo, a farmer from Opuzen; the next he was Stefan, a veteran from Koprivnica, and who knows who else he was, and when Anita told me all of this I just couldn't get over it; she was saying – and he admitted this to her – that half of those comments on forums were fake, new age propaganda, she said – can you see Maya? – and then one evening he approached her and said that he'd got something to tell her…'

When I turned to look at her, I knew instantly that Zoran and Anita's story would be left without an ending. They no longer registered on Mum's face. Her eyes were fixed on the entrance to the crematorium, unrecognisable. I cautiously turned towards the entrance, fearing I might recognise the person she'd caught sight of.

As Safet expressed his condolences, Mum, Maya and I nodded our heads mechanically, and extended our hands as if he were a neighbour we'd lost touch with after moving away. We performatively disguised our surprise at how he had appeared just as unexpectedly and unexplainably as he'd vanished twenty years ago. No one was capable of verbalising the questions posed by our eyes, and Safet, too, either out of politeness or his own paralysis, did not wish to read them.

Safet was standing before us, by now markedly different in appearance to the Safet who inhabited Mum's memories, but different again to the one I had visited in Otoka. Silent and reserved like back then, but much more commanding in his detachment. As if he'd finally made himself at home in the realm of time where we'd seen each other last. This wasn't the Safet who had met me at the bus station in Bihać, but a calm person, accustomed to solitude, accustomed to disappearing, reappearing, and disappearing again.

Mum immediately headed for the crematorium entrance, in order to avoid a polite exchange of words with her former husband, and the rest of us followed in identical fashion. A young employee of the crematorium, too young to be wearing all black, gave us the signal to enter, and we arranged ourselves by Grandad's coffin. Mum, Maya and I stood rigidly together, shoulder to shoulder, while Safet had positioned himself behind me. He was standing close enough for me to see the points of his shoes when I bowed my head. It was no longer possible to make out the colour of the suede, covered with layer upon layer of hardened, greyish-brown stains and scuffs. Over the years the soles had been moulded and flattened by Safet's wide, clumsy footsteps. If it wasn't for my memory of how they used to be, their original shape would be impossible to imagine. They were Safet's old shoes, bought in Trieste for special occasions. Those special occasions that he and Mum had been next in line for, and which both of them had long sensed were just around the corner, but which never came. Safet's special occasion shoes had walked innumerable steps along paths that were decidedly not special, all of which had left their mark. But they were still the same shoes that had walked away from us. And no doubt the only shoes he had.

Maya stepped forward, reached for the flowers in the vase, and scattered a few on the coffin. It was positioned above an opening, at the bottom of which was another, smaller opening which led to the furnace. Mum, Safet and I went after Maya. Safet allowed me to go before him, signalling with a subtle hand motion that I should step forward. We then returned to our original places. I put my arm around Mum, and caught sight of her brief glance in Safet's direction. The young man in the black suit gestured to check if we had concluded the scattering of flowers, and whether he should continue. The coffin with Grandad's body began to sink into the abyss.

I tried to focus on Safet and his shoes, and to just be a grandson beholding the sight of his grandad's coffin, but all I could think of was how, along with the coffin, the empty bottle of Grandma's medicine was disappearing too. I watched the coffin draw nearer to the crematorium furnace, and felt its burning heat under my own skin. I was back on the bedroom floor in Momjan again, crouching down and searching with one hand under the bed, feeling around on the dusty floor, touching the rolling bottle and coaxing it towards me with a finger, until it came out from under the bed. I shook it, as if I couldn't believe my own hands, and had to prove to myself that it was empty one more time. I then drew it up to my face, so that I could read what it said, checking whether it maybe used to contain just vitamins or calcium.

My eyes were seeing a slightly distorted and brown-tinted image of the crematorium and the bowing heads of Mum, Maya and Safet, as if staring through the bottle. We were separated by glass. I tapped my fingers against the brown-tinted surface, searching for a fault line so I could escape; it was as if they couldn't hear me shouting their names, like I could no longer call out to them, like I, too, was sinking into the abyss, like I was melting in the crematory flames, but nobody could see me and nobody was able to help. I would soon disappear together with the smelting, brown glass. The furnace had already taken the paper label, the darkness devouring one letter at a time, and nobody would ever know what was written on it. Everything is covered in soot. The coffin is no longer visible. The cranking of the mechanism that lowered it down has stopped. The sound of the furnace, however, grows louder. I hear the last of Grandad's secrets burning, I hear it all disappear. All that remains is doubt, for doubt is the only thing that's eternal.

'God's a bloody fool,' says Mum, like an amen concluding a prayer, calling me back.

We went outside and were blinded by the beating midday sun that had found an opening in the thick covering of cloud. Maya was rummaging in her bag for her sunglasses, and Safet was watching her, meaning that he failed to notice how Mum had approached him and placed herself right in front of him. She was looking at him square in the eyes; there was only two or three finger widths between their two faces. Safet didn't pull back. The look on his face was, in contrast to hers, gentle; almost frightened. It looked as if he was struggling not to crumble before her. We were all waiting for Mum to say something, but instead she turned to face me.

'Now might be a good time to visit Dražen Petrović's grave.'

I wanted to protest, but she was too quick.

'Safet could go with you. He was a big fan too. Maya and I will sit and have a coffee, and wait for the both of you.'

Safet and I nodded our heads, with the same combination of

obedience and submission. We both sensed that we'd received one of those offers you can't refuse. I wanted to add that I had no idea where the grave actually was, but I heard Safet say the words *We'll find him*, and then shortly afterwards, *We'll ask if we don't*, and I said nothing. I just gave Mum a kiss.

'See you.'

Walking around Mirogoj with Safet in search of Dražen's grave was fate's pathetic attempt at turning my life into some sort of Hollywood film, where in the end everyone recalls a happy moment from my damaged childhood, collapses in a tearful embrace, all wrongdoings forgiven and we all live happily ever after.

Safet accompanied me with a lowly deference. He kept his head bowed and it seemed as if he, like me, were glad of the silence between us as we walked past the unkempt graves, as if I weren't the only one to not be overly concerned about whether we'd find our way to Dražen.

Both of us had loved Dražen Petrović, but Safet had worshipped him; I had been too young to fully appreciate his rise to the top. When we watched him bring home the European Basketball Cup title, and then the World Championship, Safet was practically dead in front of the television, collapsed from the rhythmic interchange of ecstasy and despair, while my days as a fan were only just beginning. Safet was the reason I chose the number five on my Slovan shirt – the number Dražen played against Real; Safet was the reason I turned off any TV announcement about him; Safet was the reason I cried when Dražen died in a car accident; Safet was the reason I cried when rival Partisan supporters hurled chants of *We got Dražen killed! We got Dražen killed!* at the Cibona coach, who happened to be Dražen's brother.

At the time, the words I heard were *We got Safet killed!*, and when I mentioned wanting to visit Dražen's grave to Mum on the way to Zagreb, I really did think of him, of Safet, too. But Dražen was the only reason I wanted to visit the grave. For a long time my Dražen had just been Dražen; just a basketball player. One of the greatest.

At the next crossroads I went right and purposely led us in the wrong direction. Maybe Safet noticed, maybe he didn't. He'd lost interest in Dražen and in basketball some time ago, and was only following me because he hadn't found the strength to refuse Mum's suggestion.

'Strange things, those obituaries,' I heard him say.

At first Safet merely slowed down, but then he came to a standstill, at a family grave – Jelinčić, was the name – adorned with fresh flowers and peeping blades of grass. I waited for him to move, but he stood there, looking at me, as if trying to figure out where he was, and who I was; the person with eyes fixed on him in expectation. We were no longer inhabiting the same realm of time and space, and it was pointless trying to bring him back.

2.

A few years after I'd visited him in Otoka, Safet was sat down at Lela's bar. During winter, Lela left a small plastic table outside the front door just for Safet, who drank his espresso out there, bending the unopened sugar sachet between his fingers, even in the pinching December frost. These were days of vacant stares, when everyone had their own reasons for gazing into thin air, and Safet would be left to sit undisturbed for the duration of his afternoon. But that day, a newspaper thumped down on the table in front of him.

This one's for you, Slovene, Mahir's voice bellowed out.

Mahir had moved to Zagreb with his family during the war. At the weekends he renovated his old house in Otoka; it was somewhere he intended to return to if, god willing, he made it to retirement.

Someone left it on the bus, he said, going into the bar, into the warm.

Safet gave him a nod. He let the paper lie there, where Mahir had left it, and went back to staring at the undetermined point, somewhere at the end of the street, that had entranced him. Then, the sachet of sugar burst between his fingers and the white granules scattered across the table and his lap. This usually signalled that it was time to leave. The durability of the sugar sachet, in other words, was equal to the amount of time he could spend sitting outside of Lela's bar. Yet as Safet brushed the sugar from the table, his eyes fixed upon the newspaper.

The issue of Ljubljana's *Delo* newspaper was a good two weeks out of date, and he started to mechanically to turn the paper sheets. Partly out of respect for Mahir and his kindness; partly because that's what newspapers are there for. He didn't actually care what was reported in *Delo*, and it wasn't long before he'd shoved it to the edge of the table without reading a single headline or looking at a single photograph. The Slovene words, and images of Ljubljana, left him unmoved. A newspaper like any other, a stack of flimsy, grey paper that could be used to wrap up dirty tools.

But when Safet gave Lela the signal that he'd like to pay for his small beer, his eyes returned to the paper, and to the name above the largest of the obituaries. Stane Dolanc, it read, in large, bold type. He moved the newspaper towards him and recognised the former Yugoslav Minister of the Interior in the small photograph. He looked at his double chin, which blurred the edges of his face; at the thick rims of his glasses, framing two black dots for eyes; his jiggling belly and his aged bald patch that crept across his head and extended his forehead. He looked at the slightly disfigured old man, and asked himself why the sight of his photograph and name beneath it gave him a knot in his stomach, and asked why that knot wasn't unpleasant, but brought, in some strange way, a sense of comfort.

He scanned through the other names in the obituary section, but his body did not respond, and so he returned to Stane. The name didn't mean anything to him; all he had was a fleeting memory that a man with this name had existed. But his obituary had stirred something inside Safet. Something minuscule; but still there, where everything had lay dormant for so many years, and even the smallest of stimuli wielded power.

He turned away and put Stane Dolanc out of sight. He never thought about Ljubljana and about who lived and died there; he never asked himself what people he knew might be doing, how they lived, whether they were still in Ljubljana, and whether they were just like they used to be; whether they frequented the same bars and ordered the same drinks, or whether those bars were even still bars at all, or whether they'd become pawn or betting shops. His only reminder of the world up there came from people like Mahir, who called him the Slovene. They unwittingly preserved a bond that he had severed long ago.

The obituary of Stane Dolanc had roused a long-dead curiosity in Safet. He felt compelled to flick through other copies of *Delo*, to see other obituaries. He was curious to know what would happen if he were to see the obituary of someone he really did know, not just someone from the papers and the television, like Stane Dolanc; to know how his stomach would react to such a name. Perhaps he was enticed by the death, he thought. You can ignore anything in life except death, Safet believed. Because death is bigger than everyone; because there's nothing bigger than death.

Is there anywhere you can get hold of Delo in Zagreb? Safet stuck his head in and called to Mahir.

Look at you, Slovene, hooked after your first one, Mahir grinned.

Safet walked over to him, took his wallet out of his pocket and shook out all of the money he had onto the bar. With a little help from Lela's cash till, Safet and Mahir worked out that there was enough money for nineteen and a half editions of *Delo*. Safet suggested that some of it ought to go to Mahir, for his trouble. Mahir shook his head. He needed an extra pair of hands renovating his house more than he needed the money.

If push comes to shove.

Safet knew that in Bosnia, push did always come to shove, and that the Bosnian 'if' was not the same as a Slovene one; it was more a case of 'when'. But he shook Mahir's hand without hesitation.

It means a lot to me, he said to him.

Mahir nodded, though he still wasn't sure if Safet was being serious. But by the following week, he placed the first bundle of Slovene newspapers down on the table outside Lela's bar.

From that day forward, Safet spent every Saturday afternoon, after he and Mahir had completed the handover, sifting through the obituaries in *Delo*. It was a ritual that he never performed in front of the nosey regulars at Lela's. Whilst there he wouldn't take so much as a peek; he carried them home, cleared the last crumb from the kitchen table, and then spread out the pages of last Saturday's paper. He always read them in order, from Saturday to Friday. Mahir would buy the newspapers on Friday afternoon, from a kiosk run by a Bosnian woman, Amra, who put them to one side during the week, so that Safet read the Saturday paper with a week's delay. There wasn't anything else of interest to him, only the names of people who had died in Slovenia. And the dead have always got time to wait.

Why he did this, he wasn't sure, but he had stopped asking himself. And by Friday afternoon, he was already starting to think about the obituaries and the names. Now, at the end of each week, these Slovene names entered his non-Slovene life, and whenever he recognised one, it always caused some kind of reaction inside him. Every name affected him differently, and each one prised something open.

The first name after Stane Dolanc was Majda Vrečko. He couldn't recall her face, as he'd only met her once or twice, and many years ago at that, long before the fierce woman had retired and severed all ties with former employees in the Kolinska acquisitions department. He never heard a single thing about her and it wasn't long before they stopped asking. Yet years later, in the middle of Bosanska Otoka, Safet was looking at her name. She departed this life at the age of eighty-six, it read, and her life was to be celebrated on Friday, which, translated into Safet's time, meant that Majda was already buried. Majda's office was sketched out before his eyes, he could clearly picture the desk arrangement inside, with the locked drawers, hole punches and soldering irons, and the mountains of fax paper that accumulated in the corners. He felt as if his skin were being stroked from the inside. The gentle goose bumps reminiscent of the fleeting touch of a woman's hand.

It wasn't long before the eager wait for Saturday's bundle began to encroach earlier into his week, and by Wednesday he could catch himself counting down the days and hours. Over again he told himself that they were just obituaries, just the names of people he no longer knew. He tried to put them out of his mind, but time and time again he caught sight of himself, sitting before an open newspaper, and was captured by the memory of that pleasant, unsettling feeling.

There were no names that he recognised in the following Saturday's obituaries. He wasn't disappointed. He was pleased with his composure, even. He believed that his fascination with the dead was coming to an end, that he'd been liberated from this strange addiction. He thought that he'd go to Mahir and tell him that he no longer needed the newspapers.

But then it got to Monday, when Mahir was returning to Zagreb, and Safet hadn't gone anywhere near his house. Something had kept him away. If, in next Saturday's paper, he promised himself, there were no more familiar names again, he'd cancel their arrangement on Monday. He cursed himself for playing the lottery with people's lives. This is a game of misfortune, he told himself, of depravity, or sickness, even. A special form of necrophilia, perhaps. He felt a deep self-loathing, and picked up the pile of newspapers that had gathered under the stairs and carried them into the kitchen. He lit the fire which had gone out in the old stove, sat himself down on a footstool, and tore off the pages, one at a time, throwing them into the fire, until all that was left of the newspapers were tiny flecks of ash, dancing in the air. But even then, as he watched the flames inside the oven, he knew it was not the end. The unsettled feeling had returned, and it refused to go away.

That Saturday, he read the name Peter Drganc in Thursday's *Delo*. He was a mechanical engineer, it read, and Safet remembered that he used to rent a small flat on the second floor of a house on Jamova Street. He could picture it, and Peter too, standing outside. The old man's face came to life before his eyes. The sight of those wispy, white eyebrows made Safet feel something akin to sadness. His game, for the first time, had genuinely frightened him.

Sadness is no laughing matter, he said to himself, repeating the words of his father. He couldn't remember the last time he'd felt sad. But he understood that things were getting dangerous, for this very reason.

The face of Peter Drganc marked the beginning of a long period of broken promises. Walking into town on a Saturday morning, Safet swore that he was going to tell Mahir that he no longer wanted the newspapers. Yet time and again he accepted them without saying a word, giving a nod of thanks, and tucking them under his arm before heading back home. One day, the papers were already waiting for him on his table, and he assured himself that he'd visit Mahir as soon as he'd finished his coffee. But first he put off leaving until afternoon, then until evening, then until first thing the next morning, as soon as he woke up. Many a time he'd been standing in front of the post office phone box, convinced he was going to call Zagreb and put an end to what he'd been unable to do in person. Holding the receiver, he'd dial in Mahir's work number that he'd got from Refik. But he always put the phone down.

He felt like a child filling an album with footballers' faces; an album that when opened, always had new pages, waiting to be filled. There were more and more names searching for a face. This is some sort of dependency, it occurred to him, on more than one occasion. He was frequently unable to sleep and would toss and turn in his bed, terrified that he was losing his mind. Yet he was powerless to stop. He knew that he couldn't go on without the reactions stirred by the obituaries. They became stronger and stronger, and he began to note various different feelings within them, feelings that had long since been forgotten. But the reactions came and they vanished, leaving him with nothing but emptiness until the following Saturday. He'd spent years living in apathy, years of feeling nothing, but never had he felt so empty as he did now.

What are they saying, those Slovenes of yours? Mahir once asked, as he handed over the papers. Do they write about us?

It had been a long time since any foreign words had actually registered with Safet, but this question sent a chill down his spine. He never read a single word beyond the obituaries and he had no idea what the papers were saying. He was scared that Mahir was going to expose him, and discover his sick habit right there, in front of Lela and Refik, and that he, Safet Dizdar, would be known as yet another madman in the great madhouse that was Bosnia. *Crazy Slovene*, the kids would shout at him.

Luckily for him, Mahir wasn't actually interested in what was written in *Delo* about Bosnians, or anything else. He was even less interested in what Safet was reading in the Slovene papers.

I know their sort. They write about us in the Animal Kingdom section.

Mahir laughed at his own joke, and then, just like that, his head was empty of *Delo*, of Slovenia, of Safet. But the thought that someone could have found out about his obituary obsession stayed with Safet for days.

The local Otokans had always associated Safet with the foreign land he came from. To them he remained a Slovene, a newcomer. In almost twenty years of living in his father's hometown, Safet hadn't learned to be a Bosnian, and even less so a Bosniak or a Muslim, just as he'd never learned to be a Slovene in Slovenia. He sensed the unspoken demand for conformity, to not stand out from the crowd, he sensed it in every look that a true Otokan had ever given him. He sensed it, and had learned to live with it. But being derided as a Turk from Kragujevac, a Byzantine in Slovenia, or a Slovene in Otoka was one thing; he knew all that, and could handle it, but being a man possessed by obituaries was another thing altogether.

He felt shame in the presence of others for the first time in his life, and this sense of shame was the first feeling to stay with him. It was drowned out only momentarily on Saturday, by the unsettled feeling that came with the new obituaries and the name Miloš Janković, a veteran waiter from a restaurant called Čad. Then the shame returned. And transformed into tension. As he woke the next morning, he located the feeling inside, and let it wash over him. He was no longer in any doubt. Feeling had returned.

The night after he'd seen an obituary for Gordana Cvijić, owner of a stationery shop on Rojčeva, Safet had a dream about her husband, Radenko. The two of them were sat together in the garden of Šeštica, another Ljubljana institution, and Radenko kept on calling the waiter over and ordering more food. Their table was crammed, there was no space left, and the waiters were placing the silver platters and carafes of wine on the tables of other patrons, causing them to complain. But he took no notice of the complaints and carried on ordering. One of Safet's former colleagues, Jure Gostiša, was also sat at a neighbouring table. Safet asked him whether he was still alive, and Jure said that he wasn't, that he'd died some years ago, and his obituary was in *Delo*. What about your brother, Grega, Safet enquired. He's alive, said Jure, but Simona passed away. Simona Rakovec, Boris Trutkovski, Ilda Veber. Gostiša listed the names of the dead. Some were familiar to Safet, but not all. Gostiša showed him their obituaries, so as to convince him that they really were dead. Safet approached a table at which Veronika Šarec appeared to be seated. There were a few other familiar faces there too, but their names escaped him. The obituaries on Gostiša's table started to blur, and became illegible. Gostiša stood up and invited Safet to come with him to the Faculty of Arts. Radenko shouted at him to come back to the table, but he and Gostiša were already outside, on the street. They noticed the waiters running across the road with platters. The actor Polde Bibič passed them on the street, stopped one of them and grabbed a piece of meat from one of the platters. The waiter asked him if he knew Radenko Cvijić, but Polde shook his head, and with a mouth full of meat, he carried on his way. Rok Petrovič, Jure Gostiša and Safet wound up at the Nebotičnik building. Safet didn't like lifts, and so he took the many stairs alone. Gordana and Vesna Benedejčič had come to meet them. They didn't know he'd died, they said to him. He looked at Vesna and asked her if she had died too. Vesna nodded. Yes, I died in a car accident, she said.

Safet awoke from his dream. Drenched in sweat, quivering, terrified. Full to the brim. He felt as if he were being inflated by something, something which was going to shatter him into tiny pieces at any moment and come gushing out of him. In the darkness in front of him, he saw her face, he felt her breath on his lips. It was her; the one he'd been running away from for so long, the daughter of Stane Dolanc's second cousin. They were back in that office again, and he thought he could hear the sound of keyboards tapping; that he could have scrubbed the stains from the cracked lino, that he could smell the cigarette smoke that clung to the carpet tiles.

The many pieces of his giant puzzle had finally begun to arrange themselves.

Majda Vrečko was Vesna's first boss. Fat Majda, as they called her; she was horrible to Vesna every day, she was a frustrated dragon who took everything out on those below her. Safet saw her in town once, and he followed her and thought about how he could get his revenge, he pictured it right before his eyes, but she popped into a shop on Čopova and came out with a big box of nougat. She opened it right there, in the street. Safet felt sorry for Fat Majda, walking along Čopova with a box of nougat and stuffing her face with chocolate for all to see. She's unhappy, he said to Vesna that evening, to which she replied that he was a softie who felt sorry for evil fat people.

Peter Drganc was the landlord of the first apartment they ever shared together. It was in an old, crumbling house, where everything would creak, break and fall off. Their first bed was completely ramshackle and let out the kind of sounds that would disturb them in the middle of the night if either of them turned over in their sleep. When they put the mattress on the floor, they established that it was just as creaky as the bed. In that apartment even the walls would creak, but they were both young and nothing could stop them. They had neighbours who greeted them politely, and whenever they bumped into them, they'd bow their heads, embarrassed by the noise they'd made, which no doubt carried through the wooden floors. In the end they started checking whether the coast was clear, outside and on the stairs, before they would leave the house.

Miloš Janković was working at the restaurant on the evening of Safet and Vesna's wedding reception. All night long and even into the following afternoon, when the wedding guests eventually started to leave. He was a waiter of the old school, this old Serb, who nobody had ever heard speak a word of Serbian. Miloš Janković was in fact a Slovene waiter and he spoke Slovene. Only Slovene. By the time it got to midnight, the guests had had so much to drink that they were jumping off chairs, turning over tables, smashing glasses, all while he stood quietly on the sidelines, like a soldier in his well-ironed uniform, discretely sweeping up and disposing of the shards of glass and taking new orders. As if all the louts, who were throwing up and pissing in the bushes behind the pub, were all officers of the highest rank. He treated every guest as if they were Tito himself, while they, the drunken animals, spent all night encouraging him to sing one of the old favourites with them.

Radenko Cvijić had driven Vesna to the maternity hospital. Safet could see him as if it were yesterday, sitting there in his Fiat 126, parked in front of the maternity entrance, smoking and waiting for Vesna to give birth. *Let me stay*, he says to Safet, who tells him to go home, because these things can take a long time. *Just in case*, says Radenko, not that it makes any sense, as Vesna is already in her hospital bed with her son lying next to her, and no one is going to need him or his car, the only one on the street.

After Radenko Cvijić came the name Jožica Jamnik, the very same Jožica Jamnik who was duped by the pillow stuffed under Vesna's blouse and the fabricated medical note, and who allocated them the flat in Fužine. After her was Željko Drobnič, a friendly old homeless guy from Jamova, and then Vito Obrenović, the policeman who fell asleep on our sofa, drunk, whilst investigating a bicycle theft in our block.

Saturday by Saturday, the pieces of Safet's former life reassembled. Everything that he believed to have been permanently erased was now, with every photo, coming back to life. And it was bringing him back to life with it. Each familiar name in an obituary sparked individual scenes and backdrops from his Ljubljana life. He saw forgotten faces again, deserted Ljubljana streets, bars with steel stools and crammed rooms in rented flats, where student friends would get together. They were young and carefree again, resigned to making their way in a world that didn't offer much beyond packed rooms and tables loaded with cold meats, cheap alcohol and cigarette butts. Somewhere in the background you could hear music like they no longer make, and the last few echoes of laughter; the laughter of the last generation who genuinely believed that it had nothing to lose.

Each new photograph restored life to Safet. Every Saturday took him back. He had repressed an entire life inside him when he left Ljubljana. In order to survive his departure, everything inside him had to die away. His love, above all else.

And now he was reviving it once more; piece by piece he restored it like a mosaic which became stronger and more beautiful with every tiny fragment. It was only a trace of love, which was at the same time enticing and out of reach, but his restoration continued, in the faith that he would one day feel it again, stronger than ever before. Now he no longer cleared the newspapers from the table. He could sit with them for entire afternoons and evenings. He looked at the names in the obituaries and put the pieces of his story together. The pieces of himself.

When Mahir retired and came back to Otoka, Safet was left without newspapers and obituaries for weeks on end. At first he thought, superstitiously, that it was a sign, telling him to stop with this madness, but it wasn't long before he started scouring the town in desperation, looking for anyone who might be going to Zagreb or Slovenia. He stopped strangers in the street, knocked on people's doors, all to no avail. He found the sorts of people who made the journey, but not regularly, and not the sorts of people on whom Safet could rely. All the while he tried in vain to prepare himself for abandoning the search and a life without the dead. Time and time again his dependency got the better of him. He was half put together; half alive. There was no way back.

Luckily for him, Zijad took pity on him after growing tired of Safet's pestering, and promised that he'd look into the cost of getting copies of *Delo* sent to Bosanska Otoka.

No drug comes cheap, said Zijad, when he quoted his price, three times what Safet had been paying Mahir. Safet didn't give a moment's hesitation. Grateful to Zijad, he started going to his shop every day from that point onwards and bought his copy of *Delo*.

There's no hurry – no one else is going to buy it, he would say to him, whenever Safet was waiting at the door at the crack of dawn.

For a long time Zijad persisted in asking him, the Slovene, why he was never interested in what was happening here in Bosnia. But even he grew tired of it eventually, and started taking Safet's money and handing over the paper without so much as a word.

So the obituaries were part of Safet's daily life once again. Days were divided into good ones, where the dead would revitalise pieces of his past, and bad ones, where the names would leave him as cold as the deceased themselves.

Evil and twisted, evil and twisted, Safet would often say to himself, as he browsed the papers, repeating Nana's words. But the more death he found in the papers, the more he felt alive.

And then, one early autumn day, when he was sat in my room in the attic of Nana's house, looking out at the river through the window, it seemed as if he might be feeling it again. Love. It was timid and quiet, but it was love. Immediately he knew that it had returned, and that after almost twenty years he was human again. A human being capable of love and suffering, of sadness and longing.

From that moment forwards, whenever he was asked when he was born, Safet would reply the twenty-fifth of September and would think of that day. He never mentions the year. He stopped counting the years a long time ago.

3.

Eva Terčon, that was her name. Safet looked her straight in the eye and asked her why she'd done it, but all she said was that the documents were no longer valid. He told her that they were the only ones he had, and asked whether she could produce new ones for him. She would need his birth certificate, she said. He asked her if she was taking the piss, if she'd seen the news at all, whether she knew what was going on down there, that it would be insanity to go to Bosnia for a fucking birth certificate. She told him that, as a consequence, she was unable to help him.

As a consequence?! And what am I supposed to do now, as a consequence?!
She said nothing. Eva Terčon.

Sir, I've already told you what you need to do, she said, when he refused to leave.

Safet walked away from Eva Terčon's counter, and went to the post office to call Dane.

What did I tell you, Dane said to him.

What did you tell me? That they were going to punch a hole in my documents? Did you tell me that? Hm? Safet shouted, but Dane didn't answer.

Safet stood motionless in the phone booth at Ljubljana's central post office. For the first time in his life, he'd been outmanoeuvred. He, who had always outmanoeuvred the system, had finally been outmanoeuvred by Eva Terčon.

He was ashamed to go home, he was ashamed to admit what had happened to him. He stood at the bus stop by the Town Hall, the buses drove past him, but he didn't get on.

He hurried across the Triple Bridge, along Miklošičeva to the police station on Trdinova. He was almost running, as if he couldn't wait to be arrested and locked up. He marched into the station, determined to settle this with them all.

Fuck this fucking country and fuck you! he yelled, launching his hole-punched documents at the policeman coming towards him. His colleagues immediately leapt at him, pinning him to the wall. But they didn't shut him up.

You want your own country so you think you can screw up mine, separatist pricks. Why don't you take your motherfucking independence and independently go shove it up your arses?

The policeman had soon heard enough of his outburst. Contrary to Safet's expectations, they didn't lock him up. They put him in the back of a car and drove him to the border.

The Croatian border guard wanted to telephone his wife, but Safet didn't want to hand over his home number. He didn't want to go back. He never wanted to go back, ever. He was determined that for no amount of money would he ever let on what had happened to him, not to anyone. Least of all to her.

On the seventeenth of November last year, the obituary of Eva Terčon was published in *Delo*.

4.

'Strange things, these obituaries,' Safet said again, and I thought that here, in the graveyard, his story seemed fitting.

The contorted expression on his face relaxed, and the corners of his mouth curled upwards. But it was still far from a smile.

He looked up, for the first time since we'd set off to Dražen's grave, to take in his surroundings. He went up to the nearest cypress tree, loudly cleared his throat, and spat out the saliva that had gathered in his mouth. He took another look up at the sky, where a flock of birds were circling and disappearing behind the treetops. They were bobbing on the breeze, accompanied by a few tumbling leaves swaying back and forth to the ground. A static blanket of grey was all that remained above our heads. But Safet's eyes remained cast at the sky, as if trying to break through to the blue behind.

And then, still gazing upwards, he started to walk forwards, pausing momentarily to check I was following, and then continued on his way. When I caught up with him and we were side by side once more, I thought I might have seen a redness in his eyes. I walked faster, to overtake him, but when I turned back to face him, the redness had already vanished. Safet's eyes were vacant and dry. He came to another stop.

'I know this sounds wrong, but I've waited a long time for Aleksandar's death. And his obituary. I knew he would be cremated. I knew the send-off would be here. There are some things a person just knows.'

We looked at one another in silence. Standing opposite was a man whose story had just been pieced together. With Aleksandar's death, Safet became that person who had once walked away from us. Standing opposite was the Safet from 1992. A memory made human.

We went back to the car park where Mum and I had left the car that morning. Mum and Maya were already waiting for us there.

'I need to be getting back to Ljubljana too, Jadran,' said Mum, as Safet and I approached her. I nodded, and I sensed her sigh of relief.

'I'm sorry, Safet, but I really have to go,' she said, confusing him with her friendly performance. He blushed like a young boy in front of a girl. He stayed there, in the middle of the car park, and for a moment it was unclear as to whether he'd understood that Mum was saying goodbye.

'Did you come by car?' I asked him.

'Yeah, yeah,' he said. 'Over there.'

Safet pointed to a green Volkswagen Jetta parked some ten metres away.

'It'll get me home, don't worry,' he said in Slovene, and smiled.

'We'd better go,' I said, extending my hand, but he opened his arms, squeezed me tightly and whispered: 'Take care of yourself.'

Then he released me, but kept his hands on my shoulders and held them there, so that he could take one more look at me, up close. As if only now he were seeing me again, after all those years.

'Be good, son,' he said, still with a smile on his face, but this time with a bitterness in his voice.

Mum offered out her hand, reaching forwards so that he wouldn't come too close. Safet placed his hand in hers, though when Mum tried to draw hers away he wouldn't let go. He stared at her with a hazy expression, the sort seen on people who have had too much to drink. And on people who are in love.

'Nice of you to come,' Mum said, and Safet nodded. He was still holding her hand.

'Who can say when we'll meet again. But the internet's a crazy thing. Everything's on there.'

As Safet let go of Mum's hand and his fingers brushed across her motionless palm for one final time, it occurred to me that she had long been owed this farewell. He looked at her older, but still beautiful, face, and slowly moved away from us. And then he stopped, one more time, and gave us one last smile.

He saw us again, but not there, in the car park of a crematorium in Zagreb, nor in that moment where we said our sombre goodbyes.

He saw us there, in the place we used to be together; Mum, him and me. Somewhere inside him, our meeting had resonated with him, and this meeting meant so much more than the one we were witnesses to.

'Safe journey,' he said, switching back to Slovene again, and went over to his green Jetta. He took one last look back at us, and then got behind the wheel.

Can you ever feel pity for a person that's happy, I wondered, as I waved goodbye to him.

'It's a good job Dane didn't come with me,' said Maya, when he'd driven away. Neither Mum nor I said anything in response.

IX

1.

The first time Anya disappeared, there were things in our flat still in boxes. It was the end of March, more than six months after we'd moved in. The guest room, which would one day become Marko's room, was still crammed with boxes, cases, and bin bags full of her things and mine, waiting to be unpacked. Amongst the piles of books, summer clothes, beach towels and photo albums, many other things lay strewn across the flat, things that would later be shoved in the basement, and taken from the basement into the garage, from the garage out to the bin, and from the bin to the dump, synchronous with the rate at which the two of us slowly, laboriously, detached ourselves from our former lives and former homes, as we unpicked the ties to our childhoods, one at a time.

This was a lengthy and difficult process for Anya especially, during which she felt both excitement and fear over our newfound freedom. She saw our flat as a tiny, rocking boat, cast a long way out to sea. It would be a romantic image one day and a terrifying one the next, and subconsciously Anya resisted the inevitable settling down. Rummaging through boxes for tracksuit bottoms or hair rollers soothed her; she liked that false impression of a temporary existence.

Months after we'd officially moved in together and spent our first night alone in a flat of our own, Anya still hadn't made up her mind about which lampshades or coffee table she'd like. We still had bare lightbulbs dangling from the ceiling, and a white plastic stool in front of the sofa where we'd put down our glasses and the remote control. The bedside table especially got on my nerves. It was lying in a box under our bed, because Anya had since decided that she wanted something in a contrasting black, to offset the white bed linen. My books, glasses, phone, everything that ought to have been on it, were therefore in a pile on the floor, rolling around under the bed and getting dusty, and patiently waiting for Anya to abandon her monochrome ambitions.

We never knew how to discuss that sort of thing. Conversations about boxes would merely lead to all our other problems and would quickly become extensions of other conversations about other topics. And whenever I complained to Anya that she was deliberately avoiding making herself at home, she responded with the accusation that I was never at home, and so I didn't know what it was like to be alone in such a big space. She kept saying that I could at least show some sympathy for the girl who never used to be left at home on her own.

This was the point at which we'd usually stop, recognising that there was a line; a line beyond which a field of discord opened up between us, which stemmed from the differences in one another's upbringing. Which is why, at this line, we'd stop talking, and wait for those wakened memories to die back down.

Anya loved to tell stories from her childhood, and I rarely spoke about mine, but we avoided the subject and above all avoided judgement. We had an unwritten non-aggression pact on touchy subjects; for her these were rooted in a feeling of completeness that she fiercely guarded, whereas for me, feeling incomplete was at the root of it all. My defects were sacred and equally untouchable. Because those defects were who I was.

Eventually I relented and let time slip past us. I stopped seeing the rooms full of boxes and missing bedside tables. I took everything as a given, as our only possible mode of coexistence and I tried to grow to love it. Every evening on the sofa, when I put my feet up on the stool and Anya would tell me that I'd need to get out of that habit before we got a proper table, I'd feel more at home in this half-finished transition of ours and I, too, quietly hoped that it would never really come to an end. As if, just like Anya, I also wanted to resist the permanency and, just like her, was afraid to fully move in together.

I wanted to believe that this was all normal. I'd never moved anywhere before, not on my own or with anyone else, everything was new to me and I thought that our anxieties were inevitable. I told myself it would all pass, trying to protect a stability that I'd wanted for so long, having felt its absence throughout my childhood. And stability, to me, was evenings spent with Anya on the sofa, her leaning against me, no noise and no one but the two of us and the night ahead. Back then I didn't know how much instability the illusion of stability could conceal.

Until Anya disappeared. I remember seeing her phone, left on the floor by the front door, and scrutinising all the days and months that we'd spent together in the flat. She's scared, I convinced myself, she's scared of us. All I wanted was for her to come back as soon as possible, to be able to give her a hug, comfort her, reassure her that our life together was worth pursuing.

I paced around the empty flat and looked at the unopened boxes filled with her belongings, waiting to be put away on shelves and in drawers, waiting to find their new places. I began to open them, at first as a way of passing the time, but then later because searching through Anya's things calmed me down. I picked out her exercise books and textbooks, mementos from the desk in her childhood bedroom which were never going to find their way out of the yellowing tape recorder box, old clothes of hers which she was never going to wear again. I touched these things as if I were using them to get closer to her, to find a way back to her.

Then I opened a box full of children's books. One by one I went through the *Famous Five* books, a rare example of books that we'd both read as children, and I pictured the two of us reading *Five Go to Smuggler's Top* on the opposite sides of town, the detailed descriptions of food making us both hungry at the same time. I put the books down by the box, then started to line them up on the empty shelves. I opened boxes and emptied them, flicking though every book and imagining a little Anya turning the cover for the first time, for the first time stepping into the magical world of Roald Dahl or William Saroyan, not hearing the voices telling her it was time for dinner, nor the knocks on the door, and her saying *Coming!* without taking her nose out of her book.

Those books are for the basement, not the shelves.

That was the first thing Anya said to me when she returned home. I said nothing, and waited for an explanation as to where she'd been, fixing my eyes on her, visibly offended, because I believed I had every right to be. I was the one who had got the fright of my life when she disappeared. But her response was *And there's the problem right there*, stepping past me and starting to toss the books back in the box.

Something about this scene wasn't right and I grabbed hold of her hand and roughly pulled her away from the bookshelf. She angrily wrestled out of my tight grip, but she didn't move away.

You know which books are supposed to go on here, and which are for the basement.

I remember Anya explaining to me how she was going to store her childhood books in the basement so they wouldn't take up space in the flat whilst there was nobody there to enjoy them. I also remember the nod, which to her signalled that I didn't care, and that she could do what she liked.

You don't care about anything.

It was true. I didn't care which books belonged on which shelves, or about the colour of my bedside table. I didn't care where the coffee and tea would go, nor which shelf the bread would live on, just as I didn't care which pictures we'd hang in the living room and which would go in the bedroom, and I didn't care how we arranged our shoes inside the wardrobe; so many things I didn't care about, but she did. But that didn't mean that I didn't care about us, I would assure her; I did care that finally it was just me and her, that finally we were together, just the two of us.

But for Anya that wasn't enough. She was hurt by my indifference, because to her, we weren't just our bodies, entwined in our new bed; for her we were also our shoes, tidied away in the wardrobe, for her we were also a tablecloth, bought specially for our flat, and matching sheets, curtains and towels. To her, we were also a letter rack, that we could use to organise our post together.

Anya had bought this oval, wicker letter rack in a fair trade shop in Ljubljana's Old Town, years before we'd even thought about moving in together, but even then it was bought with our joint place, with us, in mind.

But that day, Anya was not going to say any more about it. Nor was she going to admit that the very thing that had driven her away from me was my reluctance to tidy away our envelopes and leaflets; my reluctance towards us. Only much later would I realise that it was a pile of post, a few bills and some flyers that she'd found carelessly discarded by the cupboard, right by the letter rack, that had taken her away. The scattered electricity bills told her that I didn't care, and it was pointless trying to convince her otherwise.

I'm home, read the message Anya sent around midday. Mum, Maya and I had only just left the crematorium in Zagreb.

OK, I replied.

I wanted to say that we were cremating my grandfather and that I'd call her when we were done, but I held back. Fortunately, my desire for retaliation quickly subsided. I've outgrown that, I thought to myself, and for a second felt pleased with myself. But my *OK* was so clearly passive aggressive, that it was just another way of playing Anya's game. Our game that never ends.

That evening, as I stepped through the door, Anya was standing at the end of the hall.

'Hey.'

'Hey.'

I knew that rigid stance. But the repentance, too, could be just a game. Her face was professing too much; her eyes were too wide open.

'How are you?'

'Alright.'

We tiptoed around one another, cautiously, like small children scared of taking a step too far.

'My mum told me.'

'Yeah.'

'I'm sorry.'

'Thanks.'

I stepped past her, and walked towards Marko's room feeling her eyes on my back, and listening out for her footsteps behind me, for her approach. I stopped at the door.

'He went down about half an hour ago.'

I opened the door and walked up to Marko's bed, bent over and gently placed my lips on his clammy cheek. Then, careful not to make a sound, I sat on the floor next to his bed.

I looked at his little sleeping face and felt that, for this evening at least, there could be no more games. I sat and just listened to the barely audible sound of Marko's breathing, looked at his tiny lips opening and expelling the air that couldn't find a way out through his bunged up, snotty little nose, and watched the trails of dribble draw increasingly large puddles on the pillowcase beneath his head.

I watched him and everything felt lighter, almost featherweight. I knew I didn't want to listen to Anya's explanations or apologies that night, let alone bring up Grandad's death and Safet's appearance; I didn't want to juggle both those things in front of her. I didn't want to elicit sympathy from her like that.

I was aware that everything that had driven her away from here was patiently waiting for me, and that I wouldn't be able to escape it. But at the same time, I knew that we could coax it out tomorrow. Or the day after.

I stood up and went over to her. She understood. She rested her head on my chest. The game was over for the night.

Anya took Marko to nursery whilst I slept, then she came back and made us breakfast. A fresh baguette, sliced diagonally so that each piece was elongated; tomatoes, basil and cream cheese.

I watched her pour some yoghurt into a glass, and imagined her departure wouldn't be broached that day either, that we'd spend another day pretending that nothing had happened. There was something in the way she was moving, easily, almost sprightly. As if nothing was playing on her mind, as if it were a completely ordinary Friday morning.

Once again I had misread her.

'Aren't you going to work?'

'No, I've got another day off today,' I replied.

I could make it easier for her to start talking, I thought. I could look her in the eye, and not look away, and that would be enough. It would be enough to tell her that I'd like an explanation. But I wasn't ready yet either. I sat down at the table and started eating.

'I stopped off at the market,' she said. 'I thought I'd make vegetable lasagne today.'

Anya's vegetable lasagne was my favourite, and I smiled at her with a mouth full of tomato.

'How was it in Zagreb?'

'Interesting.'

'Really? What do you mean?'

'Safet was there.'

'What? How? How did he know?'

'It's a long story.'

Anya nodded. She didn't wish to hear long stories about Safet. Not now. She had something to tell me. The lasagne, her apparent ease, had all been a prelude.

'What's up?'

'When you send a message on your phone, you've also got a *Recently Used* function, a list of numbers that you've recently sent messages to.'

I froze at the thought of this conversation going any further. But I pretended not to understand what she was talking about. I focused on my breakfast and tried to give the impression that I was only half paying attention to her semi-coherent story.

'Yeah, and?'

Anya stopped. She was waiting for me to give in. She didn't see why she should pull out her next move, just because I refused to admit I was in checkmate.

I had deleted the exchange with Tadea, but a trace of our exchange had remained. When Anya sent a message to Jure from my phone, I'd directed her there myself. I heard myself answering her: Yeah, Recently Used numbers, here. I pointed to the list where Tadea's number was one of several.

'You're clever enough…'

'Is this why you walked out?'

'No.'

'Why then?'

'You're not going to explain to me why you deleted messages from Tadea M.?'

'I thought you'd get the wrong impression.'

'And so you deleted them?'

'Yeah.'

'And what impression was I supposed to get?'

'It doesn't matter.'

'Doesn't it?'

'I've messed up now anyway. All you can do now is take my word for it.'

'The word of someone who deletes messages to his ex?'

'She's not my ex.'

'What is she then?'

'Someone I used to have a crush on. A very long time ago.'

'Sure.'

'I can tell you what they said.'

'If you'd have wanted me to know that, you wouldn't have deleted them.'

'It wasn't like that.'

'Well I'll never know now, will I?'

On the Sunday evening, after a tense journey home from Miro and Stanka's, we were lying in bed, each of us lost in our own unspoken regret. Our minds would not rest, and the darkness around us refused to quieten down. I didn't give her a kiss before going to sleep, and our goodnight kiss spent the night on my lips. Lying next to her, I longed for us. Distance is never more painful than when it's within reach, I discovered. Anya and I had been beyond each other's reach for some time, each absorbed in our own routines and obligations, in small grudges and unresolved squabbles; her in her unemployment, and me in my powerlessness to bring her back round. I saw how it pulled us apart, I saw it here, in our bedroom, in our bathroom, in the sighs we exhaled.

Then the darkness began to whisper. Her hand moved beneath the duvet and brushed against mine, her fingertip skated along my upper arm, over my elbow and down towards my wrist, before pausing on my fingertips, as if wanting to check if they were going to respond; if they were present. The whisper resumed and her hand reached further, it moved closer to me and paused once again. I could feel her motionless fingers, five slight tingles on my thigh, the heat of her palm radiating outwards, travelling towards my stomach and down along my leg. Then her fingers came to life. It tickled, and she knew she was tickling me. She knew how my body would respond to her touch; she already knew what would happen. She took her time. It was a night unlike other nights, a night without sleep and without dread of the coming morning. Her hand gently glided down towards my groin and let me feel restless over what might follow. It drifted across my stomach, up towards my chest, and then down again, a little further than before, a little closer. She was toying with me. How long it had been, I thought, since we'd toyed with one another; how long it had been since hunger had been nothing but an innocent game. Too long, far too long. I waited for her touch, I was ready and waiting, I was nothing but desperate for her touch, but I waited. I was playing the game; a game that was both inviting me in and refusing to let me play. I wanted her warm, trembling body; I wanted layer after layer of kisses on my lips. Yet I lay still. Only my breathing became heavier, deeper; it was the only giveaway as to what was happening beneath my composure, the only evidence of her advances. And at that moment, her hand moved away, and the whisper returned, louder than before. Anya removed her clothes. I saw her naked body, hiding beneath the covers. I sensed a glint in her eye, in the dark. I followed her lead, and undressed myself; then, just like her, I lay there, completely still. Just as we'd laid there, side by side, so many times before, but now closer than ever. As if each of our bodies bore an imprint of the other. I could feel the proximity of our naked bodies, though only touching in thought, eager and playful. Yet they were careful, too, in case our hands had maybe forgotten the way along our thighs and our legs, in case our fingertips had maybe forgotten where to find the keys that play the most delicate melody of pleasure. We would be a little awkward and impatient again; we would rush and take a wrong turn, become lost.

And so we waited. We just lay there, naked and still. It was the most precious part of the night; the most precious part of all our nights. We just lay there, waiting to give in to one another. I felt the touch of our bodies, chest gliding over chest, our legs, entangled, the softness of her neck beneath my lips, her skin shuddering beneath my fingertips; I could hear her gasps, we were making love and I was inside her and everything around us disappeared, there was only the two of us lying there, in the dark, our bodies enkindling beneath the covers; our bodies which that night, were one.

I woke up just after sunrise. Anya was still asleep, and there were no sounds coming from Marko's room. I pressed my phone on the floor beneath the bed. It was six-thirty. I turned to face Anya. She was so beautiful when she was sleeping. After last night I saw her anew, more beautiful than before. I edged towards her, stopping as my lips were just above hers, pausing to let her warm breath brush over mine. Nothing could be allowed to come between us again. No job, no dismissal, no mother and no father; this is how close we had to be, so that there was no space for anyone or anything to come between us. I picked up my phone again and opened my messages. I opened the thread of messages I'd exchanged with Tadea. I read the last one that she'd sent to me. *See you soon, I hope*, it read. I deleted them all. There was nothing in them that I wanted to hide. But I no longer wanted Tadea to be a part of our lives. That morning, I wanted to delete everything that wasn't Anya and me. Anything beyond the two of us was redundant.

'But that wasn't the reason I left,' said Anya, and that was the end of the conversation about the deleted messages.

2.

On Saturday, the day of the funeral service, Anya took Marko to her parents' and then came back for me. Patiently she sat in the living room, browsing the papers, waiting for me to be ready. Normally she would be hurrying me, but not this time. She had a soothing presence about her, as if Aleksandar's death had been a source of calm for her, too; a realisation that there was already a day set aside for her, and all she could do was wait patiently for that day to arrive.

We got in the car and drove off. I insisted that I would drive, and Anya didn't stop me. When she said *I didn't think you'd be up to it*, her voice was quiet, as if reciting a prayer. Not wishing to drown out her voice, I responded at the same, subdued volume. We spoke softly and cautiously, as if the service had already begun, so as not to let the sharp edges of our voices rupture the fragile peace that had descended between us.

Somewhere between Unec and Postojna I started to tell Anya about the time we had waited for Grandad when he was coming back from Egypt. Like forgotten lines of a poem, as one memory was stirred so the next one was prompted, as if the memories were rhyming refrains.

I was ten years old and it was the first time I'd ever been to an airport. It was the first time I had seen aeroplanes taking off and landing, the first time I'd heard the deafening sounds of their engines, and the first time I'd seen how they swept up into the sky; how quickly the sound of the engines fade, and how they slowly disappeared behind the clouds.

'That was the first time you saw a plane? So how old were you when you first flew?' Anya interrupted.

'When we went to Berlin,' I replied.

'Not before that?'

'No. Why?'

'Nothing. Carry on.'

To me, the airport was a theme park. I was running around and looking for a spot where I could watch a plane from right up close, close enough to touch.

Safet was running after me. Without saying a word he dragged me into the airport café. He dragged me in such a way that my feet swept along the floor. Mum ordered me a coca-cola. She said I had to sit still with them at the table. Feeling hard done by, I stared at the ceiling, at the old, wooden plane which hung there.

That's Eda, the Rusjan brothers' plane. They were the first people to make flight in Slovenia, Safet said.

Safet and Mum were discussing whether it made more sense to tell Grandad about Grandma being in hospital at the airport, or whether they ought to wait until we got home, whilst I sulkily stared at Eda.

Thanks to them I was never going see my first proper aeroplane. Thanks to them I was never going to get on a plane, ever. I was going to hate aeroplanes. Just to spite them. And I was never going to collect anyone from an airport ever again.

Mum and Safet were ignoring me. I could hear their conversation, even though they were discussing grown-up matters.

He'll want to go straight to Pula. It's a four and a half hour drive to Pula. God knows when we'd get there. *Visiting time will have long been over, but he'll want them to let him see her.* He'll want to see a doctor, they'll say he's not there, and you'll lose it and tell all of them where to go. *Even if they let him see her, she'll be asleep by then.* And he won't want to wake her. *He'll spend three minutes looking at her and then leave.* Let him spend the night in Ljubljana and I'll take him to Pula tomorrow. *As soon as we tell him that Jana's in hospital, he's not going to stay in Ljubljana.* We can stall him. *He'll want to ring her as soon as he gets in. He's got a phone he can use here. With some woman, Daša.* Maybe she's not working today. *We're going to have to tell him everything at the airport.*

Then they sent me to look at the big screen. It said that the flight from Belgrade had landed. This did not appear to be good news.

'Vesna was afraid that Jana wouldn't recognise him,' I explained to Anya. 'Just as she hadn't recognised her.'

Doctor Milović had said to Mum that it was normal, and that Grandma's condition would likely improve, but recovery depended on her entirely, and thus he couldn't make any promises. *It's all in…* , he said, and then stopped. God's hands had escaped him.

'Everything's always in God's hands,' said Anya.

'Even the two of us now?'

'Everything.'

It's all in God's hands. Mum kept repeating the doctor's unfinished sentence. It sounded like a diagnosis for Grandma's illness and everyone anxiously nodded their heads and let out heavy sighs.

It means they don't know anything, she explained to me.

It means your grandmother's gone from one pair of crazy hands to another, said Safet.

We were stood by the doors, where people were coming through with suitcases. We waited for a tanned and smiling Grandad, happy that he was back home again; as we prepared to give him unhappy news. I was the first to spot him, but I didn't run up to him. I felt like I had to behave like an adult.

Grandad could tell immediately that something was wrong. He stopped, fixed his eyes on Mum, and waited.

It's all OK now, she said to him.

Then she burst into tears.

Mum's had a fall and she's broken her arm, but she's fine now, the doctors have said that she'll heal quickly, she's in Pula, at the hospital, I spoke to her earlier, she sends her love, she says rest up and no need to rush over, that everything's fine, that you should rest.

'That was the first time I heard Mum tell a lie,' I said to Anya.

'And?'

'I looked at Grandad and I couldn't believe that he believed her; it seemed so unlikely to me, that he could believe her, when it was so obvious that she was lying. But he nodded. He said that he'd like to call the hospital, but Mum said to him that there'd be no one there to answer, as it was out of hours – he knew what our hospitals were like, nobody picks up the phone – and that we'd all go to Pula together first thing in the morning, and that Safet had already taken the day off.'

'Isn't it fascinating, how easy it is to lie when we believe we're doing the right thing?'

I turned to Anya, hoping that she would explain what she meant.

'Go on,' was all she said.

All Grandad asked was what time it was. It was quarter-past four.

They won't let you see Jana, Mum said. *The doctor said that the best thing for her was to rest. You have to rest, too. Jana is doing well, there's no need to worry.*

Grandad wasn't paying the slightest bit of attention.

I can drive to Pula, it's no problem, said Safet.

This rather flustered Mum.

And what will we do then? It'll be evening by the time we get there. Are we then going to drive back to Ljubljana in the middle of the night? Are we going to…

Safet stopped her. There was no point in them losing time, carrying on like this. There was a long journey to Pula ahead.

We can stay in a hotel, so we don't have to come back? said Grandad.

We'd never stayed in a hotel before.

That settles it, said Safet, picking up Grandad's suitcase and heading out to the car park.

'When was the first time you first stayed in a hotel on your own?' Anya interrupted.

'I don't know. Graduation.'

When we were all in the car, Mum told Grandad the story of what happened to Grandma. 'What she didn't tell him was that Jana had decided to leave for Momjan only two days before he was due back from Egypt. She didn't tell him how much of a hurry she was in, how she was determined to go straight away, by train, on her own, how she couldn't be persuaded to stay in Ljubljana.'

'She was running away from him,' Anya said.

'Maybe she was.'

Mum told Grandad that Grandma had fancied a train ride; that she'd slipped on the train, had broken her arm when she fell, and so she'd been taken to hospital and kept in for a few days for observation. Just in case.

She kept quiet about how the doctors suspected Grandma had had a stroke, and that she lost consciousness on the train and collapsed. She kept quiet about how she flew around the hospital in a panic, looking for Doctor Milović, because her mum was no longer her mum, because her brain wasn't functioning, because she didn't even recognise her own daughter. She kept quiet about how she had to drag Maya out of the consultation room to stop her taking hold of Doctor Milović by the throat. She kept quiet about how she and Maya were yelling at one another in the hospital corridor, *Oh for God's sake Vesna, she's had a stroke, just be happy she's even alive! Just listen to yourself, Maya! Have you lost your mind as well? Have you all lost your minds?*

'Had they fallen out at that point?'

'No, that came later. Because of Safet. And Dane.'

'But all that with your Grandad?'

'It was the final straw.'

On the way there, Grandad told me stories about Egypt; about pyramids, pharaohs and camels, about the most beautiful city in the world, where the world's longest river coursed through its uncharted bounds; about a city filled with dazzling palaces and mosques, and the women inside them, who wore long, beautiful dresses that covered their feet, which made them look as if they were floating along the streets.

It was already dark outside when we arrived at the hospital, and the reception was deserted. *Come on, what are you waiting for, let's go see her*, said Grandad to Mum, heading for the stairs. *Surely they don't think I'm going to wait whilst they're on their coffee break*, he said, which prompted a loud burst of laughter from me. But I was silenced immediately by three glaring pairs of eyes.

'I think I hated hospitals from that moment onwards. Because you're not allowed to laugh. Since then I've always wondered whether the rest of the world takes as much offence to laughter as we do. Or are we the only ones who are so suspicious of people who laugh.'

'That's because here we tend to laugh at people, rather than with them,' Anya said.

Some nurses walked past us, glancing back in confusion, but didn't say anything, and we carried on our way to Grandma's room. At the door, Mum stopped, took hold of the handle, and paused. *Is she in there?* Grandad asked, and went in without waiting for an answer.

'Until the day he died, he believed that all of this was because he went to Egypt.'

Mum was the first to come out. As she closed the door behind her, I noticed that her hands had stopped shaking.

She recognised him, she whispered to us.

Grandad came out shortly afterwards. Changed. He looked at us, but immediately turned and walked away, towards the end of the corridor. Mum tried to follow him, but Safet held her back.

Leave him.

Grandad stopped and was standing just ahead of us. He stood facing the wall, and it looked as if he were about to launch himself against it at any moment. I was scared something terrible was going to happen.

'I'd never seen him cry before, before then. Nobody had. That evening might have been the first time he'd cried in his life.'

Grandad never stopped crying. He only ran out of tears.

We drove for fifteen, maybe twenty, miles in silence. Tourist season had come to an end, the roads to the coast were empty and it didn't take us long to reach Momjan. When I came off the motorway at Koper, Anya was already rummaging in her bag for her passport, as if she were looking for something to do. Then she sat with her bag and her passport ready on her lap, even though there was still at least fifteen minutes until we'd reach the border.

'Do you remember the first time we went to Momjan? When you took me to meet your grandma and grandad?"

I nodded. It wasn't something I'd easily forget. I'd driven Anya to Momjan, hoping to charm her as the doting grandson. I pictured her admiration for the way Grandad cared for his wife, who despite being sat there next to him, drinking the coffee he'd made for her, was actually no longer with him. I pictured Anya being moved by their rituals, uttering a shy word here and there; I pictured her growing fond of something that was so much a part of me, I pictured her growing fond of my second home, and the two precious elderly people inside it.

'It wasn't the right time,' said Anya.

It really wasn't. Grandad had been looking forward to our visit, though. He'd ventured to be curious, when he'd asked me about Anya, and he couldn't wait to meet her. Jadran's first proper girlfriend, he said to her, emphasising the word proper, as if it went without saying that prior to Anya I'd had a whole host of improper girlfriends. He'd chuckle childishly when he asked me about her. It amused him to think that the slobbering little boy who had tottered around his garden had a girlfriend.

But that curious, chuckling Grandad Aleksandar was not the one who was waiting for Anya and me in Momjan. Instead, the door was opened by a dour old man, who impatiently offered his hand as if we'd come to take the meter, and told us there, at the door, to take a seat. He then gathered himself for a moment and asked Anya whether she was tired after the long journey. But then he disappeared, leaving us alone in the hall.

'All those signs,' said Anya.

The house was full of them. There were two in the hall, one stuck to an electrical cupboard, another on the door. Two sheets of white A4 paper, with an arrow and "WC" written on them. They were obviously directing somebody to the toilet, but it didn't immediately occur to me who that person could be.

'I thought they were for me, did you know that?'

'You'd probably prepared yourself for all eventualities.'

In the living room, we saw Grandad sticking a sign to the cabinet door with tape. His expression intercepted my confusion, and he smiled at us, then went back to the sign. Only once it had stuck to the wooden surface did he turn back around.

Luta naokolo ko mjesečar, ko da nije u svojoj kući. Upišala mi se u špajzi, zalutala tamo i… oh, bollocks![1]

He'd forgotten about Anya, and about how she would understand his Serbo-Croatian too. But it didn't seem like his words had been aimed solely at me, either. He'd launched the words around the room, in anger or in sadness, whatever it was, and I smiled at him, wanting Anya to think it was all a joke. But everything had left Grandad exposed, and instead of smiling with me, Anya stared in dismay at the disgruntled old man who clearly saw his home as an airport filled with travellers with full bladders.

Sit down, please, Jadran, get Anya something to drink, she must be thirsty, I'll get the coffee on in a minute, Grandad said, composing himself.

'Maybe that was the day she slipped away,' said Anya.

'I reckon she slipped away every day, over and over again.'

Grandma didn't recognise me. She waited for us to introduce ourselves and tell her what we wanted from her. I wanted to give her a hug, but it startled her. Anya offered out her hand and Grandma took it, but she didn't let go. She grasped it firmly, while her eyes asked silent questions. Anya told them that she was my girlfriend, that she was pleased to meet them, that she had been looking forward to meeting her boyfriend's grandma, but Grandma's eyes only kept on searching. They were taking Anya in, and her words, but they were vacant, and then Anya went quiet. She was distressed to see this woman, hidden far behind those eyes; that body, drawing her closer and closer. It was the first time she'd even been in the presence of someone who was senile, but I stood next to her, waiting for Grandma to say something, to start looking like herself again.

It's your grandson! And his girlfriend! Say hello, they've come from Ljubljana; tell them something, you're his grandma! I heard Grandad's voice behind me, mortified.

I shan't!

---

1 *She wanders round like she's sleepwalking, as if she's not in her own home. She wet herself in the pantry, she'd wandered in there and…*

It came out of her mouth, but it wasn't her voice. Someone else was speaking, someone irritable and brusque. There was a twinkle in Grandma's eyes again, but it wasn't her own. This sulking young girl was staring furiously at Grandad, and he looked back at her with an icy stare to match.

Fine, don't then, he said curtly.

I shan't!

Stop it!

Grandma's voice was so snappy and detached, like she was trying to bite him with her words. And so it went on – he with his *Stop it!*, and her with her *Shan't!*, and he with his *Stop it!*, and her with her *Shan't!*, and *Stop it!*, and *Shan't!* and only then did it occur to me that the language they used to share was Slovene and not the Serbo-Croatian that they'd now placed between themselves, like a wall they were shouting over.

Eventually Grandad turned back to face us. He whispered so that Grandma wouldn't hear.

She's forgotten all of us, the poor thing, he said, with a voice full of pity.

'The whole house was covered in signs, there was even one on the freezer in the pantry, do you remember?' Anya asked.

I smiled at her, even though it wasn't funny.

X

I'm fine, she said.

She insisted on this several times, before asking how his journey was. It had been a smooth flight to Belgrade, he replied, but it had been a long wait at the airport there, and he'd been bored to death without any dinars to buy a paper; he wasn't very good at making conversation with strangers and wasn't keen on it anyway.

You've aged, she said.

My little buttercup, he replied.

There was something else she wanted to say, but he drew his finger to his lips.

Sleep. We can talk tomorrow, he said, leaning over and kissing her forehead.

He didn't kiss her on the lips. That was probably significant, he thought to himself, as he left the room. And it was then that it got the better of him. Outside in the corridor he was surrounded, but he couldn't go back in to Jana. He couldn't show her his tears, nor could he show us, and he walked down the corridor until he could go no further, where there was nothing more than a window looking out on to the car park. There, he cried, and we witnessed. But at least she didn't.

After her stay in hospital, Jana didn't want to go back to Ljubljana. She insisted on being taken to Momjan, even though it didn't make any sense, because neither Maya nor Mum would be able to visit during the week. The doctors were also closer in Ljubljana, and Safet or Dane could drive her to appointments. And above all, Aleksandar had to go back to Ljubljana, as he only had a fortnight's leave having returned from Egypt, and then a new post would be ready and waiting.

But Jana's mind was set. She wished to live out her ailing years far away from it all, she said. Vesna was ready to drag her to Ljubljana against her will, and even warned Safet that he was not to try and stop her. But he didn't have to, as Aleksandar did it for him. His word was final, and his word took him and Jana to Momjan, where she was to spend the next twelve years patiently awaiting her end.

Once his leave was over, Aleksandar moved into their Ljubljana apartment and was alone once again. At first he travelled to Momjan at the end of each week, often by the Thursday evening, but later his journeys became less frequent, until sometimes he would go only once a month.

The year before he retired and moved back to Jana and his own little corner of Istria, we started to see him less and less, as if he were avoiding us. He'd make an appearance at birthday celebrations, slipping in without a sound, and slipping out unnoticed. He'd smile at us kids and stroke our hair, even though by that stage we were a bit old for that.

He was in a foul mood again, Safet would usually say the following day.

He's a cloud of misery at the moment, said Vesna, *he's miserable about Egypt, about Jana, because he's here and she's there, but he doesn't want to talk about it, doesn't want to do anything.*

Not half, he needs to bloody well cheer up, said Safet.

I don't know if anyone understood the hurt that Grandad was feeling; that sense of failure that overwhelmed him, and which had even been more powerful than the longing he'd felt for Jana ever since he'd gone to Cairo. He had arrived home ready to win back her affections, but she had rejected him, pushed him away.

Which is why he was just as lonely in Ljubljana as he had been in Egypt. He would go to see her, but would return more dejected than before. The inadequacy of those few short days to fulfil his expectations, or to fill the distance forged between them by his year in Cairo, destroyed him time and again; and when, on Sunday evenings he'd drive back to Ljubljana, it would boil up inside him. He was full of anger for the first time in his life. He woke up angry and went to bed angry. He got into arguments with shopkeepers, receptionists who answered the phone, employees behind the counters, with us.

Why is that man following that woman? asked Jana, as they were sat one Sunday afternoon in front of the television set.

He turned off the television, got up and walked out. He walked and he walked, but the anger did not subside; he thought about the man who had followed the woman in the film, and tried to find a reason why someone might not understand his simple motives. But the only one he could find was not one he wished to consider. He walked and he walked, and in his fists felt the urge to punch someone, or something; he thought about whether he'd punch Mihelčič, if he saw him now, or whether he'd be capable of killing him; he became frightened by his own thoughts, and he started to tell himself that it was just life, just old age, and that the day comes when you're watching a film and suddenly you can't understand why the man is chasing the woman, but it doesn't mean anything; the both of you just need time, away from eyes, away from the heart, he muttered as he strode on; you just need to get used to one another, because you've grown used to the distance, that's all.

The following weekend, he couldn't face going to Momjan. He stayed in Ljubljana and thought about the man following the woman. He remembered how he'd recently noticed Jana reading a book, and he'd waited for her to turn the page. Her eyes had settled as if lost amongst the letters. Minutes passed, and then some more, but she didn't turn the page. And then she closed the book, gently stroked its cover and looked up at him. She seemed surprised to see him, he thought.

The previous day, they'd been in town. She didn't want to drive and insisted that he drove.

What's wrong? she asked him, when she saw the disappointment on his face.

Nothing.

I'm not scared. I just don't fancy it today, that's all.

What will you do when I'm not here?

I'll be fine.

He knew that she'd never get behind the wheel ever again.

They drove in silence. He had stopped initiating conversations, wishing that she would decide when to speak and on which topic; he wished she'd tell him how she was feeling, or what she was thinking. There were so many stories untold, and yet they kept quiet, as if both were afraid of the unknown.

Did you want to go for a walk around town? he asked, when he'd parked in front of the shop, but she shook her head.

She didn't want to run into people. She didn't want to go to the shop, either, but he'd persuaded her, pleaded with her to go with him, said that he was fed up of going on his own. He'd tried to make her to feel sorry for him, but she didn't agree to it out of pity.

Didn't you need stock cubes? he asked.

She nodded. She was standing in front of the shelf.

How about you pick some up, then?

She took a box of stock cubes off the shelf and dropped it into the basket. She let it fall aimlessly from her hand. He lost patience and started taking things off the shelves, only checking with her to make sure he'd got the right ones. She would nod and shake her head, and so they, the two mute pensioners, made their way around the shop in silence.

Is there anything we've forgotten? he asked, when the basket was full. She shrugged her shoulders and he led the way to the till.

When he saw Nevena she opened her arms out wide, and the two of them greeted one another with a hug and two kisses. It had been so long, yes; he was back now, had been for a month or so, exactly a year he'd been away; it was hot, really nice, hot though, and too long, that was the main thing. Jana heard him speak of Egypt for the first time, and he seemed glad to talk. *You can always reach a deal with the Egyptians*, he said. *You just need time, a very long time sometimes, because time is the only thing they trust, not people*, Aleksandar explained to Nevena, and even let out a laugh.

And you let him go and see those pyramids without you? said Nevena, turning to Jana.

You think I had a say in things? Jana replied.

Nevena invited them for coffee, but they said they had to be getting home.

What was her name? Aleksandar asked, as they were driving home.

Who?

The woman at the till, what's her name? I can't remember.

He knew the name of Nevena Šergo, the dentist, their old friend. But he thought it would be easier for Jana to admit that she hadn't recognised her if he pretended to not remember her name. But Jana didn't reply. All she did was turn away and allow his question to reverberate, and slowly be drowned out by the rattle of the car engine.

And then he was transported back to their Ljubljana flat, sitting alone, once again, looking at Mihelčič who was repeating word for word that the Benedejčič family could become of interest at any moment, and that any journalist would surely be interested in the story of old Benedejčič. Perhaps someone might care to know why his daughter was so fond of her father's surname, Mihelčič said again, casually; that sort of story can land someone without a pension and goodness knows what else, he said, with a smirk, and Aleksandar felt a surging desire to launch at him from across the table, to get hold of him by the neck and thrash his slimy head against the wall, to pin him down on the floor and kick him until he stopped moving, and until his filthy blood trickled out of his filthy mouth, just as it trickles in films. Then Aleksandar also caught sight of himself, sitting there frozen, opposite Mihelčič, nodding obediently and already moving to Cairo in his head; he saw himself, convincing himself that it was better this way and there was no use in fighting it; you can never win against that sort of depravity, those sorts of unconscionable people are best left to get on with it, he told himself; let them go, let them diminish themselves, let them tarnish, terrorise, ruin. In his mind he then gets to his feet and launches at him again, at the foul, rotten lowlife; he feels his fists clench and strike the face of the faceless man; he disfigures him and eventually leaves him to lie there in the crimson pool. And then the office door opens and other Mihelčič figures walk in, all as equally conniving, with the same colourless eyes; Aleksandar beat those too, he knocked them to the ground one by one, but new ones kept on coming through the door, all filled with loathing, all clothed in it, like military uniform; there were too many of them and he didn't have the strength, his punches got weaker and weaker, more and more Mihelčič figures remained on their feet.

Jana stood in the middle of the kitchen, as if someone had pressed pause in the middle of her scene. She was staring at the worktop, at the stove, and she asked the pots on the shelves to tell her what she was looking for, but everything in the kitchen held its tongue.

What are you looking for? he asked her.

I've got it, she replied.

She left the kitchen empty-handed, and never, he thought, had a lie ever hurt him as much as this one.

Next she walked in to the bedroom with the laundry basket.

What are going to do with that? he asked her.

What do you think I'm going to do with it? she said, and stood there.

He went out to the garden with her and helped her hang the washing out. He let her laugh at his lack of dexterity, at his fingers that couldn't unfurl a tight tangle of shirt sleeves. He was reassured by her laughter, he was reassured by how they pretended that everything was normal. That it was normal that she wanted to hang the washing out in the bedroom; that it could have happened to anyone.

He couldn't keep it up. He couldn't keep turning a blind eye. From every corner of the house he'd see her, standing by their bed, staring into the full basket of washing in her hands.

He rang Vesna and asked if they could meet. So Mum and I arrived at Maximarket, for a slice of cake and to meet Grandad, who greeted me with an overzealous clip round the ear. He did a bad job of hiding how he wished I hadn't been there. He didn't think I was old enough; he didn't think I should be privy to what he had to say. His eyes told Vesna to send me elsewhere. But she chose not to understand.

What did the doctors in Pula tell you?

He continued before she had chance to respond.

I don't mean about her arm, I want to know what they said about her head.

Now Mum was looking at me, I was looking at Grandad, and he no longer knew where to turn. He couldn't look at either of us.

Did anything else happen to her whilst I was away?

Nothing happened to her. Only that.

What?

The thing with her arm.

And her head?

What about her head?

Did anything else happen to it?

What do you mean?

Vesna!

What?

Please, just answer my question.

The doctor didn't say anything.

But someone said something?

The nurses mentioned a few things. But nothing was confirmed by the doctor.

What did the nurses say, Vesna?

That her fall might have been due to a small stroke, and that's why she lost consciousness. But the doctors didn't confirm it.

They didn't have to, did they.

We sat there in silence. When the waitress brought my cake, Aleksandar pinched the cherry from the dollop of cream and ate it, just like he used to when I was small. He forgot to ask whether I was eating fruit by now. Then he took hold of my hand and held it close to his chest.

I'm going to retire, he said. *I have to be with her. Someone has to be. I'm leaving next month.*

He was still clutching my hand. He lifted it up towards his face, kissed it, and let it go.

I'll go and pay, he said.

He stood up and went to the counter. He took his rectangular, leather wallet out of his inside jacket pocket, drew out a crisp banknote and placed it on the counter. From afar he still looked elegant. When he returned to the table, he bent over and kissed me on the head.

Come to Momjan, Jadran. Grandma will be pleased to see you and will make you plum dumplings.

I had a mouthful of cake, and all I could do was nod.

One month later, he made the journey to Momjan as a retired man. It was autumn, and the sky hung low. Leaden clouds were supported by the crowns of trees, and the road was damp with misty drizzle. His emotions were rendered in the landscape outside. Everything around him was sinking and he was sinking into himself. The late summertime melancholy had dragged on into autumn and hinted at an ending. It seemed as if he were driving directly towards it, every turn taking him closer, while his life was left behind in the distance. His life had already been lived. He had inhaled all there was to inhale, and a long, painful exhale was all that was left. With her, but without her. He was driving slower and slower, and his destination grew further away. He no longer had any desire to arrive, anywhere. He no longer wished to see anyone, ever. For a brief moment, he wished he could arrive in Momjan to an empty house where he could hide away. If she, his Jana, were there, maybe things would be different; but the person he was driving to see was not her anymore. He was afraid of her, because she didn't understand what he was saying when he said nothing at all. He couldn't get used to the look in her eyes, a look he couldn't read. It was the look of memory lost. How much of him had she already lost, how much more was there to lose? How much of the two of them remained behind those eyes, now, when all that they had was each other? There was nothing else, only the two of them left, her with him, and him with her. And now that was vanishing somewhere inside her too, until it would disappear completely and he and her would exist only for him. As a beautiful, sorrowful, apparition.

During his first few months in Momjan, he spent a lot of his time following her around the house; secretly, at first, but then more openly. He kept an eye on her as she changed the sheets, transplanted flower seedlings, listened to radio broadcasts, dusted, prepared lunch. He walked behind her, watched her, and missed her. He missed her and he missed them, the way they used to be. He missed her when he was standing right next to her, too, and whenever she brushed past him. Yet whenever she asked him if everything was OK, he'd reply that he was a little bored, that was all, and she reassured him that he'd get used to it.

Just as during those long Egyptian nights, he longed for her, for the image he had in his mind, so different to the image of the woman now lying in bed beside him, telling him to turn over immediately so that he didn't fall asleep on his back and snore; so different to the image of the woman who rose before him and woke him with her coughing fits; so different to the image of the woman who, instead of saying *Good morning*, informed him that the toilet flush wasn't working as it should.

He longed for her, for the woman she no longer was, and followed her around to no avail. He hoped, to no avail, that the woman he had dreamed of, lying on his sweat-soaked bed, breathing in the dusty Cairo air, would eventually turn to face him. He longed for the illusion he was looking for, here, to no avail, in his own house in Momjan.

The longing wore Aleksandar down, and his anger made him weary. He could now go for days without thinking about Mihelčič. His bloodlust had run dry and left a cavernous hollow; his thirst for revenge had subsided, and all that remained was a transitory thought. But with the stoic calm came a fear of apathy, a fear that he would never again be roused, that he would never again feel sadness or joy, that never again would he ever really be alive.

That was also why Aleksandar clung on to the flicker of longing; tended to it, stoked it, even though deep down inside, he sometimes thought it childish, the way that he crept around after her, as if hoping to steal surreptitious glances.

He liked to watch her as she made the coffee. She made it every morning, but never had he watched her so intently, and it occurred to him that he wouldn't even know how to describe her process. How many teaspoons of coffee she sprinkles into the pot, or how long she leaves the pot on the stove to simmer, he couldn't say. For fifty years they had lived together, and now he saw her for the first time, taking the coffee jar from the shelf; he saw how she waited, spoon at the ready, for bubbles to appear in the water, how she took the pot off the flame and emptied some of the water into a cup, then stirred two heaped teaspoons of coffee into the water, before placing the pot back on the flame and then turning it off just at the right moment before the coffee boiled over; how she scraped the remains of the coffee grounds from the rim of the pot, and how they fell into the thick, dark liquid, thickening it further again.

What are you doing here? she asked.

Watching you, he replied.

Watching how I make the coffee?

Yes.

Are you scared I don't know how to make coffee anymore? That it's something else I've forgotten?

Something. Else. I've. Forgotten. Four words thundered around the room, like four giant boulders swinging against condemned walls. She had never made reference to her memory before. For the first time it was acknowledged. *Something else,* she'd said, and he caught a glimpse of the abyss. But he didn't have the courage to lean in and gaze into its depths.

She picked up the coffee pot and took it into the opposite room. He took the tray with the cups and the sugar cubes, and followed her in. Yet it wasn't like when he followed her before; they walked together this time, as if he'd finally managed to join her in moving about the house, in sharing the burden of her departure.

As he watched her pour the water from the cup into the coffee pot, taking care to ensure that the coffee did not spill over the sides, he realised that he had to let his illusion go. His Jana was here, right in front of him. Once again she stirred the coffee in the pot, skimming the creamy layer from the surface and sharing it between them, one spoon per cup, and a little more in one, then the other, each the same. It was her, and it was the two of them in the room. They were drinking coffee, each the same, down to the final grounds.

You haven't told me anything about Egypt, about how you found it, she said.

He wasn't ready to talk about Egypt. One year on, and he still didn't know what to say. He picked up his coffee cup, and drew the hot, black surface to his lips until they gently came into contact. He let the aroma reach his nose, and allowed a few droplets to moisten the tip of his tongue.

He was yet to tell anyone a single thing about Egypt. Fairytales of pyramids and camels were all that he had told. Those imagined little stories would have been fine yesterday, but today, everything was different. *Something else I've forgotten* she'd said, and everything changed. And so he slurped a sip of coffee, and said *It was awful*.

She wasn't surprised. She dipped a sugar cube into her coffee, and then placed it on her lips as if to kiss it. She let the coffee-soaked sweetness seep into her mouth, glide around it, before sucking more of the bitter black liquid from the cube.

Well I knew that much, she said. *You? And Egypt? Do me a favour! I'm not sure what you were thinking. And at that time, too. It's hard for you to get used to new underpants, yet you thought you'd get used to living in Egypt. But it serves you right, you dragged yourself there.*

She was back again, and once again she knew him better than he knew himself. And again he was without secrets, that had never been secret after all. If anyone else were to have said the same he'd have punched them, but her words made him happy; they comforted him.

He wanted to tell her a funny story, and he remembered a story that he never thought he'd tell a single soul.

In Cairo, I lived by one of the smaller mosques – everyone in Cairo lives near a mosque – but I passed this one every morning on my way to work, and

I'd look at it, on the sly: gawping at people in a mosque didn't seem appropriate, but I couldn't help but look; all those men praying on their knees, so different to here, even different to Bosnia – similar, but not the same. And each day I'd walk past even slower, and I started to feel this need to go inside; I didn't know if I was allowed, I felt awkward asking, it seemed like something I ought to know, and that asking if I could go into a mosque would make me look stupid, but something was telling me to go in, I was scared though, because I wasn't a Muslim; I thought they'd stare at me, but then again, anyone can go into a church, and all I wanted was to go in as a tourist, have a little look around, that's all. One morning, it looked to be quiet inside; from the street, the courtyard looked empty and I went in – just a couple of steps, I told myself – just to see what it looks like from the inside, seeing as I lived around the corner and heard the call to prayer every morning; in I went, feeling uncomfortable being there, somewhere I shouldn't be, and at that moment I hear someone behind me, I turn around and see a man coming towards me, saying something in Arabic, he was talking to me, and I was backing away, afraid, and because I didn't know what to say to him, I started parroting "Tito, Yugoslavia, Tito, Yugoslavia," – can you imagine? Me, Tito? But he gave me such a fright, I was scared he'd think I was some American agent; he took me by surprise, but he just went on talking and beckoned for me to follow him, while I was carrying on with the "Tito, Yugoslavia"… he seemed cross with me, like I was about to be chastised, I was shaking, I followed him across the courtyard where an old guy was sitting, I said "Tito, Yugoslavia" to him as well, and he just smiled and asked if I spoke English, and I said I did, and then he asked me if I'd like to see the prayer hall, and so he led the way, there were a few people in there, then he offered out his hand and thanked me for my visit, and I left, and at the doors I met that first, younger, guy, who nodded and said "Tito, Yugoslavia." I was so embarrassed that I never went past that mosque again, I always took the longer route to work after that.

From that morning onwards, there was no longer a Jana he was missing. His Jana was in each unfinished sentence, every trailing thought, every long-forgotten answer to a question, every one of her *who* and *when* and *wheres*, each forgotten name, every wandering stare, each rediscovery; all of this was now his Jana.

Yet he was still unsure as to how to join her in this withdrawal from life, and he remained her silent admirer. When she made the morning coffee, he'd be standing at the kitchen door. When she pottered around the garden before lunch, he wouldn't leave the window; when she watched television in the afternoon, he'd sit nearby and watch her. Only when Jana read books did he relent. He loved to go to the library and bring her novels both short and hefty, though he didn't have the patience for them himself. When she was reading, he'd relocate to the other end of the house, so as not to disturb her.

He still struggled to fill his time, and started to break it down into tiny sections. Into time for drinking coffee, time for browsing newspapers, time for a walk into town, time for listening to the radio. Yet his time was reluctant to disappear, and he was left with whole hours unspent.

That was when he'd wander around the garden. He'd forge footprints in the moist ground and then step back into them, carefully, as if they were leading the way; he observed how the trampled shoots returned to upright, and counted how many times he had to walk over them before they'd lie down; he watched how moisture was absorbed into the toes of his shoes, and how the water marks grew in size.

Sometimes he would sit beneath the fig tree and notice the mist forming in the valley below. Neither the natural beauty nor the solitude were things he knew how to enjoy, but because he didn't want to disturb Jana whilst she was reading, he sat there in silence, waiting until she finished her chapter; until she came to him and summarised the story in a couple of sentences, simplified for him, a man who wasn't fond of a long, complex narrative.

Jana's summaries became increasingly disjointed, and characters slowly lost their names, becoming merely *this one* and *that one*. But Aleksandar gave her his full attention. When she sat herself down beside him, she would take his hand in hers and he would listen to the sound of her voice, and hope that she would never run out of words.

One day she stopped short in the middle of a story, and gazed up to the top of the tree they were sitting under.

You could prune the fig tree, she said to him.

The garden and the courtyard were her domain. He merely helped her now and again, when she required the extra strength.

You've time on your hands now. Pruning a fig tree is easy, anyone can do it; you just need the time and the inclination.

She had decided – perhaps in that very moment and without prior consideration – to hand the tree over to him.

It's too late now, you can start first thing tomorrow, she said, pointing to the secateurs on the windowsill.

She also demonstrated how to cut the branches with them.

Those grey trousers must be somewhere, the ones Maya bought you in Pula, the ones you tore the seam on. I kept those back for just this sort of thing.

He didn't tell her that he tore those trousers leaning in through the window of their old Škoda when he couldn't open the door. He didn't tell her that this was nearly twenty years ago.

That evening, he spent a bit of time looking for them in the wardrobe and drawers, before telling her that he couldn't find them, and that he'd try again in the morning, in better light.

He was awake before she was. Day was only just breaking, but he got up, showered and dressed in the clothes laid out for his day's work.

What are you doing? came the voice from the bedroom.

Getting ready for pruning.

Wait for them to dry out a bit. It's still too wet at the moment.

Dry branches can be cut through more easily, he thought. But he couldn't wait any longer.

Go back to sleep, he said to her, and went outside.

He stood before the tree, counted the surplus side shoots on its branches and made a mental note. Day was yet to break under the shade of the fig leaves, and in the dark heights, where branches wound their way out of sight, his counting came to a halt.

He brought the ladder from the garage and positioned it against the trunk. He was amused by the sight of himself. An old man climbing a tree. He didn't need to do this, but nevertheless he stepped on to the first rung. It was unsteady, and as he clasped both hands around the first substantial branch, he gasped a sigh of relief, as if he'd made it. He drew the secateurs from his pocket and took hold of a branch to be pruned. It wasn't as easy as Jana had made it look the previous evening. The damp wood warped and bent beneath the blade. As he leant further forwards to get a better grip of the branch, the ladder teetered to such an extent that he was almost sent tumbling down into the depths below.

He was too old for this, and too awkward, and angry at himself for allowing her to talk him into it. Yet he couldn't stop. He pictured her disappointment, and made another cut into the branch, this time with gusto, with more force. It snapped clean. The first branch was pruned. Not so difficult, he said to himself, and he took hold of another branch, also compliant, and before he knew it he was holding a third, and then a fourth, in his hand.

Getting there, getting there, he said to himself, though by this point he was short of breath and could feel a painful throb in his hands. There was another crack, and then he climbed higher.

He first felt the itching on his palms. He thought something had bitten him, but it rapidly spread over his body: between his legs, to his back and all over his stomach, so that he didn't know where to scratch first. As if he'd been doused in itching powder.

He made one more attempt at cutting through a branch, but he couldn't take any more. He flew down the ladder like a man of half his age, taking no notice of how it trembled beneath his feet. He ran across the garden into the house, straight to the bathroom, where he tore off his clothes and jumped straight into the bath. He poured cold water over his body and scratched wildly at his skin until the itching began to subside.

I forgot to say – you'll need to wear gloves, she said.

She picked his clothes up off the floor and placed them on top of the washing machine.

She forgot. She forgot to tell him about this crucial distinction between pruning fig trees and pruning others, like apple trees, or vines. She had forgotten. And now she was standing before him, staring right at his naked body covered in scratches, and he had nowhere to hide.

I'm going to forget to go to the library today, he said.

He hurried out, but he couldn't get past her without risking a brush of naked flesh. He stopped about a metre in front of her. His clothes were folded behind her, and there were no towels on the rail that he could use to cover himself. Jana, meanwhile, didn't avert her eyes. She stared with interest at his reddened skin and the bloody traces of savage fingernails.

He felt exposed, as if he were standing in the middle of the town square. The fact that she, his wife, was the only person looking at him, was of no comfort whatsoever. Years had gone by since she had last seen him undressed; years during which his whole body had changed, years that had changed the both of them, and it was like being naked in front of her for the very first time.

Could you turn around? he eventually stuttered, feebly. He covered his crotch with one hand, wrapped his other arm across his chest, and hurried past her into the bedroom.

He slammed the door behind him as hard as he could. He wanted to lock it, but the key was no longer there. He was still wet, water was dripping from his body on to the bedroom floor. He wrapped himself in the sheets and sat down on the bed.

He was afraid she was going to come in after him. He was conscious of his naked body not being entirely shielded by the sheets, and was relieved to hear her go outside. As he caught a glimpse of her through the window, walking across the garden, he stood up and got dressed, before sitting back down on the bed. It was a pleasant feeling, being there, behind closed doors, in an empty house. The layers of material in which he'd hastily clothed his body slowly subdued his sense of exposure.

I didn't mean what I said about the library, he said, when he met her out in the garden.

I'm going to take myself today. I think the walk will do me good. You put the idea in my head.

She was ready to leave.

As you wish.

When she'd gone, he carried on with the pruning, wearing gloves and a long-sleeved top. The itching had stopped, and once the fig tree had been pruned, he sat on a thick branch, high above the ground. He loitered there, in defiance of a world that believed older generations belonged on the benches beneath trees, not on the branches of them.

He wished she were home by now, to see him there in the treetop, old legs dangling. He could never be too old to stop seeking her affections, he thought to himself. And he persisted on the branch, even though his bony bottom was starting to get sore, and his well-worn joints began to make themselves known.

As he made his way down the ladder with caution, evening was already drawing in. It was only then that it occurred to him that Jana was not yet back from the library, and it must have been hours since she left the house. In his mind he pictured her leaving with the sun high in the sky, which must have been three hours earlier at least.

He called the library, but nobody answered. It was nearly eight o'clock and the library was closed. But perhaps there was a cleaner there still; their work began when the others went home, he thought, and he rang again. This time he let the phone ring out even longer, but to no avail.

He could have called the police, but they probably wouldn't have taken him seriously. In his mind he heard the words of the officer on duty: *As long as the lady is in good health, you've no cause for concern, sir.*

He stepped outside, crossed the courtyard to the front gates and peered down the road in the hope that Jana's silhouette might emerge out of the darkness.

The evening air had turned fresh; she's cold and she'll come home, she's just bumped into someone, that's all, she had a chat, stopped for a coffee; she misses contact with other people, she's cooped up inside too often; perhaps there was a reading at the library and she stayed to listen.

It was all plausible, yet all he saw was Jana teetering down a narrow path through the maquis, growing all around her; Jana, with eyes that didn't see, fleeing, terrified, through the monotone Istrian shrubland, searching for a way out.

He was still looking out towards Buje, but he could see no further than Gini's house. And the only sound he could hear was his heartbeat. He closed the gates and walked down the street, straight into the dark.

An image appeared before him in the darkness, of the hallway in their apartment in Ljubljana. Standing in his grey trench coat, through the living room doorway he could see Jana with baby Miha, grandma and nephew, just a few months old. She was lifting up his little legs, opening her mouth, and the tiny little toes disappeared inside.

I'm going to gobble you up! I am! I'm going to gobble you up!

Maya was having a lie down in the bedroom and flicking through Burda magazine, enjoying a short breather from maternal responsibilities. Without removing his shoes, he walked through to see her, and sat down on the edge of the bed. He placed his briefcase on the floor between his feet. Maya didn't look up. He couldn't see Jana or Miha from where he was sitting; he could only hear her mimicry of his incomprehensible babbles.

Standing between him and his wife were members of the board of directors, an unpleasant array of blinkered geriatrics who were about to decide, tomorrow afternoon, on his departure for Egypt. Wedged between them were their bald heads, heads that whispered instructions and recommendations from up high, and summoned names never uttered out loud. Months of meetings, sessions and appointments had spread out between them; months of telephone calls, disagreements, agreements, extortions and threats, months of stories kept secret, all of which he carried home with him each day, and took back with him the following morning.

Everything was already decided and all he could tell her was that he was leaving. She didn't suspect a thing.

Where's Grandma's bottom? Is that Grandma's bottom? Is it, Miha?

What he planned on telling her didn't make any sense; because nobody really sends anyone off to Egypt overnight. Nobody accepts that. Nobody is without choice; nobody comes home one evening and says *I'm off*.

He sat beside Maya, who was engrossed in images of young women in beautiful clothes, and he wondered whether maybe it would be better to just leave. Without a word, without excuses.

It had been some time since he'd walked the road from Momjan to Buje, and it was hard to judge his proximity to the town. In the darkness it was hard to recognise the curves and turns of a path that his feet had taken so many times before. He no longer recognised anything.

Maybe he'd become lost himself, but he didn't care. He felt shame for letting himself be driven away from her; shame, because back then not only did he give in to threats from Mihelčič, but to his own desire for freedom, for an escape.

That freedom was now so terrifying to him that it caused him pain. It was real, physical pain – in his muscles, bones, and skin. His body itself was an unbearable pain, moving about the town, desperately fumbling in the dark for a familiar shadow.

Eventually he recognised her, even though he couldn't see a thing. He knew the sound of her footsteps and ran towards her, like a lost child running towards its mother. As if she had been the one to lose him, and not the other way round. With both hands he began to clutch her body, so as to convince himself that it really was her, that she was not just a hallucination; that he had been found, that he was saved. That he had been found.

That evening, as they were lying in bed, he felt drawn to her. He gently placed a hand on her back. He hoped that she was asleep, and would be unaware of his juvenile desire, that she wouldn't feel his tightening grip. He moved closer, and pressed his body against hers. There was a stirring of desire. A gentle pressure against her thigh. He wanted to move back before she became aware of his lust, but something stopped him. Fear was still ringing loudly in his ears. He had betrayed her, and he was clutching his body to hers, seeking her forgiveness.

Her hand moved and sought the hem of his pyjama shirt; her fingers slid underneath and touched his skin. Slowly they crept across his untamed chest. He closed his eyes, but immediately opened them again. He wanted to see her wrinkles, her grey, thinned hair and her age spots. He didn't want to embellish her with images from memory. He wanted to feel the coarseness of her trembling palms, and to stare deeply into her weathered face, which seemed more beautiful to him than ever before.

Go to sleep, she said, and he drifted off, head on her bony chest.

Fear brought him closer to her. So tight was the grip of fear in her presence that he would vanish completely, and only two of them would remain. His Jana, and his fear for her. Her eyes had always been the first to open, but now the fear woke him first. He'd get up to make coffee before sunrise, make sure the stove was stacked with firewood, go out to the shop, come back with fresh bread and newspapers, and then would peek at her over the top of his newspaper, as she wandered, bleary-eyed, around their home.

When he read that Mateja Svet was retiring from skiing at the age of twenty-two, he tried to ascertain whether her footsteps were more frail than the previous day, or whether they were just the same as today, when the paper said that Slovenia was to hold a referendum on independence. Grand newspaper headlines no longer held much meaning. At the outbreak of the Gulf War, she walked with a strange stoop in the morning. On the day Nelson Mandela was released from prison, she had an itch on her right thigh, and stopped to scratch it. When Gorbachev became President of the Soviet Union, she let out a discreet gust of wind on her way to the bathroom.

Then they would drink coffee and do their exercises. He asked the questions and she would answer. The brain needs to be active too, he explained. He had read about it in the newspaper; about how older people must fight against memory loss by doing regular mental exercises, by solving mathematical puzzles, recalling memories in detail, or reading books. She said it was a load of rubbish, like most of what was written in the papers; yet he said that it would not do her any harm, and carried on: What was the name of Tito's dog? Luks. Who's the presenter on *Give and Take*? How does the farmer cross the river with a wolf, goat and a cabbage?

The morning came when she did not respond, and he was unsure whether this was because she didn't know the answer, or whether it was all too humiliating for her. Perhaps it was a rejection of his overbearing, fatherly concern. Perhaps she sensed that their relationship had changed irrevocably and that they were no longer equals. He suspected this was unavoidable, but he forced it out of his mind, and pretended that everything he did was done at her unspoken behest.

One morning, she told him that he could do with putting a jumper on, now that summer had come to an end. That morning he was happy. He was happier still when she reminded him that he'd forgotten to call the electrician to come and look at the boiler. The care between them was mutual, it seemed. They were together at this stage of life, which was slowly erasing them both. Perhaps she was just slightly ahead in her ageing process, and by tomorrow they'd be just as helpless as each other, and all would be right again.

But then her vacant stare returned, and she couldn't remember the names of three Slovene skiers. She could list three Yugoslav national heroes: Moša Pijade, Ivo-Lola Ribar and Franc Rozman-Stane were all still there; but Bojan Križaj, Rok Petrovič and Boris Strel had gone astray.

Then she stopped recognising faces on the evening news. She was tired in the evenings, and had no wish to name those who were making history and chalking lines across roads and squares, through gardens and bedrooms.

I know who that is, she said to him, turning away. It was of no interest to her that the country was collapsing, because that was beyond her comprehension. And what she didn't understand didn't interest her. The present became increasingly demanding, and one evening she got up, said that she couldn't watch any more of it, and left the present behind.

Her world no longer extended beyond the walls of their house, and Aleksandar was left alone with the impending times, with a sense of dread; alone with everything that was happening on the outside.

Maya and Dane arrived unannounced. They came alone, without the children. Maya said that they had come to tell them something, and she then gave the floor to Dane. Slovenia was going to secede, and there would be ramifications, he said. They had to prepare for the worst. If they stayed in Momjan, they would soon be living in a different country.

Aleksandar was born in Novi Sad, he said, which was in the Republic of Serbia. If the worst were to happen, this could be an issue. Everything could be an issue. Setting up a new country did not come with a handbook, and nobody knew how things would pan out. It would be best if they could move to Ljubljana for a while, set up a permanent residence there, and Aleksandar could get Slovene citizenship. It's not every day of the week that a country collapses, and they had to be clever about things, Dane said.

Aleksandar wasn't listening to him. He was looking at Jana.

I'm not going anywhere, she said.

We're not going anywhere. She can't cope with any more moving. And neither can I.

Aleksandar's sole duty was to keep her in that house, the house which constituted her entire world. But neither at that point, nor later, did he feel obliged to explain what that house, or what those walls, meant to them. He didn't feel obliged to explain that there was no longer anything for them beyond those walls; that the world was just a view through their window.

We'll come when the bombs start dropping, he said.

When the bombs start dropping it will be too late, said Dane.

I'm sure the first one isn't going to fall on our house, Aleksandar said.

As Maya and Dane drove away, Aleksandar closed the gates and went back to Jana. Everything was calm and still again, just as before the visit.

When Vesna rang and told him that Safet had left for Bosnia, all he asked was that she didn't say anything about it to her mum. He sounded like a madman and he knew it, but he had to protect Jana from everything that he'd failed to protect her from in their previous life; everything that had caused her to be so vulnerable now.

It was a guilty conscience, and it was complete devotion to a loved one. Aleksandar built a wall around her, and after all those years of having to share her with everyone and everything, he monopolized her. This monopoly was his concluding act of love, its peak, which bordered on insanity.

Naturally, Vesna could not understand this. She put the phone down and never called again.

And so everything around them faded into obscurity. Alone they remained, as if only existing for one another. It was a lie; his great act of self-deception, but it was so appealing that he endeavoured to preserve it. He'd convince himself, every day, that those eyes of hers, which no longer saw anything but him, were not merely an illusion. He believed, he wanted to believe, that what he had missed for so long was still alive. He convinced himself that he was happy, and for a moment, for one brief moment, perhaps he really was.

Yet when the hum of the outside world had subsided entirely, and when everything, and everyone, had stopped trying to force its way in; when it seemed as if everyone had withdrawn, it was then that she started to forget it.

We've never been to Florence, she said resolutely, without the slightest shadow of a doubt.

He nodded. He stared at her in silence, and wondered how much of them was left, how much of him was still there, if at all, behind her empty eyes, if Florence of all places, had now gone. Florence, the city in which she had taken him, her greying love, by the hand; Florence, the city in which they were, for a few days, girlfriend and boyfriend again. Now that grey-haired boyfriend and girlfriend were no more, those trattorias had vanished, as had the tables shared with an American couple, elbows and knees squeezed together; there was no more wine into the early hours of the morning, no more eyes down as they stepped out into the hotel corridor in the morning, in shame, for having behaved like besotted teenagers who could be heard from the neighbouring room, and at their age, too; their Florence was no more.

From the vanishing memories came jealousy. He was jealous of those who lived on in her memory; he was jealous of the dead, the distant, the unknown. No matter who she mentioned, even if nameless, even if only a hint of a person, it caused him pain. The slightest shadow of her memory carried a sting.

What was the name of that neighbour from Rozmanova, that tall man who worked at the Geodetic Institute and whose wife died in a car crash? she asked, but he had no desire to recall any neighbour from Rozmanova Street. He was jealous of the gangly surveyor that remained, while he, who played her *Watch Out Doggy* on the guitar, had vanished.

He was being pursued by people from Jana's memory. Vesna's schoolteacher tapped on the stovetop and said that Vesna was too headstrong, and that this was a barrier to learning; Maya's first boyfriend was rummaging through their fridge in his underpants in the middle of the night; Jana's cousin from Germany peed in the bidet; whilst in the evenings, the old housekeeper would take a stroll around the courtyard, listing imaginary problems and pestering to be let inside.

Their magical moment of seclusion had come to an end. Beside them, between them, they were surrounded by phantoms, and Aleksandar was just another person she ran to for food or warmth. And in her memory, he was vanishing into a vanishing crowd.

Next to disappear was their Škoda. The old, light blue Škoda they'd been driving for twenty-two years. The Škoda that took them to their first Pula Film Festival, and in which they then slept, in the woods at Lungomare. The Škoda whose boot was used by Mum to smuggle in my first bike from

Trieste, and which ground to a halt in the middle of the night outside Postojna, where the Škoda bid farewell to its motoring soul.

When Jana said *I've never been in a Škoda*, it vanished along with all of their journeys from Ljubljana to Momjan, journeys to the Plitvice lakes, Brač, Ohrid and Budapest. All the arguments that took place in that car, on the way to and from work, so that their two young girls wouldn't hear: gone. Summer picnics on the beach, the Škoda full of parasols, deckchairs and tomato salad: gone. The smell of leather seats overheating, and the buzz of imprisoned wasps colliding against the rear windscreen: gone.

Then their old television disappeared, the television that had counted down the seconds to many a New Year, that had shown Vesna and Maya their first cartoons, and which Aleksandar so dearly loved to argue with in the evenings. It had once toppled over and fell on to little Maya, who was playing underneath it. Aleksandar had already taken it in for countless repairs, but after that incident he took it, still in working order, straight to the tip.

And then the cat disappeared, the one Vesna brought home with her one day, which they were forced to adopt, along with its ridiculous name. When he said the name *Jagger* to Jana, it didn't rouse any sort of response. She'd forgotten how it used to go astray, how she would wander around the village shouting *Jagger! Jagger!* At first Aleksandar would go after her, trying to convince her that a cat would not come running, like a dog, but by the end he'd started to shout with her, until they got stopped by a policeman, who issued them a fine because it was half past two in the morning, and the two of them were getting louder and louder.

He continued to buy a newspaper every morning, but now with a different currency, with Croatian kuna. There he read that shots had been fired at protestors in Sarajevo; that the war was spreading across Bosnia and Herzegovina.

Do you remember our visit to Sarajevo, to see Muniba? he asked her.

She shook her head, and Sarajevo was gone. The small room in Muniba's apartment in Grbavica; the trip to Jahorina; and her husband Ekrem, who after they'd got back would not let them go to bed hungry, and sliced them some cured meats and poured them a rakia. *U mojoj kući se ne ide gladan u krevet*[2], he said to them, continuing to slice and pour.

All of it disappeared when she shook her head, along with the old bazaar and the Miljacka river and the Gazi Husrev-beg Mosque; and everything that the papers said about Sarajevo was said in vain. They had never strolled, in each other's arms, along that long avenue to the spring of the river Bosna.

Jana says that she knows she's been to Dubrovnik, but he can see that her head is empty of images. For a moment, he thinks about showing her some photographs, of them standing with their arms around one another by the ancient ramparts; of her, looking so elegant, with a black sunhat and sunglasses; him, looking a bit daft in a tight-fitting nautical t-shirt. She couldn't have forgotten those photographs.

But he gives up. He reconciles himself with the fact that Dubrovnik is now gone. Now the bombs fall on the town, so the paper says, but there is no town, because Comrade Đorđević and his wife, who didn't register at the Hotel Lapad, were never there. Because Comrade Đorđević was never on a business trip to Dubrovnik; because he'd never walked along the Stradun and bathed in the warm May waters, together with his unregistered companion.

Jana remembers Zadar. She remembers the ferry and the choppy sea, the first nights on Ugljan Island, when Maya and Vesna sneaked out of their rooms and went for a midnight dip. She remembers their empty room, and she remembers the panic, and him, screaming that his children had been kidnapped.

---

2 *Nobody goes to bed hungry in my house.*

Zadar is still there, and they are saddened when they hear that it was hit by more than thirty shells overnight. Aleksandar reads what is written about Zadar to her aloud, and then both of them sit in silence. Concerned for their Zadar, where today they're waiting for the ferry to the island of Ugljan.

The following morning there's no more Zadar in the paper, but there's Gospić, though there is no Gospić, because she doesn't remember that they stopped there with Vesna, Safet and Jadran on the way to Plitvice. There was no use explaining that they stopped there because of Safet and inflation; that Safet cashed in some cheques at a bank in Gospić which would take so long to reach Slovenia that they'd be worthless by the time they eventually arrived, as inflation was too high for the cheques to survive the long journey.

Do you remember Safet, Jana? he asks her.

It's hard for him to erase Safet. Erasing Gospić was easy; but Safet, he cannot. Safet is not an afternoon stop-off on the way to Plitvice. So many memories of theirs bear the name Safet; the birth of their grandson, their daughter's wedding. Safet cannot simply be erased. There's too much of him. Too much.

The mechanisms of memory are impossible to disentangle, for they operate without working order, choosing their victims at random, as if choosing lottery balls, eyes closed, from a giant vessel. To her, all memories are of equal worth, and whilst some are left untouched, others corrode, unrelentingly. Until now, all of this had been all too familiar to Aleksandar, and was something he had come to terms with; but he could not let Safet go.

He called Vesna and asked what was going on with Safet. Vesna said nothing. The person on the end of the phone did not sound like the Aleksandar she left behind in Momjan. She had been phoned by her father, a man she had not spoken to for years.

They've driven Safet out, driven him into a warzone, they've chucked him over the fence like a stray dog, they don't care that he's got nowhere to go, that there's a war on, that they'll probably kill him, if they haven't done already...

After the tears came a fitful sob, which Aleksandar didn't dare interrupt. The world had returned to his home. Vesna's tears had burst every one of his doors wide open, forming a hurricane that was mixing their interior life with the world outside. Safet was back to being his son-in-law, and Vesna was his daughter again. But all around the house, outside, there was war.

All he said was *Vesna*, and was then at a loss. His arms tried to hug the voice that was coming out of the receiver. It looked as if he were suspended there, his entire body, in a moment forever frozen in time.

Come over. Come here, bring Jadran, he said.

Yes, she said. Barely audibly, unconvincingly. And then she hung up.

He could still hear the sound of her sobbing, which crashed down on him like a wave against the rocks.

He sat down by Jana and started to talk to her about Safet. He chattered hastily and without a pause, each time hoping that his next word might be a candle in her memory's darkness. He talked about how he first met Safet; about the resale of the stolen beds, about the wily Bosnian lad who had this likeable quirkiness about him. Others were thieves, cheats, bad guys; others were only in it for the dinars, but Safet was just playing a game. It's why he took such a shine to this lad, he told her; it's why he didn't see him off like those other hopeless cases of Vesna's; because it seemed to him that Vesna was the perfect retribution; because he was amused by how fate had brought them together. *Fate is the biggest prankster of all*, he said to her.

To the very last detail, Aleksandar described Safet and Vesna's wedding and honeymoon, from which they returned in a brand new car, the origins of which were to forever remain a mystery. He told Jana of the hysteria that set in when Safet became father to a baby boy; how he'd wanted to be the opposite of his own strict father, and how Vesna would lecture him on the importance of not spoiling a child; how he would retort with his nose out of joint, and say: *Oh don't be such a Slovene*. He told her about how the pair of them seemed so immature at the time, as if parenthood were just another of their games; she, trying to preserve some sort of order at every turn, while he would deliberately destroy it; every day he'd buy Jadran a chocolate hedgehog just before lunch, he'd let him watch television way beyond his bedtime, and Jadran was already sitting in the front seat when they came to take Aleksandar to the airport, the time he left for Egypt.

Aleksandar's story of Safet stopped here.

Do you remember me leaving for Egypt?

For a brief moment, he fell in love with her capacity to forget. For a brief moment, he was grateful for it. What had weighed him down for years and years was now gone. Jana shook her head, and his departure for Egypt had vanished. Happy memories were all they were left with. A great number of happy memories. That's the magic of their love, he thought. It has lasted so many years, that many more could vanish before they'd eventually be left with nothing.

But then Vesna's voice came back to him. He heard her saying how they would probably kill Safet, if they hadn't done so already. He was back to being a father, while she was sat there beside him, not knowing what to do with the story of Safet, already disintegrating, no longer coherent, no longer logical.

He called Vesna again. Again he asked her to come to Momjan, and once again she said *Yes*, barely audibly, and just as unconvincingly as before.

Then he made dinner, and whilst they were eating, he told Jana about Vesna and Jadran, about how alike they were sometimes, about how much he reminds him of her, when she was small.

He suddenly stopped, alarmed.

Jana, do you remember Jadran?

She looked him straight in the eye.

How could I forget my grandson?

He heard the hurt in her voice. A grandmother's hurt. He kissed her eyelids, as if soothing a child to sleep.

XI

At the cemetery, even thoughts did not speak. Our silence was a profound silence, without resonance; as if the ringing of our footsteps, coughs and whispers were muted beneath the rustling treetops, like a child creeping beneath a duvet. We stood in line before Aleksandar's urn: Mum and Maya, Špela and I, and Dane and Anya. We stared blankly ahead, and only occasionally did a hand rest on a neighbouring shoulder, or tenderly touch the nearest back; a silent reminder of its presence.

We were approached by a small number of souls, who offered their hands and whispered their condolences. They were most likely neighbours and local acquaintances; unfamiliar faces shrouded in black, who vanished as quickly as they appeared. And the silence descended again, and our glances dispersed over the still terrain. It was so peaceful, as if the wind did not wish to disturb the branches of trees in the valley.

We stood in our positions for some time, without so much as a shuffle or a glance towards the entrance, where others might have appeared. Patiently we waited, without knowing what we were waiting for. There would be no funeral service. Grandad had not allowed us to indulge in such orchestrated sadness. He had even denied us music, and the tears we fought back were left without a tune. We had nothing to tear us away from him, nothing to finally prise us from his grip.

We sensed we ought not to speak, as every spoken word would have constituted an act of ceremony, which would have contradicted the dying wishes of the dead. Wishes that were dutifully obeyed by our silence. The silence might not have made much sense, but what place did sense have, here, amid the cypress trees, in this place; a place not renowned for a prevalence of sense. In its absence, silence was the only sensible response.

Nor did anyone know how long we ought to stand there, in the fragrant Istrian frost, which was nestling in around us.

It seemed that the gentleman in gloves, who was supposed to carry the urn to the grave, didn't know either. He was waiting for our signal, casting subtle glances at Mum and Maya, awaiting permission to move. But neither of them noticed him. They were somewhere else entirely.

I tried to picture Grandad, but I couldn't. I wished he would appear before me; I wanted his image to pierce through me, to carve out a small opening in me that could drain away the pain. But all I could see before me was an obscure blotch. All I could see in the framed photograph propped up against the urn, was the glare from the low, late autumn sun. And my mind saw nothing. Grandad was not here, and I didn't know how to bring him back.

Disheartened, my eyes wandered around the cemetery, at first around the graves and the pathways between them, then through the trees. I let my eyes rest upon the neighbours and acquaintances who were keeping a respectful distance from me and my sorrow; I scoured their elderly faces, looked towards the sky, before lowering my eyes back to Anya, to Dane, to Špela, to Maya. And eventually, Mum's eyes caught mine.

Never had I seen such a dry pair of eyes. I watched, transfixed, as she opened them wide and exposed them to the gentle, but bracing wind, as if deliberately drying her eyes on the breeze. As if she had dried her tears with the help of the wind, as if the wind had blown them away.

I wanted to believe her expression, I wanted to believe the glistening droplet in the corner of each eye; two tiny, watery witnesses to her pain, which trickled away into the shadow of her hair. I wanted to believe that a part of her was still capable of crying for her father, even though in her own way, Mum had grieved for him, and buried him, long before he died.

Just as she'd grieved for, and buried, Safet. Mum buried those who betrayed her in stony indifference. Everything she had felt for him had been quashed inside her, and her husband was no longer her husband. And her father was no longer her father.

It's likely Safet knew this, he knew this better than anyone, which was another reason why he never came back. He'd never begged her to forgive him, to forgive his walking away. He knew all too well how fruitless any sort of begging would prove to be.

Grandad knew his eldest daughter very well, too, but unlike Safet, it was something he never came to terms with. After Grandma died, he asked tirelessly for her forgiveness. His pleas tasted of fig jam, carefully bottled and labelled, the only food ever to come out of his kitchen that had been cooked to a recipe. Yet she remained impervious to his attentions. Or at least that's how she tried to appear from the outside.

He would never see her dry eyes, put to the wind. He would never see how she was overwhelmed by the sadness she had renounced; how there was, for the first time, something inside her more powerful than her obstinate will. He would never see the reluctant, but irrefutable acknowledgement of a love that could never run dry. Grandad lived many long years waiting for that acknowledgement, but in the end it was something he had to die for.

Maya dabbed her puffy eyes with a handkerchief. Dane drew her close again and she did not resist. She had abandoned any pretence of composure, and her sobbing began to roll over the grounds of the cemetery like a thick fog, which embraced and constricted each of us, one by one. With every sound that came from Maya we were constrained closer together, the space between us narrowed, and soon I had the sense that something was thrusting me on to Dane, Maya and Mum, and them on to me.

The gentleman in gloves finally walked over to the urn, to be followed by every pair of eyes in the cemetery. And as if moving along with him, the wind gathered, becoming fitful. Yet we remained static, and watched him gently place his hands on the porcelain vessel containing Grandad's ashes, lift it from the ground and carry it towards the grave, towards Grandma, who had been waiting for her husband.

Dane was the first to move. He placed a hand on Maya's back and gently nudged her forwards, whilst she reached for Mum's hand, and pulled her along in tow. We were roused from our numbed state by their synchronised steps, and we moved forward, reluctantly, at a strained, soporific pace. The grave of Jana Benedejčič and Aleksandar Đorđević was no more than fifty metres away, yet this was not a short stroll. This walk was a journey.

For Mum, this was a journey into the very heart of her pain. I was walking right behind her and could feel her body surrendering. Her arms were dangling unsupervised; her steps became shorter and frailer. Her weary, unsteady legs could no longer peel themselves off the ground, and instead dragged along the sandy floor, until Mum, some ten or so metres before the headstone, came to a stop.

I took her by the arm and led her forwards. Dane put his hand on Maya, to let us go first, but Mum stopped after a few more steps. Her body was shutting down. She was shaking, and she grabbed me in panic, and clung on to me as if scared she were going to be plunged into darkness. Her eyes, which had until now been open wide, were now closing, and as her eyelashes met, everything inside her gave way.

There was a moment of quiet, barely audible sobbing, but then came a groan from within, something animalistic. Pain was screaming out of her with a voice that wasn't human; it deformed her face and constricted her limbs, as if it had taken possession of her completely.

Špela and Dane leapt to her, in an attempt to keep her upright, but she wrestled free and slumped, or rather fell, onto me. Her arms were draped around my neck and her head buried into my chest. I held her close as tightly as I could, to stop her from sliding onto the ground. Her legs hung down from her convulsing torso which emitted unrelenting screams, one after the other, which thundered around the deadened landscape.

I gestured to Dane that he and Maya come past us, and the small procession hurried along behind him. Now everyone was quickening their pace, as if desperate to be far away. They arranged themselves around the grave and waited for us. Mum was no longer sobbing as loudly, but her unruly body was still leaning helplessly against mine, and so I gave Dane a nod.

He picked up the spade and thrust it into the pile of earth gathered by Grandad's open grave. He then lifted it into the air and carefully moved towards his wife. Maya led her fingers over the moist, reddish soil. She extended her arm, fist full of earth, over the grave, and paused for a moment. She's praying, I thought, though her lips weren't moving. Then she opened her fist.

Špela followed Maya, then Anya, and then the rest. The sounds of earth falling onto the urn mixed with the fading footsteps and whispers, and then everything was silent once more.

At that moment, Mum's hand took hold of mine, weight transferred back to her legs and she steadied herself. The gentleman in gloves was the only one left standing by the stone wall, but he too was looking out towards the sea.

Mum crouched down at the graveside. She moved the spade out of her way, and started to push the earth over the grave with both hands. Clods of hardened terra rossa fell down onto Grandad's urn, but Mum kept going until the grave had been filled. Then she brushed off her hands and stood up.

With the tips of her muddy fingers she opened her handbag, and took out a packet of tissues, and placed them in my hand.

'Would you dab my mascara, please?'

I took out a tissue and started to softly wipe away the black smudged beneath her eyes, but a dried mix of mascara and tears remained on her face.

'Wet it.'

I drew the tissue up to my lips, moistened it with saliva and once again drew it back up to the rings beneath her eyes. Her eyes closed and she surrendered. I gently wiped under her eyes with the spit-soaked tissue, and felt that never before had she let me come so close.

I sensed I could have asked her anything and she would have answered all of my questions; that she might even admit that she'd told Grandad about Grandma wanting a divorce, that this had been the only reason for her final visit before he died. We were standing too close for her to have been able to back away.

She opened her eyes and my hand stopped still. Her sorrowful eyes were staring at me, as if they'd heard the questions I didn't ask.

I turned around, looking for Dane. He was standing by the cemetery gates, chatting to the gentleman in gloves. The others had already headed out to the car park. Mum took my hand and tried to hold me back.

She could sense what was rising inside me, and drew me towards her in dread. But I had already broken free, and was quickly marching towards the two men at the gates.

XII

The two of them sat at the table is one of those recurring images of my childhood. I'm standing in the hallway of Maya and Dane's apartment, shoes and coat on, sometimes with a hat and a scarf around my neck, too, leaning against Mum, half-asleep, and looking over at the kitchen table where Safet and Dane are locked in discussion, bottle there between them. Dane's holding it in his hand and filling two small glasses, the only things left standing on the table besides a brimming ashtray. During the short interludes of an evening-long debate, Safet turns to look at Mum, but says nothing. Because it's all been said already, all of us know it: Mum says *Safet*, that's all she says, and what we hear is that she's been standing with me in the doorway for an hour already, maybe more; everyone knows that the kid is tired, that tomorrow is an early start, that Maya's kids, too, ought to be in bed by now; Mum's *Safet* says all of those things. And Safet understands her too, but he doesn't get up, he just has to finish this drink and just tell Dane this one more thing, and Maya says *Dane*, which means the same as *Safet*, but once again nothing happens. Dane just pulls the bottle closer and inspects how much rakia is still inside. Then, bottle in hand, he turns to Maya, and we all know that time no longer passes by in hours and minutes, but flows like the burning liquid that is yet to run out. And Maya sighs and sits herself down on the floor, while Mum says *I'll call a taxi*. It's her last desperate attempt, because we all know she's not going home in a taxi. No woman in possession of a living husband goes by taxi. At this point Safet gets up, but doesn't move away from the table, he's coming, just a second, and Dane pours. Their rakia takes a long time to run dry, but for them it flies by, they've still got so much to say. Nobody says it, nobody even considers, that Safet can't drive in such a state; they're all hoping that he gets behind the wheel as soon as possible. Another *Safet* echoes around the room, and now, at last, Safet has had enough. Mid-sentence he stops, turns to us, and opens his arms. *Enough already,* he says; he's drunk and he doesn't look like himself. And even when Mum points at me and says *look at him, he's asleep on his feet,* Safet just smiles at me, as if he hasn't understood what his wife is trying to tell him, as if he can't see me at all. It even looks like he's about to sit down again; Dane fills his glass for him, pouring out their final droplets of time, and Mum gives up, slumps down on the floor next to Maya and closes her eyes. I hate it when Mum closes her eyes. It means that things are going to get worse, much worse, before they get better. And so I snuggle up to her and try to make her feel better, I want her to open her eyes, but she just puts her arms around me and holds me close. I don't like it, I don't want her to hug me with her eyes closed, because that means she's very sad. Whenever she's very sad, she's sad for ages, and it makes everything sad. Now I don't want to go home because I don't want to be alone with her and Safet, now I'd rather we stayed here, at Dane and Maya's, with Miha and Špela, all together. I don't want the bottle in Dane's hand to run dry, but when Safet sees Mum with eyes closed, it's a sight stronger than his drunken stupor. He realises that it really is time to go home. Dane knows it too, and they're already coming over to us, now they're saying something to us and laughing, Safet ruffles my hair so vigorously that it hurts. *What's up with you?* he asks Mum. *Alright, we're going,* he says, and she gets up, but she doesn't turn to look at him when he puts his shoes on, she doesn't look at him when he says goodbye to Dane and Maya, she doesn't look at him when he tells one last joke at the door, and she doesn't look at him as she drags me out through the door and calls the lift. Whilst waiting for the lift, Safet says *It's not that late,* only to take a peek at his watch and go quiet. He waits in silence and pats down his pockets, looking for his car keys, while Mum is still turned the other way. I don't know what she's looking at, but I do know what the look on her face means; I know that look will stay with us for some time. When the lift arrives, we get in and Mum and Safet turn to face the door and give Dane and Maya one final wave. Maya blows me a kiss, and then shuts the front door, and the lift doors close too, and the three of us are left alone, in silence, because Safet knows all too well that he'd better not say a word. Because all there was to say, was said the moment Vesna said *Safet*.

Safet and Dane. Dane and Safet. Safet, Dane. Dane, Safet. The "and" between their names doesn't suit them. It suggests a level of connection that in reality wasn't there. They weren't Safet and Dane. That doesn't sound like them. They were never really *with* each other, they were never a pair, they were just constantly together, apart. There was a bond between them and it has always eluded description. Or a name. So there was no use looking for it. Safet. Dane.

They weren't friends. They liked drinking together, they liked to quarrel over nothing. But friendship would have required honesty. Neither of them had the courage for it, and they persistently concealed their thoughts and feelings, or veiled them in stupid jokes. They enjoyed taunting one another, and revelled in finding new buttons to press. The enjoyment they took from this game of kitchen conflict was truly perverse, where they'd play the Slovene and the Bosnian, or Dane was Lardarse and Safet was Reprobate, or they were just simply Idiot and Moron. Always with dubious, false smiles, and a hint of sheer malice and schadenfreude. But an obscure kind of affection, too. Which was anything but friendly. Dane and Safet didn't look each other in the eyes often enough to be friends. They were both too cowardly to dare settle what was between them.

Maya and Mum were always telling them that their taunts were far too vulgar to be funny, but they took no notice, and we kids, too, quickly became old enough for their whole range of insults.

Yet there remained a fundamental difference in how each of them engaged in this game. Dane would spend days, weeks, preparing for a run-in with Safet; carefully collating ideas, gathering jokes about stupid Bosnians with the same passion that someone else might apply to collecting stamps; he'd work out a plan of attack and decide in advance on the best moment to strike. Sometimes he'd even rehearse his lines used to assault Safet in advance.

Safet, you heard the one about the Bosnian who catches a goldfish?

Hoping to catch a Slovene with a sense of humour, was he?

Safet improvised and came back at Dane spontaneously, instinctively. As soon as he set eyes on him, it triggered something inside and he forgot how, not even a moment ago, he had promised his wife that this time he'd keep his mouth shut. Dane would only have to pop his head round the door and Safet would be yelling *Alrightcollaborator!*

Safet used a special language with Dane, reserved just for him. The fact that Safet spoke Bosnian with him was part of the game; his little provocation. But it wasn't the Bosnian that he spoke with me and Mum, or his Bosnian mates. It was a special strain of that language, crafted especially for Dane.

Alright-you-fucking-mountain-goat-did-you-get-them-rosy-cheeks-from-all-the-steamin-beef-broth-you-ate-as-a-kid-you-did-didnt-you-admit-it-better-to-be-Slovene-than-go-hungry!

Whenever he spoke to Dane, Safet's mouth would let forth a long, continuous word, reluctant to end. But Dane waited patiently, poised for a counter-attack.

A mate saw a sign in a restaurant window that said 'No Dogs, No Bosnians.' Fuck knows what they've got against dogs.

And when their weary wives warned that things had gone too far, they instantly switched to soft and cuddly declarations.

I'm-only-takin-the-piss-Dane-knows-that, said Safet.

He knows I'm not being serious, for fuck's sake, said Dane.

But it hadn't always been like this between them.

Safet was a punk before punk rock existed; a child of many cities whose father's untimely death had been a timely release from a tight leash, which allowed him to run wild and revel in his maladjustment. Which is why he wasn't even the slightest bit interested in socialising, let alone being friends, with Dane, with the well-groomed pot-belly from Yodelling Alpsville, as Safet called all of Slovenia outside of Ljubljana. He rather resented Maya for having taken pity on this poor, timid, dumbass, which meant that he, her sister's boyfriend, was obliged to be nice to him.

Whenever they sat together, Safet was not Safet. He would formally shake Dane's hand, and was more formal still in how he said hello, and would make a few polite enquiries about Dane's health, academic performance and his mother's wellbeing. When he performed this routine for the third or fourth time at Maya's birthday celebration at the Evropa coffee house, Vesna angrily stabbed his foot with her spiky heel. The next time Dane opened his mouth, Safet listened with a performative attention and nodded at his every word like an over-keen television presenter.

Vesna stood up and asked him to come with her. He followed her to the toilets, and because there was a queue for the ladies, Vesna went into the gents, dragged Safet in with her and closed the door.

Now you know what the whole place will be thinking… chuckled Safet, but his chuckling was interrupted by Vesna's handbag, which hit him square in the face, drawing blood from just below his ear.

Safet always recounted that tale with what was left of the interrupted chuckle all those years ago. He would never cease to be amused by the sight of Vesna screeching, at the top of her voice, that he was an idiot and she'd had enough of his Bosnian antics, whilst she dabbed at the blood from the open wound and checked if he was perhaps feeling dizzy.

Mum never learned to see the funny side of that story, and all she usually said was that she should have given him a thrashing and left him there, rather than marrying him sixth months later.

What eventually changed Dane and Safet's relationship was something that Dane said, so casually and off-the-cuff, that it was only after Safet had heard it echo in his ears a few times that it sunk in. He then leant over to him across the table, until he was almost lying on it.

What did you say? he whispered in Dane's face.

It was on Safet's home turf, sat in the garden outside Čad, and the sight of Safet thrust across the table caused everyone in the vicinity to pause in terror and wait for the scene to unfold. Safet had a reputation as a bit of a joker, but also as man who'd broken a nose or two in his time, knocking over a few tables along the way. What's more, until this point, Safet had never spoken Bosnian to Dane.

The colour drained from Dane's face. He saw that something in Safet had shifted.

I just said that we all know what they're like, he stammered.

You said what Bosnians are like, didn't you? We all know what Bosnians are like? Didn't you?

Dane nodded and forced a smile, trying to hide his fear.

Safet, said Vesna, tugging him back to his seat, not that he took any notice of her.

Well? What are Bosnians like?

You know what I mean, said Dane.

I don't have a frigging clue. But I see you do, so do tell us.

Leave it, Safet, Vesna intervened, her voice louder and firmer than before. But Safet was just getting started.

You know, Dane managed to utter, but Safet shook his head.

No, I don't know. What are they like?

All activity in the garden had come to a standstill, conversations had hushed, cutlery was down. All eyes were on Safet.

Fuck's sake, will you just leave him be! Vesna shouted, shoving Safet with both hands, nearly toppling him backwards. To which he responded with roaring laughter.

I'm just curious to know what Bosnians are like, he said innocently, as if denying all responsibility.

But you know what he meant!

All I know is that there's someone sitting at this table who knows what Bosnians are like, despite me probably being the only Bosnian he's ever met in his life.

Maya, Dane and Vesna all turned away. They, along with the rest of the garden, were suspended in anxious anticipation. Safet then gestured to the nearest waiter.

Dragan, over here we're having a serious conversation about serious matters. Help us out and bring us a bottle of šljiva, would you?

Dragan nodded and people started to look away, their knives resumed cutting the meat on their plates, conversations got going again.

You're not normal. What's wrong with you? asked Vesna, now in a hushed voice.

Nothing's wrong. Why? Me and my mate Dane are going to have some rakia, loosen him up a little, so we can get to the bottom of these Bosnians.

We're going, said Maya, getting up. But Dane didn't budge.

We're going, she repeated again, but Dane stayed put.

It's alright, he said, and cast a glance at Safet.

It's alright, Maya, you heard him. Sit back and relax, Safet said.

The full force of Vesna's fists slammed on the table and the garden fell silent again.

Idiot. If you want to know what Bosnians are like, they're exactly like you are right now. They bully an entire restaurant with their games, they wind people up and don't know when to stop. There, that's what they're like. Brutes.

Vesna probably would have continued, except she was interrupted by Dragan, who arrived with the bottle of rakia and four glasses.

Pour some for everyone, Safet said, and Dragan filled four glasses. Safet raised his glass without waiting.

To brutish Bosnians and sophisticated Slovenians!

Vesna's heart sank and her eyes closed; Maya looked the other way, but Dane raised his glass, said cheers to Safet and downed his drink in one.

That was the first bottle they ever got to the bottom of, though Safet never did get to hear what Bosnians were like according to Dane. All they managed to establish during those few hours of their first drinking session was that Dane knew some guy named Mehmed, who worked at the post office in Ribnica, but he couldn't be sure whether he was actually Bosnian; maybe Serbian, or maybe even Kosovan. At some point Maya and Vesna left, exasperated, whilst at three in the morning, and with the help of Dragan, Safet managed to get a sleeping Dane on his back and carry him to the car park, where he then sat him in a taxi and paid the driver to take him home and carry him to his room. Then he paid off the rest of their tab and went home.

The next morning, Vesna had left early for Momjan and refused to answer his calls for three days, Maya wouldn't speak to him for weeks, but Dane called the next evening and thanked him for getting him home. And, he said, the next round was on him.

A Slovene getting a round in? I've heard it all now! I've heard it all! Safet repeated, laughing, and Dane laughed too, and then said that he felt like shit and quickly hung up without saying goodbye.

Drink can create the illusion of closeness; in some rare cases, it can even bring people together, but to many people like Dane and Safet, it helps to maintain a safe distance in spite of physical proximity. Their drunken states were entirely unrevealing; there was nothing, not even the slightest bit of honesty about them. They never, amid all those refills of rakia, ever teased anything out of each other that they wouldn't have shared when sober. Drink allowed them to hide in front of one another. Their endless jibes merely filled the emptiness between them, covered up their fundamental differences. That memorable night at Čad, Safet had found a way to behave with Dane, and Dane accepted. And perhaps they even enjoyed it. But even after all those years of having dragged one another home, arm in arm, across half the city, they were never any closer than they had been that first time Safet politely enquired after Dane's mother.

Perhaps it was the very distance between them that made them such an excellent team. They didn't hesitate to turn the rotary dial and ask one another for favours; the sorts of things a person needed to make life a little better, a little easier, in this day and age. They weren't burdened by feeling that they were indebted to one another, because they weren't actually friends. It was *tante za tante*, as Safet would say. Or, translated into Dane's language, you scratch my back, and I'll scratch yours. Safet was a master of black market economics: part-time handymen, amateur smugglers and short-sighted warehouse employees, he had it all covered; he hooked up maintenance guys with sales girls, mechanics and postmen. No crisis or shortage would stand in his way. Yugoslavia may have occasionally lacked coffee or bananas, but not Safet, ever. He just knew the right people, and knew who to call to get Dane out of a pickle.

Bosnians to the rescue, Dane would say, after every mission accomplished, unable to get over the extent of Safet's network.

Yugoslavia, the country, he would elaborate, *is just an illusion. All those clerks with their rubber stamps and uniforms, all the rules and regulations, all of that was just a stage, it's you people, you and your Bosnians, who are the real country. You're the subconscious of this unconscious state.*

And you lot? Safet asked him.

Needless to say, Dane, too had his own network spread throughout the Ljubljana council offices, local headquarters, and tax bureaus; he had people everywhere, there was always someone he knew who could make the impossible become possible.

What makes you and your Slovenes different from me?

Dane simply felt that he was different, that he and his fellow Slovenes were different, but all he said was *It'll all go to shit!*, to which he and Safet raised their glasses. And ordered another round.

They each had their own way of drinking. Safet never liked his glass overfilled. First he would eye it up, and run his finger around the moist edge. Then he'd take hold of it and bring it to his lips, sniff it, like wine, and let it pause there, for a moment, just on his bottom lip, before he eventually tipped the liquid in. Safet's first sip was small, the rakia only briefly touched his tongue, just enough for it to tingle, and then he'd take a second sip, longer, which would drain half his glass. He'd then hold off the glass for a bit, still holding it mid-air, and take a look at it. He'd smell it one more time, then put it down on the table, gently nudge it around with his fingers, before raising it again and emptying his glass without hesitation.

Dane liked his glass full to the brim and couldn't stand the sight of an empty glass. A full glass could sit in front of him for an eternity, untouched. But once he decided to give it his full attention, he'd fix his eyes on the glass, wrap all five fingers around it, carefully raise it towards him, pausing for a second in front of his lips for the undulating liquid to settle, and then swig it back in one swift motion. There might occasionally be a drop or two left at the bottom, but Dane never went back for those.

Once used, his glass was rejected; he pushed it away from him, which the waiters took as a request for another round, and poured him another one without any questions.

Whenever Safet and Dane met up at the bar opposite Dane's office, it was plum brandy that they drank together. At home, they'd drain pear brandy from a bottle which, throughout my childhood, housed a large, yellow, putrefying pear. But when they were celebrating, Safet would take an old sparkling water bottle from the highest shelf in the pantry, with a white label stuck on it, the sort Mum put on her jam jars.

Dunja, he read out. He opened it, and took particular pleasure in inhaling the quince aroma. *Smooth as silk.*

He poured more carefully than usual, and drank more slowly than usual, because quince brandy was his father's drink, the drink of Fuad Dizdar, the engineer.

Half a glass after lunch, along with a cigarette.

This was one of the few memories Safet had of his father, and whenever I thought about my grandfather, who died long before I was born, I pictured him sitting there, at the table, with a woollen cardigan draped around his shoulders, trembling hand bringing a small glass of quince brandy to his lips, cigarette wedged between his fingers.

Over the years, Safet and Dane's squabbling became harsher, the jokes and the smiles disappeared, and their conversations over plum brandy descended into arguments. The country was falling apart, and Dane and Safet were falling apart, too. Dane sobered up, got his own office and a direct phone line; his sobriety, for Safet, stirred up his old contempt for the rotund, well-groomed bumpkin from Yodelling Alpsville.

All I want is a country of my own, Dane yelled.

And you're happy to fuck over mine to get it, Safet yelled back.

Mum and Maya would withdraw, shut themselves away with us, in the children's bedrooms, or go for a long walk around the block during visits, whilst those two carried on yelling, undisturbed.

Your country's doing a fine job of fucking itself over.

No, you're the ones screwing my country.

Who's we?

You nationalists.

What the fuck? What nationalists?

You lot, isn't that what you are?

Take that back!

Why?

Because!

Top me up, fuck it, don't be a twat!

Just because we can see it's all going to shit, doesn't make us nationalists!

Bollocks.

It's not bollocks!

For fuck's sake! You can all see it's going to shit and what? You make a run for it?

Yes, exactly!

And whose fault is it, that it's going to shit? Don't tell me it's got nothing to do with you lot?

What's it got to do with us?

Oh go fuck yourself. Easiest thing in the world is to play dumb.

Who's playing dumb?

Seriously, cut it out. I can't deal with your crap.

What crap?

I said top me up. Fuck this. You and your inde-pen-dence. I hope your dick declares independence.

Screw you.

One day, the phone rang in Dane's office.

Oi, Mr. Independence, do us a favour and check which citizenship Jadran's got?

Yugoslav babies inherited their citizenship from parents at birth, or rather, were assigned it according to where their parents had been born. It was just one of innumerable pieces of Yugoslav bureaucratic nonsense, seemingly banal, just like all bureaucratic nonsense, until it begins to impact people's lives.

Slovenia was breaking away, and Safet, gearing himself up for the collapse of the world as he knew it, had heard that all citizens of the Yugoslav Socialist Republic of Slovenia would automatically be granted citizenship in the newly independent state of Slovenia.

Dane called back about half an hour later.

Jadran has Slovenian citizenship.

It wasn't until then that Safet recalled that September afternoon, when he had entered his newborn son into a form, translated him into letters and numbers; he recalled the pale-faced council clerk, who explained to him that his son could have either Serbian or Croatian citizenship, as his wife had been born in Croatia, and he in Serbia; he recalled thinking how unbelievably idiotic it seemed, and how her bureaucratic arrogance irked him, and how he yelled *What fucking good is Serbian or Croatian citizenship gonna be to my son when he was born in Slovenia, and is gonna live in Slovenia?*; he recalled how the other clerks came out from behind their counters when they heard him shouting, and assembled themselves behind their pale-faced colleague and told him to calm down, that it was just the way things were, that they were just doing their jobs, that those were the rules; he remembered his determination not to give in to them, because this time it was about his son and because they weren't about to screw his son over with their red tape and because neither God, nor state, nor some random lady behind the counter, was about to decide who and what his son was; he recalled how everyone glanced at him, how they couldn't believe that a person would say such things, and how they eyed the entrance, expecting, at any moment, a small contingent of policemen to march through the door and drag him away for insulting the state; he recalled how much he despised them at that moment, for allowing themselves to be dominated by some idiotic fear, to the point where the state would screw them over, would screw over their own children; he recalled how, in the end, when the fidgeting clerks realised that he was not going to accept their reasoned arguments, they dug out some subsection of the regulations, which said that in the event that neither parent could agree, the child was to be granted citizenship of the republic in which he or she was born; he recalled how the clerks expected his eternal gratitude, and all he said was *There we are, shove that up your admin twat!* and walked out.

I thought he had, I just thought I'd better check, just in case, Safet said.

What about you? Dane asked.

It was a question that Safet should have seen coming, yet he found himself unprepared.

What about me?

I can sort it for you too, if you want, so that you get Slovenian citizenship too. I'm already sorting it for Vesna.

Is that right.

Maya asked me. But she didn't know whether you'd want it or not.

What for?

What do you mean, what for? So that you'll automatically get Slovenian citizenship. So you don't run into any issues.

What issues? What issues will I have? What are you on about?

Safet was getting increasingly agitated, while Dane's voice became calmer, as if he were growing numb.

I can wangle it for you, if you want, he said.

No.

What?

No. I don't need Slovenian citizenship.

There was something else Safet wanted to say, but Dane hung up. They never drank together again.

XIII

Anya and I drove back in silence. I joined the motorway at Koper and it was as if the surrounding scenery was also choosing to hold its tongue. The monotone sound of the engine, the lines that divided lanes, the crash barriers, and Anya, who was waiting for my explanation. We had driven away so quickly after the burial, that she hadn't been able to ask. But nor did she have to. It wasn't her job to ask; it was my job to answer.

'Aleksandar killed himself.'

'What?'

Maybe I was just checking to see if she was listening. Maybe I wanted to wake her, to call her back to me. Or maybe I just had to tell someone else about the empty little brown bottle and Mum's visit.

'What are you talking about? What do you mean, he killed himself?'

'Suicide. Aleksandar committed suicide.'

'Where's this come from?'

'A few days before he died, Vesna told him that whilst he was away in Egypt, Jana wanted to get a divorce.'

'And you think he'd kill himself because of that? At his age?'

'He never forgave himself for going to Egypt when he did. He always suspected that his departure had caused Jana irreparable harm, and Vesna confirmed those suspicions. She stoked his biggest fears. Before, he could still tell himself that maybe it hadn't been so bad. But after that, he saw himself as being to blame for her illness. Death was a fairly logical choice, if you think about it; he had no source of comfort left.'

I spoke with composure, as if I were speaking about characters from a book that I'd read, and Anya, too, listened to me as if she were listening to a work of fiction. Sad, but fictional. What I was saying was too disturbing for her to believe.

'But why did Vesna tell him?'

'I don't know. But she did. She wanted payback.'

'Payback? For what?'

'For Safet.'

What did Aleksandar have to do with Safet?'

'Aleksandar did nothing to protect him from what happened.'

'But wouldn't she want to get even with Dane, too, in that case?'

'It's the biggest disappointments that hurt us the most. And the more we expect from people, the more it hurts when they let us down.'

'But you didn't get even with the person who most let you down.'

'Well, I did – on his gob. A punch in the face had been a long time coming.'

Only then did I register the blood encrusted on my knuckles, and the grizzly nature of the scene that Anya had been witness to. That they'd all been witness to. Only then did I register the fright on Špela and Maya's faces, and Mum and Anya's horror. And Dane's resignation; how he surrendered to me. As if he knew that I would come for him. It even seemed like he was relieved when what had to happen, had eventually happened.

'But Vesna couldn't have known that Aleksandar would kill himself, could she?'

'No. But she thinks he did it, too. Which is why his death has hit her so hard. She feels guilty.'

'But didn't you say that Vesna got over Safet a long time ago?'

'I used to think so. Now I think it's impossible to get over the people you love.'

'Have you spoken to her? About getting even, I mean. Or have you come up with this yourself?'

'Not directly. And she wouldn't admit it, anyway. But she was there, at his house, and she told him about the divorce. That much I know. And I know that Aleksandar killed himself.'

'How?'

'Grandma's blood pressure tablets.'

'Jesus.'

'I found the empty bottle under the bed.'

'But you didn't…'

'No. It's nobody else's business.'

'But would she really still want to get even, after all these years? I find that hard to believe.'

'Wanting to get even came from a place of love. I'm sure of it. There's no other – there can't be any other – explanation. Her love couldn't keep quiet any longer. It had been silent for too long. And Aleksandar's suicide came from a place of love. He couldn't bear the thought of having hurt the person he cared about the most to such an extent that she'd wanted to leave. He loved Grandma too much to be able to live with that realisation.'

'Love was at the heart of it all, in that case.'

'Love's always at the heart of everything. Everything except for love itself.'

XIV

Vesna arrived unannounced. After not having visited them for almost two years, she got in the car after work and drove to Momjan.

You're on the other side of the border, you two, were her first words as she came through the door.

It's like someone's drawn a border through me. They've drawn borders through us, through all of us. They've drawn borders between me, my mother and my father. It's now up to someone else to decide if I can see my parents.

Jana and Aleksandar listened to her, as if she were a teenager again, talking to them about punk, about Children of Socialism and Via Ofenziva, about a world which they'd been too old to understand for many years now. They couldn't imagine a border crossing there, where there had never been one before; their minds couldn't conjure the image of Slovene and Croatian border guards, each stopping cars on their own bank of the Dragonja river.

Vesna was talking like a person scared of silence, and it was impossible to establish at which point her story of the border crossing turned into the story of her missing husband. She was talking about Safet, but too rapidly and incoherently for Aleksandar and Jana to follow. She was tossing out words; and names, places and times flew chaotically around the room.

And so as she went on, Aleksandar and Jana were not so much listening to her as watching her, convinced that this was one of those stories that could only be understood if you managed to let the words wash over you. At some point Jana got up, went over to Vesna and took hold of her hand. It was then that Vesna's story stopped short. Tears ran down her cheeks.

You're never too old to be a child, and ever since Safet had left, Vesna had wanted, just for one short moment, to be vulnerable; to cling on to someone, seeking comfort. But when Vesna looked at Jana, there, from up close, it was another, equally vulnerable girl that she saw.

She turned to Aleksandar with two hazel question marks for eyes, wide open, hoping that her father would explain who this small child was, this child in her mother's body. But he didn't hear the question.

Vesna couldn't bear to be near the stranger who she ought to have called Mum. As she stepped out of the door, she just wanted to walk, to get away as quickly as possible, all she wanted was to carry on walking, but she was stopped by the thought of the border guards who would be waiting for her not far from here. They stopped her in the middle of the garden of the house in Momjan, and sat her down on the nearest bench. Beneath the fig tree.

She placed her palm on the thick trunk and let her fingers glide over the indents and ridges, as if to check that the world around her was still real. She felt grateful to this sprawling tree for preserving its appearance and its scent, and for resisting the madness which in a matter of years had changed everything, from the landscape to the people. Especially the people.

As Aleksandar sat down beside her, the questions vanished from her face. Times had taught Vesna that life demanded acceptance. But her words told a different story.

I'll never forgive you.

Aleksandar didn't respond. He knew his daughter and could have uttered those words on her behalf, before she even arrived. But nevertheless, they wounded him like a long, sharp thorn, which invisibly pierced through his chest and out through his back.

He looked up at his fig tree and counted the emerging buds between the branches, shielding himself there, from the pain. He knew his daughter and he knew that her resentments didn't die, that they were likely to outlive him, perhaps even outlive her and live on in Jadran, just as Ester Aljehin's resentments had lived, and still lived, in him. He knew his daughter, which is why he remained silent, conscious of the futility of words.

Down below, oblivious to the pair of them, the Gulf of Piran glistened in the setting sun. It too, was divided by an invisible and uncertain line, a line which had split mountains, valleys, rivers and seas; a line which had cut through lovers and friends, sliced through families and was even frequently capable of splitting an entire person in two. Forcibly cut off from a part of their lives, Vesna and Aleksandar now sat together beneath the fig tree, and both thought about Safet, erased from their picture.

When everything down there has settled, and Safet comes back… Aleksandar began, but Vesna interrupted him.

For better and for worse, we vowed to one another. For better and for worse. Only he decided to head into the worse without me. And he knows full well that I won't forgive him for that. He knows me just as well as you do.

Aleksandar went back into the house. Through the cracks in the shutters he heard the ignition of Vesna's car engine, and the sound of spinning wheels crunching the gravel beneath them.

The next evening he returned to the fig tree. He sat beneath it and waited for Vesna to call and tell him about Safet's disappearance, to ask him if she could speak to her mum. He held the receiver in his hand and explained to her that her mum wasn't well, and that he knew this news would crush her. He was looking at Jana and was looking at Vesna, too; he could see both of them now, and he saw Safet, too, eavesdropping on this conversation from some muddy bunker.

He was the only one that lived with her, he told them. He was the only one who had witnessed her departure; the only one who had been by her side as her words ceased to come together as thoughts, when words lost their meaning; the only one who flushed the toilet after her three times a day; the only one who chased after her into the garden to put a coat on her, when she left the house barefoot in the middle of winter; he was the only one who had to tell her, every morning, that it was Aleksandar, her husband; the only one who had to understand that she didn't like to share a bed with a stranger; the only one who helped her find the toilet in the middle of the night; the only one to be the stranger in the night who caused her to back away in fear; the only one who had to convince her that he'd seen her naked body before, and that there was no one else to call except him. The only one.

Evening after evening he would return beneath the fig tree and retell his story. He sat down under the tree, leaned against it like a tired, hounded animal that eventually gives in and surrenders to its prey. He let all of their resentments ensnare him, let them feast on him like bloodthirsty animals, gnawing at his old bones.

From beneath the tree he would sometimes see the splendour of the landscape. He looked out towards the sea and wondered how much of the gulf was still his. As he looked beyond the house, northward, he sensed a presence in the distance halting his gaze and explaining that he could look no further; that he was only permitted to look as far as the larch trees at the top of the hill. He had to secretly smuggle glances, and his yearning, across newly drawn borders; borders which he himself would never cross.

He sat beneath the fig tree and saw her trembling, veiny hands cautiously feeling at the door handle as if they'd never opened it before; he saw her eyes, wide open, scanning the wall in search of a towel; he saw her tilt her head back and stare up at the spotted pattern on the ceiling, as if it hadn't already been there for years, drawn by the damp; he saw her studying him, surprised, scouring his face for a clue that might reveal him to her.

He pretended not to hear her call of *Hey, you!* He was sitting beside her, and waited for her to use his name. But he was 'Hey You'. He got up, picked up the tray with their coffee cups and carried it into the kitchen. He tilted it over the sink and let the cups and plates slide into it. Hey You didn't care if anything got broken. He turned on the tap, letting the water cascade over it all, causing the coffee dregs to splatter all over the walls. He watched as they dried, and saw how the tiny dirty flecks would stay there, forever.

Hey You let the dirt build up everywhere; he let oil splatter out of frying pans that were still wet. He carelessly shovelled vegetables into a pan, not peeled nor scrubbed; he left the simmering liquid to spill over the sides and flow into the crevices, spoiling the wood and steel.

She was frightened by the cockroaches that crept around her, but they no longer signalled to her that her house needed cleaning. Those disgusting little things never seemed to repulse Hey You, much like the moths, maggots and spiders and their other cohabitants that quietly crawled around the house. *There's room for everyone*, Hey You would say.

The back garden was so overgrown that it was no longer possible to fight your way through. Tending to all those stalks and stems that no longer served any purpose became senseless – Hey You was ambivalent about how they looked; it all came out of the ground and it was all living, and who was he to restrict and interfere with nature. Hey You didn't care if others would pick his raspberries over the garden fence.

Hey You cooked whatever he liked. Everything was cooked in water until it was soft, and everything was fried in oil until it was brown, or even better, black. And everything went with everything, because it all ended up together in the stomach and there was no point in complicating things for the sake of a couple of pensioners with tired old taste buds.

She made her way along the hallway slowly, as she couldn't find the light switch and couldn't see where she was putting her feet. Hey You watched her, illuminated by the dim light of the gas flames, flickering in blue beneath the pot, and causing her to stop there, in the doorway. She was looking at the stove, she thought it strange that something was cooking in the dark, in an empty house. There was nobody around and she didn't want anything cooking. She didn't see Hey You, as he drew nearer, and stopped right behind her, touching her gently.

Boo!

She leapt into the air. She wanted to scream but couldn't summon her voice. The air was expelled from her lungs and she took desperate gasps of breath as if choking. She backed away from him and almost tumbled to the ground. She wanted to run away, she didn't understand his laughter;

she was trembling and was holding on to the walls with both hands. She still couldn't scream. She was choking and she opened her mouth, but she couldn't breathe.

Jana! It's me, Jana! I'm sorry! It's Aleksandar! Your husband!

It was too late. She was in flight, but rooted to the spot. Her feet were incapable of moving; she found her balance and glared at him as if he were a monster, and a thunderous roar from her throat was the only eventual sound.

Aaaaaarrrggghhhhh!

Aleksandar put his hands up.

I'm not going to hurt you, Jana, it's me, Jana.

Get out! Get outttt! Shoo! Shoo! Out! Outttt!

She spun around, and her arm spun round with her, pointing in all directions.

Jana, it's me, can you see me, it's OK, it's me, your Aleksandar.

Her left arm was still pointing away from her, but she had lost her voice again. Now she was taking quick, shallow breaths. He tried to get closer to her, but he saw how her right hand softly clutched her chest, and he didn't dare move.

He didn't go to bed that night. The sun was rising as he drifted off to sleep, propped up against the door to the bedroom, where she had hidden herself away. He listened to the silence, waiting for her voice to emerge. But the night remained deaf.

He woke up in pain. His body resisted every movement and he could barely get himself up. The bedroom door was still closed.

He opened it carefully and peeked at her lying there on the bed. She also fell asleep with her clothes on, he thought to himself. But from where he was standing it was impossible to tell whether she really was just sleeping. She was lying on her back, with her mouth open, but he couldn't hear her breathing.

His heart was already pounding dangerously as he got closer. He hovered his hand over her mouth and his body froze. He waited for his trembling palms to be touched by her warm breath; he waited for blood to flow through his veins. He waited for death to return him back to life.

She's alive, he eventually sighed.

She's alive, he said again.

He tried to move his hand away from above her face, but it disobeyed him.

He was struck by the smell of stale urine. It was a foul stench that clung onto a person, got under their skin. As if the bed-wetter had been lying there for days. On the bed beneath her he felt a large damp stain. Then he noticed her eyes, open and bulging.

They gave him such a fright that he darted backwards.

You've had a little accident, he told her. *Stand up, let's get you washed and dressed, so you're not lying there in the damp.*

Jana didn't move. She showed no sign of understanding what he'd said. The only thing that showed was the horror from the previous night.

It's not good for you to lie there in the damp. You'll catch a chill.

She didn't react. Her clenched fists gripped the sheet beneath her, probably with every bit of strength she was still able to muster. Aleksandar took a further step backwards.

Have a feel, you'll see that it's wet.

By now he had one foot out of the door, and her left hand had let go of the sheet and slowly moved down between her legs. He watched her touch the patch of damp beneath her.

He was stood only two, maybe three metres away from her, but it seemed as if he were watching at a boundless distance. The body that felt at the sheets no longer belonged to anyone. It was just an image of a body.

Shut the doooor! Shut ittt!! the body cried, and he closed it.

The body came out, wrapped in a sheet.

The bathroom's the second door on the left, he informed it.

He pointed his hand in the direction of the bathroom, but the body didn't move. It merely turned its head and looked around the room.

Shall I bring you some clean clothes, so you can get dressed?

It didn't answer him.

It stood there for a little while longer before going back into the bedroom.

After a while he peered around the door. Jana was sitting on the bed, still wrapped in the sheet.

Are you coming for some breakfast?

No! she said. Sharply, brusquely.

A little while afterwards he brought a tray over to her, which had a few slices of bread and jam on it, and a cup of cocoa. He placed it down next to her on the bedside table.

Jana got up from the bed and sat herself down on his armchair. He didn't remember her ever sitting down there before. It was strange to see her sitting there, attempting to make herself comfortable.

You have to eat, he said.

She shook her head.

You have to eat so you can take your tablets. Do you hear me? You have to eat something so you can take your tablets.

She shook her head once again.

Fine. I'm going, but eat this. Please, Jana, eat this.

When he came back, he noticed that she'd eaten the smallest piece of bread and taken a big slurp of cocoa. Less than usual, but on that day it constituted a lavish feast. He took the leftovers back in to the kitchen, and brought her blood pressure tablets and a glass of water. She shook her head then, too.

You have to take your tablets. Please, Jana! This is serious, stop messing about.

This was the first time she'd resisted taking her tablets. Aleksandar stood in front of her, with a tablet in one hand and a glass in the other, while she was turning further and further away from him. Until she had eventually buried her face into the arm chair.

Christ's sake Jana, don't do this to me, please. We can't play games with tablets.

She tucked her legs under her bottom and was kneeling there on the chair. She curled up into a ball like a child, and her head disappeared completely.

Jana! Jana! Stop it, Jana. Please, stop!

Get out!

Jana, this is your medicine, not some bloody joke!

Leave me alone!

Jana!

Get out! Shoo!

Jana!

Shoo! Shoo!

He put the glass down, took hold of her hand and pulled her towards him. He squeezed her cheeks and prised open her lips, placing the tablet on her tongue. Next he reached for the glass and poured some water into her mouth.

Swallow! Swallow, I said!

She swallowed.

There we are! Good job.

As he left the room, he shut the door behind him. As he left the house, he locked the door. He did so just in case, as he didn't know how long he would be. Because he didn't have any idea where he was going.

The books had been sitting on the table next to her, untouched, for a long time. For a long time he'd been returning them to the library unread, and bringing her new ones, but all she would do was open them and then close them again. She'd occasionally hold one in her hand, but it was as if she didn't know what to do with it; as if the letters no longer came together as words. She'd sometimes place her hand on the covers and stroke them. When he came home that day, her fingers travelled over the embossed lettering on the cover of a book by Ivan Turgenev *Sketches from a Hunter's Album*.

Shall I read it to you? he asked, as a way of bringing her back round, and severing the melancholy that he'd brought into the house.

He was surprised when she nodded, and he took the book from beneath her hands and started to read. He thought he'd just read a page or two, but when he went to return the book to the pile, she said *More*, and so on he read, and then she said *More* yet again, and he carried on reading, until the light had faded and he could no longer see the letters, and was forced to stop in the middle of a page. Mid-sentence.

The following morning, it was she who placed a book in his hands. Another book. A book by Somerset Maugham. *Of Human Bondage*. She's remembered yesterday, he thought to himself, she's remembered him. It moved him, and his voice faltered as he read.

He felt, for the first time in a long time, that something had occurred between them again; that his voice was getting through to her. Maybe it was only individual words that were getting through; maybe, for her, reading was only a pleasant murmur, a slight variation on silence that she longed to hear. But there was something between them again, which had spent the night in her memory and which had awoken with her the next day.

And so he kept on reading. The sun shone through the window and the letters on the page bathed in the light. She was calm again, and it seemed as if she were listening, as if she were present, with him once more. He couldn't have wished for any more; any more would have been too much.

I'd like to go home, she said.

Once again he stopped mid-sentence. Half a word remained on the tip of his tongue.

But you…

No, it wasn't a sentence he could complete. He couldn't go any further. He could no longer keep calling her back from her imaginary worlds.

Sutra te vodim kući[3] , he said, to this stranger, who lived in his home.

That woman wasn't Jana, and it made no sense to speak in the language that he and Jana had always spoken.

---

3 *I'll take you home tomorrow.*

XV

The first night marked the death of a great poet. I'd never read his poems before, but his death made it seem as if he snuck his way into our family and joined us that very day. He became a part of the story, and for a moment I contemplated going to his funeral. Marko was our great story, and the great poet had unexpectedly, and irrevocably, become a part of it. The night that we decided on Marko, and the night that death had decided was for the poet, bound us together and paved the way for me to read a few of his poems. They were intriguing, a little unusual perhaps; I liked a few verses, and there were many I didn't understand. But his words didn't befit that night; they didn't suit it. That night was different from the poems of the great poet. It sounded different. There was rhyme. It seemed to me as if the words of his poems came together by happenstance; that they'd fallen onto his page from somewhere, they dissolved and were absorbed by the paper; but our night had been planned all along, considered, calculated, there was nothing poetic about it; it wasn't so much a poem as a shopping receipt. But it was nevertheless infinitely beautiful, more beautiful than any poem. Though in actual fact, that wasn't the evening that Marko was made. And yet I still remember it more than the night when he was. I forgot that night a long time ago. And with it, all of its deaths, even the significant and memorable ones, if they happened; I've forgotten everything. That's how it is. Some nights and some deaths stay with you, others don't. The night that marked the death of the great poet has remained, and Anya still lies next to me, looks at me and says *Are we really going to do this?* I nod and she laughs, a laugh full of fear, *you'd rather just have sex*, she says, and I say *It doesn't work without it*, and she shakes her head; *Are you nervous*, I ask her, because I like to ask questions that I know the answer to, and she says *I am a bit* and I say

Well it'll be over before you know it, an old, rehearsed joke, and she hugs me, grateful for my patience, and we lie there for a long time in each other's arms, likely thinking about whether that night really is the right night, and if right nights actually exist. Then she whispers *Let's do it* and starts to remove her pyjamas and my hand caresses her body, tickles her, she's always ticklish when she's nervous, but I don't say anything now, now is no longer the time for my jokes, now it really is time to undress and get down to business, and I think to myself, in that very last moment before her hand reaches down between my legs and my mind quietens down, how funny it is that we call this business.

The second night, Anya stayed wrapped up in her red shawl. Late that afternoon she'd wrapped it around her neck before leaving the office, and there, around her neck, it awaited morning. Her office had just completed its first big project, which she'd collaborated on, and her time had been a commodity; she had been a commodity. But that evening – it was around six thirty – after eleven hours of work, she stood up from her desk, said to her workmate that she had a dentist's appointment at seven, and left. She wasn't expected to be anywhere, not even at home; she just wandered around the stalls with a mulled wine, weaving through crowds gathered before the New Year, amongst the Chinese tourists, amongst the Bulgarian Roma playing Christmas songs, she walked past all that merry December madness and the whole time it seemed as if she were standing still, and everything else was moving past her. She walked and watched the happy, drunken people and the fairy lights framing the buildings, and it seemed as if she wasn't there at all, that this was all unfolding somewhere else; as if the Ljubljana she was walking through was a giant twinkling illusion. *I don't feel like coming home. Do you fancy coming into town?* she said, when she eventually returned my call. It was around nine-thirty in the evening and she was waiting for me in Prešeren Square, in our spot, right where we used to meet when we would still go on dates and hold hands; yet the fact that she was standing in that very place didn't even occur to her. She was too cold, but she didn't want to go anywhere;

all she wanted to do was keep on walking. *We could head towards Tivoli park*, she said. She had a feeling that if she were to so much as step over the threshold of any bar, she'd suddenly become a part of the celebrations which had swept over the city. *I can' do it*, she said, and so we walked, until there were no longer any stalls nor happy people or fairy lights around us, and we walked where people never go for a walk; we veered away from Tivoli, on to Prešeren Street and then towards Rožna Dolina, and I was afraid to ask what was wrong, while Anya just kept on repeating that the fresh air and the silence of Ljubljana at night was doing her good, because she was sick of the sound of keyboards and coffee machines; she said that she'd forgotten how beautiful and peaceful it was out there, and I looked around the street at the heaps of slush along the edges of the pavements – all those parked cars, plain houses with worn out facades, lit by the ugly neon glow of the streetlights – I looked around and I didn't know what beauty she was talking about, but she was smiling. *My phone's turned off*, she said, as if triumphantly announcing her great victory over availability. That night she'd wrapped her red shawl around her neck and turned her phone off at six thirty. *I've turned my phone off*, she repeated, and I said *High five!* and raised my hand, which she slapped and then on we walked, Anya, me, and her phone that was turned off; we walked in silence past the student dorms, and I didn't like to ask where we were going, or if she was cold and if everything was alright, because I knew that she wouldn't answer.

The third night I watched her as she dozed on the sofa. I watched her, and I saw those who had sent her to sleep. Prior to this I'd watched her coming in through the door, lacking the strength to hang her coat on the hooks in the hall, kicking her shoes off, her bag sliding out of her hand and along the floor; I watched her gobble down her dinner gone cold, without even tasting it; I watched her stare absent-mindedly at the television without following the changing images; watched how she uttered empty words; how she didn't even pretend to be listening to me, and turned away; how she lay there on the sofa, how her body relaxed and how her eyelids covered her eyes as she said *I'll go get changed in a minute.* I watched her and I saw them saying goodbye to her at the office door, smiling, satisfied; they would have invited her for a beer if it hadn't have been so late, always good after work, especially after such a long, tough day; if they complete this project, if they're in this together, if they're a team, this project is theirs; the redesigning of Naklo Technical College means a lot to them and they could talk about it for hours, but now they're just standing by the exit, saying their goodbyes and talking about sewage systems and the colour of tiles in the canteen; they're smiling, Anya's smiling too, she's full of energy, which will mysteriously vanish on her way home; but there, at the exit, I heard her talking, she was repeating certain words just she always does when talking about important things, and the redesigning of Naklo Technical College is impossibly important to all of them and to her, which is why all day long she keeps a close eye on the clock in the corner of her screen, and hurries to the toilet; it's why they order food to the office, it's why they avoid their superiors who shout for no reason, it's why they have extra coffee in the afternoons and someone drums their fingers on a neighbouring desk, while someone else pushes an empty cup around theirs. I watched her and I saw her leaving early, into the darkness, rushing, and instead of a kiss she leaves with the excuse that she didn't want to wake me; she prefers to get to the office early when everything's still quiet, when nobody pesters her, before there's a queue at the coffee machine and when she can stand and stare out of the kitchen window, or check the news on her phone, from Celebrity World and other gossip; the feeling that she has time for mindless activity is a comfort to her, it eases the exhaustion she wakes up with every day. I watched her and I saw her sleeping, exhausted by the dreams of others, on the sofa in front of me. I felt like shouting, waking her up and telling her how stupid this tiredness of hers was, how pointless this sleepy evening was, how sad it was that I was watching her sleep; and maybe I really should have woken her and told her of all of that, but I left her there and I slept alone in our bed, on the night when I was supposed to be giving her a child.

On the fourth night I held my tongue. She had things to say and I was waiting. I waited for her to eat her reheated pasta with smoked salmon and leeks. *You go ahead and cook something; I'll heat it up when I get back.* I waited for the washing machine to finish and for her to hang the washing out to dry. *You could do some washing too you know, if you can see that I'm short of time.* I waited for her to finish talking on the phone to Stanka. *What is it?* I waited for the evening news to finish. *Are you not interested in what's happening in Syria?* I waited for her to come back from the toilet. *What did they say – what's the weather like tomorrow?* I waited for her to reply to an email. *Fucks sake, I've explained all this to her already.* I waited for her to finish looking at a photo montage of ten cities to visit before you die. *I'd love to go to Luang Prabang one day.* I waited for her to check Facebook. *No way.* I waited for her to put the kettle on. *Do you want tea as well?* I waited for her to browse the television channels. *There's nothing on.* I waited for her to turn and look at me. *Are you alright?* I waited for her to stop asking questions. *Why are you so quiet? Are you annoyed or something? Are you coming to bed?* I waited for her to get ready for bed, to get into bed and turn out the light. *Are you not tired?* I waited for her to turn over to her side. *Night night.* I waited for her to fall asleep.

On the fifth night I was thinking of running away. I didn't wait up for her, and I turned off the television and went to bed, disappointed at yet another identical day. We continued to pass each other like ships, and when I entered the silence of our empty flat, I felt abandoned, for the first time in a long while. I had forgotten that feeling of betrayal which thrusts itself onto you, through the pores, exerting pressure on your bones; it takes hold of you, isolates you. You always revert back to childhood when you're alone, and it's when you think your most childish thoughts. And that's why I was thinking about revenge against everything and everyone, about walking out, about running away. That evening I considered running away; that evening I understood Safet. I was Safet. Betrayed, cheated, abandoned. I considered leaving just as he had done, to some place far away, by the sea where people speak another language; to a town where eyes would travel with me, the stranger, who would spend his days on the beach, launching himself into towering waves, who would yield to the ocean current, as if each venture into the water marked a farewell, a farewell to someone not known to anyone here, but everyone would sense it, because they see it in his face, in his posture, in his silence. At first they'd watch me, but then their eyes would grow tired of looking and they'd turn away, pretend I wasn't there; only children would occasionally acknowledge me, but I'd soon stop being of interest to them too. Children quickly get tired of things. I'd be left alone in the waves, I'd become increasingly reckless in surrendering to them, as if asking the water to take me, but all it would do is wash over me, flow under me, protect me from the solidity of the sandy floor, teach me freedom, I'd surrender to it and discover the infinite freedom of my naked body gliding along the surface of the water, just above the seabed; nobody would understand what I was doing, day in, day out, and with such perseverance; nobody would understand why no wave could be frightening enough to keep me on dry land, why I set out time and time again; nobody would understand that running away never ends, that I hadn't arrived anywhere, let alone at this seaside town amongst these unknown people, at these waves, that I wasn't even there, just like Safet was never in Otoka; I'd never be short of waves because I'd never wash up on the coast. Running away is the ultimate voyage, and that is why, that evening, it was such a tempting prospect, I was drawn to its very infinity; the fact that there would never be anyone there on the coast who would offer me their hand and help me out of the water; the fact that I might meet someone in that town, but we wouldn't know each other, we wouldn't put our trust in one another, we wouldn't get carried along in the same direction. I heard her coming in, I heard her carefully open the door and check whether I was already asleep, and close it more carefully still, take her shoes off; I heard the trickle of her urine, I heard her get changed and lie down next to me in bed. I felt her lips place themselves on my face. I don't know which one of us was the first to fall asleep.

On the sixth night I started talking. *What is it now?* I said, and my expression echoed the same question. What is it now? I looked and sounded like an idiot, I realised that. The conversation I wished to begin was deserving of a more refined opening line, but yet again I was incapable. Words abandoned me when it mattered most, and left me with just a few remaining characters which I struggled to put together as 'yes', 'no' and 'I don't know'. At the height of our most serious conversations, all I could do was grunt and garble and stammer, and on a good day, I'd mumble something incomprehensible. Then Anya would give up hope and put the conversation on hold indefinitely. *What do you mean, what is it now? What? What is it that you want?* I knew that she knew full well what I was asking her, and that she didn't need other, alternative words, that I had merely chosen the wrong moment to press her. She planted her feet on the ground, thrust herself backwards, and her swivel chair skidded away from the desk and found itself in the middle of the room; she turned towards me and glared at me. *Nothing.* It was all clear, to the both of us, but now Anya was swinging from left to right and avoiding eye contact. She was shielding herself with silence. *You're not going to say anything?* Without answering she turned back around to face the monitor and stared at her plans, both feet dropped to the floor and stopped the swaying of the chair. Everything calmed down and I could hear the water coursing through the radiator. The tension in Anya's posture told me that I should have held my tongue that night too. The conversation was hers, she ought to start it when she was ready for it. She drew herself closer to the desk, her hand reached for the mouse and the sound of her typing was soon reverberating about the room. I ought not to have said anything to her, and I ought to have turned away, taken myself away from her, but in such a way that wouldn't have made my exit seem like a protest against her decision to say nothing; maybe I ought to have said something to alleviate the unbearable silence; that was the moment I ought to have said something, but it was already too late; her hand slid from the mouse and fell to the desk. *Fucks' sake, Jadran, can't you see that I'm working! You know how much work I've got on! And you're still giving me a hard time!* She couldn't find the strength to turn and face me, and was instead talking to the computer. And I couldn't stand the sight of her back, so I got up and went into the kitchen, opened the fridge, poured myself a glass of apple juice. Then I sat back down on the sofa and turned on the television. Meanwhile Anya had turned the computer off. *I'm going to bed*, she said, and went into the bedroom. As she walked past she took care to step over my outstretched legs, but she didn't make eye contact.

On the seventh night, it was Anya who started talking. *I can't do it. I'm not ready to have children*, she said.

XVI

Look, I'm not breaking the silence that has engulfed us since we returned from Momjan, Anya; I observe you from afar, always, even when you're right next to me, and it's then that I think of Grandad's words. *You don't have to be alone to be lonely*, he said, if you remember, and now his words are the only sound reverberating in our silence. I keep my distance, I stay on my side of the invisible barrier and wait for you to come to me, for you to tell me what I already know, and then everything else: the reasons for your silence and the reasons for mine. Safet used to say *some days last longer than years*, and now it seems to me like these are the only kind of days we are up against, with mornings and evenings never further apart, evenings in which our silence subsumes countless silences, each of them painful because I still don't know why you went away. The only thing you said was that Tadea was not the reason you left, and since then I've felt even more afraid, and the unknown keeps me quiet, keeps me from breaking our silence; instead I choose merely to observe you as you fold Marko's clothes into a little pile by his bed so that he can dress himself in the morning, probably wondering whether he'll manage to tuck his top into his trousers rather than his trousers into his socks, and I hear you calling me to come and have a look, pretending to be cross and asking me to tell him to tuck his top in, as you turn away to hide the fact that you're smiling, because he's just like you when you were small. Now I'm observing you and picturing you in that hotel room – you see, I know which room it was, Anya, I didn't let on, but I know where you went, I know you went there, to the room where the view from the bed is only sea and sky. That's the only memory I have of that room, all other memories of that long night and what little was left of the morning were overwritten by the sight of your naked body lying on the bed as I stepped

307

out of the bathroom. Our bodies slept and celebrated on that bed, and when I revisit this place in my mind I feel nothing but lust. It was our first anniversary – something else I remember, Anya, though I don't often remember the things I should – and as a gift we gave ourselves to one another, though I know we described it differently at the time, but that's what it was, because back then we were just two bodies drawn together, yet to be joined by the invisible threads of love, and we had to cling to one another so as not to get swept apart by the currents; we had to constantly touch, hold, caress, and, in case you were wondering, I miss that quiet doubt and distrust in us, which time and again we pushed aside, I miss our insatiable nights, I miss how simple it all was, when all I could see in you was a naked body waiting for me on the bed; yes, Anya, I miss that naïve idea that being together in bed is enough. I also miss that room where the view from the bed is only sea and sky, I even miss that heady morning aroma of love-making which contrasts with the fresh, glimmering view on the other side of the window pane. And no, I've never wanted to go back there, to the room where we were doubtful and distrustful, where so many things were yet to be known, where so many things were yet to be, where everything was all so uncomplicated and where there was so much we were without; because that wasn't us at all. We came later, Anya, because we don't wake up in hotel rooms to a heady aroma of love-making; that aroma dissipates when you take me to the dentist and wait for me in the waiting room, angry, because I didn't do as you said and put on a winter coat when I headed out to the embankment that evening; it dissipates when I manage to guess what you're thinking and decline an invitation to a birthday party so that we can have a night in, alone on the sofa, in front of the television. That's us, Anya, and when I recall that room, I don't see us there at all, I just see you; your young, proud breasts, my fingertips making their way down from your belly button, to the first downy hairs; I see your face, with its barely concealed, bashful expression; your mischief, which I didn't yet know, at that point, was all for show and that there isn't a mischievous bone in your body. We were still enticing one another, back then, Anya, there was nothing but enticement in that room, and now we've long since been enticed. Enticing one another was good, I admit; trembling at every touch is good, being mischievous was good, and yes, I miss it, but who wouldn't miss that, who wouldn't be tempted to go back there, but I wouldn't go back there and I'm lost as to why you would go back; I'm lost, it's eating away at me, but I can't ask you because our brittle, fragile silence could not withstand such a thundering question. And so I just sit at the table next to you and I watch how you eat, you've never been that into food and neither are you now; you were used to listening to your father who would tell you stories at the table, now the stories are inside you and you're trying to hide them by looking over at Marko, keeping an eye on him, taking care of him, but I know that's not what you're doing, that it's just a guise to save you from having to look at me. There was a time when I didn't know how to hold my tongue, but I learnt this from you and I came to love silence, as it covered my weakness so well, and even now it's covering the fact that I don't know what to say to you, which is why I'm waiting for you to speak first, because yet again I have no words of my own, and because I know that when we're sat side by side, everything I'm feeling will remain unsaid, like so many other things in my life, a life which remains beyond the reach of words.

'You don't know why I left, Jadran. Maybe you think you do, maybe you're guessing, but you can't know. I left to try and summon the courage to tell you that I got a job. That Miro got me a job. A good job. In the Department for Urban Planning. At the Council. Yes, I got a job and yes, Miro landed it for me. Daddy landed me a job and that wasn't something I could tell you. When I came back from the interview… see, I couldn't even tell you that I'd had an interview, I didn't tell you because I went there as the daughter of Mr Černjak… I came back from the interview really pleased and I wanted to share that happiness with you; I waited impatiently for you to get home from work, but then it occurred to me that you wouldn't be happy for me, I saw you, pretending, I saw your fake smile, I saw you looking at me with disappointment, with contempt, almost, and my happiness vanished; I was sad, I felt so alone because I couldn't share my happiness with you, and then it was impossible to sit there waiting for you, I knew that I wouldn't be able to tell you, I couldn't stand your silent judgement, your contempt, I couldn't stomach it, not then, not on that beautiful day; I had to take myself away, I had to work though that disappointment within, disappointment in the fact that I can't share everything with you; I needed time and space, because I was hurting, really hurting – the slightest suspicion of what you might do, suspicion of what you might say, can get to me too, because I know you so well that there's no doubt about what you'll say, because it's not actually suspicion at all. I knew what was coming and I didn't want to see it, just as I knew that you would be quiet now, as I told you everything, because you're always quiet when there's a need to speak, when it's time to shout you lose your tongue. And then I talk and talk and I have no idea whether I'm talking to myself or whether you're even listening to me, or if you're off in one of your worlds. What was it you once said, about your problem being that your world – the one that really is yours – holds no footsteps of your own, only the footsteps of those you follow. Maybe that's what you're doing at this very moment, running away again from the here and now, as you do, because you're too cowardly to be here and now, because it's not your world. All that going back of yours is nothing but running away from here, you're scared to forget because then all you'd be left with is what you fear the most. And what you fear the most is the present: it terrifies you, you don't know how to exist in it, because you've never tried to, not with me. Forever absent. The present requires courage, courage which you don't have. The men in your world can't muster courage; the men in your world run away. I'm sure running away is something you've already considered, that you feel it inside you, and I don't know what's stopping you, what's keeping you here next to me. Marko? Maybe. Maybe me as well, a little bit, but maybe just fear; the realisation that you have nowhere to run to. That running away, even from me, will solve nothing. And so you're holding out here and retreating into yourself. Where are you running to, Jadran?'

I go back to the old house, open the creaky door, I let the cold doorknob rest in my hand, I turn it and push forward, and I look down the hallway towards the living room, the edge of the easy chair just visible from behind the door, with its worn, wooden back; I let my eyes travel across the empty walls, tinged yellow from Grandad's cigarette smoke, then I lower my eyes to the floor, to the rug, which is a little bit too wide and curls up along the edges and rests against the walls. There are shoes on it, Grandad's gardening shoes still carrying the remains of damp earth, and Grandma's black shoes with a low heel; and when I look up again I feel the warmth coming towards me from the kitchen stove, there's someone there behind the door, I hear the water bubbling in a pan, maybe it's plum dumplings, Grandma in a red apron with her back to me, she has her hair tied back when she's cooking, I can hear her, greeting me without taking her eyes off the pan, and then I sniff the air, anticipating the smell of damp and the smell of wood smouldering in Grandma's old stove; that's what my childhood smells like, that's what my first memories smell like; I hear the sound of the television coming from the living room, not a clear sound, the indoor aerial needs adjusting, the sound of Grandad coughing can be heard in between, I listen to him, nobody coughs like he does, and now I see him, Grandad sitting in his place, the midday sun beats through the window behind him and his face is in darkness, hard to make out; he puts his paper down on the pile by the armchair, changes his glasses – reading glasses go on the window sill – I'm there, I feel the creaking of the floor beneath my feet, I'm in Momjan, where everything is calm and reassuring; I feel someone stroke my head, and through the window outside I hear a voice calling me; mine and Safet's cardigans make for goal posts on the grass in front of the house, I'm so small again, it's so warm, like someone's holding me tightly, and I open the door to the Golf – it's Dane's Golf, parked on the road, surrounded by darkness; it's white, a Golf Mk2, a posh car, as we called it – I try to see it through my eyes back then, to admire it, just as we admired it at the time, it's nicely rounded, the doors open so smoothly, not like our Renault 4, not like Grandad's Škoda, not like Aunt Katarina's Yugo Skala 101; in the back seat I can see Mum's blue sweater, my duvet for the night ahead, I feel the fresh night-time air, I hear the crickets, I listen to them, I can hear an engine approaching from a distance and I guess whether it's a lorry, or a Vespa, or a Fiat, it's still too far away and I'm going to shield myself from it in the car, away from the growing rustle of tree tops and bushes beside our little parking space, our roadside room for the night, away from everything that's in the bushes, it's full of sounds; but when I lie down on the back seat of the Golf, the doors close behind me and everything goes quiet, Mum turns and leans over to me, draping her jumper over my legs and her jacket over my body, I kick my trainers off, they're black and white and they've got L.A and something else written on them, I tuck my knees up so that my feet aren't touching the door; I see Safet opening the door and getting in the front seat, his door closes too, and now we're all inside, it's quiet, the only sound is breathing, Safet's breathing is easy to recognise, the seat tips back, over my legs, Mum's seat tips back too, both of them are just above me, Mum's head is just a centimetre or two above mine, I can sense her, I hear the sound of her breathing, so quiet and peaceful; Safet turns round to look at me, it's dark and I can't see his eyes, I just sense them, it's as if the three of us are sleeping in the same room again for the first time in ages, like they're by my side, like they've got me, each from their own side, nobody can get to me and I can close my eyes, the two of them are here, so close, I'm so calm, I open my eyes again, the inside of the Golf is lit up by headlights, Safet's eyes are closed and I close mine again too, it's nice and calm like a shelter, and I hear the pounding of hammers, iron striking upon iron and steel, I can't understand the voices trying to make themselves heard over the pounding, the workers pace along the scaffolding, some high above, some lower down, they grind, they weld, and then someone's shouting again, it all goes quiet for a second, a loud burst of laughter is heard, and then more pounding; I'm in a large empty flat, only bare walls and dusty windows through which the sounds of the building site break in, there's parquet flooring which is buckling in places, dust is gathering in the cracks, the main doors close automatically, slamming shut and reverberating up the staircase, the bathroom door is ajar, I walk into the biggest room and look through the window, I see the street below, busy with people and cars, I'd need to get closer to the window to see Pražakova but I don't want to, someone might see me pressed up against the window, and so I step back, I feel the dust in my nostrils and the agitation, a pleasant aggravation, how good it feels that no one can see me as I back away from the window, I become invisible to everyone, to the builders and people on the street and the agitation grows, I sense I'm growing there, down below, but you can't tell yet, thanks to my trousers that are hanging halfway down my backside with my belt across my crotch, I lean against the wall and feel the cold on my back, it arouses me, like a naked body arouses me, because I'm there in the empty flat on Pražakova, I see the windows on the other side of the room and the radiators beneath them and the blood travels down, my hands seek bare skin, I can feel it, that you're here, I see your brown Airwalk trainers, laces untied, everything is drowned out by the pneumatic drill and it seems as if the walls are shaking, or I'm the one who's shaking, too aroused, unbearable, uncontrollable, I travel upwards from your feet, past the torn knees of your trousers, I go up to your belt, where there's a slither of your skin between your blouse and your trousers when you raise your arms, it's so soft and I can't handle any more, I'm trembling and I don't dare look up at your breasts, or feel your skin on my fingers, or travel up from your belt under your blouse, I couldn't handle it, I'm already way too aroused; instead I listen to the builders yelling, I try to pick out individual words, they're speaking Bosnian, someone's singing, someone who's extremely close by but can't see us, because we're hidden, hidden away from everyone, alone, finally alone…

…and then I'm back, I'm here and I'm now, where there's no house in Momjan, where there's no Golf parked on the road and no empty flat on Pražakova, I'm far away from all of those things that make me who I am, as if I've been driven from those places, which are me; as if the doors have closed and I can no longer go back in, and it's as if I can no longer get back to myself and I'm no longer me, that everything is over, that I'm sitting here and now and I don't know who I am anymore, because I don't have anywhere to return to, I no longer know who I am, sat here beside you, waiting for you to start speaking again.

'Do you remember what you said to me, when I confessed that I was scared to have children? You do, of course you do. I'm spoilt, you said. I'm entitled and I expect life to keep me wrapped up in cotton wool. You said that. You had a go at me for being a bourgeois Ljubljana princess with holiday homes, a de-nationalised apartment and a family fortune safely protected in stocks and trust funds – I was entitled, you said. You might be ashamed of those words now, but you were just being honest. Maybe you were hurt because I'd changed my mind about pregnancy, but you were only saying what you thought. That was the first time I'd felt your loathing, not that I realised at the time, because of the guilt I was feeling; I knew that I'd let you down and I thought you were entitled to those insults. You had a right to be angry with me, I had to understand that you were hurting because I'd said I was afraid to have a child with you. That's why I kept quiet. Why I didn't respond. I thought I understood your pain and I had a guilty conscience because I was the one who had caused it. Jadran, I'd give everything for this not to be true, but Marko – our Marko – is not the fruit of our love, but merely a result of my guilty conscience. After that evening I didn't change my mind about anything, I didn't get over the fear, my life didn't become any less uncertain, I didn't calm down nor accept anything; I just couldn't bear to disappoint you like that again, never again did I want to be that awful spoilt princess in your eyes, like I was that evening. It's true, Jadran, my guilty conscience is the reason we have Marko. No realisations, no transformative experiences, no conscious dismissal of dreams and desires. And still I'm terrified. I just couldn't find the strength to tell you yet again that having a child didn't seem like a good idea to me. I believed, then, that what I'd said had made you hate me; that it was just that evening, that the hatred was just anger born of hurt that I had caused. What a mistake that was, Jadran, how naïve, how blind. I couldn't see that you were full of hatred, which doesn't actually have anything to do with me, with what I said or with who I am, or who my parents are. You were hurt before I met you, Jadran, with such a deep, boundless hurt, that you didn't even realise yourself. You told me the story of Safet, told it with such anguish and you led me to believe that it was just your past that was full of sadness. But it was never the past for you, Jadran, I know that now. I saw it that night, so very alive. Now it seems as if I just wasn't prepared to believe what I was seeing right before my eyes, that it was too alarming, and instead I chose to pack everything away, call it by another name, dismiss it and thrust it far out of reach. I was too scared to confront the fact that you hate me. I needed time to admit that, to admit to myself what I'd seen and heard that evening; I needed time to admit to myself that you hated me and you will always hate me, that you will hate me and love me at the same time, because that's who you are, Jadran, father to my son. And now you're keeping quiet and you probably hate me for saying all this, too, because I've exposed you, maybe now you hate me more than you ever have, but this was something I had to tell you.'

On the eighth day after my father's disappearance, I got home from school and found Mum on the living room floor, slumped against the wall. *I've spoken to him*, was all she said. She was wrapped in her dressing gown, which wasn't quite covering her bare breasts. I turned away, thinking that she would cover up now that I'd got back, but all she did was sit there, and I stood in the doorway staring at the floor, not daring to look at her any longer, at her naked body, not daring to ask her what Safet had said; they had spoken, it was the first time they'd spoken since Safet disappeared, which is why I stood there staring at the floor as if shackled, waiting for her to talk, to keep going, waiting for her to cover her breasts, but nothing; all she did was sit there, and even if I wasn't looking at her, if I kept on staring at the floor, I could still see nothing but her bare breasts as if she were parading them; I wanted to tell her to put some clothes on, but that would mean acknowledging that I could see her, and I was ashamed, so, so ashamed, of her and of myself, I thought I was going to throw up, it seemed as if her dressing gown was becoming looser and looser, that she was now completely exposed; I slowly raised my eyes over her out-stretched legs and upwards, I had to convince myself that her gown was still covering her thighs and her groin, I had to, otherwise I'd probably just collapse on the floor; Who had done this to her? I thought, who had stripped her in front of me, who? I wanted to avenge her, I still want that even today, I want vengeance for her, for my mum, stripped bare, for her being so exposed that she wouldn't cover her naked breasts, for her not covering herself, for her being so helpless, like an abandoned child. That naked woman has stayed with me, that image has never left me, that feeling of shame has never left me. That's my hatred, Anya, that's the moment you're talking about. My hatred is my mum's naked breasts, looking out from underneath her dressing gown, her motionless body that says *I've spoken to him* and offers no further words. The image of my hatred is this, an image that hasn't faded with time, instead getting stronger and stronger, her breasts become more and more exposed. That image will always be with me, she will always be naked and I will eternally stare at the floor. When I look right into your eyes, too, Anya. *You don't have to be alone to be lonely*, Grandad said to me. I finally understand what he meant.

'I believed, for a long time, that it was pain at the root of your hatred. I knew Safet had been erased and that he'd abandoned you, that it hurt you and still hurts you today, and I believed it was this pain that had led to the hatred – but now I'm not so sure. Now I think that you've woven your life into one great big story in your head; you've spun a huge, hefty tome in order to create a connecting thread in all the chaos, you've woven us all in with you, me and my family too, just so you can find sense in your own nonsense, to prove to yourself that what happened to Aleksandar and Jana was connected to what happened to Vesna and Safet, and that all of it is connected to us and to you and what you're feeling. I think you've convinced yourself that you are the logical conclusion of everything that happened in Momjan, Otoka, Ljubljana, in Buje and wherever else; that all those lives join together in you; all the regret, remorse, longing, despair and disappointment, all of that is now within you, and lives on inside you, as if none of those people had ever died, as if all of those people were trapped inside you, like in a closet, frozen in time. And you're here, you're sitting next to me and looking at me like you always do, as I tell you things you don't want to hear, and as usual you say nothing because you know that what I'm saying is right; you're sitting here, feeling all of their pain, as painful to you now as if it were your own, as if what happened to them had happened to you. You see – it does really hurt you, I believe that; I believe you truly do relive their pain, and that you had to weave it all into a story so that the scattered fragments wouldn't fester in the corners of your mind, so that it wouldn't just be full of meaningless details, you had to give all of it a higher design, with an introduction, a core and a conclusion; a story to sate your feelings of hatred which would help to convince you that everything has conspired against you – all of this so you can play the victim and feel justified in hating your executioners. Isn't that it? What you've made is one giant story of your hatred. Your feelings of hatred are your creation. Which is why nothing can remain separate in your world, there are links between everything. But that is childish, Jadran, what you're doing is childish; adults accept that there's no such thing as meaning in this world, that it's all coincidence and things happen independently of us, and that there's no use in searching for reasons, the world is chaos and it's childish to force it all together into a story; I don't know why you can't understand that, Jadran. I mean, I know that you understand, you just refuse to accept it, because you need that story because you can't, and won't, give up your hatred – it's a part of you and you love it, but at the same time you're scared to be alone with it, to be without justification for it; it's a scary thing to hate without reason, to be full of hatred with no excuses, it's scary, it's a scary place to be, and I understand that you're scared and that the only reason you tell yourself stories is to excuse yourself and perhaps to excuse yourself to me, because you're full of fear, Jadran. Your entire being is pure fear.'

I admit it, Anya. My story is an invention; with the help of my imagination I found connections between my memories, that disorderly collection of images and voices, I put them in a logical order that suited me. All the gaps in Aleksandar and Safet's stories, gaps I couldn't have known, I filled in with figments of my imagination, and I did it to build a more appealing whole. I admit it, Anya. The whole story was put together so that within it I might find what I was looking for. Justification for my actions, for my fears, disappointments and longing; reasons for my sadness, for the anger. Yes, you're right, the story is my conspiracy theory designed to excuse me from myself and from others, most of all from you, Anya. It offers an explanation for me, shifts responsibility away from me, onto circumstances beyond my control. In it, I am merely a consequence of what happened to Aleksandar and Jana, to Vesna and Safet. I am merely a consequence, but the causes are inventions, Anya, I admit, but such is the nature of autobiographical stories. At the end we arrive at ourselves, at ourselves as we are, we can't change the eventual version of the story, or embellish it, because we're here, before everyone's eyes, with all of our faults; it's why we have to adapt what is no longer here, that which cannot contradict our lies; we can imagine our past because it doesn't care, it won't begrudge us a few alterations. I admit it, Anya, but hear me out. There are too many things about Aleksandar, Jana, Safet and Vesna that I don't know. I don't know what Safet's arrival in Otoka looked like, Aleksandar's in Buje even less so; I'm not familiar with the life and death of Branislava Đorđević, I don't know why she changed her name to Ester Aljehin; nobody ever told me about how Vesna and Safet met, nor did Aleksandar ever speak to me about Egypt. The story of Safet and the obituaries is a product of my imagination, too. *Strange things, those obituaries*, was all he said. I know hardly anything about what it was like for Aleksandar to experience the gradual departure of Jana, I doubt that anyone could ever have asked him about it; nor did Vesna ever speak to me about their arguments, or the time when Safet disappeared. I admit, Anya, my story is a great big lie, a typical bedtime fairytale to soothe my conscience, because it's so logical and easy to understand, all the pieces fit together and follow on and in the story the present is merely a result of the past. In this story, Anya, in such a beautiful, orderly world, I understand myself; I understand what I feel and I understand how I behave. This story enables me to be what I am; to be me. It really is a conspiracy theory, a theory of how life has conspired against me, Jadran Dizdar. I admit it, Anya, I admit all of it, but what am I left with, when left without my story? What's left for me when I admit that I've invented a story about myself, one that I've used to understand what I feel when left alone with my own self? What's left for me if I now reject my story and am left alone with feelings that I don't understand? What will happen to me, what will happen to us, when I'm left alone with my anger? If I reject the story I invented, we're left alone, Anya, you and I, with everything that's crying inside me, everything which ought to be laughing; with my clenched fists which ought to softly caress you; with everything that says nothing whilst you wait for me to speak; we're left alone with all of that, and all we can say is that I am what I feel, that what I feel is the two of us, that's who we are, and that all of these things constitute our love. We can call all of it love and we can hide everything behind it, it's big enough to devour all of my anger and fear. But would you really want to be alone, Anya, with me, and with a love which is not purely love? If that is what you really want, then I'll concede to you, my story is no more. Maybe Aleksandar didn't really kill himself, and that little brown bottle on the floor was just a coincidence; maybe Vesna's final visit was also just a coincidence and she never actually told him about how Jana wanted a divorce. And maybe – yes, Anya, this is also possible – maybe Safet disappeared of his own accord, because he wanted to disappear, because he'd had enough of the life he was living, maybe he erased himself from a life that had placed limitations on him, maybe he longed for freedom and merely took the opportunity; all of it is possible because I know nothing about it. Everything I know is invented, and I'll admit all of this to you if you want, here and now, Anya. I admit that Safet might not have ever actually had his citizenship erased, he might have been the one to leave, for a place where there was no Vesna and no me. And Aleksandar might have just been tempted by the freedom of Egypt, maybe there was no Mihelčič to drive him away, from his Jana, at all. Maybe freedom really is a fatal attraction for all of us, which is why we constantly run away from the people we love, and maybe that's why love can never be love alone, because love is beautiful, but binding; because it ties all of us to those we love, and which is why love can sometimes make us feel like we're chained to the floor, we sense our wings withering away. Is this what you want me to admit, Anya? To admit to you that just like Aleksandar and Safet, I also long for freedom, for some place beyond, where there's no you and no Marko, that I long to run away, and which is behind what happened with Tadea? Would you like me to confess that all my stories are just a map of my fears, fears that try to drive me away from you? I'll admit all of it to you, but only if you, Anya, can love someone who is full of anger without a name, anger without a story, anger which you will never understand because not even I myself will ever understand it. Maybe you're right, Anya, maybe I'm not my past after all, maybe it's just my childish need to make sense of the nonsense, maybe my invention of stories is a naïve form of madness, because nothing is that simple and we're not that simple, and maybe there just shouldn't be stories in this world at all, because all stories are only here to explain the unexplainable to us. Maybe your look, Anya, the look you're directing at me this very moment, hateful and loving at the same time, is stronger than the story of Safet's life; maybe, if I now take you by the hand, your touch will leave an impression stronger than all of Aleksandar's words and maybe I really am just scared of not knowing who I am, maybe I really am scared of just being someone who loves and hates, of being someone who clings on to you, Anya, as if clinging onto the final throes of life, someone who doesn't wish to be left alone, without you. Maybe I really am just scared of being a regular guy who lies next to you in bed at night and who kisses his sleeping son before he goes to work. But admit it, Anya, you're scared of that too, you're also scared of being someone who loves me deeply; admit it, you're also scared of a love that isn't only love, admit that it's also the reason why you ran away from me. Let's admit, Anya, that all of us are scared of love, because love is so binding, so terrifying. So good and so terrifying. So good and so terrifying. So good and so terrifying. So good.

XVII

With his will, Grandad attempted to simplify everything which life had made complicated. The apartment in Ljubljana and the house in Momjan were left to Mum and Maya, with the suggestion that they sell the apartment and split the money, while they keep the house as a holiday home for their families. It was, he wrote, what he would do in their position, but he knew that the two of them would decide to do otherwise, and that his only wish was that they did not fall out about it. That his will so clearly overlooked just how argumentative his daughters actually were, even without involving his inheritance, was the final trace he left behind; the trace of a need to see the world in a more beautiful light. That sentence in his will conjures him before my eyes so clearly, as if he were standing right beside me in his vest, telling me that once again his tomatoes hadn't lived to see the rain.

Luckily, Mum and Maya agreed to ignore his suggestions and found their own way of solving the joint ownership issue. Maya needed a place in Ljubljana for Špela, and suggested that she give her half of the house in Momjan to Vesna, in exchange for her half of the apartment. It seemed to make sense, except that Mum didn't feel like going anywhere near the house. She never wanted to go there ever again. And so she passed the decision on to me.

If Maya takes the flat and you take the house, does that seem about right to you? she asked me, casually, as if she were asking me if I'd like a glass of wine with my lunch.

To her, inheritance was a burden. She didn't want anything. She didn't even want to transfer the seven hundred euros that were left in Grandad's safe into her own account.

I said to her that before we started exchanging Grandad's real estate, it would be a good idea to go to Momjan and establish what sort of condition the house was in. I was stalling, in the hope that she might change her mind. I couldn't picture Anya, Marko and me spending summers in Momjan; having a house in Istria, with all that astonishing scenery, was surreal. I could hear Anya asking me: *And what are we supposed to do there?*

The house was too far from the sea, too far from the town, too far from our routines. I could hear Anya saying that we didn't even use Miro's cabin at Lake Cerknica, somewhere else we could spend time on our own, amidst stunning nature. The house in Momjan meant something to me, but for her it was just a house that needed maintaining, maybe even renovating, a house that needed money we didn't have. But I couldn't sell it, either.

Marko would quickly get bored of running round the garden, I heard her say, and so I told her that I was going to Momjan for Mum's sake, to help her decide what to do with the house. I kept quiet about how Mum had already handed it over to me.

I can't see Vesna in that house, Anya said as I was leaving.

Me neither, I replied.

On the way there, Mum and I said no more than a few words to one another, but it was easy to see that she was not going to change her mind, and that this was her final journey to Momjan. When I pulled up outside the house, she took the keys from her bag and thrust them into my hands. I thought she was going to stay there in the car, but whilst I was opening the gates, she crossed the road and walked through the damp grass. She took carefree, childlike steps through the undergrowth, towards a small clearing which opens up onto the most beautiful view over the bay.

I never did see the beauty in sunsets. When I was a kid, it was just a day disappearing, leaving me alone with the night-time; and as an adult, too, I often felt that same melancholy as evening drew near. Yet now, as I watched my Mum saying goodbye to the coastlines of her childhood, I didn't feel sadness. Neither hers, nor my own.

I felt relief. She would go and I would stay, with the warm breeze, withered vines and overripe figs. As if Mum's departure had already played out, I looked over to the figure in the clearing as if peering into a distant memory. The house she was born in was now just another house above the bay, and she was just a woman who used to live there, many years ago.

We walked through the house as if through a gallery, as if merely wishing to pass through. We were both trying to pretend that what surrounded us was just an empty shell, with all traces of the past scraped from inside.

'Maya's late.'

'Just like her Dad.'

She used to call him Grandad when I was little, then later he became Aleksandar. He'd never been Dad.

'Shall I make coffee?'

'I've had one already this morning. You have one, if you want.'

I gladly took myself off into the kitchen. After Grandad, there were only a few teaspoons of coffee left behind. It was strange, pouring the water into his Turkish coffee pot, now, when all of this was mine; when the sugar grains encrusted inside the small tub were my encrusted sugar grains. I would have to replace the gas canister when the gas ran out. Just like I'd have to replace the boiler under the sink, which hadn't worked for years, and which is why only cold water flowed from the tap. Cold water that was now bubbling in Grandad's coffee pot. The coffee pot which was now mine.

'Are you sure you don't want a coffee?'

There was no reply. Mum was no longer in the living room, but I didn't want to move away from the stove. It felt good to gaze into the water and wait for the bubbles to surface. To be alone in the house. In it, I started to see the makings of a hiding place. Nothing would burst in uninvited. Here there would always be silence; silence in which I could hide.

When Mum and Maya came inside, I was sat at the dining room table. In Grandad's place.

'Is there any milk left in the fridge?' Mum asked.

'No worries, coffee hasn't agreed with me recently,' Maya said.

They stood there in the doorway, as if waiting for me to invite them in.

'You look just like him. Especially sat just there. All you need is to play patience.'

'When did he play patience?'

'He used to, sometimes.'

'We all used to play at one time.'

Maya thought twice and kept her answer to herself. She came forward and sat down next to me.

'I don't really know why we're all here. Everything's settled, as far as I'm concerned. This house is yours, Jadran. For the two of you, I mean.'

'It was Jadran's suggestion that we had a look round together, to see what state it was in.'

'I thought that before you made any final decisions...'

'My mind's made up.'

Those words were the reason that Mum and I had come to Momjan, but now, when Maya said them, it seemed as if I'd already heard them months ago, maybe even years. Our journey had been redundant. Both Mum and Maya had already bid farewell to their childhood home a long time ago.

'Yeah... mine's made up too.'

'And if I sell the house?'

'What you do with it makes no difference to me. That's your decision.'

'Exactly.'

'You won't change your minds?'

'Don't worry, Jadran.'

Now Mum sat down too, and I felt a sudden, strong urge for them to leave. I couldn't stand their presence any longer, nor our performance of bureaucracy.

'Maya, would you be able to take Mum back to Ljubljana?'

'Yes, of course.'

I didn't want to make excuses and come up with reasons. I didn't feel obliged to be tactful. I was past caring.

I didn't care about the opinions of others for the first time in my life and I decided to enjoy it. Mum and Maya left at my request. I no longer needed to pay attention to anyone.

I sat down beneath the fig tree and watched the two of them pack things into Maya's Clio. Maya was moving things from the front seat into the back, so that Mum wouldn't be sitting on her sunglasses or expired parking tickets. I didn't go up to the gates to guide Maya out of the drive, or to wish them a safe journey and wave them off as they drove away. I just watched the purple Clio disappear over the hill from a distance.

I tipped my head back against the tree trunk. Figs were decomposing on the damp ground beneath me, the same unpicked figs which had driven me to tears a few days before, but that night now seemed distant, like a childhood memory, as if Grandad had died in some previous life, one that ended long ago. Everything that had until recently been mine, now seemed to be separate and far away from me. I, Jadran Dizdar, was an exile from my own life.

If I could stay frozen in this feeling, I'd be free, I thought to myself. If I didn't feel scared of memories, I could move in and I could be on my own. Without those who are no longer here, and without those who are still waiting for me.

I'd sit in the garden at midday and wait for another day to sail out of the bay and disappear into the distance, just like the containers vanish out of the port of Koper. I'd get up early, head down to the salt pans and walk along the soft, cracked earth. I'd watch as my feet stepped over the meandering lines in the ground, and I'd wonder about all that had flowed through those narrow depths.

When anyone who might have recognised me was no longer around, I'd take a walk through Buje and buy a paper at the kiosk, I'd drink an espresso at the café on the square; I, the stranger, who'd be left to depart without a goodbye. The shop assistants wouldn't guess what I had come for, they wouldn't memorise my preferences. I'd be a stranger and I could go unseen, hidden from the all-knowing whispers.

In the evenings I'd shut myself up in the house and watch games, one after the other, and each one would be tense, and critical, just like when I used to train and basketball was my entire world. I wouldn't just be doing it for the money any more, but because I'd started to enjoy the game again. I'd cheer and I'd wait, on my feet, for the final attack, and there'd be nothing else, only the ball soaring towards the hoop, and me, watching, alone in front of the television, in the quiet night.

There'd be no more minutes and seconds; winters and springs would pass by undetected. There'd be no more countdowns, because there'd be nothing to count down from. Everything would be over, finished; all farewells and partings far behind me.

But I wouldn't be free then, either, I know. Freedom is the illusion of all illusions; just another name for loneliness. Even now, as I sit beneath the fig tree, as I tip my head back against its trunk, not feeling any of life's pressures, I'm not free. I'm just lonely. Just alone.

I bent down and picked up a fig from the ground by my left foot. It must have fallen from the branch that day or the day before, as it hadn't yet started to rot. Maybe there's still a few up there on the tree, I thought to myself. A few more figs that I can pick and take back for Anya.

I don't remember the last time I ate a fig, but it always was my favourite fruit. Perhaps for the very reason that figs were never something I picked for myself, but always for others. When I was a kid I would pick them for Mum, and later I picked them for Anya. She adored figs, and so this tree was, for me, the delight with which she bit into the freshly picked fruit. This tree was, in my head, her small, but great pleasure. That's why I loved it. It helped me to make her happy; it helped me feel my love for her.

Rarely did I feel it; all too rarely. It was a feeling rarer than anger, sadness, or hatred, even. Which is why I was grateful to Grandad's fig tree. Beneath it, I was the kind of person I could only dream of being elsewhere. As I reached for its branches, or climbed up it, I was in love with Anya.

I could no longer remember where best to place my foot, if I wanted to climb up to the thick branch around head height. It was too dark to see the indents and ridges in the trunk, and so my hand felt around in search of the best place to start my ascent. The last time I tried I was nearly two stones lighter and much more nimble. It had also been light enough to sufficiently judge the distance and thickness of individual branches. But it was too late to change my mind. Something was drawing me to the tree and had taken away my power to decide.

After several unsuccessful attempts, I managed to prop my leg on a small ridge. I held a branch above my head in one hand, and pulled myself up with all my might, while my other hand fumbled in the dark for a new, higher handgrip to help steady me. But I was waving in mid-air and all I clung on to were a few leaves left in my hand after I'd swung sideways.

I was clutching at the air in a panic, knowing my foot could slip from the ridge at any moment, but luckily, I managed to find a cavity in the trunk and clung on to it tightly. I quickly got my leg up onto the thick branch and let it take my weight.

As a child I would scale the tree with such freedom, as if walking along broad forest footpaths, but now I was holding onto branches with both hands to stop me from tumbling backwards. My body, taller and slightly more rounded, was worn out from heaving itself upwards and I leant against the trunk to catch my breath.

I was now wedged between branches and no longer worried about falling. I let go of one and with my free hand began to search for fruit. But leathery fig leaves were all I could feel. Even when I was brave enough to stand on my tiptoes and extend my arm beyond its reach, I couldn't find a single fruit. I had to go higher.

My fingers assessed the branches above, considerably narrower than the one I was standing on, though it seemed as if they ought to support my weight, and that I'd be able to climb onto them. During the day this would probably be relatively easy, yet in the dark it was a risky move. But I couldn't get down from the tree without Anya's figs. I had no doubts, and even the fear had subsided. All I knew was that I had to go up, up where there was a fig for me to take back to Ljubljana. A fig that would make her happy.

I raised my right foot. My right hand assessed the thickness of the branch in sight. I couldn't be certain that it would support me, but I didn't want to think about it too much. What will be, will be, I thought, and I stepped onto the branch, lifting myself up.

The branch seriously bowed under my weight and it felt as if it would snap; the entire tree was swaying with me, but at that moment I didn't feel scared, just a certainty that I was going to get to where I was meant to be. My other foot sought out a nearby branch and balanced my weight, and then I waited for the swinging branches to settle.

I was far too high up. The crown of the tree would shake at the slightest movement and I could have plunged to the depths below, but I extended in all directions without a care, just like when I was a child and believed that I was invincible. I was now leaning over to one side, then to the other, feeling all of the branches within reach.

I was determined to leave no leaf on this tree unturned. I knew that my fig was hiding behind one of them and that if I could just stretch a little more, if I just shifted a little further, if I just managed to reach and grab that one bushy branch at the end, then I would find it. I climb just a little higher. The fig that I'm looking for is definitely up there, on that sturdy branch. The fig that I will find, and pick, tonight.

THE AUTHOR

GORAN VOJNOVIĆ is a film director, writer and columnist. His first novel *Čefurji raus! / Southern Scum Go Home!* (*Beletrina* 2008) was a bestseller and won Vojnović an award for the best Slovenian novel of the year, which he also received for his next two novels, *Jugoslavija, moja dežela* (*Yugoslavia, My Fatherland, Istros Books* 2015) and *Figa* (*The Fig Tree, Istros Books* 2020). His novels have been translated into more than twenty languages and successfully adapted for theatre and film. For the last ten years Goran Vojnović writes a weekly column in one of the biggest Slovenian newspapers *Dnevnik*, while also contributing to many other news and cultural forums, at home and abroad. He lives and works in Ljubljana.

THE TRANSLATOR

OLIVIA HELLEWELL is a translator from Slovene to English of literary fiction, children's fiction, and non-fiction in the field of arts and culture. She received her PhD in Translation Studies and Slovene literature at the University of Nottingham, and has translated works by Jela Krečič (Peter Owen 2016) and Dunja Jogan (Tiny Owl 2020). In 2019, she was awarded first place in Asymptote Journal's Close Approximations Translation Contest, and is the recipient of two English PEN Awards.